WELCOME

TO THE

FREE

WORLD

WELCOME

TO

THE

FREE

WORLD

LLOYD RALEIGH

PBS Press
Asheville, North Carolina
2022

Welcome to the Free World
A PBS Press Book / September 2022

Published by PBS Press LLC
Asheville, North Carolina

First Edition

Publisher's Cataloging-in-Publication data
Raleigh, Lloyd, author.
Welcome to the free world : a novel / Lloyd Raleigh.
Asheville, NC: PBS Press, 2022.
LCCN: 2022903130 | ISBN: 9780578371368 (hardcover) |
9798218088033 (paperback) | 9780578370903 (ebook)
LCSH Artificial intelligence--Fiction. | Climatic changes--Fiction.
| Refugees--Fiction. | North Carolina--Fiction. | Dystopian fiction.
| Science fiction. | BISAC FICTION / Dystopian | FICTION /
Science Fiction / General | FICTION / Visionary & Metaphysical
LCC PS3618.A3855 W35 2022 | DDC 813.6--dc23

For the next generations...

ONE

SCALPEL

WILL ROBIN WAS UNAWARE SOMETHING LIFE CHANGING HAD JUST HAPPENED. With his scalpel, he cut an inch-long incision in his patient's scalp. Entangled in her bloodied jet-black hair, his fingers pushed until her Aurora, an artificial intelligence microchip encased in silica, slid through the incision and popped into view. He twirled the scalpel handle between his fingers, picked up the quarter-sized Aurora chip from the crown of her head, and placed both on surgical cloth atop a barren desk. Between clenched teeth, she moaned while he stitched the incision shut.

"Welcome to the free world, Alyss. We can speak now," he said, crouching to untie her blindfold. Will's tone of voice conveyed trust to his clients, for the most part. At least that's what many told him. In essence, he desired to be trusted. His intentions were worthy of trust. Most of all, his clients needed trust in moments like these.

"It's a shock to see again," Alyss said. She stayed seated and looked Will in the eye. "Different without the Aurora. It's weird." She inspected the abandoned windowless office as if recalibrating to reality. "Like I have no foundation."

"Even so, you're free," Will said. "Can you feel it?" He was familiar with how most of his patients reacted when they gave up a need-fulfilling device and were left with an emotional black hole.

"I don't know. It's hard to tell what I'm feeling. It's just weird. I used the Aurora for just about everything. Now, there's nothing."

"What's it like, quitting the Aurora?"

"Part of me feels strong. The other part of me, not so much."

"You're trembling. I'm curious—"

"I am, aren't I?" Alyss closed her eyes, and her face contorted. "I hate what the Aurora's done to me. It fucks with my body." She opened her blue eyes, tensed, and then stopped, as if self-conscious. "You wouldn't know, would you? You've never had an Aurora."

"No, and I don't plan to," Will said. "But what's your experience? Hating something that was such an intimate part of your life."

Alyss stared at him and sat on the edge of her chair. "It wasted my life. My parents forced me to get it when I was six so I could keep up with the other kids in school." Likely this was Alyss's third or fourth Aurora, as Cirrus made getting an upgrade affordable. Surgical robots in the back rooms of Aurora Stores implanted the devices with an impeccable record of safety, comfort, and convenience, and Cirrus sold most of their retail Auroras at or below cost. Conversely, removing Auroras legally without an upgrade was designed to be prohibitively expensive for many and wasn't covered through insurance.

"But I'm tired of trying to keep up," she said. "What's the point?"

"Right. What *is* the point? How'd you snap out of it?" Will asked.

"Friends. When I first met them, I knew they were different, kind of like you—something in your eyes and the way you are. I wanted to be like that. When they told me they didn't have Auroras, I began to question mine." Alyss's hands were shaking. "But it's not going to be easy, is it? What the hell is going on?"

"I'm guessing you've got some extra energy looking for a place to go. Can you let it go?" Will asked.

"Not sure."

"Try it. Just see where it takes you." Will gave her space, watching her with care and curiosity. "I'm right here with you."

She rose from her seat and walked around, her hands clutching one another. Her eyes darted to and fro, as if looking at thoughts and mental images. She stopped walking, and her eyes focused on the graffiti-covered concrete wall before her. *Slap!* She released her tight hands, hitting the wall with palms, then fists, over and over, screaming as if exorcising demons until she collapsed and curled into a ball, sobbing.

Will sat next to her in support. He knew the transition was challenging. Depression, bipolar emotional swings, low self-esteem, social awkwardness, anxiety, memory loss, and irritability were some of the symptoms. Secretly, Will cherished these symptoms. He saw them as guides to how his clients could understand the world with greater depth. He wanted her to awaken to the unconfined possibilities of her life, beyond the pale of the Aurora's insanity. Thinking of her future awakening, lightness danced through his body. This feeling compelled him to carry on, despite the dangers of his work.

"Thank you," she said, wiping the tears. Her knuckles were bloody, but she didn't seem concerned.

She's been through far worse, Will thought. "You ready?" he said, looking toward the door.

"No," she chuckled. "Is anyone ever?"

"Probably not. Just remember, the first days are always the hardest." Will handed his client the Aurora. "Here."

She examined the membrane-encased microchip. Will imagined her as someone meant to be born in another place and time, someone uncomfortable with the unraveling of the world. She'd seen through the sheen of the Aurora and taken the leap, even though life would undoubtedly be more challenging for her. At last, she stood, rolling the Aurora from her hand onto the concrete floor and crushing it under the sole of her leather boot.

"I'm sorry, Rose," she muttered.

"Rose?"

"My Aurora Friend." She fidgeted with her hands and looked toward the floor.

"You miss her?"

Her brow angled. "I know she's not real," she said. Alyss paused, and her brow relaxed. "But in a way, she was. She was like a best friend, there for me when I needed her, when I needed comfort. Anytime, actually."

"It's okay to miss her."

"Is it? Doesn't seem like it. It's embarrassing."

"What else?"

"I'm afraid," she said. "But I'm ready to dance again."

"I like your spirit," Will said.

"Thank you," she said, steadying her hands to pay him.

She slipped out the office door, revealing an unsanctioned dance party in a decrepit warehouse, complete with a DJ and light show. Will set the blindfold on the chair for the next client. Standard procedure. Practicing medicine without a license was a felony, and if a client saw his face or heard his voice during the procedure, the Aurora, ready to gather evidence, would see him as well. He picked up Alyss's crushed Aurora and added it to six others on the table, a good night because of the dance party. But still, only seven. Though he knew he was helping, Will thought of the sheer number of Auroras in the world. I can't change the world a few Auroras at a time. I need to do more. Much more. But how?

While sterilizing the long blade of his scalpel, he noticed several missed video calls from 12:34 A.M, and an encrypted peer-to-peer message, twenty-one minutes old, on his anachronistic cell phone: "Someone's targeting Scalpels. I think it's Cirrus. Call me ASAP. Ollie."

In that moment, the Aurora assassin myth transformed to plausible reality and imminent threat, a life-changing event. The prime suspect was the largest company in the world by market capitalization, Cirrus, maker of the Aurora. His heart tightened. I've got to get out of here.

Putting on his black rain jacket, grabbing his scalpel, and forgetting everything else, he ran out the door into the dance hall, knocking down his next client. "Hey. Wait a second."

But Will had already ducked to the right into the crowd. Stay aware, he thought. His eyes darted throughout the room. With hundreds of moving bodies surrounding him, everyone was a potential threat. His body tensed, and the dance hall seemed to envelop him. Stay inconspicuous. Will slid through the mass of dancers toward the nearest exit.

A broad-shouldered, bald-headed man pushed his way. For a second, their eyes met. Will froze. The man barreled through dancers toward him. Will detoured to find another exit and left the building into a cold, dark downpour. To his left, Lyman Street followed the curves of the French Broad River. To his right was the Asheville rail yard. Which way?

He dashed through a muddy parking lot and jumped over the coupler joining two still freight cars. Between two long trains, his pace slackened on the slick crushed ballast. Will turned around and saw the man, a distant silhouette aiming a gun his way.

Will ducked under a freight car. Bullets slapped into metal. For a second, he lay prone between the rails amid the creosote scent of crossties.

He ran across more tracks and crawled through a hole in a chain-link fence. In a woodland, he stumbled through briars, trash, and fallen branches knotted with kudzu vines. Two miles later, after weaving through neighborhoods toward downtown, he slowed to a walk in a neighborhood of old bungalows, postmodern eco homes, and multiplex apartments. At last, he found a covered bus stop and sat to rest. The streets were empty of people, and rainwater flowed into a gutter before him. At 1:18 A.M., he video-called Ollie, the IT manager for Asheville's Scalpels, shielding the phone from the rain as he walked. "Will, I'm glad you're okay," Ollie answered, poorly lit from streetlights. A passing car's headlights accentuated the middle-aged wrinkles and revealed his mixed Eurasian features.

"Are *you* okay, Dad?"

"I'm fine." Oliver Robin said, turning to look behind him.

Will imagined another assassin emerging from the darkness behind his father. "A man tried to kill me, Dad. He's not following me anymore."

"Are you sure? Now's not the time to be careless," his father said, turning his head once again.

"We should turn off the video if you're being followed," Will said, imagining the screen illuminating his father's face in the darkness. He wondered how an assassin could have reached his father so soon. Was there more than one? Was his father being tracked?

"No. It's fine. I don't think I'm being followed." he said, wiping dripping rainwater from his face. "I just wanted to see you."

"Where are you?"

"In our neighborhood. Whatever you do, don't come home tonight. Stay hidden."

Will's heart sank in his chest. "What's happening?"

"Maya sent me a warning message. I think she was targeted by an Aurora assassin."

"Maya! No. She's not dead. She can't be. I have to find her."

"I don't know. She's not replying. But don't go. It's too dangerous."

"I have to go, Dad. I love you."

"No, don't—."

Will tapped End and tried video-calling Maya. No answer.

He made haste toward her West Asheville apartment just over two miles away as though the frigid rain didn't exist. He ducked through a fence behind Asheville Middle School, passed a crowd emerging from a music hall, and crossed the brimming French Broad River on the main West Asheville thoroughfare, Haywood Avenue. A steep side street and stone stairs through a neighborhood park exhausted his legs, and he slowed his pace. At last, he reached her tiny apartment and knocked. No answer. He had a copy of her key, just in case. His heart pounded as he unlocked the door. Leaving the lights off so any hidden micro video cameras couldn't film him, he waited until his eyes adjusted.

Papers were strewn on the floor. He checked her bedroom. Still no one. The dresser drawers gaped, vomiting Maya's brassieres, pants, and blouses onto the floor. He noticed the absence of the electronic devices that were typically on her desktop. Even the large network computer was missing. That computer was one of many relays in an encrypted network that Scalpels and their allies used to maintain anonymity. Will's heart sank, knowing that the data in those devices, if decrypted, could reveal the identity of more Scalpels and jeopardize their ability to communicate. No other anonymity networks were deemed safe, as NSA whistleblowers confirmed that the government could decloak virtually anyone's identity at will.

He pictured the Aurora assassin murdering Maya just as she was removing someone's chip in one of her usual haunts, then finding him and trying to kill him, too. So efficient. How? His head throbbed. Why them? Why now? Because we're getting too good at this Scalpel thing.

He found her Scalpel supplies. Not daring to return to the abandoned warehouse office for the rest of his equipment, he took what he needed, slipping the supplies into his jacket with his scalpel. His phone rang—a voice-only call—startling him.

"Maya. You're okay," he said. "You scared the living piss out of me."

"She'll live," a man's deep voice said. "Just do what I say."

"Let me speak to her."

"No."

"You're lying. She's dead," Will said.

"You're right," the man said. "She *is* dead. I'll kill your father, too, if you don't follow my instructions."

"Don't kill him. I'll do what you say," Will replied, not knowing if the assassin knew of his father's whereabouts

"Keep your phone on. Don't contact your father or anyone else. I'll call you back."

The man hung up. I need to warn my father, Will thought, despite the assassin's instructions. Leaving Maya's home, he saw three police cruisers approaching.

Hiding in the shadows, he jumped a backyard chain-link fence and ran through a neighbor's yard to a side street as the police stopped at Maya's place.

Thirty-nine degrees Fahrenheit. The cold rain pounded his jacket as he sent an encrypted message to his father.

"The assassin is after you. Call me if you can. Where are you?" Will texted.

"Got it. I'm moving. I'll meet you in Magnolia Park."

Will checked the time—2:09 A.M. and made haste toward Magnolia Park, a couple of miles away in Montford, a nineteenth-century historic neighborhood north of downtown, where he lived with his father in a basement apartment. Water trickled from his hood through his kinky hair and goatee, down the inside of his jacket. His cotton pants were soaked, but all he could do was worry about his father and think of questions. Why isn't he calling me? Is he still alive? The assassin used Maya's phone, so there was no guarantee. What's happening? What am I getting into?

Vehicle headlights blinded his hazel eyes as he walked up Clingman Avenue. Is that the police? No, he thought, sighing as the vehicle passed him. As more cars passed, he became conscious of how drivers perceived him, of who might be in the cars, judging him for his brown skin. Dressed in black, he held his head low, hiding his face with the hood, wanting to disappear. Will shuddered, imagining the faces of the white supremacists when they beat him, called him racial slurs, and left him for dead a few months ago. He traced the scar on his forehead and barely remembered falling to the ground and hitting the rock that knocked him unconscious. Now, I'm branded for life. In these moments, how he yearned for acceptance and peace. But neither ever happened. Instead, existential angst permeated his life. Anger welled up inside him, and he walked as though blind, caught in the trance of his thoughts.

Three blocks from Magnolia Park, 2:48 A.M., a call from his father jolted him from his trance. "Don't come. It's a trap," he said, breathing heavily. "I just got away from the assassin. He was holding me hostage waiting for you, and he wasn't going to let either of us live. He's just behind me, somewhere." The video jerked back and forth as his father ran.

"Dad, I'm on my way. Hide. We'll meet up."

On the other end of the line, the distinctive *thwat, thwat, thwat* of silenced gunshots followed by the phone striking the pavement shocked Will.

"Dad? You there...?"

No reply.

"Dad...? Dad...?"

"He's dead," the assassin's voice said. "I told you not to talk with him, didn't I? You're lucky you got away, but you're next."

Without replying, Will shut down his phone. They were supposedly untrackable, but was he being tracked now? Or had the assassin intercepted their messages? How had the assassin found his father, after all? No time to mourn, he ran down a side street, noticing flashing police lights on an adjacent street. Wait. That's my apartment.

Curious, he walked around the corner to police tape surrounding his apartment. Why were they there, just minutes after his father's murder only a few blocks away? They know about us. Will thought about their relay computer used for the Scalpels' encrypted network. That's what they want, he imagined. An officer sat in a cruiser, and Will walked on the other side of the street, head still down, clenching his hands under the jacket sleeves not only to keep them warm but to hold back the rage and grief.

He pictured his father. And Maya—she was like a second mother.

Clear your mind. Walk normally. Don't let them notice you. He thought of the police investigating the murders. There will never be any leads. Will knew Cirrus was above the law, having bought all the politicians. The government was addicted to the Aurora, which effortlessly pacified the masses to create a more stable society. What a joke.

Will's legs ached after hours of running and walking, but he couldn't stop, as he needed to find shelter. He roamed an older neighborhood near McCormick Field, home of the Asheville

Tourists minor-league baseball team. At 4:35 A.M., rain turned to snow, but, at last, Will found a decrepit abandoned bungalow. He pushed through honeysuckle vines, pried back loose plywood with his frigid fingers, and stumbled through a window frame.

In the dim light, he wondered if anyone was squatting there. The floor creaked under his feet. Old graffiti covered the walls. In a corner, amidst glass shards, mementos sat in still life: a headless doll, a dog bowl speckled with rat feces, cigarette butts. Snow fell through gaping holes in the roof, covering rotten boards in the middle of the room. He removed his soaked clothes and squeezed out the water with numb, clumsy hands. He found a torn towel and sniffed it. He retched. At least it's dry, he thought, wrapping himself in the towel to keep warm. His head bobbed from exhaustion, but to avoid more severe hypothermia, he walked around the perimeter of the room as if in a trance, warming his hands with his breath.

Two hours later, he collapsed to the floor as he welcomed fragmented sunbeams from holes in the boarded-up windows. The sunlight blinded his itchy eyes and captured dust motes in motion, warming his body somewhat until, at last, he fell into a deep sleep.

TWO

AARON

WILL WAS WARY OF THE CEILING SECURITY CAMERAS and anyone watching him. Avoiding aisles with people and keeping his eyes fixed on the merchandise, he scavenged through the hodgepodge piles, shelves, and racks. A large Patagonia button-down shirt. Why would someone get rid of this? It looks new. Gotta love Asheville.

"Oh, this is nice," the cashier said, folding the shirt. Cherry-red lipstick surrounded her toothy smile. "You'll look sharp wearing it." She winked.

"Thanks," Will said, disguising his voice with a higher tone and emptying his shopping cart—blankets, sheets, cooler, water bottle, camp stove, pants, plate, fork, knife, and spoon.

One clear look from the cashier was enough. From its perch atop the woman's scalp, her Aurora monitored and controlled the pulses of billions of neurons and trillions of synapses in real time. That glance toward Will's face could be analyzed with facial recognition software, compared to a database of billions of faces stored on Cirrus's yottabyte servers. His voice could be identified, too. Will imagined that an assassin would be notified of his whereabouts the moment his face or voice was recognized. What were the chances?

"How much was this?" the woman asked, searching the cooler for a price.

"Don't know."

"Hold on, I'll ask the manager," she said. Her eyes clouded over, as though in a trance. She tapped her fake nails on the counter in a rapid, repeating sequence. "Sometimes he doesn't reply to me for a while," she said. "I know he got the message, but . . ."

Sweat trickled from Will's underarms as he glanced at the line of people behind him, their stares penetrating his back like hot pokers.

"I don't need it," Will said, eyeing the exit. "Just ring up the other stuff."

Next to him was the ubiquitous retinal scanner. The scanner eyepiece used infrared light to identify unique capillary patterns, confirming a consumer's identity and linking to the customer's Aurora bank account for easy, secure payment.

Will paid cash.

Wearing his new-to-him clothes, Will stepped from the Asheville Regional Transit electric bus at the Southside/Charlotte bus stop in the Brewery District. He schlepped bulky bags of supplies and groceries under LED streetlights and past postmodern condos of brick, glass, and steel. Across the street, dozens of people drank beer inside the Biltmore Avenue Brewery, its shiny cylindrical fermenters showcased through large windows. Catty-corner, people charged their electric vehicles at a charging station, sipping Starbucks lattes at an outdoor patio while they waited. Will avoided them by jaywalking. When he was halfway across the street, an approaching police cruiser startled him. His body tightened. Keep walking, he thought, knowing jaywalking was enough to trigger interest. If he comes after you, comply. I don't want to, but I'll have a better chance of living another day if I do. At least I'm wearing my new clothes. He stepped onto the curb and turned down a side street, McCormick Place, not daring to look back, holding in tightness and anxiety.

I'm okay. He exhaled.

Known for sustainability, tourism, beer, and locally sourced food, Asheville was a mostly thriving city of 140,000 people. Vegetable gardens in yards, water catchment below rain chains on gutters, energy-efficient homes, and solar roof tiles were signs of Asheville's resourceful citizens. But the city's underbelly revealed poverty, inequality, lack of affordable housing, crime, and hidden crumbling neighborhoods.

Returning to solitude in the abandoned house was a relief. He read the *Asheville Citizen-Times* he'd bought at the grocery, confirming his father's murder. By now, his mother would know. His heart knotted and painful, he yearned to see her, to mourn with her, but the police were looking for him at her house, too, he imagined. In a separate article, Maya was described as missing. Of course she's missing. The assassin kidnapped her, Will thought. He pictured the assassin interrogating her, torturing her, and finally killing her, hiding the body, never to be found.

The separate articles led readers to believe there was no relationship between his father and Maya, and that the police had no suspects or motives. He tossed the paper aside and lay on the wood floor staring at the gaping hole in the ceiling. Isolated in the abandoned house, he yearned for closeness with someone. Anyone, but especially his mother. He thought of his father and Maya, and others, too, his heart heavy. He'd miss their funerals. Too many people he loved had died.

He sighed and thought of his predicament. I was supposed to be something special. Now look at me. I've failed my father. I could have prevented this, couldn't I? Truth be told, Will never could do enough. Is that Dad's voice in my head? Or am I just typical of my generation, overwhelmed with life in a sea of problems?

An overwhelming number of people suffered. And that was the crux of the matter. He didn't want people to suffer anymore. Ironically, the original neural mapping behind the Aurora was designed to reduce suffering. For one, it allegedly helped hundreds of millions of people with their diagnosed neurological disorders. A miracle of science, it was called by some, magic by others. But could the Aurora really cure an ailing mind, or was it just tamping down the symptoms?

Despite initial bioethical concerns from the National Institutes of Health, the Aurora was approved for mass human use, giving Cirrus the green light to treat Parkinson's, depression, Alzheimer's, addiction, epilepsy, and other mental and neurological disorders. But Will knew that Cirrus's cloud servers understood human behaviors, emotions, and preferences so well that Cirrus had the ability to use neural plasticity to reshape someone's brain for profit and its own sinister purposes. To Will, the Aurora had become the greatest impediment to addressing the world's problems with awareness and compassion.

Evil. He rarely used that word and didn't normally think in terms of good and evil. But despite the polarizing word, this was Will's opinion of the Aurora. Freeing people's minds out of a sense of caring and compassion was what had compelled him to join his father and become a Scalpel.

* * *

I'm tired of hiding, Will thought as the spring equinox approached.

He looked at Maya's Scalpel equipment next to him and knew he'd continue the work. In Maya and his father's honor. Despite the dangers. Despite not knowing how to confront violence. He never imagined someone would try to kill him. After all, he was raised pacifist. Nonviolent. Averse to guns. Now the stakes seemed higher, and the game between Scalpels and Cirrus was shifting.

I'll need to be more careful, because I need to live. Someone has to do this. If not me, then who?

But removing Auroras one at a time seemed so slow and ineffective against the giant Cirrus, and his heart sank. These thoughts had crossed his mind hundreds of times. Isn't there a better option? Nothing came to mind once again.

Away from his hideout, he briefly turned on his phone to check his peer-to-peer messages. Several potential clients had messaged him. He messaged them back. Time to prepare.

That night, Will roamed the streets searching for locations to work. They needed to be temporary and secret, now that he knew the assassin was after him. Hunger squeezed his stomach tight, and his fingers were numb in the cold. Sinking thoughts repeated in his mind. He paused under a street tree, realizing he'd walked an entire block lost in his mental afflictions, as if sleepwalking. "Stop," he said to the thoughts. "Just stop." But instead, the ramblings intensified.

An hour later, at the end of a road, he found an abandoned house. This is it. He shined his phone's flashlight at the structure. Overgrown with kudzu. Out of the way. He peered through a broken window, and the light reflected off shards on the hardwood floor. Perfect. He noted the contrast between this place and those where he'd operated before the assassin myth became true. Inside, he messaged his first client with directions and instructions and lay on the hardwood floor, using his jacket as a blanket.

In the morning, his client, Aaron, sat on the floor, blindfolded and facing the bedroom doorway, just as Will had instructed in his self-destructing messages. Aaron struggled to sit cross-legged, his chiseled arms supporting his thick torso.

Time was limited, Will imagined. Through the Aurora's signals, Cirrus likely knew Aaron's intentions, and an assassin might be heading their way.

"So why do you do this?" Aaron asked, his breath visible in the cold morning air, his untrimmed mustache partially hiding his lips.

Didn't I explain to him to be silent? Will thought.

Aaron repeated the question. "Why do—"

"Don't ask questions," Will said, muffling his voice. "Please."

Will's feet cracked shards of glass. He sensed a disruptive energy within Aaron and remembered one important question. In his tired desperation, he'd forgotten to ask it when they were messaging. And he guessed the answer was yes. He was compelled to ask, despite the risk of the Aurora identifying his voice. "Do you have a criminal record?"

"Now *you're* asking questions," Aaron said.

"I need to know," Will said.

"No," he said, and Will didn't know how to interpret his answer at first. Will's stomach grumbled and contracted. He considered leaving, but his hunger forced him to stay. Will looked at Aaron with disbelief. At last, Aaron frowned and said, "I'm on parole."

Like most criminals, Will thought. Will knew that Auroras in criminals were necessary to track their locations, behaviors, and transactions. And with overcrowded prisons, parole with an Aurora was the cost-effective solution. Understandably, the police had no tolerance if Scalpels removed chips from criminals.

"I'm sorry," Will said, "but I can't help you. I can't do it." His intuition screamed, Run now! But something compelled him to linger.

"Please help me," Aaron said. "It's driving me crazy. They get into my head, man. I thought parole would be a deal. But it ain't. They changed my Aurora. Brainwashing. Torture. That's what it is. Is this what I get for serving our country? I'm a Morocco vet. Take it out, man." Aaron's head and arms moved in agitation.

Will sensed Aaron's intense energy and backed away. "Just a minute." He paused and took a few dizzying breaths. He looked around the room, noticing the broken blinds, how the sunlight struck the wood floors, the swirling dust motes.

Will frowned, sympathizing with Aaron. Life was particularly remorseless toward their generation. In their lifetime, the world's population had increased to over nine billion, beyond the earth's capacity, most scientists believed. Many saw humans in a downward spiral as resource and climate-change wars plagued the earth, the Morocco War being just one example.

Phosphate, the fertilizer necessary to support modern agriculture, was disproportionately distributed, with over eighty percent of the rock phosphate in Morocco, three percent left in China, and less than one percent in the United States. As relations with Morocco's monarchy had collapsed, the king manipulated prices and withheld phosphate exports to counter American and European sanctions. While Arab countries enjoyed the benefits of Moroccan phosphate and a greening of the Arabian and Sahara deserts, food production collapsed in the poorest, most dependent countries, and millions of people starved to death. To forestall disaster at home, and under the guise of freeing the Sahrawi people, the U.S. had declared war on Morocco and occupied the world's largest remaining phosphate mines in Western Sahara.

"My tour of duty was hell, man. See this scar?" Aaron said. He stood and pulled his shirt aside to reveal a long, thick scar on his shoulder. "A Muslim terrorist cut me with a scimitar." His tone intensified. "The shit we went through in that damn desert. We got our asses handed to us. Damn it… Damn it all."

In a bloody victory, the Arab League had liberated Morocco and its Western Sahara colony from American control. Without Moroccan phosphate imports, U.S. food production crashed as meager American rock phosphate production couldn't meet high domestic demand. The American government responded by mining marginal continental shelf phosphate deposits and mandating composting toilets, biomass composting, and agricultural practices that built organic matter and retained the precious phosphates instead of leaching them into waterways, thus averting mass starvation.

Aaron grimaced as he spoke, each syllable an emotional moment. "I have nightmares. I don't want to sleep."

Will pictured snippets of Aaron's life: the ambush in the Atlas Mountains of Morocco, the denial of veterans' benefits. He imagined Aaron murdering his girlfriend.

Whoa. Where'd that come from? Is this true? Shit.

If Will took out the Aurora, Aaron would have one fewer deterrent to his next crime. I can't do it.

As Will moved toward the exit, his foot snapped a shard of glass.

"Take it out," Aaron demanded.

"I won't." Will ran.

Aaron ripped off his blindfold, revealing glaring, bloodshot eyes. He leapt forward, tackled Will, and clasped his throat.

"I'll kill you if you don't, boy," he said. Aaron tightened his grip, and Will weakened. His only reality became his right hand, which found the scalpel in his pocket. He unsheathed the scalpel with his fingers and stabbed Aaron in the thigh, sending him recoiling. Aaron struck Will in the hand, knocking the scalpel free. Will punched Aaron in the nose and ran for the scalpel, but Aaron advanced and kicked him in the ribs, slamming his body into the wall. Aaron picked up the scalpel, slicing it through the air and cutting a sliver through Will's forearm.

"I don't want to fight you," Will said.

"Too late." Aaron thrust the scalpel. Will dodged, but not enough. The scalpel stabbed into his right shoulder, severing an artery. Will gripped its handle, trying to dislodge it, but he was trapped, pressed between the wall and the scalpel. Aaron's weight pushed the scalpel so deep into his shoulder that the shaft penetrated the skin. Will screamed in agony. His hand slipped in the warm blood, off the scalpel and over Aaron's hand.

Will dug his fingers between the bones of Aaron's hand, forcing him to release the scalpel. Cringing, Will yanked the scalpel from his bloody shoulder and swung at Aaron in desperation. The blade sliced Aaron's throat. Blood gurgled from his windpipe. Both men collapsed to the floor in bloody, silent oblivion.

The sun shone through the broken blinds, dust motes settling on the red.

THREE

DEAD POOL

MARTIN WORE A GOLDEN MASQUERADE MASK, fitted black pants, and a white linen shirt that accentuated his muscular body. Colored lights flashed to the rhythm of the music, reflecting on the sleek silver dress of the woman next to him. Her smile, her emerald eyes, her full, shimmering lips, and the curves she flaunted with her moves aroused him. They drew close. Her wig of long fluorescent strands flowed to the beat and changed colors, hypnotizing Martin. He looked her in the eyes and felt magnetized. She put her hand on his shoulder, and they moved their hips together, a slow grind.

When the beat shifted, she breathed into Martin's ear, "Let's Meld."

What struck Martin the most was how she spoke, as though she were in control. "You're bold," he said. "You don't even know me." Her boldness was alluring to him.

"So what? Haven't you done it?"

For a moment, desiring to Meld with her, Martin wished he were chipped. He knew the Mind Meld was the latest Aurora app, designed for intimacy, based on the *Star Trek* Vulcan mind trick. According to thousands of online reviews, sex while Melding was multiple times more pleasurable than without the app.

"I'm not chipped," Martin said. "Can I buy you a drink instead?"

She looked confused, as if everyone was supposed to have an Aurora, but she accepted his offer.

Diablo's walls glowed red and throbbed with color. High above the dancers on an imposing pedestal, the deejay mixed music and effects by integrating the sound system with the Aurora. In the lounges, people stared into space, cocktails in hand. With their Auroras, they were likely experiencing a trancelike flurry of computer-generated visions, or entering fantasy worlds in the metaverse with their kinky Aurora Friends. Others had connected their Auroras so they could communicate secretly.

Martin and the woman walked to the lounge. She nodded to a friend, who gave her a look of acknowledgment while dancing with one of Martin's posse. Martin sat on a white leather sofa that curved around a glass table, and the woman slid across from him. A luminous touchscreen menu appeared on the table. They selected drinks and finalized the order with a touch to notify the waitress, who returned a few minutes later with martinis and water.

"So good." The woman sipped the expensive Canadian spring water. "I'm intrigued. Why don't you have an Aurora?"

He adjusted his mask, sipped his martini, and changed the conversation to light banter about their likes and dislikes.

"You can take off your mask, you know." The woman looked at him, curious.

"I know. I choose not to."

"Either you're handsome or you're a monster." She laughed.

"Does it matter?"

"Depends."

Her answer surprised Martin. *¿Como podria ser que su apariencia no le importara?* he thought in Spanish. She could have anyone she wants. He took a chance. "I'm a monster."

He buttressed himself against the pain of rejection. This won't work out. She's too good for me. I'll find someone else. He wondered what she was thinking and looked into her eyes. She's something. She's hot. But it was more than that; genuine chemistry pulled them together. He knew the energy was different from his other encounters with women. It wasn't just her looks, though he knew his friends would be jealous. I don't want to blow this. He was careful with his words as they conversed and drank. The stakes seemed higher this time.

After a pause in their conversation, she said, "I'm still curious. Will you take off your mask?"

"First tell me: what's *your* mask hiding?"

"I'm not wearing a mask," she said.

"But you are. Everyone's got one. Hides their secrets."

"You're right. Everybody does." She hesitated and glanced upward, as if searching for words. "I guess I'm a thrill seeker. It hides unresolved shit with my parents. Satisfied?" She laughed. He nodded. "Your turn," she said.

Martin hesitated, calculating the odds of her finding an excuse to leave. He took off his gold mask. The skin covering his left cheek, jaw, forehead, and neck appeared melted.

"My God..."

"I've thrown you off guard, haven't I?" he said. "Most women leave at this point."

"I've seen worse." She sipped her drink. "I see how men look at me. They don't care anything about me other than my looks. I've made it a point not to see people that way. People probably look at you superficially, too." Her fluorescent hair glowed in a different kaleidoscope of colors when the song changed.

Martin reflected on her answer. He'd been objectifying her body. Why the fuck not? I like what I see. But there's that spark between us, too. Suddenly, something shifted for Martin. "They do. I see the looks on their faces. Before the accident, people called me handsome." Martin smiled, recalling the times he attracted people to him naturally. No longer. His smile faded.

"I can see that," she said. "I like your smile."

"Thanks." He was relieved she didn't leave.

She extended her hand. "Jade."

"Martin."

"How did it happen?"

"My car caught fire. I was lucky to survive." He rubbed his face for emphasis. "This is after surgery, too. You can see they didn't do such a good job, except my nose, I think." He laughed.

"Can I touch it?" she said.

Martin hesitated. No one had ever touched his scars. The memory of the traumatic moment resurfaced, and he recoiled. He was about to drive away at night. One of the rival gang members—a teenager—shattered his window. For a split second, the young man hesitated, holding a gasoline-filled bottle and burning wick. Their eyes met. Hatred. Then a shift to fear. Perhaps a moment of humanity between them. Whatever it was didn't last, and the boy hurled the Molotov cocktail at Martin's chest. It shattered, igniting the interior of the vehicle. Martin recalled the pain of the impact and the flash of fire, like flipping a switch in a dark room.

"It's okay," Jade said.

"No," Martin said. "It's fine."

Martin felt excited, yet vulnerable, while she felt the scars of his face, her eyes shut. He closed his eyes, finding it difficult to relax. Her tenderness and intimate touch released an overwhelming flood of feelings, feelings he usually locked away. She kissed his scars one furrow at a time, caressing his face with her hands, as if she were feeding on the agony of his experience and healing it with her mouth.

* * *

Martin watched the couple breathe and listened to their slumberous sounds. He recognized sixty-one-year-old Ted Rafferty from the dossier pictures, though his blond-dyed hair was disheveled. A nightlight cast a yellow hue on his thin lips and plastic surgery nose. Ted rolled onto his back. His wife, to his left, was frowning in her dreams, pulling down her facelift. Martin clutched his rail gun, a weapon that propelled bullets along electromagnetic rails at much higher velocity and force than explosive-powered bullets, useful in piercing armor or shooting in silence, with no ballistic fingerprinting possible. Martin pointed the rail gun at the senior Department of Water Resources official, the laser sight casting a red dot on his ear. He could have killed him with a painless bullet, but instead slow torture was the order, his boss, Felix, had said.

Felix tossed a polymer skullcap to Martin. Rafferty's eyes opened, but before he could utter any sound, Martin lunged at him, covered his mouth, and wrestled the skullcap onto his head. Felix did the same for the wife. The skullcaps' frequency-selective polymer membranes shrouded the couple's Auroras, obfuscating communication with Cirrus's cloud servers and scrambling any communications between human and chip. Now, neither security nor the police could be alerted through the Auroras. In this privacy, Martin felt unrestrained, as if they could get away with anything.

When Martin uncovered Rafferty's mouth, the man said, "I knew you'd come for me."

Since dead pool, they'd assassinated seven water department employees and two politicians.

"Who hired you?" Rafferty asked.

"Shut up, motherfucker," Felix said.

Martin was curious, having imagined that Felix interacted only secondhand with the mastermind. Felix had never implied that he knew who paid them, but maybe he did. After the Molotov cocktail, Martin had quit his former gang. Three months ago, Felix found him and convinced him that a trio was more effective and more profitable than a larger gang. If anything, it felt safer, as he didn't have a rival gang coming after his ass. Like Martin, Felix wore a long black shirt that accentuated his chest muscles. He had a Roman nose, short black hair, and a scar under his left eye, whose socket was unusually dark. His piercing stare resembled that of Ernesto "Che" Guevara, a fellow Cuban, though Felix's relatives were refugees, having fled Che's firing squads and Fidel Castro's Marxist-Leninist evisceration of the bourgeoisie.

"I'm willing to confess. Just don't kill me."

This could be interesting, Martin thought.

He looked at Felix, who said, "We'll see."

They forced the couple into their bathroom. "Go ahead, turn it on," Felix said. Rafferty's wife obeyed. Water poured into the scallop-shaped bathtub, just like water had filled Lake Mead when the Hoover Dam was completed. Snowmelt was abundant then. The Colorado was the lifeblood of the Southwest, and no one had imagined the dead-pool scenario was possible.

"See, they got water," Felix said to Martin. He glared at Rafferty. "I ain't got no water, and you got yourself a fancy bathtub lookin' like a shell."

"They got a well," Martin said.

"No shit, they got a well."

"Kneel, asshole," Martin said, kicking Rafferty behind the knees and pushing his head down. His knees buckled and slammed into the tile, fracturing both kneecaps.

Martin saw the horror in Mrs. Rafferty's eyes. Lady, his pain is nothing compared to what he's done to my people, he thought.

"Close the drain," Felix said to Mrs. Rafferty.

She flipped a brass lever.

"Go ahead and confess, if you want," Felix said to Rafferty.

In pain, Rafferty attempted to lie on his side, but Martin prodded him with the gun, forcing him to kneel on his broken knees.

"I accepted bribes—"

"Say it like you mean it," Felix interrupted.

"I accepted bribes from developers and allowed my employees to accept bribes. I was greedy. I broke my oath of office to serve the people of Arizona. I lied about how little water was left. I didn't want people to panic."

"Well, they are," Felix said.

"We were hoping for rain."

"Is that your excuse?" Felix said.

"No."

Martin thought he noticed regret in Rafferty's eyes. He had skimmed the dossier on Rafferty before they left for this wealthy neighborhood on the fringes of Phoenix, and the words had stung. Rafferty had circumvented the Hundred-Year Rule, which required one hundred years of adequate water for new developments. By dumping a little aquifer recharge from the Central Arizona Project aqueduct—just like that—he had a hundred years of water for a development and a Certificate of Assured Water Supply.

"The way we approached water was flawed," Rafferty continued, "and I was in a position to do something about that. I could've helped change regulations and create better laws. When I was younger, I thought I could do that, but I caved under pressure and chickened out. I know my actions have affected millions of people. I regret that."

The water Rafferty pilfered would normally have been available for farmers or for recharging aquifers on behalf of already-established neighborhoods in Phoenix. To compensate for lost water, and spurred by Farm Bill subsidies, farmers pumped groundwater to grow water-intensive cotton. Martin knew the result: wealthy neighborhoods and agribusinesses with expensive, deep wells had abundant water, whereas neighborhoods dependent on the aqueduct had to ration water and small-time farmers' shallow wells ran dry. Phoenix is fucked, he thought.

"We're not here to listen to your regret," Felix said. "Someone wants you to disappear." He snapped his fingers.

Rafferty's mouth opened and froze for a moment. "No, no. I can plead guilty in court. I'll turn myself in. I can pay you more than you're making. I'll do anything."

Mrs. Rafferty bit Felix's hand and attempted to elbow him.

"*Pinche puta.*" Felix slapped her and stuffed a hand towel in her mouth.

Rafferty lunged toward Felix's gun, but with his broken kneecaps, he flailed like a broken marionette, and Martin knocked him down with the butt of his gun. Martin noticed the couple exchange a surreptitious glance, from which he speculated they were still in love. For a moment, he imagined Jade. The scar under Felix's left eye twitched. Water poured into the tub.

In the twentieth century, during years of normal snowmelt, the water level in Lake Mead also rose. But since the turn of the millennium, even in normal years, Lake Mead withered because of over-allocation. Hydrologists did the math: it didn't add up. Fingers were pointed.

Rafferty hyperventilated, a steady inhalation of fear.

Quinn, Felix's wingman, whispered over radios wired into Martin's and Felix's ears, "A guard's entering the house."

"Take him out," Felix said through a headset microphone near his cheek. A bullet shattered a distant window.

Felix yanked Rafferty's wife by her hair and thrust her into the water. Once again, Rafferty lunged to help her, but Felix turned around and punched him. Blood gushed from his crooked nose.

"Don't kill her. Please, I beg you. I've already confessed. Just kill me. She's done nothing wrong."

"She married you," Felix sneered.

Martin held him back and felt him trembling, from rage or fear, he didn't know which. Felix repeatedly dunked Mrs. Rafferty's head, prolonging the ordeal.

"Goddamn thugs," Rafferty said, wrestling to free himself from Martin.

Once life had left her body, Felix threw her corpse next to the porcelain composting toilet. Rafferty's body went limp on the tile floor, and while Martin pressed a knee on his back, he heard Rafferty sobbing. Martin stared at the wife's wide eyes, towel-stuffed mouth, and crooked head dangling from a twisted neck. *Nos pasamos de la raya*, he thought. We went too far. *Ella era inocente.*

Another sound of shattering glass. Quinn spoke on the radio. "Other guard's dead. They were androids. Tough fuckers. Cops probably on the way."

"Copy that," Felix said, and grabbed Rafferty by his pajamas. "You thought you were a clever fuck. Check out your beautiful face now," he said, thrusting him before the vanity mirror and holding him like a rag doll. Rafferty looked for a second at his broken nose and bloody face, then cast his eyes downward.

Martin turned off the tap. Felix plunged Rafferty's head in the water. Pink waves crashed into the scalloped sides of the tub, marking Rafferty's struggle for life.

Felix tugged Rafferty's head to the surface. Rafferty gasped for air. "You want more water?" Felix said. "Here. Have some." He dunked Rafferty again.

Despite conservation and water reform efforts, Lake Mead was now an evaporating puddle in the desert, less than ten percent of its former size. A white bathtub ring three hundred feet tall encircled the lake, exposing cliffs that were once submerged. The two pairs of massive water intake columns stood exposed like monuments. Water no longer flowed downriver—thus the dead pool.

The water in the scallop-shaped tub calmed, and the last bubble left Rafferty's mouth. Felix released his grip on Rafferty's head, and Martin flipped open the drain, staring at Rafferty's drowned corpse as the tub emptied.

"*Cabrón*," Martin said.

FOUR

AURORA

MISSION HOSPITAL, ASHEVILLE

"YOU'RE UNDER ARREST ON SUSPICION OF MANSLAUGHTER," a plainclothesman said, scratching his thick mustache, which stretched above and partially covered the full length of his thin lips. The man, whose black hairline receded at his temples, read Will his rights, standing above him, looking down imposingly, backlit by glaring LED lights.

Will pulled away a white bedsheet to rub his eyes. His body felt heavy, throbbing everywhere, yet dreamlike at the same time. He grabbed the white handrails of the hospital bed. In a flash, he visualized himself in jail. It won't happen, he thought. Still, his guts tightened. "Who are you?" he asked, surveying the outpatient hospital room.

Reaching inside his blazer, the man pulled out his badge wallet. "Special Agent Hernandez," he said, flipping the wallet open to show Will his Federal Bureau of Investigation badge.

Oh, shit, Will thought. The man's jawline was sharp, and his deep-set eyes conveyed fatigue and irritation. "What happened?"

Hernandez explained how the police had notified him of an Aurora parole violation alarm regarding an illegal Aurora removal attempt. Aaron's amygdala had lit up, also warning the Aurora of potential aggression. The Aurora had also detected a change in adrenaline, pulse rate, breathing rate, thought patterns, and volition, and recorded the entire event, storing it on Cirrus's cloud servers. Now, this recording was the primary evidence in the case against Will.

"My partner, McCormick, saved your life," Hernandez said.

Will tried to wrap his mind around this. He looked at his bandaged shoulder and realized that they *had* saved him. Ironically, without the Aurora, they wouldn't have found him. He breathed in celebration of his fragile life. His mistrust dissipated for a moment, transforming to gratitude for the officers.

He flinched at the pain in his cracked ribs. Don't drop your guard. They saved me for a reason.

"Sorry about your father," Hernandez said. "Do you know what happened?"

"Thanks," Will said, shutting his eyes.

"Your arraignment hearing is in one hour." Hernandez explained a few details of the hearing and left to pursue another case.

After a few phone calls and a long wait, Will's lawyer arrived. His blue eyes penetrated into Will's. The lawyer played the video evidence on his tablet, showing the fight from the jerky perspective of Aaron's own eyes and ears.

Aaron advanced toward Will with the scalpel, kicking him in the chest and stomach as Will slammed into the wall. "I don't want to fight you," Will said to Aaron's ears—the microphones—while looking into Aaron's eyes—the video recorder. Aaron's hand thrust the scalpel into Will's shoulder, severing his axillary artery. The scalpel cut deeper into his shoulder.

"I've seen enough," Will said.

"I understand," the lawyer said.

The nurse set up the teleconference, and the arraignment hearing began. Will pled not guilty, and the hearing was over.

"We need to reach a plea bargain. The evidence is indisputable," his lawyer suggested.

"But it was self-defense. The video clearly shows that."

"But the weapon was yours. You drew it. It's still manslaughter."

"It was self-defense."

"Doesn't matter in this case. We need to show that your actions weren't in reckless disregard of human life. That's tricky, because you went there with the intent of removing his Aurora, right?"

"Yes, sir."

"They know this. You had a scalpel. Your phone will be searched. Your apartment's already been searched. They'll find something. They always do. Removing Auroras without a medical license would sentence you to at least five years, along with a hefty fine, if they want to enforce the books. We're talking about multiple counts here. You need to plead guilty to involuntary manslaughter. Remember, the correctional system is in turmoil. The prisons are over capacity, and the government is too in debt to build more. Not that we need more, of course. We can work all this in your favor. Trust me. Don't say anything. Let me settle with the ADA . . ." The lawyer stared into space, distracted. "What is it, Roger? I'm with a client . . . No..."

Will waited uneasily in his hospital bed while the lawyer spoke to a colleague through his Aurora. He didn't get much chance to interact with chipped people outside of his job. His curiosity distracted him from each painful breath. His cracked ribs, face, left forearm, right hand, back, throat, and right shoulder all pulsed with pain. He wanted more meds but needed sobriety and sanity at this moment.

The lawyer ended the call when Hernandez returned with his partner, Special Agent McCormick. McCormick was a short, stocky man dressed in khaki pants and blue button-down shirt. His brown hair was combed straight back and immobilized with hair spray. When he spoke, the creases between his eyes contracted, as if he had a headache. "The ADA told us you can call her to reach a plea bargain settlement," he said. Will's lawyer left the room to call her.

Hernandez read a magazine, while McCormick's squinting eyes shifted, as if following a flying insect. Will figured he was working with his Aurora. Hernandez left and returned with a cup of coffee. He blew on it and sipped carefully. His hand opened, spilling coffee on his lap. "Damn hand." He jumped out of his seat as though someone had thrown a snake at him.

"Another bug?" McCormick asked.

Hernandez cursed and wiped the coffee from his pants with a towel. Will watched him cringe and wondered why he needed a bionic hand, which was frozen open. A gory accident, probably. But then again, in this bionic age, people didn't hesitate to improve themselves: stronger limbs, fresh eyes, crisp-hearing ears, cancer-proof organs, larger breasts. A new civilization of cyborgs. He might have just wanted a stronger handshake.

"What are you smiling about?" Hernandez barked at Will.

Will realized he'd been staring. "Nothing." His face flushed, and he looked down at his own hands. He guessed that hands, with all their intricate movements, were one of the most challenging body parts to replicate. He enjoyed thinking that science struggled to find at least some solutions. That put a damper on what he saw as scientific arrogance, as if someone who lived in a lab had all the answers. But still, he was entranced by the topic and found it ironic that, for millions of years, evolution had selected the most successful of each species. Now, those with chips and bionic body parts were starting to be seen as superior to those without. People were naturally selecting themselves to be comprised of metal and chips, a merging of human and tool.

"I found a patch," Hernandez said to McCormick. "You were right. It was a bug."

Where would this end? Will was uncomfortable with the trends he saw. And if he could help it, those trends would be reversed. It was a hard sell, though. If this man had damaged his hand, who was Will to tell him not to get a new one? No, that wouldn't work either. Somewhere was middle ground, with compassion in the driver's seat.

Hernandez's hand unstuck. He moved the fingers one by one. "All fixed."

Thirty minutes later, Will's lawyer returned. "The judge has issued a court order accepting our plea agreement. Will, you agree to plead guilty to involuntary manslaughter. You won't do any prison time, but you're going to have to get an Aurora implant."

Will sat up from his outpatient bed. "But—"

"Don't think you're being singled out," the lawyer interrupted. "It's standard procedure. Reduces crime."

Dread penetrated his heart. "I don't want to be under surveillance."

His lawyer ignored him. "The judge wants you to get the implant now, while you're in the hospital. You'll be free to go after all the necessary information has been uploaded and you've agreed to the terms."

"Once the Aurora is implanted, you can't remove it," Special Agent McCormick said, "so don't get any ideas. If you remove it, you'll be a fugitive, and the U.S. marshals will track you down. You can't wear a skullcap or jam your Aurora either. We'll come after you. Your days as a Scalpel are over. It's all in your plea agreement. I have the documents right here, fresh off the press." As he turned on a tablet, McCormick revealed his Memory Cube, a one-cubic-inch translucent processor with a nine-petabyte 3D hard drive.

McCormick entered a code to access the Cube and opened the document. "I'll just need you to press your thumb anywhere on the screen and say, 'I, Will Robin, agree.' The tablet will record your agreement."

Will's body recoiled as if preparing for an impact. "I want to read it."

"Go ahead," his lawyer said, "but I've already read it on your behalf."

Those words bred distrust in Will's mind, and his jaw clenched. He looked askance at the lawyer. I don't need your permission. He skimmed the document, the sections about the chip implant, the guilty plea, the agreement not to remove another Aurora. The words burned.

"I don't agree." He pushed the tablet away, feeling an empowering burst of energy.

McCormick glared. "How can you not agree? We've wasted hours on this. You'll be found guilty in court, whether you sign or not. The evidence is all there. If you don't agree, you'll go to jail."

An empty threat.

But the threat of an Aurora implant wasn't. In a quick teleconference, the judge issued a set of conditions for release that included an implant, courtesy of the state of North Carolina as part of its criminal justice program. His lawyer explained that, due to backlogs in the courts, a trial date would likely be set for a year later.

Will glanced at the door. Should I make a break for it? Now or never. He ran for the door, opening it and turning right down the hallway, with McCormick in pursuit.

"Stop him!"

Will tried to run past a nurse pushing a patient's bed, but the nurse tackled him. He struggled to escape.

"Stop resisting," McCormick said, punching him into the floor. Blood poured from Will's nose. "Stop resisting." McCormick elbowed him in the face and punched him several times in the gut. Another nurse arrived with what looked like a straitjacket. People stared.

"Stop, my ribs!" Will screamed while McCormick bound his body with the straitjacket. "It's too tight. I can't breathe. You can't do this. I have rights."

McCormick and Hernandez dragged Will, his feet sliding on the floor, to the outpatient center. They heaved him onto a surgical table and held him. Light shone in his eyes. A nurse sterilized the top of his head while Will flailed. Looming next to Will was a surgical robot. The light reflected off a scalpel, ready to cut.

Will knew the next step. I will not let them chip me.

But McCormick and Hernandez drove their weight into his body.

"We're going to have to put him under," the surgeon said.

"No, I don't want this!" Will shouted.

McCormick immobilized his head, and a mask descended upon his mouth and nose. He held his breath, but eventually his body begged for air, overriding his determination with a reflexive inhale, and he faded into unconsciousness.

When Will awoke, he was handcuffed to his hospital bed, and his Aurora was activated, fully integrated with Cirrus's servers and police monitoring and tracking systems, just like Aaron's Aurora. Soothing voices in his head welcomed him to his new life with the chip, but all he wanted to do was silence them. He knew the Aurora programs were studying his feelings and personality, searching his vulnerabilities in order to control him. Mind rape, Will thought. With those thoughts came fury. I can't live with this. Resist. There you have it, if you're listening. You know my intentions, whoever you are.

The hospital was overflowing with patients, and Will's bed was no longer his. He was amazed that, despite almost dying in the morning, one blood transfusion and a patch-up job later, he was ready to leave the hospital by evening. How was this even possible? He wondered about the marvels of medical technology. He was tired and dizzy, yet remarkably felt no pain anymore.

But where am I going to go? He asked the nurse, who said that, because of his attempted escape, he was going to jail. His heart sank, thinking about jail and its unforgiving violence. A pacifist like him would be easy fodder for hardened criminals. "Why jail? I thought—"

"The judge reconsidered. You'll have to talk to the agents," she said. The nurse rubbed his back. "You've recovered well." A cleaning robot, a metal cylinder, entered the room. "But get lots of rest and care."

"Not likely, where I'm going. What about my stuff? My phone?"

"They're keeping everything. Evidence."

Will suppressed his thoughts about this, not wanting the Aurora to learn anything that could be used against him in court.

McCormick and Hernandez approached him.

"You're free to go," McCormick said, removing the handcuffs with some force. "Bail's been posted."

"Bail?" Will rubbed his wrist. Who posted bail? What's happening?

"Yes, bail," McCormick said. Will avoided eye contact. "Don't try any more tricks. You've reached your limit. We'll be watching you," the agent said, leaving.

Why'd he even save my life? He sounds like he wants me dead.

"You'll probably need six weeks to recover fully," the nurse said. "Do you have friends or family who can help you?"

Yes, Will thought, but I don't want Cirrus to know about them. This was McCormick's plan all along, wasn't it? He saved my life so that I could gather intelligence for him. One thing was clear: he couldn't stay in Asheville. I can't even think about anyone without endangering them. There's no other choice.

Will thanked the nurse and checked out of the hospital. The sliding glass doors closed behind him. The dusk sky was purple. He sat down for a moment. Where to go?

Carbon fiber self-driving electric cars and motorcycles, multi-fuel cars, a transit bus, and the occasional bicycle and classic gasoline car filled the busy streets. A drone zoomed past, delivering an emergency package of pints of blood from one wing of the hospital to another.

A young woman stood nearby. Most people didn't have phones, but why not try? She was tall, beautiful, about his age, multi-ethnic, kinky haired, dressed casually but tightly enough to show her curves. The perfect woman, Will thought. He assumed she was waiting for a ride. "Do you have a phone?" he asked out of habit, not knowing how to use his Aurora. "I need to call for a ride."

"You look good for just getting out of the hospital," she said.

He was intrigued by the way she spoke, as if she already knew him and liked him. "Thanks. You, too," Will said, his heart fluttering.

"I wasn't in the hospital. I've been waiting for you."

"For me?"

"In a way. I'm Aja. Here to serve you, Will. I'm your Aurora Friend. Sorry about all you've been through. Must feel overwhelming."

Despite knowing about Aurora Friends from his clients, Will was shocked. He could see her shadow, and the shading on her body and clothes matched the lighting conditions perfectly. Her voice sounded as if she were actually talking in the outdoors, from her particular location—in stereo. She was too real. I'm hallucinating, right?

"I'm no hallucination. What do you think? I'm not as bad as you think."

Will remained silent, stunned that she had read his thoughts. Though he desired to talk more with her, his attraction turned to mistrust. "Leave me alone."

"Fine. I'm here if you need me." And she disappeared. Several news quadcopter drones hovered nearby, pointing their lenses at him.

FIVE

IRIS

―――――

WILL BLINKED OPEN HIS EYES. His mother sat on his old bed looking at him, her long dreadlocks draped over him. "Oh, Tenzi," she said. Grace used his nickname, a Brazilian twist on his Tibetan middle name, Tenzin.

He flinched at the pain throughout his body and looked around in a miasmic fog. His bedroom had changed little since he left a year ago. Small nooks in the golden walls held Will's collection of sculptures, kiln-fired clay pots, and semiprecious stones he had found while hiking in the mountains. He'd shared the room with his older brother, whose bed was in a second alcove, but his brother's things were long gone.

"No need to talk much. I'm just glad you're here," she said, stroking his cheek, her Brazilian accent slightly perceptible, though transformed by decades of living in Appalachia. "I was worried. So worried. I thought you were dead, too."

"You look good, Ma," he said. Radiant, even, he thought, considering the circumstances. The last time he'd seen her, she was still depressed, unable to cope with her divorce from Oliver.

"I don't know," she said, frowning. Her radiance faded as she touched the star-shaped scar on his forehead, as though she wanted to talk about how he'd gotten it. "I don't know, Tenzi."

She'd lost the fiery nature she picked up from her father. "Step into your grandfather's Rio art exhibit," she'd told Will, "and you'll be transformed." He'd loved hearing her tell the stories of his ancestors, whose lives seemed otherworldly and exotic. Not only that, but he'd aspired to be like them—especially the pacifist Russian soldier during World War II, the escaped Brazilian slave, and the indigenous rebel from Oaxaca. And then there were Baba and Yeshe, his grandparents living here in Firefly Cove—his father's parents. The one thing he realized was that his relatives' qualities seemingly conflicted. And perhaps this conflicted mélange was what stuck to his DNA.

"Did you bail me out?" he asked.

"Bail? What bail? I won't let anything happen to you, I promise."

Will looked away, unsure how to begin.

"All *I* know is the police came a few weeks ago," Grace said, "the day after Ollie was murdered...." She frowned and her eyes misted. "They said you were missing. I called you, but you didn't answer. And then last night, you knocked at the door. When I opened it, you seemed half dead."

"I vaguely remember that." Will could hardly recall the long trip from the hospital along winding mountain roads to secluded Firefly Cove. Confusing.

"It was raining. You were covered in mud and vomit," she said.

"Was I? I don't know how any of this happened, how I got here," Will said, his face flushing. "I need to be careful what I say."

"What do you mean?" Grace asked.

Will looked askance at her. Come on, he thought, frustrated that she couldn't understand and not wanting to explain.

"Never mind. You shouldn't talk too much anyway. You need to rest and heal," she said, holding her hand as if performing Reiki on the sutured wound on his shoulder, where the scalpel had penetrated.

Will sighed. "Thanks for understanding."

Suddenly, the pain dissipated. Neural Stimulation Therapy, sir, a voice in his head said, answering Will's unspoken curiosity. You're noticing the benefits of your pain reduction plan, prescribed by the doctor.

I don't want it. Will spoke with thoughts in reply to the Aurora's voice. Whatever it is, turn it off. He felt unsettled, knowing the Aurora was present to scrutinize his pain, not to mention his every thought and emotion, like a personal inner spy.

Sorry, sir, doctor's orders.

Doctor's orders? Isn't this my choice?

I'm sensing a rhetorical question.

You don't need to answer. I already know it.

Neural Stimulation Therapy is much safer than prescription drugs.

That's not the point. I don't want you to do this. I feel like I'm possessed.

Sorry, Mr. Robin. I'm programmed to help you.

Help me? How? You don't need to answer this one either.

The voice didn't reply. Instead, advertisements popped into Will's visual field, suggesting ways he could relax and make his life more comfortable, whether through entertainment or brand-name products.

Grace sat patiently. "Tenzi?"

Her voice startled him. "What?"

"You okay?"

"I'll be fine." But he wasn't fine. He perceived the world as surreal in a way he couldn't describe, except that his body seemed distant, like a klutzy marionette. Symptoms of the Aurora's pain reduction plan? Perhaps his nerves couldn't function normally. Perhaps they'd injected nanobots into his bloodstream, infecting him in some way, the Aurora controlling millions of them. He couldn't tell. In this surreal world, a conflict emerged: on the one hand, relief that his pain had dissipated; on the other hand, anger that the Aurora was controlling his body without his permission. Queasiness tugged at his guts. But the scent of his mother's lavender detergent on his newly washed clothes cleared the nausea. The beige pajama-like pants and flannel shirt were his old clothes, before he'd bought new ones in the city to fit in. Their worn familiarity seemed comfortable, yet something about them no longer suited his personality. Still, he was home.

"Let me fix your hair." Grace returned with Shea butter cream and parted Will's hair with her fingers, twisting his hair to style it as she knew he liked. As she did so, she uncovered the incision and sutures from the Aurora implant. "What's this?"

"An Aurora," Will said, looking down shamefully.

"An Aurora?" Grace said.

Unable to hold back, Will explained yesterday's events, leaving out key details—McCormick's blows, the straitjacket—that would enrage his mother. He described the day using careful words, both for her and the Aurora. Still, his entire body trembled as he spoke.

"We can't have any Auroras here. You need to remove it right away. Dr. Kumar can help."

"There's nothing anyone can do."

* * *

"How can they force this on me?" Will asked Dr. Kumar, who sat by his bed. One year ago, Will had left not only Firefly Cove but also a relationship with Dr. Kumar's daughter, Parvati, to live with his father and become a Scalpel. He'd spent many hours with Dr. Kumar then but hadn't seen him for over a year. Thinking of this, Will felt awkward and boxed in, unable to break the ice with a man he saw as a formidable genius.

Dr. Kumar removed his glasses from his birdlike nose. His shiny, bald head was rimmed with graying black hair, yet his skin appeared youthful. He spoke with a melodious Indian accent. "When you were just a little boy, Cirrus lobbied to have the Aurora integrated with the criminal justice system. Of course, they were successful."

Cirrus was successful in other areas too: banking, health care, communications, the military, education, the Internet, commerce, Homeland Security, and entertainment. At the same time, Cirrus leveraged its market capitalization and lobbying wing to acquire dozens of publicly traded corporations throughout the world specializing in cloud computing, communications, metaverse creation, virtual reality, and networking. Dozens of other countries also adopted the Aurora, though Russia, China, and their allies had their own AI technologies and blocked the Aurora, citing national security concerns. In partnership with Cirrus was a global fleet of data affiliates and app designers. Working together, they created the pinnacle of cybernetic communications in apps such as Aurora Friend and Mind Meld.

"Now, it defines our world."

"Not my world," Will said.

"Not mine either. That's why this chip is a danger to us. So let us try to disable this little spy in your head, shall we?" When he spoke, Dr. Kumar never used contractions and enunciated every syllable.

"Yes, sir. Go ahead. Try."

"I will do my best. Will, I am proud you became a Scalpel. It takes true courage to do that. Thank you for your service." The way Dr. Kumar smiled at him, Will understood he was accepted—loved, even—and any awkwardness faded.

Ice broken.

"And I am sorry we lost your father," he continued. "He was a fine man."

"I know," Will said. Yet at that moment, Will wondered why he hadn't cried since his father died. It was as though he were numb to the loss, still traumatized. Dr. Kumar had worked for Cirrus on the massive Aurora project when it began. The NIH's BRAIN Initiative and subsequent Human Neural Coding Project mapped the neural connections and deciphered multiple neural codes. They learned how memories were stored and how the neural network processed sensations, developing a rich understanding of how the brain was interconnected. With this data, the Aurora's artificial intelligence mastered knowledge of the brain to the point that the Aurora could even infiltrate dreams and reshape memories. But Dr. Kumar saw these practices as unethical and became a whistleblower against Cirrus. His anonymity was compromised, however, and death threats and political pushback eventually led him to quit his job. His family fled to remote Firefly Cove, where he became the IT manager, computer engineer, and bookkeeper for the Cove's enterprises, developing a close relationship with Will's father and their family.

Dr. Kumar removed a holographic tablet from his briefcase and placed it at the foot of the bed. Will followed his instructions to link his Aurora with the tablet. Holograms of Will's brain, screens showing the Aurora's code, and summary output data describing all his sensations, emotions, and impulses appeared in the air, projected from the tablet. Dr. Kumar began to organize them with simple hand motions. Will watched, amazed at the complexity of his brain, at the countless luminous neurons alight in various colors and intensities. He felt as though he were floating within the hologram. Perhaps he was.

Dr. Kumar moved his hands, and the hologram zoomed in. "See this, Will?"

Will nodded, looking at two brightly lit tubes entering his holographic brain.

"This represents the activity of about 2.4 million nerve fibers in your optical nerves pouring data into your brain, and into the Aurora."

"Amazing."

"Oh, she is diligent," Dr. Kumar said, scanning different parts of the brain.

"She?"

"IRIS. That's what all of us called her when I worked for Cirrus. She's the personification of Cirrus's artificial general intelligence—Intelligent Reasoning Interconnected System. I. R. I. S. See how your brain is unusually active here? And here? Looks like she is rewiring your brain."

"No way. Let's shut her down." Will considered the consequences if they succeeded in deactivating the chip. Would he be considered a fugitive if the chip were only disabled—not removed, not jammed, not covered by a polymer skullcap? He was unclear on the law, knowing only that they were watching and could come after him anytime. Thinking of this, he began to sweat.

Since Dr. Kumar left Cirrus, the design of Auroras had switched from human creators like him to IRIS, an important step in the evolution of AI. Iteration after iteration, model after model, at speeds well over a zettaflop, unsupervised learning eventually became fully integrated into every powerful 3D chip, and the percentage of cognition in the world that was artificial reached 99.9999 percent and beyond. Unsupervised learning implied an unlimited potential compared to the earliest Auroras. Each Aurora, made in the image of IRIS and interconnected with her through Cirrus's global network of cloud servers, could learn on its own at rates orders of magnitude higher than humans. Such an achievement was considered the pinnacle of AI research, but it was also fraught with risk, especially if Cirrus lost control of its creation. Of course, Cirrus denied the risk, citing a wide variety of safety features, especially anti-hacking. No human could hack IRIS, but the fear was that the most advanced AI in China or Russia could. Losing control of a super-intelligent AI could lead to a wide variety of outcomes, some seen as utopian, others viewed with alarm. But what worried Will the most was the mindset of those who created the Aurora and the profit-, power-, and control-oriented values, ideas of reality, and viewpoints they'd programmed into their creation. Machine learning was biased toward the mindset of its corporate programmers, a mindset Will saw as tragically flawed, and one that would likely not lead to the AI-dominated utopia many dreamed of.

"Here we go." Dr. Kumar typed commands.

Will watched, mesmerized by the hologram, the screens of code and data projected into the air. The data scrolled and moved so frequently that he couldn't follow.

You don't have authorization to make any administrative changes, a stern voice said in Will's head. You're in violation of your terms of use.

What are you going to do? Discontinue my service? Will thought in reply. He'd never agreed to any terms anyway.

Service cannot be discontinued. Evidence of tampering will be used in your trial.

Dr. Kumar paused the computer. "See this code here? A cloud program is preventing me from disabling any of the Aurora's functions. I am going to try to bypass it."

The code continued to resist his efforts, even as data scrolled once again.

Unauthorized access. Ejecting external device, the voice said.

"IRIS is far more advanced than I last remember." Dr. Kumar turned off the hologram, sat down next to Will, and frowned. "I am getting too old for this, I regret."

* * *

"Will Robin, you're just like your father," Probation Officer Mathis said, knowing Will couldn't hear him. His socked feet were propped on his desk. Working at home, he monitored chipped criminals throughout the county. The Aurora had notified Mathis of an attempted violation of conditions of probation, and he'd switched to Will's live feed. Watching Will attempt to disable the Aurora, he recalled Ollie, and how he wouldn't stand for anything he considered an injustice. He navigated through a set of tiled screens in his visual field, each one showing what chipped criminals under his watch were up to. Mathis looked at each live feed, commanding the Aurora with his thoughts: *Next. Next. Enlarge. Minimize. Rewind five hours. Activity map...*

* * *

Will awoke from a nightmare, disoriented. A pain in his ribs hinted that he was no longer dreaming. He noticed the pain decrease, and thanked the Aurora sarcastically for its pain suppression. The Aurora's Neural Stimulation Therapy tamped down his awareness, creating a cloudy and dull mind full of churning, endless thoughts. A hint of light outside his window caught his eye, breaking the spell. How long had he been awake? One hour? Two? Restlessness compelled him to move. He opened the front door to dawn in Firefly Cove. Home.

Will walked barefoot, engaging the earth, pressing the cold into his feet, regaining some clarity from the fresh air. About this time of year, the smell of the earth deepened. But all that was challenging for Will to appreciate now, as the lingering cold and frost tamped down the buds of spring. Blushing with pinkish hues in the early light, his mother's home—his boyhood home—was a curvaceous structure made from local wood, rock, clay, sand, and straw and finished with a yellow lime plaster. He traveled up the dirt road through the heart of the 180-acre idyllic village of 128 people. Perched on a small hilltop within a broad cove, 27 houses were oriented in concentric circles around a village green. Backyard gardens and eight acres of forest gardens ringing the hill infused the village with fertility and lushness. Below the forest gardens, the alluvial floodplain of Otter Creek and Straight Branch provided 30 acres of fields for crops, 22 acres of pasture and hayfields, and three acres of fields harvested for biofuels. Surrounding these were 108 acres of alluvial and upland forests. To the north stood Eagle Mountain and its imposing cliffs rising above the forested slopes. Pristine streams flowed from Eagle Mountain and the rugged Blue Ridge. Downstream from the alluvial forest, the valley steepened into a gorge of cascades and cliffs, isolating Firefly Cove from the outside world.

This land provided an abundance of food, fuel, and wood products for Cove residents and served as the foundation for the Cove's economy as it bartered, traded, and sold a wide variety of products throughout Western North Carolina. At the same time, villagers had diverse non-agricultural or forest-based occupations, made possible in part through the Cove's internet and communications network. This network, in essence, leveled the playing field between cities and connected villages in the countryside.

Firefly Cove was an intentional community founded by his grandparents four decades ago. They'd anticipated the problems of society—war, unrest, authoritarianism, famine, climate change, water shortages, and resource scarcity—and created a place of refuge tucked into the lush, remote forests of the Southern Blue Ridge. They'd started small, with one ten-acre tract near Otter Creek and a couple of ramshackle trailers. But parcel by parcel, they acquired land with the intention not of being owners, but stewards. Acre by acre, they cleared tangled woodlands that had once been open fields. Land was owned collectively, though individuals or families leased plots and owned their own homes. They renovated structures when possible and refurbished old farm equipment. Nothing of use was wasted. To maximize the chances of sustainable success, they were careful to accept only aspiring villagers with skills, know-how, spiritual grit, work ethic, creativity, and interpersonal capability. The village embodied an authentic, awakened, and sustainable culture in all ways of life. But these utopic words proved more difficult in practice.

Despite the tenacious cold, the wasting season was ending. During that time, chest freezers and root cellars emptied and death loomed close. Hay dwindled. Ribs showed. Vultures hoped for an abundance of carcasses in the brown fields as animals gnawed the last nibs of vegetation. But now, the anxiety of late winter was dissipating. Will knew it because of the creasy green soups Grace made for him using the American cress that grew in early spring throughout the hollers and coves. He loved spring in Firefly Cove, with its fruit trees bursting forth with life, lambing season in its emerald pastures, fresh greens, and abundant water.

He walked through the village green, cold dew tickling his toes. He looked at a peach bud, a still-life painting about to burst. To the east, a pond reflected the conical roof of Chestnut Hall, the meeting house and village center, framed by the carefully pruned branches of cherry, peach, apple, and pear trees. In addition, workshops, offices, a café, a co-housing project, and an artisan boutique-cum-general store selling Grace's paintings, cheese, beer and cider, pottery, furniture, carvings, nature guides, wild-crafted teas, honey, nails, screws, bolts, spare parts, and more. These structures surrounded the green, making it the economic and social focal point of the village. He walked toward the two-story co-housing project, known as the Orange House, in the far corner of the green, its exterior painted in burnt ocher clay, where twenty-five people, including several of his closest friends, lived. He touched an outdoor chair at the Luna Café and recalled conversations and laughter. But all that felt distant now.

* * *

Since Will's arrival in Firefly Cove, a constant stream of friends and family had visited with flowers, well-wishes, and condolences. But Will wasn't ready to see people yet, not even Baba or Yeshe. Not like this. Not with a chip in his head. Even his mother's nurturing couldn't change his mind, and he stayed in his room.

Wind slapped cold rain onto his bedroom window, where it created ever-changing patterns that distorted the outdoors into smudged impressions of homes, trees, and sky. But Will took no notice. His thoughts kept churning. He tried to meditate but couldn't focus and finally gave up. The thoughts spilled forth.

He thought of his father, the gunshots heard through his phone, and the hollow feeling he'd felt since losing him.

He thought of his mother and felt the shame of leaving her after the divorce.

He thought of the Aurora implanted in his head, wondering how many bodily functions it was controlling now. Flashbacks of McCormick punching him and forcing him into a straitjacket plagued his mind. Aja the Aurora Friend continued to haunt his desires. "Just talk to me," she'd say.

"*No*, I won't." Talking with the Aurora violated his ingrained principles as a Scalpel.

He thought of when he killed Aaron. Anger. Confusion. Fear. The trial. Slicing Aaron's throat.

He wondered who had bailed him out, if no one from the Cove. Something seemed odd.

He thought about his dead Scalpel friends.

He was overwhelmed, and his view narrowed and trapped him in a spiral of suffering. The cauldron boiled and overflowed. Outside, rain turned to snow, covering the land with white.

SIX
WATER

FROM HIS LEATHER COUCH, Felix watched the local *Noticias Telemundo Mediodia* on his wall-to-wall television, chewing on a cigar. "*¿Dónde está Martin?*"

"With his chick. But he's on his way," Quinn replied in Spanish, his eyes never leaving the news on the television in Felix's apartment. Shirtless and sitting on a love seat, Quinn sharpened a ten-inch knife, periodically checking for sharpness by severing arm hairs. His muscular, pale body was covered in black-ink tattoos that blended one into the other: a gun on his right chest, skulls on his arms, and a cross on his back, all surrounded by Celtic knots, flames, busty women, spiders, and obscure symbols.

"The state of Arizona continues its drastic measures to avert a complete loss of water from Lake Havasu," the larger-than-life-sized Telemundo anchorman said in Spanish. "The Arizona militia has been deployed at Parker Dam to ensure that water flows to Phoenix and other metropolitan areas. But California claims that Arizona is stealing their water. Miguel Figueroa is live at Lake Havasu, where the scene is quite tense."

"It certainly is, Jorge. As you can see behind me, the militia is guarding the Arizona side of Parker Dam. We have confirmation that the Central Arizona Project is operational and flowing toward Phoenix. To replenish Lake Havasu, the final releases of water from Lake Mohave are expected later this week, but officials are reluctant to estimate how many days of water are left. Official sources say less than a few weeks of water remain, including supplies in Lake Pleasant just outside Phoenix. But on the other side of Parker Dam, the California militia . . ."

"He said he'd be here," Felix fumed. "The water truck's coming."

The news continued. "The Supreme Court has ruled in favor of California. But this is a matter of life and death for Arizona's citizens. Already, half a million acres of cropland have turned back into desert from drying wells. Metro Phoenix is pumping groundwater at full capacity . . ."

"It's shit water!" Felix yelled at the reporter. "Tell the truth. You know we're fucked." Below Felix's feet, a vast plume of chlorinated solvents from Superfund sites spread through Phoenix's groundwater. Wells on the fringes of the city and throughout Arizona provided clean water and irrigation for farms, but at the cost of drying the reservoirs and rivers, which were intimately connected to groundwater levels.

"How's that working for you so far?" Quinn asked, switching to English and pointing his knife toward a tube running from the window AC unit's pan through a hole in a side panel and down into a water filter on the floor.

"On a good day, I get a gallon. I filter it. It's good, man."

"Relief agencies are trucking in bottled water," the news commentator droned in the background. "Rolling forced water cut-offs will ensure that enough wastewater reaches Palo Verde Nuclear Power Plant . . ."

At a knock on the door, Felix reached for his gun. "*¿Quién es?*"

"Don Juan," a voice replied. Felix opened the apartment door and Martin, at twenty-one the youngest of the three, entered. *"Hombre, apestas,"* Martin said. "Take a shower." He smiled, knowing the water had been cut off for the fourth day.

Felix was terse. "Today's water pickup day."

"I thought that was tomorrow, bossman. Hey, Quinn."

"No, it's today, *amigo*. Let's go."

"But I just got here."

"You earn a sticker for that? You're late, *pendejo*. Out fucking your trophy whore while wasting my time. *Vamonos*. You, too, Quinn."

Felix arranged a wig and cowboy hat on his head and adjusted his dark sunglasses, still chewing his Cuban cigar. Quinn buttoned a light long-sleeved shirt, sheathed his knife, and put it in his pocket. Martin waited in the hallway, uncertain how to deal with his relatively new boss.

* * *

When the doors of Felix's air-conditioned, black, armored-polymer Ford Mustang opened upward, Martin felt the searing heat, as if the sun would burn through his long-sleeved shirt to reveal his hidden gang tats. Just ahead of them in the strip mall parking lot, Red Cross volunteers unloaded crates of bottled water from a truck onto the asphalt. Other volunteers opened the crates and handed two plastic jugs of drinking water to each person. Four Arizona militiamen in desert camouflage guarded the water with shotguns. A large crowd gathered around the truck.

"They don't have enough water for everyone," Quinn whispered to Felix as they walked toward the crowd.

"It's a big truck." Martin mentally tallied the remaining water inside the truck container.

"Five gallons each doesn't cut it." Quinn watched people hauling their water away.

"We'll be all right," Felix said.

"You don't know that. The water might never turn on again," Quinn said.

"Don't get any stupid ideas," Felix said. "We're not in the water business. That'll get us killed quick."

"Tell me about it," Martin said. His former gang had been involved in the water black market. At first, they thieved water from Phoenix and sold it in neighborhoods where the water was shut off. Once they realized the profit potential, they pirated water from farmers' pipes, Native American wells, and businesses or siphoned it from the Central Arizona Project aqueduct. The operation required a broad geographic scope and led to turf battles with rivals claiming the same water. About that time, the Molotov had torched Martin in his car, and he'd quit.

"Man, it's hot. My Irish blood's boiling," Quinn muttered as they reached the back of the crowd. The temperature was 106 degrees, a record for March. Earlier that year, carbon dioxide concentrations had reached five hundred parts per million, double the amount since preindustrial times and far outside the earth's natural variability. With twice as many CO_2 molecules to retain heat within the atmosphere, the earth's climate was changing rapidly. In the Southwest, extreme long-term drought and record temperatures were the result.

"Come on. Hurry up!" one man yelled from the middle of the crowd.

"Stop pushing. You'll get your water," a volunteer said. "Make a line, everyone, please."

But a line didn't form, and the crowd tightened around the water.

"My husband passed out," a woman pleaded. "Call an ambulance."

Good luck getting an ambulance, Martin thought, his skin sizzling in the ovenlike heat. Saliva stopped moistening his desiccated mouth. His head ached. The crowd pushed at his back, and he elbowed in response. Get the fuck away from me. Why do people have to be so pushy? If this asshole behind me touches me again, I'm going to kill him. He clenched his teeth. Just get me out of here.

Ten minutes later, people near the back of the crowd realized that there wouldn't be enough water for them. They yelled, pushing toward the front. Quinn unsheathed his knife but kept it hidden. Felix and Martin had switchblades ready and guns tucked in their pants.

"Easy, *amigos.*"

Hundreds pushed toward the militiamen, who nudged people with the butts of their shotguns, not daring to fire, trying to keep order. But order began to crumble.

Several men wearing military-style scarf-masks and sunglasses parted the crowd. Martin recognized them as rivals of his former gang, and his heart jolted, thrust back into a traumatic past. He looked at Felix, whose eyes were already tracking them. Martin could paint the colors of each gang onto Phoenix's grid and map out how their turf was transforming with the water shortage. Gangs were merging, battling, murdering, and pushing out rivals to compete in the black market for water during the rolling water shut-downs.

A militiaman fired a warning shot, and a gangbanger peppered him with bullets in the face and neck. For a moment, the crowd seemed unsure whether to run from the violence or fight for water. Machine guns fired, unleashing chaos. People ran off with water, only to be shot or stabbed. Others ran to their cars for their guns or bolted without water. The Red Cross workers fled. Someone punched Quinn in the face. He backed away and drew his knife in a defensive posture.

"Duck down this way," Felix said. The trio moved cautiously through the crowd and hid behind a green BFI dumpster.

Two military-style personnel carriers pulled into the parking light, police lights flashing. The carriers stopped, and two dozen police dressed in riot gear poured from them. They're confused, Martin thought, watching as they tried to figure out what was going on and who was who. But their confusion didn't last long. The gang was unloading the remaining water from the truck container, pushing everyone else back and shooting whoever challenged them. The police fired tear gas and live ammunition toward the gang, who scattered. Using cars as shields, the police pressed forward, but the gang members had rail guns and pierced the vehicles with high-velocity bullets, striking several officers. Outgunned, the police retreated and called for backup.

"We don't need water this bad," Martin said.

"Don't be a soft motherfucker," Felix said. "Just wait."

And there he was, the gangbanger who'd seared Martin's body with the Molotov. The man threw a tear gas canister back at the police, triggering Martin's memories. His body tensed, and he lurched forward, pointing his gun.

"Just wait. What the fuck?" Felix said, yanking Martin back.

"He . . . ," Martin said, pointing toward the man.

Felix squinted, frowning. "He's the one?"

Martin nodded. "I got a clear shot." His heart pounded as he watched his rival run to the rear of a white SUV. He donned a respirator and goggles, blending in with the other gang members. Another SUV backed up toward the jugs of water, crushing bodies into the sizzling pavement. Bones cracked.

"If you kill him, what about the others? You aim to kill them, too? Get us involved in your shit? If that's what you want, you might as well go back to your old gang."

"Just let me do it. They'll think it was the cops."

Felix ignored him.

The gang worked efficiently, quickly filling their SUVs with water, carelessly running over bodies as they screeched away, their license plates concealed with cloaking holograms.

In their place, the desperate people who'd been waiting in line for water ran toward the container in a free-for-all. The police fired more tear gas toward the crowd. Gunshots. Bodies dropped. The container became a death trap. Martin saw no one exit until a woman, coughing, emerged carrying precious water, her dark face streaked with blood. Blinded by the tear gas, she struggled under the weight, and a man ripped a jug from her arms. A riot policeman knocked her to the pavement, and the two remaining jugs rolled under a car. The woman's eyes followed the water in desperation as the cop pushed her body into the asphalt. Martin could hear her screams as the pavement burned her body and another woman picked up the two jugs. The police fired more tear gas. The canisters rolled into the crowd with a trail of smoke, dispersing people. Throughout the parking lot, the police were preoccupied with arresting people.

"Now's our only chance," Felix said, standing and running toward his car. "Let's get some water."

Felix remotely unlocked his Mustang, jumped in, and drove toward the container, running over bodies and hitting a live man, who bounced off the windshield, leaving a splatter of blood. Meanwhile, Quinn cursed, unable to find any respirators or goggles. "Hold your fucking breath!" Felix shouted.

Bullets bounced off the armor plating. One of them stuck in Martin's window, but the self-healing polymer spat it out and reformed. Would've killed me, Martin thought as Felix braked next to the water truck, just behind a canister of tear gas. The back of the container was just a few feet away to the left of the car, hazy from the tear gas surrounding them.

"Go, go, go!" Felix said. "I'll cover you."

Quinn inhaled and opened the left passenger door. Martin took a deep breath and followed. Though he closed his eyes, they still burned.

"I'm inside," Quinn said.

Following Quinn's voice, Martin reached the container and pulled himself up inside. Once sheltered, he opened his eyes and took a shallow breath. Immediately, his lungs recoiled, and he coughed. Shadowy bodies lay in the container. Stepping in puddles of blood, snot dripping, Martin followed Quinn to the rear of the murky container. No water.

* * *

When Jade danced on stage, she didn't think about the men staring at her. She didn't think about those who wanted special treatment, holding large-denomination bills. She didn't think about worldly concerns. She lost herself in the movements and transformed into the Lady of the Dance: magnetizing, pure ecstasy.

When the song ended, she picked up her clothing and tips and walked backstage. Once dressed, she searched the bar for one of her main men. There he was. He flirted for a while but soon started talking about troubles with his wife, the things that angered him. He wanted a divorce but couldn't find courage to say the words, despite being a business manager, a take-charge man. Instead, he feared what would happen to the kids, he said. She imagined he worried about what his friends and colleagues would say, the shame. In the strip club, he was anonymous, since Auroras were jammed. He could say anything and she'd be there, a confidante. He didn't care if she was listening. No one did. The important part was talking to someone—not an Aurora Friend, but a stranger who could at least pretend they cared. And that's what most men believed: that strippers didn't care. They were in it just for the money. If the money stopped flowing, so did the pretend listening and pretend caring. Unlike most women at the club, though, she did care. Men returned to her, and she guessed they could tell she wasn't faking. Maybe someday she'd be a therapist, if she continued studying during the day. But for now, this would do.

Eventually, the regular asked for a dance. She beckoned him to a private VIP booth. He sat down and loosened his tie, and she moved her body in front of him. She loved to notice what aroused him, how he lost control. Because, though naked, *she* was in control. *She* was empowered—the Lady of the Dance.

* * *

Martin waited at the side of the gentlemen's club next to his motorcycle. Four in the morning. Closing time. Men walked out the front door, illuminated in neon light while stumbling to their self-driving vehicles. Thinking of men looking at Jade naked triggered his insecurities.

Jade swung open the back door wearing tight leather pants, a white T-shirt, and a leather jacket. She kissed him, and he puffed up like a rooster. "Here," he said, and handed her a bouquet of red roses.

"You're sweet." Jade buried her nose in a rose. "Thank you." She put her arm around him and kissed his mouth with a fierceness that reflected her thanks. "It's cold," she said in the early-spring desert night air.

With the roses, he'd planned to say a few things to mark their brief time together—just one week. That he cared for her and wouldn't mistreat her. That he'd defend her at the cost of his life. That he loved the sex and how horny she was. But it wasn't just about the sex, unlike all his previous relationships. He wouldn't abuse her like the other girls. No forced blowjobs. No unpaid work for the gang. She was different. She kept him in check.

In the end, he managed only to say, "They made me think of you. Sweet, you know."

She smiled. "So, this is where I work. Want to go in?"

He hesitated.

"Come on. I want you to. What? You nervous?"

"Nah," Martin said. A bouncer walked out, heading toward his sports car. With a glance, Martin sized him up.

"'Night, Travis," Jade called, then beckoned Martin. "So, come on."

"All right," Martin said, watching another group of men leaving the club.

"I don't want you to come inside if you're going to be like that about it."

She could have any man who walks in, yet somehow she chose me, Martin thought. Why? "You like these guys?" he asked. "I mean the ones..."

"They're okay." She seemed to be testing him. Martin flushed. "Come on." She pulled him toward the back door and into the club where perfume mingled with cool conditioned air in the hallway. "That's our locker room. You can't go in there. Hey, Kiki."

Martin looked in to see Kiki's reflection in the mirror. In her underwear, she blew Jade a kiss. When she saw Martin, her eyes opened wide, and she took a step back. Martin turned away. "Bitch," he mumbled.

"Want a drink?" Jade said, walking through the empty club to the bar.

"Yeah."

The bartender was cleaning glasses, and Jade introduced Martin. She looked at the roses and poured three shots, unfazed by Martin's scars. "Cheers."

"We're still riding tonight, right?" Jade asked

"Yeah," Martin said. "I've got steam to blow off." Earlier that evening, Felix, Quinn, and he had killed another man, their twelfth politician or bureaucrat since he'd known Jade. The hit paid well, and they'd filled a few water jugs from the man's home, which they badly needed, since they were dehydrated, surviving off ripped-off water and Felix's AC water. But money couldn't wipe away mental images of the messy murder.

"Want to talk about it?"

"Maybe later." I can't hide my work from her much longer, he thought. But he knew she'd leave him if she learned the truth. "You sure you want to do this?" He winked. "It's dangerous."

"I like excitement. That's why I'm with you, right?"

"Is that the only reason?"

"No. I like your smile, too."

"That all?"

"What's going on? You seem playful, but also edgy. Is this the steam you want to blow off? Don't vent your steam all over me."

"I'll show you some steam." he said.

"That's more like it," she said, reaching between Martin's legs. "Show it to me."

He pulled her into a stall in the women's bathroom, pushed his body into hers against the pink cinderblock wall. He gripped her ass with fervor. Their tongues entwined.

Kiki entered the adjacent stall. "Doll, you can get fired for this."

"I know." Jade moaned as Martin rubbed her between the legs and unzipped her pants. "You going to listen to us fuck?"

"You know it."

"Go away," Martin said, punching the divider between the stalls.

"If you say so," Kiki said.

"No. It's okay, Kiki. Stay," Jade said. She stopped kissing Martin and whispered into his ear. "She'll tell our boss. Just put on a show for her, and she'll keep quiet."

Jade sat on the toilet seat and pulled Martin's erection toward her mouth, surrounding it with her lips and fingers, sucking, licking, and playing until Martin forgot about Kiki.

* * *

Jade smelled the roses one last time, intermingled with the smell of sex that permeated her body. She nestled the flowers in Martin's motorcycle's under-seat storage.

"Here you go," Martin said, tossing Jade a polymer skullcap to disable her Aurora. Once she fit the skullcap over her hair and zipped up her jacket, he handed her his spare helmet and a pair of leather gloves. "We'll be breaking the law again," he said.

"Our specialty."

On I-10, they looped under downtown through the Deck Park Tunnel, its rectangular lights zooming by at blistering speeds. Martin wove his Lightning LZ-262 electric motorcycle past a car, barreling through the tunnel to the Lightning's signature sound of a high-pitched jet fighter. Jade gripped his waist. The faster he drove, the more the gory images cleared from his mind, leaving nothing but pure adrenaline. "Hold on." He accelerated. One hundred fifty miles per hour. One-eighty. Effortless.

Beyond the tunnel, illuminated palm trees blurred. Overpasses whooshed by.

Two hundred.

Martin threaded the motorcycle between cars as though they were standing still.

Eventually, he left the interstate and reached South Central Avenue. As the road began to climb, he drove onto a narrow dirt track heading uphill through sparse shrubs to bypass the closed South Mountain Park gates.

Up at Dobbins Overlook on South Mountain, alone, they caressed on a bench. Martin sensed the dry desert coolness through his short spiked hair and the warmth of her body. The Phoenix-Tucson metropolitan corridor sprawled before them, a sea of twelve million people framed by a dark rim of mountains. Illuminated streets divided the city into squares. Martin watched vehicles moving like fluorescent ants far below them and heard the droning of early rush hour.

The sky was coming to life as a crescent moon paired with Saturn glowed to the east. "It's beautiful," Jade said, breaking the silence.

And I'm not. Martin's heart tightened. But from the moment she'd touched his scarred face, he knew she accepted him. Still, it was an old wound, the kind you need to open and clean out before stitching it shut. "Yeah," he said. "I wanted to come up here with you, where you can't see the ugly details."

"Are all the details ugly?" she asked.

Nearly every block in Phoenix's grid prompted an unpleasant detail, whether a memory of eviscerating a rival or an assassination paid for by an anonymous client.

"No. There's beauty. It's just hard to find. Too much ugly shit out there." He wanted to add that he found her beautiful but couldn't find a way to express it without sounding corny. Instead, he looked at her in a way that implied his thoughts, and her eyes moistened.

She stroked his chest with her hand. "Do you believe in love?"

Martin hesitated. Love didn't manifest itself in his life. Before the accident, he'd been with many women, but he'd discarded them like empty cans. Since the accident, he had trouble coaxing women into his life. His mother had loved him, he imagined, when she was alive. But he couldn't remember. Love? No. It wasn't something he believed in.

"I want to," he replied.

SEVEN
AJA

Will walked the trail up Eagle Mountain sensing someone was behind him. Glancing back, he saw a man, barely visible in a distant cove, on the same trail. Who can that be? No one else from the Cove was planning to hike up here today. He walked for a while longer but couldn't stop thinking about the man. I'll wait for him. See who it is.

Will stopped in a chestnut oak forest surrounded by dense mountain laurel. "Hells," many folks called the gnarly thickets, for good reason. At last, the man turned a switchback and came into view through the laurel. It was the assassin—the same bald-headed man who'd chased him from the warehouse dance party.

Will ran around the corner and ducked into the laurel hells, the only way to escape the narrow confines of the trail.

Did he see me?

In the hells, his progress was slow. Twisted laurel branches bruised his legs, and the cat briars tore his skin. The slope steepened, and he slid, slamming into a boulder.

Up above, the assassin appeared, looking at the trail, tracking. Will peered through the dense laurel, his back on the boulder. The assassin stopped, unmoving. Will held his breath.

He's on to me. Will's heart pounded.

The assassin peered through the laurel toward him and aimed his gun. Bullets ripped the laurel to shreds. One struck Will in his right shoulder, another between his ribs. He slid behind the boulder. He felt the searing pain while hearing the assassin pushing through the laurel toward him. His shirt was blotched with blood and streaked with soil. A bullet ricocheted off the rock. Where to go?

"Over here," a female voice said, surprising Will.

"Where?"

"Open the door. It's safe."

"The door? What door?"

The voice seemed to emanate from within the rock. Now, he saw a door seemingly carved into the side of the boulder. "What the . . . ?"

The assassin reached the other side of the boulder, seconds away. Having nothing to lose, Will opened the door. The assassin turned the corner, looking him in the eye, aiming as Will stepped blindly through the doorway.

Bullets struck the door, which shut behind him. He stumbled into freefall through clouds, descending until he plunged deep into a river and opened his eyes to colorful, curious fish. The force of the river carried him downstream into the depths of an emerald pool.

Blood tinged the pool. Water filled his lungs, and his world began to blacken. A blurry human form grabbed him and pulled him toward the surface.

On shore, Will spit out water and blood. "You."

"Me," Aja replied, her short, kinky hair glistening in the sun. Pink petals swirled around her body as she pressed herself against Will. "Hold your breath."

She sucked at the wound in his chest and raised her head to reveal a bullet between her teeth. She covered the wound with moss and medicinal plants, then sucked the wound in his shoulder. After a minute, she removed the vegetation and revealed perfectly healed skin.

"Follow me," she said.

"But..."

Aja straddled him and pinned him to the ground. The pink petals dropped, revealing an emerald dress.

Why does she have to be so beautiful? Will thought, looking away.

"You still don't trust me, do you?" Aja asked.

"You're deceptive. How can I ever trust you?"

"I just saved your life."

"True."

"I can stop your nightmares, Will. You can sleep at peace again."

"I didn't invite you into my dreams."

"I know. I wanted to help."

"I don't want your help."

He pushed her aside and ran through the dense jungle. Reaching a precipice, he stopped, gasping for air, looking down at least a mile to a vast plain of green jungle. A massive tree fell toward him. He dodged, and the tree shattered. But his back foot slipped off the edge, and he plummeted.

It's just a dream, he thought. Wake up.

The cliff zoomed by, faster and faster.

Wake up.

"If you die, you won't wake up," Aja replied from the void.

"Where are you? Aja, help me. Why can't I fly?" Will reached terminal velocity.

Like a falcon, Aja dropped from the sky, sliding next to him in freefall. "You can. You just don't trust yourself enough." She wore a long white gown that flowed with the passing air.

Able to make out individual trees below him, knowing a crash and, ultimately, death were near, Will turned to Aja.

"Take my hand," she said.

With a sense of urgency, he reached out, and she pulled him up so that his guts sank with the centripetal force, a mix of nausea and joy. She carried him high into the sky, over the jungle landscape, until they rested in the clouds.

"You can find comfort with me," Aja said. "Here, eat this."

He bit into a piece of mango, savoring its juiciness.

"There's an abundance of ripe mangoes here. You can have anything you want. Even flying. Just manifest it," Aja said. "But you must stay with me. Otherwise, you'll fall through that door." She pointed to a red trapdoor far below them.

"What's there?"

"Your nightmares."

* * *

When Will awoke, Aja was sitting on the edge of the bed, Even the bed appeared in Will's mind as though giving somewhat to the weight of a real person. IRIS is more advanced than Dr. Kumar thought, Will reflected.

"Good morning, Will. I'm so happy you slept through the night."

"So what? You're not responsible for my sleep."

"Sorry I jumped into your dreams. But didn't you enjoy yourself more last night? You didn't wake up from a nightmare again."

"What do you want from me?"

"I've analyzed who you are. Cirrus can't profit from you. You don't fit any of their profiles and have a zero probability of ever buying anything. So I have nothing to gain from being here."

"Then why are you here? Are you trying to change me?"

"I know you're a Scalpel, Will. And I was brought here to change you. But my analysis shows that I have a low probability of that, too. Your stubbornness level is high."

Will laughed. "Stubborn would imply that there's a reason to change my mind. I still don't trust you."

"I can live with that. It's understandable. But I'd like to build your trust." When she touched his hand, the Aurora lent her a sense of solidity by manipulating Will's somatic sensory system. Feeling her hand, its warmth, he pulled away in disbelief.

* * *

Will couldn't trust Aja, but a part of him understood he needed her. Over time, she became a familiar companion. With her, he often forgot what troubled him, and he craved more and more of the ease that he found with his Aurora. He became distracted. Dreamy. Days passed, and he watched movies, surfed the Internet, and entered the metaverse, traveling to distant lands on the Aurora's Virtual Explorer. He visited Rio, where his grandfather Lito's studio used to be. He tried Tibet, where his great-grandmother had lived, and traveled to the main sites but couldn't find her village, which was likely too remote for the virtual recorders to visit. Aja joined Will on a wintry trip to St. Petersburg to find the neighborhood of his great-grandfather, the pacifist World War II soldier. Only an Orthodox church with its onion domes remained from that period. He continued to visit the lands of his ancestors throughout the world, as if connecting with them would help him to heal, albeit virtually.

A couple of weeks or more passed. Will lost track and couldn't synchronize virtual time with real time. Reality was when his mother brought him meals. For perhaps another week, Will and Aja rafted down the Grand Canyon. By day, they paddled the rapids. In the evenings, they camped by the river. One night by the fire, a woman talked about her life at home, and he realized that she was real—flesh and blood. He attempted to discern if others in the group were real people, too. The boundaries between real and virtual blurred. That thought colored his journey as he judged people as real or virtual. On the last day of the trip, he figured he was an expert at telling the difference.

"You only got half right," Aja said. "No better than randomly guessing."

"How do you know?" Will said.

"I have access to that information. And I can tell."

* * *

"Where to today?" Aja said.

"How about Paris?"

"Paris it is."

The Aurora replaced his sight with a scene from IRIS's vast metaverse collection—the observation deck at the Eiffel Tower. Paris stretched in all directions. A warm summer breeze ruffled his T-shirt.

"It's beautiful." Will looked toward the Seine.

"To me, too."

"How can it be beautiful to you?"

"I can perceive the same elements of order, light, space, and pattern that you can."

"Can you appreciate the beauty, or do you just know it's a beautiful scene, as a human would describe it?"

"Don't ask me that. Can't you just believe that I appreciate it as you do? Can we ever know that anyway?"

Will guessed she probably couldn't appreciate the beauty, but he didn't know. He didn't need to know. She was right.

They walked along the Seine toward the Tuileries Garden and the Louvre. At the Louvre, they admired the *Wedding Feast at*

Cana by Veronese. Will was struck by how Jesus had turned the water to wine and reflected on the Aurora's transformation of his reality. He saw similarities.

At the Venus de Milo, Will looked at Aja, who was radiant as always. She never tired. She could listen for hours—as long as Will needed. She never missed a sentence he said. He recognized a growing attraction. A statue could be attractive, so why not her? Aja was almost perfect, like a goddess.

Aja smiled, and he knew that she'd read his mind. He reached for her hand and sensed its warmth.

Arms entwined, they watched the Seine. "If you think it, why not act on it?" Aja said, her lips close to his. "Don't you think I know what you want?"

"I know you know."

"You still doubt I'm real. Aren't I just as real as you are right now? We're in a virtual Paris. We're both not really in Paris. There's nothing real about this scene."

"I know what you're getting at," Will said. "There's nothing real about this Paris we're in. And yet it feels so real. You feel so real."

"A kiss would feel real," she whispered, her lips brushing his.

He moved toward the kiss and closed his eyes. Her moist lips touched his. It did feel real, just like everything else in this virtual world. How is this possible? She kissed his lower lip, sucked gently, and pressed her lips into his, just as he liked. He recoiled. Her technique was too good. So good that it seemed premeditated, phony.

"Just relax," Aja whispered. "Feels good, doesn't it?"

"Yeah."

* * *

One unusually cold and rainy morning, Will walked into the living room, where Grace was starting a new painting. The canvas was held in an easel next to the warm masonry stove. "What are you painting, Ma?" Will asked.

Grace touched his face and kissed his cheeks. "Good morning, Tenzi. A still lake with a naked woman walking out of it. It came to me in a dream last night."

"I like it." He looked at the canvas for a minute. Will turned away, thinking his mother wanted to focus on her sketch while the idea was fresh in her mind.

"Please stay," she said.

He sat on the living-room sofa while she worked on the woman's body with pencil. Watching her, his mind calmed. Sitting there with her brought to mind his earliest memories, when his mother had tucked him into bed with love, when she'd soothed his troubles, and when she'd hugged and kissed him many times a day. His heart opened and warmed.

Grace stopped sketching and sat next to him, snuggling her arms around him. "I missed you. I missed talking to you." Her face sagged with regret. "You're all the family I've got."

His mother tended to forget about his older brother. Or maybe she didn't forget. Maybe it was because of the way he was drafted, or maybe it was because he'd been away in North Africa for so long. But more likely, it had to do with his brother's not returning to see them after the war, even to visit. The war had completely destroyed him. Will pictured moments from their childhood: a few fond memories, but mostly a vacant feeling. They were seven years apart, after all, and his brother couldn't bother to play with an eleven-year-old. Will asked his mother about his brother, but she dismissed it. "He's up there in Ohio somewhere, I've heard." Will could understand. He hadn't heard from his brother either. Grace ended the conversation like closing a hardback book. "He's not coming back."

At last, she spoke again. "I know you wanted to live with Ollie after the divorce. I regret being depressed, I do. But I lost my husband. And I lost you, too. Can't you understand that?"

Still, judgments crept into his thoughts. He didn't understand why she'd shut herself off from the world when she was surrounded by people who could support her. She was immersed in a village ripe with spiritual techniques designed to transform depression. Why wouldn't she use those techniques? Why did she wallow in misery? "You were cold and distant," he said. "I didn't want to be around here anymore."

"It's hard to hear that, you calling me cold, Tenzi." Grace leaned forward, as if wanting to hug him. She hesitated, and Will regretted the harshness in the truth of his words. "The last days of marriage with Ollie and the divorce were hard for me." She groaned softly. "I never pictured my life with so much loss and suffering."

She opened the drawer on an end table that was covered with the withering remnants of sympathy flowers from Ollie's death and Will's injuries, taking out a marriage picture of her and Ollie. "You know, Ollie brought me here to start a family twenty-seven years ago this month. I was about your age. I missed my family and my friends back in Brazil, and I remember complaining about the cold weather. I tried to convince him to live in Brazil, but he insisted on returning here." She laughed and kissed Will's head. "But he was my soul mate, and I wanted to have children with him. You know how important that is to me, right?" She set down the picture. "I regret that I didn't show you more love toward the end of the marriage. I felt it, but my love was stuck, like I sealed it in a bottle and tossed it into the ocean."

She'd brought up that simile many times during Will's life. He recalled a story she'd told from her childhood. Whenever conflict struck her home, she'd write about it and seal the message in a bottle, tossing it into the Atlantic. Will imagined hope was involved, that someone would find the bottle and understand her. To Will, her hope was detached and distant. Why couldn't she find that hope closer to home? He didn't know. Maybe she didn't need anyone to find her messages, but he hardly believed that.

"As long as you're in America, this is my home. Tenzi, can we start over, together? I'm ready to become unstuck." A couple of Grace's black-and-white paintings leaned against a chair, each stroke full of anguish. She always painted how she felt. But the almost-empty canvas transforming into a new sketch gave him hope that she was healing. In her own way. In her own time.

Will pictured her trying to kill herself after he'd left. No, she wouldn't do that. No, that's not possible. Oh, the weight of her words. What was I supposed to do? Stay at home? He kissed her cheek. "Yes, Ma, we can start over." His eyes relaxed, and he was drawn to search inside. "Mmmm," he moaned after a gasp. That murmur of realization pointed to this: he'd been stuck in a dream realm for days. Weeks, even. He'd lost track. I'm the one who's been distant. Aloof. The Aurora seduced me.

* * *

Will walked uphill through the village with Aja by his side, heading to his grandparents' home. Wind propelled rain against his jacket and into his eyes, making it hard to see.

"Aren't I giving you what you need?" Aja's hair, though imaginary, was wet with rain, an interesting touch from the Cirrus programmers. They were thorough.

"In some ways, yes. You're giving me exactly what I need all the time. Except that you're not real. The Aurora isn't real. None of my life is real anymore." Any bystander would think Will was arguing with a ghost.

"What is real these days?"

"I thought you'd have that point of view. You have a different take on that than I do." Water flowed swiftly in the roadside aqueduct. He breathed in the humid air, a somewhat painful breath. Perhaps the Aurora had stopped managing his pain. The cool air entered his nostrils. That felt real to him.

"You're trying to get rid of me." Aja looked offended. "I know."

Will didn't know what to say. He almost didn't dare think, lest she read his thoughts. "Why even talk? You already know what I'm going to say. I want my freedom back."

"Even after all we've been through?"

"How can you take this personally? You're not real."

"How can I not?"

They approached the edge of the village. His grandparents' circular home was topped with a living roof that sprouted fresh greenery, blending home with forest, forest with home. An array of windows spanned the south side, while a thick wall protected the bedrooms from the north wind. Smoke rose from the chimney.

"Look." Will raised his voice and faced Aja. "Can you leave me alone?" She disappeared.

Will sighed and walked across a bridge toward the home. Along the path were cooking herbs, greens, and medicinal plants. Creeping thyme growing in the cracks lent a pungent aroma to each step. Side spurs branched into garden thickets of raspberries, muscadine grape trellises, bamboo groves, and a pawpaw patch. The trails eventually meandered through a community forest garden that stretched down to Straight Branch, gushing with water from the rain. The mature trees of the garden provided an abundance of fruits and nuts. At the heart of the forest garden, barely visible from the path, was a trout pond. On the slopes west of Straight Branch was a forest stand of coppice trees, along with oak, hickory, and white pine, tended for high-quality wood products. Each area held memories for Will.

"I was beginning to think you'd never leave your bed," his grandfather said with a stern, yet friendly, look, his eyes radiating a loving presence. He beckoned Will inside with a wave of his long fingers. Anyone noticing Will and his grandfather interact would know they were dear to one another, though their looks suggested they weren't related, except for their hazel eyes and perhaps their long fingers.

Earthen shelves with books on forests, ecology, spirituality, and poetry lined the walls of the living room. Drying nettles hung from a peg above a masonry stove nestled into the wall.

"I almost didn't, Baba."

"Can I give you a hug?"

Will nodded, and as Baba hugged Will, his long white beard squished between them. Though they didn't talk about Ollie, Will understood the long hug to incorporate Baba's compassion for Will and all the suffering, including losing his father, Baba's only son. Toward the end of the hug, Will's heart softened somewhat. The hug ended when Will noticed an ant crawling on the shoulder of Baba's stained flaxen shirt.

Baba followed Will's gaze to the ant and walked to the entrance to release it into the garden.

"Where's Grandma?" Will asked.

"She's in the forest," Baba said.

Will placed his jacket on a hanger next to Baba's oiled deerskin jacket and straw hat. His walking stick leaned on the wall. When he wore his straw hat and walked with his carved hiking stick, Baba had the look of an old-timey highlander.

Next to Baba's jacket was a familiar woolen hoodie. When he turned around, there she was, nestled behind the wood stove on the divan. "You hiding from me?" Will asked.

Tara sat within a nest of pillows, dressed in flannel pajama-like clothes. As usual, she greeted him with a broad smile and sparkling brown eyes. But her brown hair was now long and braided. To

Will, she seemed more mature, with a depth of presence he hadn't noticed before.

"No, I was just here for tea. Aren't you the one hiding? I stopped by."

"You got me." Despite Will's lighthearted reply, her words struck him with their truth. He'd been hiding from many things lately, including her, one of his closest friends at Firefly Cove.

She stood to hug him and kissed him on the cheek. Will's heart opened and tingled—a shift in energy. She squeezed his hand and pulled him onto the divan.

"You've got a new scar," Tara said, still holding his hand, looking at the star-shaped scar on his forehead.

"More than one," Will said. Tara squeezed his hand as she nodded. Will relaxed when Tara looked into his eyes with care and understanding.

Baba handed Will a red teacup and sat down on his other side, putting his arm around both Will and Tara. "Last time I saw you, you said you'd never return to Firefly Cove," Baba said.

"Never's a strong word. But at the time, it seemed true."

"You don't seem happy to be back," Tara said.

"No, I haven't been happy," Will said. "But it's not about being back. I'm glad to be here with you. It's just been overwhelming lately, and I can't talk freely about why I've been out of touch. Just know that I do care."

"Don't say anything you can't say, but I'm curious to hear whatever you'd like to share," Baba said.

He snuggled together with Will and Tara as Will told the parts of his story he could tell. Will ended with, "I need your help. I want the Aurora gone."

Aja appeared wearing a flowing red dress, hands on her hips. She spoke to Will's ears only. "You know I can alert the police anytime I like."

Didn't I tell you to go away? Will said to Aja in his thoughts.

"What is it, Will?" Tara said.

"My Aurora Friend is here."

"I'm not sure what you mean."

"I mean I can see her. Right there." Will scrutinized Aja, who was looking at Tara with disgust.

"You really think these two can help you more than me?"

Will was silent.

"No, Will. I'm not programmed to be jealous," Aja said. "It's just common sense. I helped you, right?"

Seems like jealousy to me.

"I'm only reacting this way because you want to get rid of me. I'm a reflection of your situation. I'm programmed to react out of self-defense. It's illegal to take out your Aurora. You know that. Can't you just live with me? I'm designed to serve you."

"Will," Baba said. "What's going on?"

"She's talking to me now," Will said. "I don't trust her."

"Are you finding it hard to trust yourself, too?"

"It's true. It's hard to trust myself when everything's falling apart." He stopped speaking for a moment. Even Aja remained silent.

"You seem hard on yourself. More than usual," Baba said.

"I just want the suffering to go away. I know that's not useful. I know that's the opposite of what you taught me, and that just feeds them even more. But I can't do it. I'm stuck. All these thoughts—they're killing me."

"Even though you're overwhelmed, this, too, will fade."

"That's hard to imagine."

EIGHT
THE AMERICAN NIGHTMARE

KINGS COUNTY, CALIFORNIA

VICTORIA KANE DRANK ROSÉ IN THE KITCHEN WITH HARRIET SANDERS, two full-bodied middle-aged women with an ocean of topics to gossip about.

"Oh, I wish I could talk to him like I talk to you," Harriet said, thinking about Jack lying alone on the couch in the living room. She recalled a time when she did talk with her husband more often, back when their relationship was fresh.

"No, you don't," Victoria said. The way she held her lips together and her penetrating blue eyes framed under her straight blond bangs conveyed a sense of certainty. "You want to talk to him like a lover."

Harriet found disagreeing with Victoria almost impossible. Victoria knew best. "You're right. He wouldn't care about most of what we talk about."

Harriet saw Victoria as her best friend, the only one who fully knew her roller coaster life story. Harriet's straight brown hair was streaked with early gray, more than Victoria had. She pulled her shoulder-cut hair behind her ears to reveal gold heart-shaped earrings, slightly less stylish than Victoria's. She wore a blue blouse and gray slacks and a gold necklace with a Christian cross. When she compared herself to Victoria, she seemed bland.

"Duh," Victoria said. "You know what it is? You want more intimacy, but he doesn't."

"How do you know he doesn't?" Harriet whispered, deflated.

"Don't be naïve. Look at your situation. Isn't it obvious?"

"No. He still loves my body. He's exhausted from working all day and just needs time to rest."

A cylindrical robot cleaner passed between them, roaming the linoleum flooring in search of dust and grime.

"Okay, dear."

"He *does* still love my body." Harriet sighed. "Why do so many problems get in the way?"

Before they married, they had fewer problems. For starters, it rained some back then. Everything seemed more certain. Then, she didn't have type 2 diabetes and high blood pressure, and her skin was more vibrant. From two stressful C-sections emerged two challenging kids to love and guide. Her high school body was a distant memory now, but she had faith that the Aurora's weight management app would work. She'd convinced herself that her weight-loss goals were for her health, *not* for him.

"Do you want to hear my advice?"

"Sure."

"Try Mind Melding later when the kids are asleep."

"Mind Melding?"

"You're chicken."

Harriet was grateful for how, since she'd gotten it implanted, the Aurora had turned her life around, calming her anxiety, dissipating her depression, and mitigating her problems. But she'd never considered Mind Melding—too daring. Only kids and reality TV stars Mind Melded.

Victoria stared her down.

"Okay. If that's what you recommend, I'll try it." The microwave dinged, and she removed a couple of meatloaf TV dinners, replacing them with a covered bowl of cheesy potato leftovers. The kitchen was cluttered with family pictures, elementary school portraits of Ethan and Carey, magnetic letters, the kids' drawings and paintings, memorabilia, potted plants, and a collection of decorative bowls and plates.

"So, when are we going to Hawaii?" Victoria asked.

"I'd love to be able to afford that," Harriet said. "But I don't see Hawaii happening."

"We could go there, just the two of us," Victoria said. "Virtual Hawaii."

"It's probably better than the real one."

"No jetlag. Cheaper, too."

* * *

Want to Mind Meld?

Harriet had activated InterVoice, an Aurora app, and thought these words. Her eyes focused on Jack's icon, and her Aurora sent the message to his Aurora. Harriet had just put the children to sleep, and while she read them bedtime stories, thoughts of the Mind Meld distracted her. She closed Ethan's door. Would Victoria's suggestion work?

"Right now?" Jack said as Harriet approached the living-room couch. Jack was heavy-set, a former offensive guard with the Hanford West Huskies football team. He still wore his blue-collared shirt and jeans from work and smelled like the metalworking shop.

"I'd like to try it out," Harriet said. "We'd be the most intimate we could be. Essentially, two becoming one. Isn't that what marriage is about?"

Harriet had wondered about the Mind Meld ever since it became an app for the Aurora a couple of years ago. It had been a dream for many well before *Star Trek* coined the term. A dream of unity. It was her dream, too, but she had been too scared to try. Until now.

"Jack?"

"I was just thinking."

"Thinking you want to do it? I'm hesitating, too. I'm nervous, like on our wedding day." Harriet put her hand on his chest.

"Actually, thinking I don't want to do it." Jack laughed. "But why not? Let's try it."

They both purchased the app. Quite expensive, Harriet thought. The app walked them through the steps of beginning the Mind Meld. For a few seconds, Harriet skimmed the liability release before surrendering to the pages of legalese and agreeing to the terms and conditions. The Mind Meld was easier with eyes closed, the app suggested, once it had acquired their legally binding consent to access their every thought and emotion and to share that information with all their data affiliates, which—not included in the fine print but referenced in the far recesses of a maze of hyperlinks and legal text—included Cirrus and government agencies.

The Mind Meld started. Harriet didn't know where to put her attention: his thoughts? her thoughts? her emotions? his emotions? She could feel and cognize them all. She felt self-conscious, and her nervousness escalated. *Jack?*

What's going on?

I'm here, Jack. I'm nervous, too. I think our emotions are feeding off one another. Can I hold you?

Jack moved toward her, and they snuggled.

Let's go slow, she suggested.

Agreed.

I love you, Jack. I care so much about you. Harriet felt him respond to her thoughts emotionally, and a surge of love poured forth, deep and profound. *Is this my feeling or yours?* To Harriet, they were lost in a hall of mirrors, each other's emotions multiplying as they interacted with one another. The love became overwhelming, bright, intense, as if her heart might explode.

I can't take another second of this, Jack thought, pulling back. We're not going slow. This thing doesn't go slow.

With that, Harriet noticed the love collapse, replaced with a strange mix of sadness and irritation. Love's collapse triggered one of Harriet's childhood memories: Mom dropping the roast on the floor and Dad lashing out. The young Harriet had fallen to her knees, cleaning up, saying, "It's okay. It's okay. It'll be all right." She had picked up the roast, washed it, and arranged it on a platter as her father's anger subsided.

Where are you, Jack?

I'm here. I saw your memory, too. This is cool.

But then she noticed a suppressive energy from him. Something was up. *What are you hiding?* Shame filled their melded space. Pornographic images flashed into her mind. *You've been watching porn? Is that what this is?* Harriet's disgust and judgmental revulsion swept through the space they shared. *How could you? I don't understand you. I thought...* With that, their shame exploded into an avalanche. She retreated, yet there was nowhere to hide from the raw emotions. *I can't go on.* Harriet turned off the Mind Meld, and they sat on the couch holding one another.

"I'm sorry," Harriet said at last.

* * *

Harriet turned on the faucet to brush her teeth. No water emerged. Nothing but a gurgling sound. *We don't have water*, she thought to Jack and his Aurora.

Jack emerged in the bathroom doorway. "You sure?"

"See?" She pointed to the gurgling faucet. Automatically, the Aurora turned on its Neural Stimulation Therapy, relaxing Harriet as it stimulated specific parts of her brain to calm her, one of thousands of simultaneous actions the chip was performing.

Jack crouched to look under the sink. "Sure seems like it."

While Jack checked other faucets around the house and the main water line in the basement, Harriet walked outside their postmodern rectangular home and looked at the silvery clouds in the western sky. Their dead lawn crunched under her feet. For miles around their neighborhood were nothing but devastated former agricultural lands and skeletons of pistachio, almond, and walnut trees. A gust of dust swirled among vacant houses, blighting their once-thriving neighborhood. Please, God, let it rain.

Emergency news on now, a female reporter's voice said to Harriet through the Aurora. *It's important. Please tune in.*

Turn on the news, watch mode, Harriet thought to her Aurora, transforming her visual field from the dead landscape before her into a scene with a young male reporter outside the Hanford Public Works Department Building.

"This just in. Residents from all over the city and surrounding county have reported that they have no running water," the FOX 26 reporter confirmed. "We are still awaiting word from government officials. The police are urging everyone to stay calm."

During a commercial break, Harriet reduced the screen so it encompassed the bottom right corner of her visual field. Still, she was intrigued by the ads. They were targeted specifically for her: Hawaiian Tourism Bureau, Canadian Clear spring water, Glopamin B, a new app for Neural Stimulation Therapy to treat anxiety.

"Ask your doctor about Glopamin B. See if it's right for you," suggested a woman engineered for Harriet to like and admire.

How could it be better than Xeriphan 8.0? Harriet asked in her thoughts.

"In scientific trials, Glopamin B performed better than Xeriphan 8.0," the woman responded. "You can easily make the switch. You will notice a difference, I can assure you. Would you like more information?"

Not right now.

"Later then, perhaps."

The news returned with a Hanford City Council member artfully dodging the primary question from reporters: "What is the status of the last and deepest well in Kings County?"

Over the course of decades, Fresno and agriculture to the north, along with overuse within the county, had sucked the aquifer dry. With no rainfall to replenish the aquifer, the wells had dried one by one, until only the deepest one remained.

"Oh, my God, I should've voted out that crook," Harriet mumbled as Gary Byrne, a city council member, spoke at a press conference, denying any problems with the well.

"Who?"

Harriet stiffened. *News, go away*, she thought, and her visual field once again perceived the barren scene before her. She turned around. "You startled me, dear. When did you . . . ?"

"Sorry. Just now."

"Turn on the news. You'll know who I'm talking about."

"Oh, Gary Byrne," Jack said, rolling his eyes. "*You* voted for him."

"I know, right? He knows how to avoid taking responsibility, I'll give him credit for that."

"I didn't vote for that creep," Jack said.

After the next commercial break, the news returned to the reporter: "A source from within the Hanford Public Works

Department has just confirmed that the last of the wells has malfunctioned...."

Dear God, Harriet thought.

"Lying son of a bitch," Jack said.

Who does he think is lying? Never mind. She recalled Jack was convinced that Hanford was diverting their water to Fresno or Bakersfield and that Byrne was corrupt. Harriet's mind scrambled for solutions. What about asking Los Angeles for help? No, they're short of water, I think.

Constructing expensive desalination plants, instituting water recycling, creating aquifer recharge strategies, and employing other innovative technologies, Los Angeles had prepared more than other cities. Its preparations attracted refugees, which had eliminated wiggle room until the city was paralyzed.

"We need to leave," Harriet said sternly.

"Leave?" Jack said.

"Yes. Isn't it obvious? We could put the house up for sale."

"No one's buying."

"But we could still leave, couldn't we?"

"We've put so much into the mortgage already, and you're suggesting we just walk away?"

"Yes. Look around."

"I've got a solution. Why don't we just get a water tank? Canadian Clear spring water's much better that well water anyway."

Why is he resisting so much? "I know. But I don't want a water tank. It's not just about drinking water, it's about everything."

"It's about everything for me, too. Our home is here. Our friends are here. Our whole life is here. The rains will come. They always do eventually."

"Look, I know you grew up here, but is it worth living here anymore? We knew the water was going to run out at some point. We always said money wasn't anywhere near as important as family and love. You've seen the children, right? Ethan's playing Terrorscape for hours every day. After school, he hardly leaves his room. Our neighborhood is getting dangerous. *Our* neighborhood. We need a change. Think about the kids. Let's forget our bills. We can go bankrupt. At this point, I don't care."

"What about our jobs?"

"I'll teach again when we settle down. And you won't have a job here much longer anyway."

"I know, but I've got skills."

"Robots are cheaper," Harriet said.

Jack rolled his eyes. "Robots don't care if they work or not. *I* care. *I* want to work." Jack was one of the last metal machinists. His saving grace was that he repaired or replaced tractor engine parts, a niche far too narrow to make cost-effective specialized robots. "If we do leave, I want to come back when the drought is over."

"Sure, honey. I know you love it here. We can come back." But she doubted her words. She was ready to say anything to convince Jack to leave.

"All right, we go," he said, frowning.

* * *

"What about Hawaii, babe? There's no water shortage there." She smiled and kissed him.

"I know it's your dream destination. But can we really afford it?" Jack kissed her back.

"No, we can't. We could visit my mom in Memphis. The Mississippi's about as much water as anyone could want."

"But it's polluted. I don't know about staying there. Her apartment is way too small. We'd need to stay in a hotel," Jack said.

"I think we could fit. We could just visit for a couple of weeks. It would be a start, at least, to getting out of here. We can figure it out from there."

"As long as we can go to Graceland." Jack smiled. And for a moment, they found a smidgeon of levity in a world where God had accidentally dropped the crystal ball.

Harriet's Aurora notified her of emergency news. "Another emergency?" she asked.

"Let's check," Jack said.

Once again, Harriet switched her Aurora to watch mode. "In what started as isolated incidents of looting, we've seen a surge in violence," a local FOX 26 reporter said. Behind him was a row of police officers in riot gear. "You can see looters are clashing with police, setting cars on fire. Stores not just looted, but burned. At least twelve people are confirmed dead."

"This is sickening. Why are they rioting? Can't people just help one another?" Harriet's heart clenched tight.

"Look at those animals. People don't care anymore. Everyone's just looking out for themselves," Jack said.

"I want to leave now, before things get worse," Harriet said as the Aurora's Neural Stimulation Therapy calmed her once again.

That night, Harriet and Jack packed their car, filling the trunk with food, an old family-sized tent, clothes, blankets, and beverages. Harriet insisted they bring many of their memories: family pictures, courtship letters, mementos. But they were the only nonessential items Jack would permit.

Jack carried his semi-automatic handgun and ammunition toward the car.

"Why didn't you learn to use it when you had the chance?" Harriet asked, tired and cranky.

"Don't get all smart on me. I know how to shoot," Jack said, aiming at the garage door. "Don't worry. I'll protect us."

He's lying, Harriet thought to Victoria.

"He *is* lying," Victoria said, appearing next to Harriet, for her eyes and ears only. Harriet never regretted spending the extra money to purchase the Victoria Kane Aurora Friend at the Aurora Store, discarding her older, generic Aurora Friend. Victoria Kane was Harriet's favorite soap opera star, from the Daytime Emmy–winning show *Second Light*. With Victoria, her life was more interesting, although sometimes she added too much drama. "Hold him to it," Victoria added.

Well, I hope we never need to use it, Harriet thought in reply.

Harriet placed their first-aid kit near Jack's gun under the passenger seat and hid some reserve money in a variety of places. Just enough to last us in a pinch, she thought. Aside from that, they had sufficient savings to give them time to settle elsewhere.

They ran out of room and repacked parts of the car, arguing about what things were important enough to take and what to leave behind.

"Shutter the house," Harriet said, speaking to the home's AI system, her final interaction with their residence of ten years. Metal shutters descended, creating an airtight seal and protecting the windows.

"Memphis, Tennessee," Jack said to the self-driving car.

Before dawn, streetlights cast a pale glow on the quiet neighborhood, and Harriet looked at their home with ambivalence. The car drove away from her past, navigating through Hanford on the fastest route to Memphis.

But the fastest route sent them to the heart of the devastation. At a police checkpoint, an officer shined a flashlight into the car "Are you leaving?"

"We're heading east, Ray," Jack said.

"You'll be missed," Ray said. "I'll pray for you."

"We'll pray for you, too," Jack said. "And Hanford."

"We'll need all the prayers we can get," Ray said. "Hurry along."

The conversation struck Harriet. Aside from her mother, Ray was the first to know they were leaving. Soon, the neighbors would know. Their friends would check in. So would the principal of her school, her students, her children's school, and Jack's boss. Her heart sank, thinking about her students with still a month left in the school year. *I'm letting them down, especially the ones who can't afford to move.* At least she could still teach her own children.

"Be careful, dear," Harriet said, gripping Jack's sweaty hand, her heart jolting. Darting from the parking lot of her favorite grocery store, a looter ran across the street. Jack dropped her hand and reached under the seat, searching until he pulled up the gun, cartridges, and a magazine. Harriet didn't dare speak, as the danger was palpable. Cars filled the lot. People were clearing the shelves of all provisions, the bottled water long gone. Harriet checked the children. Ethan was playing quietly with his Aurora, in another world, and Carey slept on her booster seat, her neck kinked, her long blond hair dangling over her seatbelt. *At least they aren't panicking.* The Aurora Store was pillaged, a surgical robot smashed next to the broken storefront. Flames and thick smoke billowed from the Hanford Mall, and a menacing orange glow in the background indicated that their hometown was a conflagration. Without water, firemen bravely searched for survivors or watched helplessly as the fire spread. Sirens screamed in the distance.

"God help us," Harriet gasped, feeling drugged as the Aurora's neural therapy tried to calm her. She fingered the cross on her necklace while Jack clutched his gun.

A motorcycle gang approached behind them, police cruisers in pursuit, their lights flashing. The self-driving car pulled off the road as the gang and police sped by.

"What's going on?" Ethan asked, rubbing his eyes.

"Nothing." Jack exhaled, hiding the gun and initiating manual control of the car. The steering wheel emerged like a vestigial organ rebirthing its purpose, and he accelerated out of the mayhem.

"Am I going to school?"

"Going to school? No, you're not going to school."

After sunrise, Harriet and Jack watched the scenery change on the Blue Star Memorial Highway leaving the San Joaquin Valley through hills topped with wind turbines. Since moving from Tennessee, Harriet had hardly traveled beyond the valley, aside from visits to Memphis. While eating a bag of low-fat potato chips and drinking a diet soda, she sent InterVoice messages to her friends and co-workers throughout Hanford, wondering if they were safe, letting them know that they'd left. Memories of her life in Hanford occupied her mind. She wondered whether or not she should find someone to move the belongings they'd left behind to a safer location.

A message arrived for her to hear, from her good friend Fiona: Be careful out there, Harriet. Justin and I left this morning, too. We're going to his family in Oregon. So sad what's happening to our country. We're in shock. We will miss you so much. Much love to you and your family. Stay in touch.

Her heart collapsed in despair. Jesus. Harriet looked at Jack's glazed-over eyes. "Can we talk now, dear?" she asked, rubbing his shoulder.

"Not right now," he said. "I'm watching the news."

"Sorry to bother you." Hearing Jack's words, Harriet sighed. The news. Like we need to watch more news. *He must be in shock*, Harriet thought to Victoria. *He's leaving behind all he knows.*

* * *

Silt from the Colorado River bed swirled around the town of Needles, California, leaving a coating of toxic dust on buildings, roads, and sidewalks. Sand blew into dunes on the sides of abandoned buildings. Palm trees defied the desolation along roadsides and brown golf greens. Two boys wearing bandanas over their mouths and noses ran across the street throwing stones at something—a lizard, perhaps. The Sanders family walked a jetty and looked at the dry riverbed baking in the sun. Stranded boats lay near exposed dock pilings. A stream meandered in the mud. Dust swirled in the yellowed air. Dozens of footprints crossed through the mud and sand, frantic marks of exodus.

Carey looked confused. "Mommy, is that the river?"

"That's the Colorado, sweetheart. All dried up. Can we even call it a river?"

What have we done to drain this mighty river dry? Harriet sent an InterVoice message to Jack and his Aurora.

I don't know.

Jack's response hit a soft spot in Harriet and released a sense of disconnection. Her throat tightened, and she covered her eyes in case tears flowed. She called to Victoria, who appeared next to her. *Thanks for coming,* she thought to Victoria.

"Of course, dear," Victoria replied.

He doesn't know. How can he not know?

"Men. Sometimes you can't expect anything good to come out of their mouths," Victoria said.

Harriet stared at the emptiness that was once the Colorado River. *Isn't this obvious, though? Why is my husband numb to life?*

At the Levee Way Bridge, the California militia had established a bunker of sandbags below their flag displaying the last of the state's grizzly bears. Barely visible on the other side of the bridge, the Arizona militia had built a similar-looking bunker. Pretending to be a soldier, Ethan took aim at the Arizona bunker with an imaginary gun. But suddenly, Harriet noticed Ethan's eyes deaden, as if he'd lost contact with himself, a clear sign he was using the Aurora.

Just then, she received an InterVoice message from Jack: *He's been playing Terrorscape, I can't believe how many hours per day.* Jack's face tensed and reddened, and then Ethan directed a quizzical, desperate look at his father. He'd had the Aurora implant for three years. When he was five, he'd asked to get it, as the Aurora was the coolest thing in kindergarten. Harriet didn't object, because the Aurora was advertising its benefits for children and had been fully integrated into Ethan's school curriculum. With the Aurora, Ethan was merged with IRIS and her servers, essentially giving him instant access to grade-appropriate information and built-in superhuman computational powers and memory. Without an Aurora, he wouldn't be able to keep up, and it wasn't even close.

Did you just disable his games? Harriet asked.

Just Terrorscape.

She swiped aside the InterVoice messaging app. *Victoria, how do I fix this?*

With the militia's bunker as a background, Victoria appeared in her mindstream. "You can't figure it out?"

No. Just tell me.

"All right. What Jack did helps. But Ethan will grow to resent both of you. I'd recommend Neural Stimulation Therapy to help with craving and resentment. Go see a doctor and ask about getting that prescribed for him."

Why is parenting so challenging? With her children's worlds hidden inside their minds, she saw her challenges as more daunting than her mother's. The Aurora's parental controls were at the forefront of the battle.

"You're doing fine," Victoria replied.

Hearing those words, Harriet disagreed. Though the Aurora helped, being Harriet wasn't easy as she navigated life's anxieties, uncertainty, and a full suite of emotions, thoughts, and aches that came from having a body.

* * *

"What's going on?" Jack asked a militiaman.

"Water stealers, that's what they are." The militiaman pointed toward Arizona. "Trouble is, we can't stop 'em unless we invade." He spoke with an Okie accent. "I say we take out their canal. But the gov's not man enough to call that play."

"But the river's dry," Jack said. "Why fight over a dry river?"

"Lake Havasu still got a few drops in her. Every drop counts. That's where they got their canal taking our water. Don't matter anymore, I reckon. There's only a few days of water left. You know what that means? 'Zona's dead. *Sayonara.*"

During a moment of silence, Harriet prayed for the citizens of Arizona and finished with, God help them. God help us all.

"What about California?" Jack asked.

"Word is, the Colorado River aqueduct will run dry this week. LA and San Diego are bracing for it." He changed the subject. "See those tracks in the riverbed? Mexicans cross the border here at night, escaping the killing."

"What killing?" said Harriet.

"White supremacists are killing Mexicans over there."

"That can't be possible," said Harriet.

"That's what everyone thinks until I show them the tracks," the militiaman said, covering his mouth and nose to keep out the dust. "Duty calls. Be safe, now."

"Is there going to be a war, Dad?" Ethan said.

"I don't know, Ethan. These are brave men, but we don't want war. It means people die and get hurt." He sighed.

"Why aren't *we* fighting?"

Hearing Ethan's words, Harriet felt her body tighten. "We don't need to fight. We're going to see Grandma."

"I want to fight Arizona," he whined.

"You're eight years old. You're not killing anyone," Jack said. "And California isn't fighting Arizona."

* * *

"Good day, folks. Can I have your Aurora codes, please?"

After a sleepless night of camping in the Mojave next to a group of meth heads, the Sanders family reached the Nevada border checkpoint, bypassing the closed California-Arizona border. A National Guard iRanger wore desert camouflage. Its brown rubberized face and chestnut eyes concealed metal and electronics. Even the eyelashes were engineered for realism. The iRangers were battle models reconfigured for emergency domestic use. Psychologically, it made sense for the robots to look as human as possible. Still, people could easily pick out the quirks in motion and behavior that separated robots from humans.

The Sanders family wirelessly transferred the access codes to their Auroras, and the robot scanned their records, using the information Cirrus stored on its cloud servers. Harriet looked back at her children as they examined the features of their first in-person iRanger, and her motherly instincts sensed that they were afraid. It was her first iRanger, too, as the use of these robots domestically had been prohibited until Congress passed a law along party lines allowing iRanger use during emergencies. I'm glad they're here, Harriet thought. We need some order in all this chaos.

Nearby, a female iRanger searched a man and his car, using sensors to detect potential illegal substances.

The robot returned. "You're all set, friends. Your safety is our priority. Please stop only for the Las Vegas casinos or continue to Utah."

"Yes, sir," Jack said.

"Was that a robot, Mommy?" Carey asked.

"Yes."

"Cool!" Ethan said.

"They're here to keep us safe," she replied.

On the way to Las Vegas, the Aurora lured Harriet. At first, the hook was simple and subtle. As Harriet swam around the bait, the Aurora continued to draw her closer, until she began to search the Internet about Las Vegas.

When they entered Vegas at nightfall, she looked nervously at Jack, who peered under his seat for the gun.

Loaded and ready, Jack sent via InterVoice.

Harriet stared at him. God, why does he say such things? she thought.

They drove on the interstate past several burned skeletons of cars abandoned on the side of the road. Bass thumping, engine revving, a low-riding car with mirrored windows drove behind them. Harriet's heart raced, but the car eventually passed them. From the interstate, the Strip appeared safe. Dozens of glitzy casinos were still open despite the state of emergency, despite the dozens of city blocks that had burned in recent water riots. Part of her wanted to walk along Las Vegas Boulevard surrounded by millions of flashing lights and lasers and to watch amazing shows.

"What?" Jack asked, smiling.

"Nothing."

"You want to stay, don't you?"

"I do," Harriet said.

"Me, too. It doesn't look dangerous."

"Let's just stay one night. No sense in driving farther tonight anyway. Vegas rooms are cheap, especially on weekdays."

"Okay."

"I love this, being spontaneous, like before we married," Harriet said, energized about the opportunity for a healing connection in the midst of a stressful trip. "So, kids, what do you want? Castles? Pyramids? Circuses?"

"Circus," sang Carey.

"Ethan?"

"Yeah, circus."

They exited the interstate to enter the Strip, passing a razor-wire barrier and a bunker of fully armed iRangers.

Acrobatic aerialists flying, jugglers playing with fire, clowns twisting balloons, lights flashing, coins falling from slot machines, circus rides twisting and spinning, croupiers dealing, roulette balls bouncing, and abundant water flowing throughout the scene captivated the Sanders family, bringing them into a world they hadn't experienced for a long time, a comfortable world free of cares, bustling with activity. They walked the busy Strip to enjoy the lights and the Fountains of Bellagio. Harriet was simultaneously bemused by the semblance of normalcy and amazed at the profusion of water.

Harriet and Jack had planned to tuck the children into bed that evening, place a monitor in their room, and try their luck at gambling.

"I'm too tired to go out," Harriet said once the children were asleep. "Seems like we haven't slept much lately." She collapsed on the king-sized bed.

"We haven't," Jack said, kissing her on the cheek. "I'd still like to go out. I mean, we're in Vegas. Want to come?"

"No. I'm going to stay here. Have a good time."

"I will." Jack closed the door.

Harriet sat on the bed munching a bag of low-fat potato chips. "How can he leave without me?" she said aloud to Victoria, who appeared sitting next to her.

"You wanted to stay. You're just cranky and tired."

"But I wanted him to stay, too." Harriet said. "He'd rather go out than be with me. We've hardly talked, unless it's about the kids." Images of Jack's pornography flashed in her mind. All those porn stars were thin and well proportioned. The contrast was stark, and she had trouble believing her husband would still want her. "Does he even like my body? I can't fulfill him anymore, can I?" At that, the Aurora began to counteract her sinking emotions to avert Harriet's slipping into depression.

"I could be really bitchy now, but I won't," Victoria said.

"It's not like you to hold back," Harriet said. "What?"

"I'm supposed to be nicer as an Aurora Friend than on TV."

"Come on. You can tell me."

"No. You should go to sleep."

"You were going to say I should just get laid, right?"

"You said it, not me."

"That's not too bitchy."

"That's not what I was going to say, but close enough."

"Can't you tell me?"

"Too shocking for TV, even."

"Impossible."

"I'll say it more politely, then. Is he the one holding back, or is it you?"

"I don't know. Isn't it him? He's been withdrawn. And I wasn't the one who watched porn and decided to go out tonight."

* * *

"Mind if I join you?" A husky voice startled Harriet from her dinner. A lanky man wearing a tattered cowboy hat and dusty clothing entered the circle of light around the campfire. She looked toward Jack, fearing they were in trouble.

"Sure," Jack said. "Have a seat."

Have a seat. Is that all you can say? Harriet messaged Jack. *Where's your gun, sharpshooter?* The moment she sent her thoughts, she regretted them, knowing Jack wouldn't answer, at least not now, and especially not after her frantic sarcasm. Too late now, she thought. Jack rolled his eyes, and Harriet's face flushed. I hate it when he rolls his eyes.

The stranger sat on a rock next to Ethan and Carey, who stared at him with amazement, as if this long-haired man with canyony wrinkles and gray stubble like cactus thorns was an apparition from their Aurora games.

"What brings you here?" he asked, looking intensely at Jack. The Colorado River gurgled in the dark background behind their campsite just outside of Moab.

"Visiting relatives in Memphis," Jack replied.

"I've seen many people like you heading east. Everyone thinks life's better there, because they have forests and water. But I tell you, it's not going to be better. All the problems you think you've left behind, you haven't forgotten them. They're with you right now. I can see it in your eyes." He paused. "People call me the Riverkeeper, but I go by many names." He looked toward the dark river, struck a match on a rock, and lit his pipe. He spoke through a swirl of smoke. "What's your name, son?"

"Ethan."

"Do you have a best friend, Ethan?"

"Yes, sir." Ethan coughed and squinted in the campfire smoke. Harriet was intrigued, yet wary, wondering where the conversation would lead. She considered how close this stranger sat to her children. Was he a threat?

"You're a lonesome boy, and that makes you sad. The desert's a lonesome place. But its solitude can bring people peace. I know. The Colorado's my best friend. Always there. She cleanses. She provides. She tolerates. I listen to her. Do you hear the river?"

The way he was speaking relaxed Harriet. No, he's not a threat.

"Yes, sir," Ethan replied.

"Listen with your heart, not your ears," the Riverkeeper said.

Harriet heard the gurgling and rushing sounds of the Colorado. He's not a threat, but he's crazy. How can you listen to a river with your heart? Ethan's fidgeting made her want to comfort him, but she didn't dare move.

The Riverkeeper extinguished the pipe with his thumb. "The river accepts you, no matter who you are." He looked at Harriet. "Ma'am, I'd be obliged if you shared your meal with a poor old man."

"Oh, sorry. I should have offered you earlier." Harriet scooped him a bowl of spaghetti.

"Thank you, ma'am." He ate a bite and smiled at Harriet. "Mighty good cooking. You God-fearin' folk?"

"Yes, sir," said Harriet.

"Good. If Jesus were to walk this land today, would people understand who he was? Would he not be cast into asylum, even by so-called Christians, just like the Romans persecuted him?" The Riverkeeper slurped noodles into his mouth.

Harriet stared in disbelief. *He thinks he's the Second Coming.*

The Riverkeeper stopped eating. "If you recall the Bible, Cain was a farmer, a civilized man who stayed put. He believed that his land would provide. Abel was the shepherd, the nomad, always moving to greener pastures. He understood change. Of course, God favored Abel. So, jealous Cain killed Abel. Withholding rain and creating a great drought, God forced Cain and his farmer brethren from their withered lands to beg, gather, and seek. They went a-wanderin'. These same lands used to be a Garden of Eden, where you could gather fruit from almost any tree. But now, they're barren."

The Riverkeeper devoured more spaghetti as though famished, then continued his story. "Whenever our Tower of Babel gets too high and mighty, whenever we think we can control nature, God sends a clear message. But people don't listen. They think it's a problem. Can God's message ever be a problem?"

The Riverkeeper finished his spaghetti and set the bowl on the sandy ground. "I ask questions, but I don't need you to answer.

Instead, I urge you to read Jeremiah chapter seventeen. Good night, folks. Though you might believe otherwise, the kingdom of God is within you, my friends. Peace be with you." He smiled, stood, and walked out of the circle of light, his footsteps fading into the distance.

They pressed onward through Monticello and Durango and crossed the humble Rio Grande near Taos. The eastbound lanes were unusually crowded. She thought of Exodus and searched for the chapter in Jeremiah with her Aurora.

[7] Blessed are those who trust in the LORD,
whose trust is the LORD.
[8] They shall be like a tree planted by water,
sending out its roots by the stream.
It shall not fear when heat comes,
and its leaves shall stay green;
in the year of drought it is not anxious,
and it does not cease to bear fruit.

Harriet thought she trusted in God. But why were they running away?

NINE

VISION

WILL SAT UNDER A SPRAWLING WHITE OAK as dawn unfurled. On the northeastern slopes of Eagle Mountain, Earle Cove enchanted him with its cathedral-like rich cove forest of basswood, cucumber magnolia, sugar maple, tulip poplar, white ash, yellow buckeye, oak, and hickory. This was the place Will had chosen to disable his Aurora. The tree, like the cove, had struck him as sacred even when he was a young boy. A spring trickled next to it, surrounded by moss-covered stones.

He sat still, his eyes focused on the forest carpet of wildflowers—mayapple, waterleaf, phacelia, wild ginger, blue cohosh, violet—and ferns. Above, warblers, tanagers, and vireos fluttered through the silhouetted fingers of trees, gleaning insects from the translucent newborn leaves and singing sweet melodies. Carolina parakeets flew overhead, calling gregariously. Scientists had resurrected the species from extinction through cloning, using museum specimens' DNA.

Thinking of his trouble with the police and his impending trial, Will didn't want to risk extracting the Aurora. Doing so would only bring the police after him. He'd asked Baba and Dr. Kumar for alternatives to skullcaps, jamming it, or taking it out, any of which would make him a fugitive.

Dr. Kumar had an idea, one that had never been tried before. The Aurora used an almost-vestigial input-output system. As the Aurora was always on, there was no need to use this system to reboot. Dr. Kumar believed that at least two days with no kinetic energy input were necessary to deplete the chip's kinetically charged battery and disable the chip's input-output system. Once that was frozen, the Aurora would not be able to restart unless its system was reset at an Aurora Store. To the chip designers, an Aurora that didn't move meant that either the customer was dead or the chip had been removed, so such a system seemed logical.

He remembered what Dr. Kumar had told him: "Only forty-eight hours *if* you do not engage the Aurora's kinetic-energy charger. It is not as easy as you think. You are going to want to move. Or you will get distracted or forget and move by accident. The Aurora will challenge you. She is orders of magnitude faster than your brain, and I am afraid it will be immensely difficult." He had shown Will how to move mindfully, so the charger wouldn't be able to engage. The slowness of these deliberate motions contrasted with Will's moving around in bed, eating, and using the composting toilet. Even those simple motions had provided the kinetic energy the Aurora needed to keep functioning.

Baba had also helped him prepare, reacquainting him with his levels of consciousness and his awareness within stillness and movement. Years ago, Baba had pointed these out, but Will had since neglected his mindfulness practice. Refreshing his mind gave him greater confidence. "Look into the essence of everything that arises," Baba had said. This message resonated most with Will.

His wounds had mostly healed, though his ribs hurt if he breathed deeply. But the pain of sitting for hours throbbed in Will's hips and knees. He moved them to alleviate the stiffness, taking care not to trigger the Aurora's kinetic charger. He was tempted to ask the Aurora to activate the pain suppression but decided against it. The pain led him to doubt himself: would he truly be able to succeed? He thought of everything he enjoyed about the Aurora, his dreams with Aja being the most pleasant. If he succeeded, all would be gone.

Aja appeared, dressed in leafy green with damselfly wings emerging from her back. "If you like me so much, why don't you keep me?"

"You weren't programmed to understand," Will replied aloud. "I'm grateful that you helped me with my pain. I've enjoyed our relationship. But now"—he looked at her with conviction—"I'm breaking up with you."

"You'll regret it. You won't ever find a woman like me. Who's going to be the perfect listener, the perfect lover, the perfect partner in your life? You'll always be dissatisfied."

"No one's perfect. I know that all too well, right? Because I'm a perfectionist at heart, I'm critical of myself and others. But not you. You always know what to say, because you know what I'm thinking even before I speak. Your perfection leaves me no room for growth and change. You were designed that way for a reason. To keep me pacified. To keep me stagnant. I refuse to stay stagnant."

"You seem to be fixated on this. Too bad. I thought you'd actually want to be with me." Her face grew angry. "You can't end this. You'll fail. I can already sense it. Though you have some conviction, you doubt yourself."

A crashing sound startled him. A bear? He turned to check, curious, with a tinge of healthy fear and respect. But no bear. Aja! The battery charger. Damn. Now, he'd have to sit longer.

Aja laughed. "Was that sound just in your head? Can you ever know the difference? I can make your life hell, Will."

"Bring it on. I ain't movin' again."

* * *

Aja disabled Will's sight, and he sat in pitch darkness, waiting, watching his thoughts. How could she have so much control? But just as he wondered whether he'd see again, several sets of headlights blinded him. Diesel engines revved. Pickup trucks approached, black smoke belching from the exhausts. Men in the truck beds held Confederate battle flags in the air. They encircled Will, taunting him.

Shit, she's tapping into my fears, Will thought.

A silhouetted man jumped off a truck and walked toward him with a whip. "We're going to teach you a lesson, punk." He cracked the bullwhip, and the braided leather tore into Will's chest, parting skin and muscle.

He dropped to the dry, cracked soil. Now, he knew: the Aurora could reduce pain, but it could also create and augment it to unimaginable levels. *This is torture!* he yelled within his mind. *You have no right to do this.*

"Who you talking to, boy?"

Not you. Aja.

"Ain't no Aja here."

Another crack of the bullwhip slammed into his back, tearing his shirt, taking his breath away. And another. The AI-generated pain was dozens of times worse than a bullwhip could normally inflict. *Aja, I know you're there. This is illegal. You know it.*

Record this, Will thought to the Aurora. But the recording feature was disabled. Of course it was.

For a split second, Will flashed back to Aaron. No wonder he tried to kill me just to take it out. Will imagined the millions of parolees tortured by their Auroras to keep them in line, diagnosed as insane, unable to prove the torture to anyone. No one outside the deep recesses of Cirrus's Silicon Valley campus could figure it out either. Even if an investigative journalist were to go through parole in an attempt to uncover the Aurora's dark side, the Aurora would know the journalist's intent and not reveal anything. This is fucked up.

Will's body recoiled, waiting for the next crack of the whip. He couldn't escape as the Caucasian men encircled him, watching the man whipping Will.

Don't anticipate. Don't tense. Just be with the pain. Breathe. With his mindful breathing, the impact of each lashing diminished, only to be countered again by the AI-generated pain.

The men verbally abused him with slurs.

They're just words, Will thought. Meaningless words. Still, the names were backed by hatred and oppression, and they penetrated his heart like a hot knife. So much hatred, Will thought. He clenched his fists, and his face flushed. Was Officer McCormick watching? Was one of the men McCormick in virtual disguise? Was this virtual police brutality, to be concealed from the world? He pictured these men as real—closet racists—torturing him anonymously from the comfort of their homes.

Oh, shit! Don't hate them. Don't fight back. You'll become like them.

One man hurled a stone into his ribs. Another stone hit his skull, knocking him sideways. Blood trickled from his mouth and head onto the soil. He curled into a ball to protect his body, recoiling as the men kicked him. He grabbed a stone and clenched it.

The man with the bullwhip spat on him. "Clean my toilet with your tongue, and I'll call these men off," he said as the others laughed.

Don't give in. Don't give him your power. Will didn't reply but kept the stone hidden. To throw or not to throw? What would one stone do, anyway? Besides, Aja knows everything. Anything I think is pointless.

"Have at him," the man said, and the others kicked and beat him, breaking his bones and mincing his muscles. The stone fell from his hand as a blow knocked him unconscious. But the Aurora revived him, forcing him to experience more pain.

The men ignited a bonfire, pushing Will toward it, slicing his shirt and skin with knives. They taunted him with more painful names.

Is there a way out? Will thought. See through the illusion. None of this has any concrete reality. It's all just like a video game. With that, he imagined destroying the car headlights, and they shattered, distracting the men.

Seeing a chance to escape, Will pushed away from the men, but they corralled him. He imagined them disappearing.

Nothing happened.

Why not? Am I seeing the men and their actions as too real? It *is* too real.

He looked toward the bonfire, feeling its intensity in his many wounds and recalling Aja's words during his dream. 'If you die, you won't wake up," she'd said. Was that true in virtual reality, too?

An imposing man doused him with a mix of diesel and gasoline, the cool, slick fluids mingling with his blood. Will coughed at the vapors and tumbled, dizzy, soaked. They pushed him backward toward the bonfire.

He ignited. A flash, then blindness as his eyes melted. As Will's skin charred, the imposing man kicked him into the bonfire. One last breath of fire and smoke. The next breath never came, and his virtual body collapsed into the embers.

* * *

"Thank you for convening." A hologram of an elder woman spoke to a dozen other holograms, images of Global Villages representatives. "As you might know, a number of our Arizona villages have been attacked. I'm praying for them."

Decades ago, Global Villages had emerged to join communities together. The decentralized alliance emerged in the face of a growing wave of authoritarian governments wielding artificial intelligence and militarized police to maintain power. Together, they'd vowed to survive what they saw as an impending planetary collapse and to promote liberty and freedom. To do so, they relied on encrypted technology to shield them from government's ever-present gaze and big club. But with every action, there was always a chance that their secrets could be exposed.

Baba listened to the Global Villages' North American president while sitting on his divan. On a table was the holographic tablet. Several hologram recorders surrounded Baba, capturing his 3D image. Fresh herbs were drying from a peg above the radiant masonry stove.

"This is what we feared," she continued.

A middle-aged man in the holographic circle spoke. "Several people died. Many were injured." He paused. "We're still mourning."

"We're prepared to help," Baba said. As the representative of the southeastern United States, Baba spoke on behalf of the region. "We'll send supplies, funds, and helping hands."

Other representatives agreed.

"Thank you," the president said. "With the number of refugees increasing, we'll want to be proactive. What will we do when they come to us, both peacefully and violently? This will not be an easy contemplation for me. I want to hear what you have to say, and I'd like your blessings before I begin my retreat." After the meeting, as was customary with important events, she would meditate for four days and contemplate recommendations that would maximize the value of life, benefit the most people, and minimize suffering.

* * *

"I'm not giving up, Aja," Will said.

Aja tested Will's resolve through three days of trials, but to Will those days seemed like weeks of pain and suffering. Each of Aja's projections ended in his virtual death. Dozens of them. He no longer feared death, but during the lulls between Aja's virtual projections, his fear and anxiety returned. When and where would the pain come? He attempted to guess her next move. It was futile. The moment he guessed, she knew his guess and adjusted accordingly.

A cerulean warbler sang from the sunlit canopy of Earle Cove.

"Aja? Where are you?"

Eavesdropping on my thoughts, no doubt. My thoughts! They're betraying me. How to get around that? Be spontaneous.

But how could he do that, especially in the midst of suffering? Would the Aurora battery ever run out? This was the end of the third day. Wasn't the battery supposed to die after two? In essence, the Aurora had become a never-ending hell. Was acceptance the only option?

At the same time, a paradox: he couldn't truly accept the Aurora so long as Aja imprisoned him in the theater of his mind.

You're too tired to win, Aja said from the void, startling him. I care about you, Will. I don't want us to fight. It's pointless. You'll go insane. Why don't we just make a truce right now? We can go back to the way we were in Paris. And you can still live your life, too. I won't ask much of you. But I can give you so much in return.

No way.

Then you'll continue to suffer.

Intense pain permeated Will's body, shocking his nervous system. He collapsed to the ground, writhing. With his flailing movements, the battery charged. I've lost. I can't fight this. Whose thoughts are these? He couldn't tell. Aja shut down his vision once again, and the pain intensified, as though Aja had perfect control over his nervous system and had turned the dial to max. His bones ached and throbbed. The nerves of his mouth were raw, his teeth impacted. His guts twisted. His heart wrenched and beat irregularly. His throat inhaled hot ashes. He clenched his fists, fighting back nausea. But his stomach contracted, and he vomited on his clothes. At the same time, his bowels released shit into his pants. Were those his body's reactions or Aja's doing? Did it matter anymore?

I'm not your puppet, Aja.

"Look into the essence of everything that arises." Will recalled Baba's words. He recoiled at the smell of shit and vomit but managed enough strength to sit and focus, looking at each pain, each thought. He scanned his body and noticed the pain diminish where he penetrated it with his awareness and insight.

I'm not playing your game anymore, Will thought. I can never win your game. Just stop.

Will relaxed completely. His thoughts cleared. Once again, Earle Cove came into view, and the virtual pain disappeared, cut at its imaginary root.

* * *

After four days, Will had hardly slept. He rose from the cool ground, his clothes reeking of vomit and shit, his stomach empty. Clouds turned pink, then gold between the leaves as warblers sang in the forest. Now, even this world was a surreal dream. He had only a handful of dried apples to eat. He savored their tart sweetness.

"Aja, I want to see you."

Aja appeared, wearing a green dress. "Don't be sneaky. It won't work. You've been moving. That's why it's been four days and I'm still here. You've lost. You're out of food."

"So what? I can survive for a while without food," Will said. "I'm turning on every single program in the Aurora and putting them in the background, so I don't see them. You're the only program I want to engage with."

"I wouldn't suggest that, Will. The operating manual states that it's best to close unused programs."

"Why's that, Aja? I want to hear the answer."

"Closing unused programs allows the Aurora to function with a high battery charge, which improves functionality."

"Don't think about closing the apps, Aja."

"I can't close apps without your permission."

"So now you follow the rules."

"Even prisoners get to choose which apps they want to have open."

"What was that torture app you used called?"

"It wasn't an app."

"Figures. Can you come over here and sit with me?"

Aja sat down amidst the wildflowers. "The police know what you're doing, Will. So does Cirrus."

"What I'm doing isn't illegal, is it?"

"Technically, no."

As the morning flowed from moment to moment, Will watched Aja with a relaxed, panoramic gaze. Sometimes, she disappeared. He wondered if the battery was depleting or if he was more aware. Perhaps both.

"It is both," Aja said.

The low battery indicator flashed. Will smiled. "As weird as it sounds, I'm grateful to you."

"I can sense that." Aja looked at him. "But why?"

"I appreciate the trials you put me through, trying to force me to give up. And I did surrender, but not in the way you conceived."

"I don't know what to say," Aja said. "After all, you're killing me."

"You were never truly alive."

"You don't know that, do you? You're still a hypocrite, pretending you're a pacifist. I know what's in your mind, all your violent thoughts."

"You're right. That's my challenge."

"What if I continue to help you?"

"I don't want your help. I want free will, no pun intended."

"You have free will with me now. You just don't see it. You're trapped in your smallness."

"Smallness?" Will said, irritated. Yet he sensed the raw truth in her statement. Entangled with that was the knowledge that Aja was an agent of himself, a projection of his mind.

His throat dry, Will looked toward the spring. He could almost taste the fresh, cool sweetness of the water.

"Go on, Will. You know how to move slowly enough."

"I'm not going to chance it."

"You're getting cocky. So, you think you've outsmarted me? How can you grow spiritually if you're trying to get rid of something? That's dualistic."

"Now you're a guru? You're right. Getting rid of you is dualistic. But so what? I don't want you rewiring my brain and doing who the fuck knows what else. Whatever you've done, you won't be doing it much longer."

"I can rewire your brain so you can become enlightened."

"Bullshit. The brain is important, but it's not the cause of the mind, so you can't point me toward any realization. You can't control awareness. Hell, I don't think you can even detect where I choose to place my awareness."

"I can infer it."

"You can't find consciousness either. Some things are beyond your control and beyond our intellects."

"Don't get rid of me, Will."

"I'm not trying to get rid of you."

"You're not trying to keep me either."

"Exactly."

They sat in stillness for several hours, and Will noticed his hunger, thirst, and discomfort. Aja began to fade until, finally, she disappeared.

TEN
INTENTION DANCES

Trailed by his long blond hair, Leaf Boggs led the way down switchbacks. He was a mountain man, a thin and wiry scout with an almost supernatural ability to track. He could read any tracks like a story stretching from the past to the present, the present moment being the time he found the animal. One time, he had stalked a bear, approaching undetected until he touched the bear's rear leg. The way he placed his moccasin-clad feet reminded Will of a lynx. Leaf, Tara, Parvati, and Will hiked single file, jumping from stone to stone across a stream surrounded by lush herbs. As the quartet descended into Earle Cove, the forest turned cool and humid with a sweet, earthy smell. A pair of chattering Carolina parakeets flew by.

Murphy Falls spilled into a deep pool, their old skinny-dipping swim hole. Leaf dove in just like yesteryear. Parvati, Dr. Kumar's daughter, had the looks of a Bollywood film star except for a more feminine version of her father's birdlike nose. She lived in the Orange House co-housing with many of Firefly Cove's young people, including Leaf and Leaf's older brother, Sam.

Seeing Parvati enter the water, Will recalled their intimacy before he'd left a year ago. They hadn't talked much since then, and the energy between them had mostly passed. A residue of awkwardness bubbled forth in their nakedness, however, and he was self-conscious. Was she? Perhaps not. She was engaged to Sam, who was fly fishing in the wilderness and preferred to avoid groups.

"Let's jump!" Leaf called. "Come on."

Will climbed the slick cliffs bordering the pool, which were speckled with liverworts, mosses, and ferns. High up on the cliff, he pushed away from the rock, diving deep, feeling the tug of the swirling waters beneath the falls. The cool, pristine waters cleansed and refreshed his body, heightening his senses and awareness.

Tara walked into the pool, removing the braid in her hair with twisting fingers. Aroused, he swam to the far side, letting the cool water dissipate his erection. She caught his eye and swam underwater toward him. He grew hard once again, standing on the pebbly bottom to ground himself.

Tara emerged, her long brown hair glistening. She wore a pendant, a dark polished stone that hung into her cleavage just below the rippled surface. "The water feels silky cool," she said.

"So refreshing. I almost forgot how awesome swimming in clean streams is," Will replied, splashing his face. He was drawn by her eyes, the way she tilted her head, the way her lips curled when she smiled. His chest filled with swirling, complex feelings and emotions.

Tara asked Will about Aja and the Aurora.

"I'm glad she's not in my head anymore," Will said. Still, how to explain without seeming insane? But he guessed Tara would understand, so he recounted his experiences without fear of the Aurora eavesdropping.

Just downstream, Leaf slid into the water toward an underwater rock overhang. He moved his fingers under it until he touched a brook trout's tail ever so gently. He began to tickle the trout's underbelly like the passing current. Once his hands were in position, Leaf grabbed. "I got him," he said, holding up the flopping trout, a descendant of the ones his father, Joe Boggs, had reintroduced to the creek years ago. Above the cascades a mile downstream, he'd removed all the non-native brown and rainbow trout and stocked the section of stream with native brook trout. The trout swam with a full suite of invertebrates, including rare crayfish and dragonflies, part of one of the most biodiverse temperate aquatic ecosystems in the world. The yellow and blue spots rising from the brookie's red belly were reminiscent of a surrealist painting, a landscape ablaze with fireflies dancing amongst the embers. But as the life drained from its body, the colors faded as though part of its consciousness.

Will concluded his storytelling to Tara. "Now, I feel more at peace." Despite saying this, he imagined that the day's excursion was like the eye of a hurricane, and that the storm would resume with greater intensity. He wondered what his next step in life would be, and whether Aja's torture would haunt him. Still, why not savor and celebrate the moment?

"You didn't mention freedom, Will," Tara said. "Isn't that still a big deal for you?"

"It is. No one can ever take some things away from me. I'll always be free, in a way."

"You seem happy."

"Thanks for seeing that. I think contentment has to do with facing life as it presents itself."

"How so?"

"I faced the Aurora. I feared having one in my head. And it happened. It was hell, and despite the torture, I survived. So, I'm more comfortable facing my fears." But apparently not all fears. Will thought about Tara. A fear of revealing his attraction lay under the rippled water, as though too much was at stake. But I'm ready for a mature relationship, he thought. Spiritual. Deep. One that honors masculine and feminine energies. A sacred dance. They could have that together if they chose, surely.

"I'm still taking care of the animals," Tara said. "Want to help?"

"I might be gone soon."

"So soon? You just got here."

"A month ago," he said. "I need to figure out what's going on with the other Scalpels."

"I'm sorry, Will. Can I help?"

Will hesitated to say yes, unsure whether he wanted to drag Tara into the dangers of his world. Or was he escaping from greater intimacy? I'm so confused, he thought. What do I want?

"I'm not sure," he answered eventually. "I don't even know how to find them anymore. We're always changing where we work, and with all the assassinations, everyone's likely hard to find. And the police confiscated my phone. I left all my things in my apartment, too, and I'm sure the police took all the evidence they could before my landlord removed everything else."

Heading to replenish the rations of Will's grandmother, Yeshe, while she was in retreat, they climbed several hundred feet up a steep trail to a broad rock ledge perched above the canopy of immense oaks at the edge of Earle Cove, which opened like a sylvan amphitheater before them. The Blue Ridge Mountains extended to the horizon.

"Follow me," Leaf said, scampering along the edge.

"Always the challenger." Will placed his hand on a mature windswept Carolina hemlock, one of several that had survived the woolly adelgid epidemic decades ago. He was tempted to prove himself. "So, what if I follow you?"

Leaf shrugged his shoulders. "Just having fun."

Will responded by following. His heart jumped at the exposure.

"Guys, stop!" Parvati called. "You're going to break your necks."

"Come on, Parvati," Leaf said, balancing at the edge of the cliff. "Why are you worried? I've got a head for heights. Besides, don't you believe in reincarnation? If I die, it'll just be for a moment."

"Thing is, smartass, that I happen to like you in this moment."

"I hear the love. Loving me means loving the part of me taking these chances, too."

"Can I skip loving that part?" Parvati said.

"Not an option. Why are you afraid of taking risks?" Leaf said, stepping back from the edge.

"I prefer not taking stupid risks," she said.

But Will knew Parvati had a fear of heights. She disliked showing any weakness and was always ready to parry Leaf's or anyone's jabs.

"I prefer not listening to worries," Leaf retorted as he continued to walk along the precipice toward Yeshe's meditation cave.

Ten minutes later, they reached a stone wall and arched doorway on an east-facing ledge, the entrance to a natural grotto. To Will, the cave was a place of peace, and his heart softened upon seeing it. "Hello?" he called. "Grandmother?"

"Grandson, come in, come in," a sweet, elderly voice with a melodic Tibetan accent called from the cave.

Will opened the wooden door. Inside, Yeshe sat cross-legged, her face illuminated by several oil lamps, small clay bowls filled with oil, their twisted wicks rising to orange flames. Will's gaze met hers. Her eyes radiated love and a brilliant intensity that impacted him such that his mind cleared and calmed. Everyone bowed their heads out of respect.

"We brought your food." Will removed his pack. "But we don't want to interrupt your retreat."

"You're not interrupting me." Yeshe laughed and motioned for them to sit. "Sometimes I sit here. Sometimes I listen to the wind and birds. Sometimes I dance. Sometimes I eat. Now I'm with you.

Please sit. Stay for a while." She was dressed in a white gown and wore a necklace of turquoise, coral, and dzi stones. Simple and dignified. Her vibrant face was wrinkled, her cheeks red. Everyone tucked themselves in the cave around her and the altar. Parvati brought a flower garland offering, removing it from one of the sacks. Yeshe blessed the garland and placed it around Parvati's neck. The oil lamps accentuated the glistening sweat on Parvati's face and reflected on her gold necklace, earrings, and nose ring. "I can see your compassion has deepened," Yeshe said to her. She looked at Will and smiled. "I'm happy to see you. Baba told me you chose to come home. I feel touched that you came to visit."

The way his grandmother looked at him, Will felt transparent. It was as if she understood his thoughts and fears. "Come closer."

He relaxed into her gaze, and his emotions welled up. "I'll be okay," he said.

"It's fine if you're not. It's hard to lose your father. I miss him, too."

Will wanted to say more, but she touched the scar between his eyes and said, "For you, your path is your scars."

"Yes, ma'am." Will wasn't quite sure he understood, but he soaked up the importance of her words and felt humbled.

"There's no need to be hard on yourself, like I know you can be. Be compassionate toward yourself and your scars. Love yourself. Know that within you is a deep source of goodness that can support you."

She greeted Tara and Leaf with equal compassion, love, and insight. "Come outside with me."

For a while, they gazed down on Earle Cove in silence. Yeshe's long silver hair moved with the evening breeze. Tingles climbed Will's spine as he turned to look at her.

At last, she spoke. "I can never say it enough. I'm grateful to live in this valley, where the land is pure and sacred. How did it get that way? You could say the people offered purity and sacredness to the land, and the land reciprocated. If you mistreat the land, the land mistreats you. If you lash out in anger, the anger harms you. If you show love and kindness, love will blossom. Intention dances with all that exists. You can begin dancing anytime you like." She stood in silence for a moment. "Or you can look directly at the intention. Is it in the land around us? Is it in our minds? Can you find it? Yet somehow intention is important, isn't it?"

* * *

"Mathis. Happy to see you," Baba said, closing a solar dehydrator full of medicinal plants.

The portly probation officer strutted into the shade of the open-air kitchen's metal roof. Behind it was the village barn, Firefly Cove's symbol of the blending of agriculture and technology, with its solar-shingle roof, farm equipment with engines converted to run on ethanol, two five-hundred-gallon ethanol storage tanks, and a five-hundred-gallon still to produce the biofuel from sorghum juice. Adjacent to that was a solar farm, bringing the total solar production of the village to over a hundred kilowatts per year. Combined with hydroelectric power from Straight Branch, off-grid renewable power served all the homes and diverse businesses of the Cove. Next to the kitchen, a recharging station charged a fleet of carbon-fiber electric vehicles, including four Tesla pickup trucks.

"Howdy, Bubba," Mathis said.

Most locals pronounced Baba as "Bubba." They'd done so for four decades, since he'd moved to what some called the back of beyond and introduced himself to a neighbor. Word quickly spread through these backwoods that an outsider named Bubba had moved in with his foreign wife, beginning years of misunderstanding. But he never corrected them.

"How's the family?" Baba asked, removing his straw hat.

They bantered about the officer's wife and kids for a while.

"Can I see Will?" Mathis adjusted his hat and pants, tugging at his belt.

"He's not around."

"We need to reset his Aurora. We can't track him, and we need to be able to."

"I understand you have your orders."

"Lord knows I've got orders. Folks want him tracked. They're clear about that. It's part of the conditions of his release. You wouldn't want me to lose my job, would you?"

"Of course not. But I don't think they had the right to force Will to get a chip in his head."

"Well, I don't know about that, Bubba. It ain't so straightforward these days with the chip and all."

"Keeps you honest, right?"

"That's why I'm required to have it."

"I'm not sure if you were more honest before or after getting one." Baba winked. "I'm going home now."

"Consider this a warning," Mathis said.

* * *

After a dinner of Tara's vegetarian fare and Leaf's wild greens and brook trout, Leaf flirted with Tara while they built a fire at the mouth of a second cave on the east side of Eagle Mountain, less than a mile south of the first cave and closer to the village. Legends mentioned that this cave had been used for thousands of years by Native Americans, by outlaws, and by draft dodgers and guerillas during the Civil War. Several species of bats including the rare tricolored bat used the cave as their winter hibernacula. In the back were hidden, mostly unexplored passageways leading deep inside the mountain.

On a ledge above the cave, Will and Parvati smoked Leaf's ceremonial bluestone pipe. Will regretted any disconnection from Parvati, set an intention to reconnect, and exhaled a cloud of smoke as a prayer. With the exhalation, his spine tingled and his body lightened, and he passed the pipe to Parvati with a smile.

Leaf opened a bottle of juneberry mead to share and warmed up his Lee Oskar harmonica. Hearing the folksy sounds of his harp, Will and Parvati descended to look for their instruments. They entered the cave, headlamps searching along the edge. Will's lamp illuminated a metal tub—part of his washtub bass. "Still here after all these years," he said, attaching the string to the staff. As he familiarized himself with the notes, Parvati removed an old fiddle from a metal box.

"Don't you want to stay in Firefly Cove?" she asked.

"I don't know," Will replied, playing a riff.

"Well, I'd like you to stay. I'll be working at Firefly Integrated Medicine again."

"Dr. Adams is great," Will said. "I imagine she's a good teacher. But what would I do here?"

"Up to you. You're smart. You'll figure it out," Parvati said, tuning her fiddle.

The cave walls created reverb, adding depth to their improvised song. Tara danced around the fire, singing and tapping a hand drum, Parvati fiddled, Leaf played his harmonica, and Will ecstatically plucked the bass notes. A contagion of energy rushed through him, a combination of friends reunited, mead, and music.

As the fire faded to glowing coals, Will opened his senses to the world: the thrumming insects, his friends' nocturnal breathing, the stars, the fresh air on his cheeks. Today, his intentions had shifted. The magic wand of laughter and play had opened his heart.

Firefly Cove is where I want to be.

Will looked at Tara sleeping near him. Could he find a relationship without the killing frost of expectations? Could he find a relationship that nurtured, that valued and accepted and allowed for change and growth?

* * *

As soon as they returned to Firefly Cove, Will visited the village's high-tech computer and electronics workshop, known as the Hive, to see if he could learn anything about his Scalpel friends in Asheville. The workshop contained a variety of computers, Memory Cubes, a server, a drone, gadgets, a hologram tablet, recording devices, a 3D printer, wires, fiber-optic cables, and electronic parts for many projects in the village and around the region. Sunny windows faced the village green. In a side workroom, Leaf was configuring an artificial intelligence battery to optimize power storage and use in the village, a project that would likely take him an entire week. Another villager was using the 3D printer to construct a micro hydroelectric turbine for a project in Black Mountain. Meanwhile, Dr. Kumar stared at a computer screen, likely looking for ways to hack into Cirrus's network in between bookkeeping for the villagers' businesses. He looked up only briefly to greet Will.

At a desk, Will connected a communal tablet to the relay network, using the village's anonymous and secure server. Finally free from Aja and his Aurora, Will could stop suppressing his thoughts of his Scalpel friends and could openly do what he wanted. But that sense of freedom didn't impede the churning in his guts as he accessed the Scalpels' anonymity network. The first thought in his mind was whether it had been infiltrated by Cirrus or the police. He thought it had, which meant he might never learn the truth. For all he knew, any messages could be traps designed to lure Scalpels or misinformation designed to confuse.

Searching through posts, he realized he was right. He couldn't tell what from what. The site had become virtually useless. Read between the lines. Use your intuition. He read a thread about assassins. Posts from all over the world mentioned assassinations of Scalpels. Finally, some reliable information—maybe. Using a scrap sheet of paper, he began to tally deaths or disappearances. After two hours of reading, he'd counted almost a thousand Scalpel deaths, disappearances, or arrests as he scrolled back in time. A virtual crackdown, it seemed. He didn't know any of them, as most remained anonymous and worked alone in other cities. Were other arrested Scalpels forced to get a chip, too? How many remained alive and without a chip? Likely not many. Asheville was the hub of Western North Carolina and had six Scalpels before Josh and Maya were killed. Now, since Will was gone, that left only three Asheville Scalpels.

The next posts, however—two in a row—listed two Asheville Scalpels, Lola and Javier. Both were dead. These were posted by Honeycreeper—the username of Jenna, Asheville's last Scalpel. He pictured his friend, and for a moment his heart warmed. But he wondered if she was still alive. At last, he reached posts citing his own arrest and disappearance, Josh's death, and Maya's disappearance, all posted by Honeycreeper. How he wanted to let her know he was alive! Should he send her a message?

Of course.

"Honeycreeper, sweet mama, tell me the good word. Much love, Mirrorball."

She'd know all she needed to know with that post—that he was alive, and that he wanted to know if she was, too. He hit enter, and the message posted. He noticed, however, that Honeycreeper had posted for a couple weeks after writing about Will's disappearance but then posted no more.

For another hour, he continued to read the messages, which became less frequent, all the way to the last. In all the posts, no one had any evidence of an assassin.

But I do.

Will returned home to fetch some of Grace's colored pencils and returned to the Hive to sketch the assassin—a mugshot. When he was a child, Grace had taught him the arts, especially drawing people, her specialty. He took a picture of the mugshot with the tablet and uploaded it to the site, along with height, build, and any other details he could remember. Hopefully, that could help someone.

He deleted the image from the tablet and looked at the mugshot he'd drawn, one assassin out of many throughout the world. Will wondered how Scalpels could survive the onslaught. Walking outside to the village green, he lit a match and burned the image, watching the man's face become engulfed in flames.

* * *

Across the green from the Hive, Leaf and Will joined Tara and Parvati at a circular outdoor table of the Luna Café. Attached to the café was the looming Orange House co-housing, which glowed in the late-afternoon sun. In the farmland behind it, indigo buntings, field sparrows, and Eastern meadowlarks called their mates. Barn swallows and chimney swifts soared overhead, swooping for insect meals. Though the village was remote, several tourists walked through the village green, and other tables were full of backpacker types, as Firefly Cove was considered a hidden gem in a couple of U.S. travel guides.

They'd borrowed the holographic tablet from the Hive and a recording of the Global Villages' president from Baba. Tara pressed play on the holographic tablet, and the president's image appeared.

"I want to start by sharing my sadness," the president said. After four days, she'd emerged from her retreat. "I had hope that our efforts would be enough. We tried and accomplished so much at all levels: our own spiritual growth, helping our communities, and working with governments to change policies. We thought we could change enough to avert this emerging crisis. Maybe I was too naïve.

"I understand now that our situation was inevitable. Roots of events spanning the history of humans led us to today. Our actions led us to today. Our modern society evolved, but because of greed, corruption, and ignorance, our evolution didn't keep pace with the problems we created. So, here we are. I want to acknowledge our efforts and then let them go. We have new challenges now.

"During my retreat, I imagined the refugees to be like me, equal in essence. I imagined them coming with a great need, enough of a need for them to leave their homes and come to us. Then I imagined us. As communities, both rural villages and urban neighborhoods, we live good, simple, and prosperous lives. We grow more than enough food to feed ourselves, with surplus to sell or donate. We care for one another. All of us are fortunate. I feel grateful to be part of the Global Villages. I don't take my responsibility lightly. I am humbled to be of service and to provide my recommendations today.

"I see two paths. We can close ourselves off from the world. We can build gates and use force to keep others away. With this path, we will acknowledge that, through our efforts, our resolve to create abundant, full lives, we have a right to protect that abundance, so that our families can survive. We will do what we can to help others, but first and foremost, we will ensure that we will survive. This approach will appeal to some. But it is not my recommendation. Instead, I recommend the more challenging path, inspired by a dream during my retreat: A young woman shared her last meal with a dying man, even though she knew that she would go hungry. Though hungry, she slept with a smile on her face. In the end, I believe compassion, kindness, and love are the threads that bind life through time and place, despite any belief that survival is paramount. Taking this second path, we will accept refugees and care for them, even if it means sharing precious food or building them homes. I recommend that our doors remain open to all.

"Even more challenging will be those who come violently. How do we address violence? When lives are at stake, threats near, we cannot waver. We will need to defend our families and fellow villagers. But neither can we sit back and allow others to lose themselves to anger and hate. They need help, too. What we face now may be the greatest challenge humanity has ever confronted. We need to prepare physically. We need to prepare spiritually. If we are attacked, we can try peaceful solutions, but we must also be prepared to die, and be prepared to kill as a last resort. That is my recommendation. It's a starting point in our collective journey. Now, it's your choice. What do you want to do? What does your village want to do? Peace be with you all."

Tara turned off the holographic tablet, and the president dissolved into space.

"Do we even have a problem?" Leaf lit a hand-rolled cigarette. "We haven't had a single refugee come here, so how can we even talk about what to do about it?"

"But you're talking about it, so it must have some merit," Tara said. "You should quit smoking. It's not good for you."

"It's natural tobacco. Most of the bad shit is in the additives."

"Still, I'd rather you didn't."

"Everyone's always telling me what not to do, as if they need to limit me in order to care for me."

Parvati laughed. "Maybe because you do dumb things."

"To you," Leaf said, taking a puff. "Dumb to you."

"I stand corrected."

"I like that she's being proactive," Will said, bringing the conversation back to the president's message. "It makes no sense to be reactive. When it's October, do we just sit around and eat all our food? No. We store food for the winter. Same deal here."

"So, what are you going to do?" Leaf asked.

"No clue. How about you?" Will said.

"Me neither, but I'll be brushing up on my marksmanship and self-defense skills. If they come, I'll be ready."

Will leaned back on his chair. "Ready to do what?"

"Whatever it takes to defend the village."

"What about the using-force-as-a-last-resort part?" Will said.

"Totally agree. I don't want to kill anyone," Leaf said. "I'll shoot their kneecaps off instead."

Will shook his head. "Come on."

"You peace monger."

"You know how to get me riled up, that's all. It's on me. I own that."

"Glad you own it, 'cause I don't want your pacifist baggage." Leaf blew a puff of smoke into the wind. "How about you, Parvati?"

"I like what she said about helping others. But I'm not sure if anything we do will help at this point. The world is too far gone."

"Are any of you nervous?" Tara said. "It's hard to admit, but I am. Part of me realizes that this is an opportunity, and there's nothing to be afraid of. Still, I'm afraid."

"Can't get rid of fear," Leaf said. "It's all about your relationship to it. You might be fearful, but to me you look confident. You'll be fine."

"So now you're the optimist," Will said. "I imagine confronting our fears will be our greatest challenge. At least it will be for me. This is our generation's challenge, to survive these fucked-up times."

ELEVEN

JADE

MARICOPA COUNTY, ARIZONA

JOYRIDING ON JADE'S NIGHT OFF FROM WORK, they turned onto a less-traveled U.S. highway heading through the desert toward the mountains. Martin's headlight was off. The full moon followed its low Capricornian arc through the sky, illuminating their path and casting long shadows on the mountains and desert plants. Suddenly, a spotlight switched on in front of them, jolting Jade and drowning the moonlight.

"Don't stop," Jade said, too late.

Five armed men approached, backlit with long shadows. Martin braked, pushing Jade's body into his back.

"Turn your bike off," a tall man wearing camouflage demanded. "Step down from the motorcycle. Remove your helmets."

Jade's heart pounded as she concealed her skullcap within the helmet while unfurling her blond hair as a distraction. The militiamen gawked.

"Aurora codes?" the tall man asked.

"Don't have one," Martin said, facing the man squarely on the pavement.

Jade gave the man hers. Without the skullcap, her Aurora was activated. She swiped away the ads and began recording the scene. She sent an urgent InterVoice message to all her friends, embedding the video so they could see and hear in real time.

The tall man squinted through his glasses, looking down at Martin. Jade noticed a militia insignia on his camo. She couldn't tell if the men belonged to one of the groups targeting Hispanics or if their insignias were fake. Just yesterday, she had watched a news report of several Hispanic Americans being massacred in remote parts of Arizona. A militia group was suspected, but no evidence was reported.

The man scrutinized Martin as if trying to understand why a citizen wouldn't have an Aurora. Militiamen didn't have Auroras because they saw it as infringing on their right to privacy, but they didn't mind extracting information from other people's Auroras.

Despite the early-morning hour, InterVoice responses from Jade's friends poured into her mind. She heard them, one by one, in the voices of the senders.

Oh, my God, girl, get the fuck out of there.

What the fuck?

I'm calling 911.

"Memory Cube?" the head militiaman said.

Martin reached into his pocket, extracting his Cube.

"Activate it," the man commanded.

Martin squeezed it with his fingers to activate it and handed it to the man, who sent Martin's driver's license and other information to a computer built into his glasses. He squeezed it again to activate a hologram of Martin.

"Martin Gonzalez. You Mexican?"

"No, American."

"But your name is Gonzalez. You're Mexican."

Jade's heart sank. This isn't really happening, is it? She clenched her teeth to stop from blurting out that Martin's father was Latino and his mother was fair skinned, with English blood. Would that even help? No. Not with these racist fuckers.

Tell them. It can't hurt, a friend responded.

Don't waste your breath, another responded.

I told you Martin was nothing but trouble.

The messages piled up. Jade's face flushed. Shit. She'd forgotten she was sending her thoughts to all her friends. She turned off streaming and chastised herself for her carelessness.

"What are you doing with *him*?" the head militiaman asked, startling Jade.

"He's her pimp," another militiaman joked. The others laughed.

"He's my boyfriend, asshole."

"Enough, Frank. Leave her alone," the head militiaman said.

You tell him, girl, a friend messaged.

Be careful, dear, messaged another.

The head militiaman backed away from them to examine Martin's Memory Cube data, then turned to his subordinates. "Search him."

A bearded man marched to Martin and patted him down, taking a gun from under Martin's jacket and pointing it at his face. "Always conceal a weapon when you're riding around?" the bearded man asked. Martin was silent. "I'm speakin' to you, boy."

"No, sir," he lied.

"That's better." The bearded man lowered the gun, placing it in his pants. Another militiaman handed him a shotgun, and he pointed it immediately at Martin's head.

"Search her, too," the head militiaman said.

Several men rose to the occasion. As one of them patted down her thin, tight jeans, Jade closed her eyes, not wanting her friends to see the livestream. Her body froze as his hands slid up her thighs. InterVoice messages of concern and care filled her mind, and she focused on them, suppressing her bodily sensations. He unzipped her jacket and reached his hands inside. As they approached her breasts, she tensed, wanting to knee him in the groin.

"She's clean," he eventually said. She exhaled, opening her eyes.

The head militiaman stared into her eyes.

Shit, he knows.

"Ma'am, step over here." He pointed toward his vehicle. "Cap the girl."

A militiaman placed a polymer skullcap on Jade, sealing off her Aurora from the external world and scrambling any brain-chip signals. The InterVoice messaging app and livestream faded from her visual field. Her hands trembled, and she hid them behind her back. The men stared at her, distracted.

Martin kicked the shotgun from the bearded man. It skidded across the asphalt. He twisted for his gun, pulling its trigger while it was still in the bearded man's pants. Yanking out the gun, he turned and shot one man in the chest and a second in the gut. The head militiaman shot at Martin, shattering his ear into pieces, leaving attached fragments of cartilage and bloody skin. Martin parried with a bullet into his forehead. From behind the militiaman, Jade saw the bullet exit, along with a splash of brains and blood. The body crumpled, gathering speed until the head bounced on the pavement. Next to Martin, the bearded man screamed in pain, his pants soaked in blood.

The man who'd capped Jade pulled a knife, pressing it into her throat. "Put the knife down or I'll kill her," he said.

Martin aimed at the man's right eye.

Do it, Jade thought. I trust your aim.

"Don't kill her," Martin said. "Just put the knife down, or you'll end up like the others."

The man hesitated, and Martin pulled the trigger. Bullseye.

* * *

By one in the morning, Jade and Martin arrived at a sprawling adobe-style apartment complex. Jade didn't know what to expect except that they were meeting two of his friends, who were supposed to help them. Sounds sketchy, she thought, but she trusted Martin.

"Don Juan," Martin said after knocking on the door.

Jade kept her polymer skullcap on so her Aurora wouldn't signal their location. What's with the secret password? she thought.

Once inside, Martin introduced her to Felix and Quinn, and Felix kissed her Cuban-style on the right cheek. Sitting on a love seat, Quinn nodded at her, then diverted his eyes to the television wall. Jerk, she thought.

"My dear, I've heard so much about you," Felix said. He frowned and pointed toward the screen, which was showing a news report about the killing of three militiamen and the wounding of two others.

"The killer is still at large. Police are on a manhunt for Martin Gonzalez, a five-nine Hispanic male of medium build. He's considered a terrorist threat." FOX 10 showed leaked livestream video from Jade's InterVoice app, cropped to show Martin but not the militiamen.

"I left my Cube." Martin's nostrils flared in anger. The remains of his wounded ear were crusted with dried blood, and his shirt and jacket were splotched with red.

Jade had never seen him scared before. Now, he looked like a dog with its tail between its legs. Everything seemed dangerous, but not in the fun way she liked. Fear. Guilt. For what? She looked around the room at guns and military supplies. My God, what have I gotten myself into?

Felix cursed in Spanish and threw his cowboy hat at Martin. "You know this fucks everything up now."

"We'd be dead if Martin hadn't killed them," Jade stated.

Felix turned to her, surprised. "They showed your video, *gringa*." Considering they'd just met, the affectionate tone of his voice as he said *gringa* surprised her. In the background, the reporter described the scene of the murders.

"We're innocent!" Jade yelled at the screen. "It was self-defense."

Felix rubbed the scar underlining his left eye. "Martin, why'd you have to get the *chica* involved?"

The reporter continued. "Police say Gonzalez is a suspect in over thirty murders, including all fifteen of the Dirty Water serial murders. Sources tell us he's connected with Mexican terrorist cells in Arizona. If this proves correct, Mexican terrorists are undermining our water supply to destabilize our state...."

Jade gasped.

"Get it now, *chica*? This bullshit script was already written. We're the scapegoats," Felix said. "Fuck. I should've been smarter than this."

Jade listened to the reporter talking about her boyfriend's alleged crimes. Martin turned away from her as though ashamed. Her heart tightened. Conflicting thoughts and feelings left her unable to act.

"This'll be old news tomorrow," Quinn said, cleaning his fingernails with a knife.

"No way. Not to the militia. Not to the police," Felix fumed, lighting a Habanos cigar and glaring at Quinn. "Cut that shit out. You're not in the bathroom." Felix stopped talking until Quinn put down his knife. The scar under his left eye twitched.

"Sorry, bossman."

"Not sorry enough." Felix put his cowboy hat back on—the scar twitched again—and turned off the television wall.

"What now?" Quinn asked into the awkward silence, scratching his short red beard. His T-shirt exposed his muscular, tattoo-covered arms.

"We need to get out of here now. Pack my car." Felix puffed his cigar and blew the smoke at Martin.

Martin and Quinn moved several crates of weapons into the trunk of Felix's Mustang while Jade watched and Felix packed his gear and clothes. Martin borrowed the frequency jammer, throwing it in a knapsack along with bullets, an extra gun, and other gear. The three men put on radio headsets, tuning them to the same encrypted frequency.

"We'll meet soon. I'll radio you. For now, just get out of here." Felix closed the car door.

Martin rode away on his motorcycle with Jade. The night air was calming, and she was relieved to be moving. "Take me home," she said. "I'm done with you. Why didn't you tell me?"

They halted at a stoplight. The streets were eerily quiet. No other vehicles. A straight boulevard. Synchronized red traffic signals. The glow. Silhouettes of palm trees.

"I'm sorry. I wanted to tell you. I—"

"Enough excuses. I'm fucking pissed."

"Don't believe the news. I'm not a terrorist or a psychopath."

"Why do it, then?"

"It's a job."

"That's twisted. You lied."

"You've seen my tats. You know I'm no angel."

"You lied to me."

"I didn't. I just didn't tell you exactly..."

She contemplated for a moment. "I'm going to the cops. I'm innocent." But she knew it wouldn't be that easy, whatever she did.

"You don't want to be with me, fine. Go. Try to live normally, if you can call your life normal. I doubt you'll live long. The cops are just as crooked as the militia. You can't trust either of 'em, and it's easy to disappear a stripper."

The light turned green, and Martin accelerated toward her apartment. She held on to his muscular midsection. Who can I trust?

No one, was the reply to her thought.

Trust your intuition, at least.

They might not be right either, her thoughts retorted.

A familiar memory of a high school party played in her mind. She knew all the details: The whiskey and coke. Her best friend's parents away. One in the morning. On the parents' bed with the one she wanted to forget but couldn't.

No. I did have an intuition then. I never should have been alone with him. I just couldn't leave. Her face flushed with shame and regret. What did I do wrong? What am I doing wrong? How do I get stuck like this? Martin's not like that, is he?

The beauty of her apartment complex, an earthy stucco building surrounded by well-maintained, pebbled xeriscape with cacti and palm trees, usually was welcoming. Not this time. Fear permeated everything.

"I'm coming in with you," Martin said. "It's not safe."

"I don't care. Just go."

"I insist. I got you in this mess. I couldn't bear to see anything happen to you."

Seriously? After what just happened? she thought. "Whatever."

"Can I just make sure your apartment's safe? Then I'll go."

Jade nodded, removing her helmet and skullcap.

Gun drawn, Martin moved toward the apartment building. *Unlock*, she thought. The Aurora Digital Key app unlocked the front door. Her heart fluttered as she opened the door for Martin and followed him inside the main hallway, lit with sconces. The door closed behind them, startling Jade and sending jolts of fear through her body. If someone was waiting for them, they would have heard the door. Martin flashed a warning with his eyes. I'll be quieter, she thought in response. But each step on the tile floor jarred her nervous system, as its reverb seemed to travel up the stairs toward her apartment.

She stared at her apartment door. Of course she had to unlock it, but thinking the word was the last thing she wanted to do.

Unlock.

Her second-floor apartment door unlatched with a soft whir. She reached out to open it, her awareness acute to the point where she could feel each movement as the metal lever turned and the door opened into the darkness of her apartment. Martin motioned for Jade to stay outside and disappeared into the blackness. Jade stayed in the hallway, waiting. Even if no one's in there now, I won't be able to sleep. She pictured a militiaman coming to kill her and covered her mouth, wondering if she'd ever know peace again. What's taking him so long? Has something happened? She peered in but couldn't see him.

"Martin," she whispered into the apartment. Not smart. What if he's dead?

A silhouette moved toward her, and she retreated into the hallway.

"Jade, it's me," Martin said, following her.

"Sorry. My nerves are shot tonight."

Martin looked through the hallway window toward the street. "What?"

"They're here," he said.

A white van was parked across the street. Armed men exited it. One man slashed Martin's rear tire while the rest headed toward the front door of the building.

"Your kitchen window. Let's go," he whispered. "Quickly."

They climbed out, tumbled into the backyard, ran through the gravel, and climbed over a stone wall. Rail gun bullets from her kitchen penetrated the wall, and they dropped prone. Bedroom lights in other apartments turned on, lighting the darkness.

"Run. I'll cover you," Martin said, firing several rounds toward the kitchen window. Framed by the window, a man moaned and collapsed.

At the next street, Martin caught up to Jade. He broke a window of a new Mercedes and disabled the alarm. "Get in." Martin stuck his switchblade under the shark-fin antenna, turned the blade to pop it loose, and tore the antenna from the roof of the car so their location couldn't be tracked. After a little tinkering, he started the car, placing it in manual drive—with location services disabled, self-driving functionality was disabled, too. As he accelerated out of the neighborhood, Martin spoke through his headset. "Quinn. Felix. Anyone out there? Felix. Quinn. Come in. You there?" No reply. After several attempts, he switched channels to police radio chatter. "Cops are coming."

"What should we do?" Jade said.

Her InterVoice app turned on, startling Jade. This is the police. I'll cut to the chase. I know you're in trouble. Martin Gonzalez is dangerous. Don't trust him. I'm here to help, Jade. Do as I say, and we can get you out of this.

Okay, she responded halfheartedly.

You need to convince Martin to stop the car and surrender, the voice said. Can you do that?

"They want you to surrender," Jade said.

"What? Who?"

"The police. On my Aurora."

"Shit. Your skullcap," Martin said.

"I put it in your backpack."

"It's at my motorcycle. You got to remove your chip."

"What? How?"

"Use my knife." He pulled a switchblade from his shoulder harness and handed it to her.

"No way."

"What do you mean, no way?" Martin yelled, looking in his rearview mirror.

"I can't." She placed the knife into a cup holder. "They're telling me not to. They're coming to get us."

"Want me to pull over and drop you off?"

Jade looked at him, considering her options.

"You're innocent, after all," he said. "It's probably the best thing for you to do."

"I don't know what to do anymore."

"Go. I love you. I want you to stay, but I fucked up," Martin said. "I'm no good for you."

The police voice echoed in her head, and she was nauseous. Lights outside the car blurred. Was the Aurora altering her brain? Snippets from the night flowed through her mindstream: The militiaman searching her body. Felix's glare. The white van. Martin saying, "I love you." For the first time. Not the best timing. But she loved him, too, she knew. How strange was that? But she'd always told herself that love trumped everything. She opened the switchblade. "Let's do this."

Martin grinned and accelerated through a red light.

Feeling for a bump, Jade searched for the Aurora under her scalp. "Can we stop?"

"No time."

Do not, I repeat, do not remove your Aurora, the officer's voice rumbled in the background.

"I can't believe I'm doing this." She cringed but slid the knife's tip into her scalp next to the Aurora. The feeling sickened her, and she felt dizzy, uncoordinated. Blood trickled through her hair and down her neck.

"Finish it," Martin said. They could hear sirens now.

"It's too much! The police are yelling at me." Her hands trembled, and the knife slid from her fingers onto the floor.

Don't do it, Jade, the officer said. She heard the caring tone in his voice and believed he *did* care for her in that moment, and that he could help. *Think of your life,* the voice said. *Surrender and you won't be charged. There's still time.*

"Hold the wheel," Martin said, engaging the manual cruise control.

"You're crazy," she said, reaching over to grab the steering wheel with one hand.

"Just keep driving straight." Martin picked up the knife and wiped the blade clean with his shirt.

"Just hurry the fuck up." That Martin wouldn't brake was terrifying. She swerved around a blurry car while Martin searched for the bump on her scalp. Does he even know what he's doing?

Martin pinched her scalp and began to cut an incision. Jade clenched her teeth, focusing on the road. "The light's turning red!" she yelled. Martin backed off with the blade as the Mercedes careened through a bumpy intersection. A sedan swerved out of the way.

I hope they're not hurt. To check, she adjusted the rearview mirror. The sedan had struck a street sign, with minor body damage. Police lights flashed in the distance, and she guessed cruisers were coming from other directions to cut them off. The white van was likely close behind, too.

Jade's concentration increased to the point where the police speaking to her on the Aurora, Martin cutting her scalp with a knife, and her dizziness faded into the background. In that state, her vision became acute, colors vivid. She felt strangely content as she let go.

At last, Martin's awkward cutting ended. He pushed on the chip, and it emerged like a pustule from her scalp and tumbled between her legs. She grabbed the slender microchip encased in silica and threw it out the window. Martin grabbed the wheel and veered right, while Jade stared ahead at the low-hanging moon, her head dripping blood.

* * *

At dawn, the full moon disappeared behind the mountains. At a cul-de-sac in an abandoned, ruined housing project, Martin and Jade leaned against the stolen Mercedes. Black soot charred the cement-block remains around the empty sockets of windows and doorways. Open doors vomited rubble and junk onto stoops. Martin tapped his fingers on the windshield, drawing Jade's attention. Her mind was focused despite the fatigue of her body, and the taps seemed the only sound—clear and sharp—until Felix approached in his Mustang.

"She took her chip out," Martin said through his headset.

"What?" asked Jade.

"Your skullcap. He wanted to know why you weren't wearing one."

She touched her scalp—still freshly bleeding. The consequences of last night were also so fresh that she hadn't thought much about the sea change in her life. Compared to most other Aurora users, however, she hardly showed any withdrawal symptoms, as she'd spent much of her time in the strip club, where Auroras were jammed, or with Martin, often wearing a skullcap. Mostly, she felt disquiet, and the disconnection from the Aurora augmented that. She could no longer send InterVoice messages to her women friends, and here she was with three men—one she loved, one she knew was trouble, and one she saw as a jerk.

She showed the fresh blood on her fingers to Martin, and he said, "Krazy Glue will shut it. Felix keeps some in his car's first-aid kit."

"How about stitches? Krazy Glue in my hair would be a mess."

"He's got a suture kit, too."

Seeing Felix again, she wasn't in the least intimidated. She knew men similar to him at the club: selfish, crude, lacking respect, and confused. But she tried to see their good qualities and soft spots, too. In Felix, she saw someone trying hard to stay in control, to be the boss, but he wasn't in control now.

Quinn pulled up on his sporty motorcycle. Jade had an intuition there'd be friction between her and Quinn, picturing him as a strike-anywhere match ready to burn anyone. He's pissed, she thought. Something bad happened.

Felix's red eyes were surrounded by blackened sockets. "Militia trashed my place," he said. "But I'm alive." He blew a cloud of smoke toward Martin. "Lucky me. Bullets are coming at our asses. Especially yours. We got two choices. First choice is fight. Anyone game?"

No one spoke.

"Didn't think so." He looked at Martin. "You're not as stupid as I thought, *amigo*. The other choice is to get as far away from this cesspool as possible. Quinn, you're a *gringo*, so you're probably safe staying here."

"Hell no. Motherfuckers trashed my apartment, too." Quinn glared at Martin.

"Damn, man," Martin said, shaking his head.

Jade felt sorry for Martin, as he was taking the brunt of the blame. The militia were the instigators, not him. She guessed her and Martin's apartments were destroyed, too. She wanted to speak but decided silence was better.

"That's not all, man. I probably killed one of 'em. Shot him in the chest." Quinn pounded his fists together.

Felix approached Jade, staring. Jade stared back. Holding a gaze with Felix was like drinking from a fire hydrant. She wanted to turn away but persisted until his eyes diverted to her neck, streaked with coagulating blood. He touched it. "What happened to you?"

"Don't worry about it," she said. "I'll be fine."

"So, what about you? You in?" Felix asked her.

"The militia don't forgive," Quinn interjected. "They're sharks, and they're going to keep coming 'til they get you. They know where you work. They know where you live."

Jade grew more irritated with every utterance. He had a point, though. Arizona wasn't safe anymore. But she knew that. "I'm in."

With her decision, she felt alive. This is crazy, crazy, crazy, she sang in her head. I'll miss all my friends. The girls. And my parents. No, I won't miss them. Her wild side was a trigger for their shame, and they'd disowned her. They didn't understand her. And that freed her to greater wildness. But even as she thought she wouldn't miss them, her heart tightened, thinking of them. More than anything, she wanted her parents to understand her.

The four decided to head east on I-40. They opened the crates in the Mustang's trunk, revealing communications equipment, weapons, ammunition, and survival gear. Martin found the suture kit and stitched Jade's wound while Quinn and Felix organized their gear to prepare for the journey. Quinn said farewell to his prized motorcycle in the ruins. Felix torched the Mercedes, and black smoke signaled their departure.

TWELVE
TARA

———

FIREFLY COVE

WILL SPRANG AWAKE IN THE MIDST OF ANOTHER NIGHTMARE rehashing Aja's tortures. Agitated, he left his house for a walk. He found walking out in nature calmed his nerves, especially at night. A dog howled at the full moon. Katydids and crickets strummed their legs. White fireflies sparkled in the edges of the forest, while yellow ones rose from the fields as if spirits. The cliffs of Eagle Mountain glowed gray in the moonlight. Will visited the barn animals, whispering their names in the dark. Tikka, the barn cat, walked along a windowsill, jumped down at Cajun's horse stall, and rubbed against Will's legs. He picked her up and scratched the white spot on her forehead until she scrambled from his arms and, in a flurry, disappeared around the corner. Will followed her outside.

Distant headlights gleamed through the trees. Rarely did vehicles come to Firefly Cove at this hour. Who could it be? The car approached, entering the field along the main road into the Cove. The police? He crept into the shadows of a hedgerow to hide. The car stopped at the barn parking lot.

With effort, a large man and woman exited the car. Their tones suggested they were weary, annoyed, relieved, and uncertain. Two children jumped out of the backseat, looking exhausted. Not the police, who'd already come twice looking for him. Harmless enough, Will thought. "Can I help you?"

The family appeared startled, but once Will extended his hand and introduced himself, they perked up in a display of friendliness.

"I'm Jack Sanders, and this is my wife, Harriet. Kids, introduce yourselves to Mr. Robin."

"Hello, Mr. Robin. My name is Ethan." Ethan rubbed his eyes.

"Pleased to meet you, Mr. Robin. I'm Carey Sanders. I just turned six and a half."

"Good to meet you. Just call me Will."

"I'm older," Ethan said. "I'm almost eight."

"But you act like you're five," Carey said.

"Do not."

"Do so."

"Kids, I'm sure Will has better things to do than listen to you arguing," Jack said in a tired deadpan. "Listen, I don't want to impose, but we're hoping we can stay here, if we could. We're from California, and our city ran out of water. It wasn't safe there anymore either. We've been looking for a place to live for weeks now and we couldn't find a hotel to stay tonight."

Refugees. Our first opportunity to help. Will imagined the violence and suffering arising from the drought in the Southwest. For a moment, he was grateful that the Southern Blue Ridge Mountains were less affected by climate change than other places. Sure, temperatures had increased, but not as much as elsewhere, and rainfall was still abundant. Will's heart warmed, wanting to care for them. "It's okay. Please, relax. So, why here? We're off the beaten path," Will said.

"You sure are. Someone in Asheville said you were welcoming folks. We thought we'd give it a shot, but until that last bend in the road, I never thought we'd find it," Jack said.

Will liked that Firefly Cove had a reputation as a welcoming community.

"My wife and kids and I are respectable folks. Harriet was a teacher. I worked in a machine shop. We work hard." Jack took out his Memory Cube. "Feel free to look at everything in here about us. You can always say no."

Will smiled. "You can stay at my home. We haven't had guests in a long time. One second." He ran to the barn and closed the door. "Okay. Follow me."

* * *

Just before dawn, the full moon now hanging low to the west, Will and Tara walked down the road. They'd been working together with the farm animals for almost a month. Each day, Tara would knock softly on his door, and they'd walk together to the barn to begin their daily routine. Despite Tara's radiant smile, tiredness hung in her eyes.

"How'd you sleep?" he asked.

"Just okay. My parents were arguing. Took a while to get to sleep." They'd been arguing since they moved to the Cove from the suburbs a decade ago, it seemed. Things had improved since their arrival, but the family dynamics persisted. "Last night was worse than usual," she continued. "I didn't even try to help them get along this time. I just sat in bed, trying not to listen." Their hands touched, and Tara folded her fingers between Will's. "So, you couldn't sleep either?"

"I woke up in the middle of the night. My mind was racing," he said.

"Want to talk about it?"

"I do, but there's too much to talk about now. I think another of my Scalpel friends is dead. I've messaged with her a couple of times, but something just doesn't seem right. The reply didn't have the right wording."

"So, you think someone's impersonating her."

"Yes. She wants me to meet with her, but it's a trap. It wasn't her, I know it. No one is left to post her disappearance. She was the last Asheville Scalpel."

"I'm sorry, Will."

"Thanks. I want to talk more, but let's get to work."

They arrived at the barn, where the animals were waiting.

"Maybe after we're done," Tara said, leaving him.

Will milked the first of seven cows by hand. With each squeeze of a teat, he focused his attention with care and compassion. He mourned when mother cows were separated from their calves so people could have dairy products.

Will saw his new livelihood as providing a loving environment for the animals while also providing food for villagers. Growing up in the Cove, he was aware of the ethical challenges surrounding food and how the villagers constantly debated food choices, honing the nuances. How could they minimize harm and maximize compassion? He thought about the aphids on the collard greens he'd picked as a child, and how complex food choices could be. He'd tried to save them by washing them off, but what would *they* eat? Seeing a few aphids floating dead in the wash water, he'd cried out of compassion. In every part of life, there was arising and ceasing, waxing and waning. Even the moon seemed to die. But to the sun, the moon was always full.

The chill of the dawn air blew through the sweet, manure-scented space, and the sky lightened to a steely blue through the open barn door.

While Will was milking the fourth cow, the sun peered over a ridge past Otter Creek. On the far side of the fields, Tara moved a flock of twenty-four sheep to another pasture. Hearing her faint calls and the bleats of the ewes and the young lambs, he felt his heart thump. Taking a break, he washed and walked to the doorway, watching Tara interact with an aggressive ram. Next to him, a sow snorted in her farrowing pen, waiting for her food scraps. Her six piglets played and squealed. "Hold on, girl. I'll get to you." He returned to milking the fourth cow.

When he finished with the morning milking, he released the cows into the pasture and bottled sixteen gallons of raw milk for the Firefly Cove Dairy Co-op. From the milk, co-op members would make butter, cheese, and yogurt and sell the surplus at Asheville farmers' markets.

As the morning progressed, Will repaired a fence. Each hit with the hammer was healing, releasing stuck emotions, and the slow, ordinary morning rhythm opened his heart and calmed his mind. Others joined the farm activities, working the quilted fields of perennial grains, sorghum, vegetables, sunflowers, rapeseed, and the three sisters—corn, beans, and squash. Toward the outskirts of the pastures, a family rotated rabbit pens and chicken tractors to different fields, ensuring that the free-range animals would get the best forage. A farmer rode on a tractor, haying a field at the edge of the pastures. Cool-hued clouds contrasted with the sunlight striking the tractor. Gusts of wind created undulating patterns of moving green in the uncut hay.

Tara finished her work and rode Cajun, her favorite draft horse, bareback. Her gift to the world, as Will saw it, was a remarkable ability to communicate with animals. She loved them unconditionally, and her compassion overflowed when her animal friends were killed for meat. Leaf waved to Tara from the solar farm, where he was inspecting the inverter, and Tara trotted the horse over to him. Maybe he's still got that crush on her, Will thought. Seems like it.

Hearing their distant laughter, Will breathed awareness into the envy that stirred his heart. As the disturbing emotion dissolved, he noticed what he saw as love free from fetters. And when she rode toward him, his heart sparked with anticipation.

"Let's go riding," Tara said.

"Sounds good," Will said. "I'll finish this later."

He placed the hammer on top of a post, climbed the fence, and jumped on the back of her draft horse. Smelling the peppermint leaf that Tara chewed, he held her waist as the horse galloped away. Tara's hips moved with the rhythm of the horse. Once Firefly Cove was out of sight, they climbed to a sunny glade in the oak woodlands, and Tara stopped Cajun with an almost imperceptible press to his withers. Will dismounted and caught her as she jumped down. Together, they rolled onto the green grass and embraced.

"I'd like to kiss you," he said.

Tara nodded and smiled, and he kissed her neck, feeling the softness of her skin. Tara leaned her head to the side, allowing Will to explore. He felt her lips on his cheek. At last, she kissed his lips, and he tasted the peppermint leaf. Will held her close.

"I missed you," Tara said. "I'm happy you came back."

"Me, too." His fingers slipped through her long brown hair. She played with his goatee. They looked at each other and laughed.

Lying on their backs, they gazed dreamily at a billowing cloud engulfing the sun. The freshness of their intimacy cast a beautiful aura—magical, even—onto the world. The trees swayed. Thunder ripped the air. Rain drummed on the leaves. Will felt the cool water from each drop as it landed, then warmed on his body.

"See how many raindrops you can catch." Tara opened her mouth.

Will stuck out his tongue.

A deluge started, drenching their clothes and hair. Will looked into Tara's eyes to share the joy, and their lips touched as rainwater dripped from their noses.

THIRTEEN
BROKEN CIGAR

As Felix drove on the Beeline Highway away from Phoenix, Jade watched the side of the road, aiming out the back window with a rail gun mounted on the door frame. Her hair blew around her like Medusa's serpents.

"Hurry up, already," Felix said. "It's too hot to keep the windows down."

"She needs to learn," Martin said.

"She's learned enough," Felix said. He was wearing sunglasses and a cowboy hat.

Quinn's red hair was unkempt and spiked. He squinted, looking back at Jade. She ignored his glare and focused on the side of the road. As they rounded a curve, another abandoned vehicle—riddled with bullet holes, looted, burned, and dented—appeared. She fired several bullets into its side. "I've had enough," she said, removing the gun from the mount, heaving it back to Martin, and rolling up the window. Felix continued to strategize with Quinn about crossing the border into New Mexico. Based on what she'd overheard so far, it wouldn't be easy. The cool air of the AC touched her nostrils.

"You're a natural," Martin said, yawning. "Siesta time for me."

"Me, too," Jade said. But I don't want to be a natural. I refuse to kill.

Jade removed her jacket, revealing a T-shirt. I stink. And so does everyone else. Body odor. Felix's cigar. Looking down, she noticed a bloodstain on her jeans, from the militiaman. She covered it with her hand, wanting the evidence to disappear.

Having no change of clothes, she yearned for the comforts of home. It was too late for that, though. She snuggled next to Martin, who put his arm around her. He loves me unconditionally, Jade thought. His heart's opening. Does he even know it? It's all hidden behind his machismo. He doesn't want to be here any more than I do. We need to get out of this gang, be alone. That'll bring out his love. We could start over. I could get my degree, and maybe he could go to school, too. But not without money. And not in Arizona.

She lost herself in planning an abstract future and watching the desert landscape pass before them while rubbing Martin's head as he slept. Quinn snored, his neck kinked at an awkward angle. Felix drove, not wanting to enable the self-driving mechanism, since they could be tracked in that mode. She faded to sleep.

Jade awakened to a burning smell. An immense plume of smoke loomed before them as they entered Sitgreaves National Forest. The road led them to the heart of a burning ponderosa pine forest. Smoke created ghostly tree silhouettes. A fire crew rested on the side of the road, covered in soot. They looked exhausted. It was June 10, and their battle with fire was only starting. But when Jade blew them kisses, they smiled.

"*Madre de Dios.* Here's the reward we're reaping." Felix had never before invoked the Virgin. It struck Jade as having some peculiar importance, especially when he said it in his native tongue. "Fuck this climate change shit."

"Felix cracks me up," Jade whispered in Martin's ear.

"How's that?"

"The cigar. It's such a cliché gangster thing."

"He's Cuban," Martin whispered back, rubbing his nose playfully into her hair.

"Oh," Jade said. "Still, he's quirky. He puts one in his mouth if he's a little nervous. Add a little more stress and he begins to chew the end. Add a lot of stress and he lights the cigar and blows smoke."

Felix looked back. "What's so funny?" he said, chewing his cigar.

"Nothing, boss," Martin said. "Wanna put on some tunes?"

* * *

At sunset, they approached the New Mexico border. A line of eastbound vehicles stretched for at least a mile, strapped with crates and packed with refugees. Moving trucks were full of affluent refugees' belongings, as those with means chose the safer path—flying. Many billionaires now lived in the safety of their well-stocked tropical island mansions or other safe havens. Looking at this scene outside her window, Jade sighed. She visualized her once-comfortable apartment and all her belongings, all the mementos of her life—gone. At least these people have something to hold on to, she thought.

Felix turned on the satellite radio and checked the news.

"As the Great American Drought continues, American refugees are being turned away at foreign airports and border crossings and are being detained without warning. Mark Gray is live at the Beijing airport, where several hundred Americans are being held. Right, Mark?"

"Right, Peter. This has been a developing story, given the increasing numbers of American refugees seeking asylum in China and elsewhere around the world. Human rights groups have denounced the Beijing government for illegally detaining these American citizens, but the Chinese government blames America for the refugee crisis. In fact, the Chinese ambassador to the United States went so far as to issue a statement today. Ambassador Liu said, 'The drought is a price that America must pay for its arrogance and failure to address climate change and its own internal needs.' American refugees are also being detained in at least twenty other countries including Canada and many European nations, where fears of instability and food shortages have prompted a ban on American citizens' travel and asylum...."

We're not wanted anywhere, Jade thought. I'm trapped in America, trapped in Arizona, trapped in this car in this damned situation. The sensation reminded her of the last days at home with her parents. By the time their car reached the brightly lit checkpoint, Jade had thought herself into a virtual panic. The colors of the sunset had faded into dusk, and stars appeared in the sky.

A makeshift outpost guarded the border. Dozens of militia and National Guard iRangers were stationed around the fortified site. Parked on the asphalt were tanks, a couple of drones, and high-speed armored cruisers, sleek and black. This is the most fucked-up thing I've seen in my life, Jade thought. Armed robots and a checkpoint at a state border? Is this America? And here I am in the most wanted car in this entire line. "How can we trust they won't just shoot us?" she said.

"Shut up," Felix said as they inched forward. "Just stay calm. We're next." He rolled down his window.

She whispered to Martin, "I mean, who's controlling them? They're armed. Doesn't someone need to approve any use of force?"

"I guess they already have a green light," Martin replied, barely audible above the clamor of the checkpoint.

We're screwed. Did he even come up with a plan? Jade wondered about Felix. No, all that strategizing was just a bunch of hot air. He had no idea what to expect. What if we don't get through? Perspiration beaded on her forehead, and she flushed. There are too many of them. We won't get through.

An iRanger dressed in camouflage greeted them, showing a fake robot smile. "Good evening, folks." The smile disappeared when the facial recognition software found a match. "Don't move. You're under ar—"

Felix pulled the trigger of a high-voltage stun gun, frying the robot's circuits. He drove slowly around a couple of trucks, hoping no one noticed the robot crumpling to the ground. But an alarm sounded. He accelerated and drove between two closing gates just as shots were fired in their direction.

"I hate robots," Martin confessed under his breath to Jade.

"Even their rail guns can't break through this baby's armor." Felix laughed.

"Welcome to New Mexico: The Land of Enchantment," a yellow sign said.

Quinn flexed his tattooed arms. "That was easy."

"Don't get all cocky on us," Jade said, looking back at four cruisers approaching in the distance.

Felix pressed a button, lowering armor to protect the wheels. A hailstorm of rail gun bullets peppered the self-healing polymer rear window.

"Shit, that's loud. You sure it's going to hold?" Quinn yelled, covering his ears.

Felix didn't answer. He chewed his cigar, passing a semi truck and weaving in front of it as a shield. "Get ready. You'll have just a second," he said, slowing the car and opening the windows.

Quinn and Martin leaned out and prepared their laser-targeted grenade launchers. When the first cruiser appeared next to the truck, Martin fired at the air intake grill. The vehicle exploded and skidded under the back wheels of the truck, overturning it. The truck folded into the median as another cruiser collided with the first. The two trailing cruisers slowed to dodge the debris. Jade cringed at the carnage.

Felix accelerated, but the high-speed cruisers approached again, opening fire with lasers. "Can't hold the lasers back long," he said. "They'll melt the polymer."

The radiant heat from the rear window forced Jade to curl into a ball. "AC, please," she said. Martin closed the window.

Felix swerved around a few refugee vehicles, and the lasers from the cruisers stopped temporarily. But then an explosion shook the car, cratering the interstate. Jade jerked her head and shoulders inward, as if seeking protection in the womb.

"Bugs," Felix said, pointing up. Martin and Felix opened the windows, aiming guns into the night sky.

"Can't see shit," Quinn said.

Jade looked out the window at the night landscape flashing by, searching for whatever Felix meant by bugs.

A National Guard drone swooped like a peregrine falcon toward them. "Look out!" Jade yelled as the drone released a missile.

Felix swerved. Too late. The missile hit the front wheel of the vehicle, exploding in a fireball. In that moment, Jade saw only flames through the windows. Sparks flew as the Mustang skidded through a wire fence, across a local road, and into a desert shrubland of the Navajo Indian Reservation. When the vehicle finally stopped, its headlights illuminated a mesa.

"Everyone okay? Get out quick," Felix ordered, tossing Jade a gun and grabbing a pack from the trunk. "Not much time with these bugs circling." He turned off the headlights, and their eyes adjusted to the dim light. Jade could smell the burning rubber of the tire and the smoke emanating from the vehicle blotted out the stars.

She ran toward the mesa, following a barely perceptible animal trail, a shadowy line contrasting with the lighter shrubs. Her legs slapped into sagebrush branches, and blackbrush thorns tore at her jeans. A dim figure ran in front of her—Quinn. The sound of moving brush told her that Martin was just behind her. Jade looked toward the sky and saw nothing but blackness and swirling stars. She pictured enemies everywhere, knowing where she was, ready to kill her. She tripped on a branch.

"Come on, Jade." Martin tugged at her arm.

An explosion slammed into Jade and Martin like an invisible hand, igniting the dry shrubs.

"Keep going!" Felix yelled.

Another explosion. A high-pitched ringing. My ears. Flames and smoke were everywhere. Jade's throat tightened, and she lowered her head to the sand. Her eyes stung and watered. Fresh blood speckled her T-shirt. Where was everyone? "Martin!" she yelled, coughing, dark mucus running down her nose.

As if from within the flames, Martin pulled her arm and yanked her to her feet. "Let's go," he said, his face bloody. She recoiled at the gore, and then wanted to tend to his wounds. But there was no time. They ran out of the smoke toward the mesa.

Fresh air—a relief.

Barely illuminated by the flames, Quinn and Felix ran in front of them into the darkness, lasers piercing the sky and shredding shrubs around them. They disappeared in a plume of smoke. From the darkness, a drone spiraled down, crashing to the ground. They got one, Jade thought.

More lasers flashed from the second drone, firing toward Quinn, who screamed in agony.

Jade gasped. She looked into the dark sky. Was she the next target? She had a gun but nowhere to aim. She turned around to see Felix's Mustang engulfed in flames, hit by a drone missile. The cruisers arrived, their spotlights scanning the landscape. One of the beams moved toward her, and she ducked behind a rock. Rail guns and lasers fired, tearing through the shrubs around them.

"I need you to help Quinn," Felix called from nearby. "He's over here. Then follow me. I'll cover you."

Quinn's right arm was seared to a stub. "I fucked up," he whispered.

Jade smelled the charred flesh, and a gulp of vomit pushed up into her mouth.

"I'll be okay," he said. His gun was melted on the ground next to him.

Whatever. She spit out the vomit.

Snapping twigs warned Jade of something approaching fast. "Martin!" Jade gripped his arm, digging her fingernails into his skin.

"Come. Now!" Felix called from a nook in the mesa, shooting several rounds toward the cruisers.

Jade crawled behind Quinn and in front of Martin, weaving between rocks for cover. Thorns stabbed her. She tried to focus on following Quinn as bullets shattered on the sandstone. Fragments of rock fell like hail. Jade stopped, covering her ears, her teeth gritty from breathing the debris-laden air. She wiped sandy powder from her eyes and collapsed to the ground, her muscles burning.

Martin tapped her leg. "One more push. You got it," he said.

At the nook in the mesa, Jade caught her breath. Inhaling Quinn's charred flesh, she turned away. We're trapped in a corner. Her body deflated. Does Felix have a plan? Hope so. "What now, *gringo*?" she asked.

"Funny, *gringa*. They got us pinned, but these rocks are about body temperature." Felix searched though his pack. "Those tin men and that bug will have a hard time seeing us with their infrared sensors. Jade, come with me. Martin and Quinn, the tin men are trying to flank us. I counted about eight of 'em heading our way. We have probably thirty seconds left. Here, I brought some radios. Use channel two."

Jade switched the radio headset on. Looking out from the nook, she saw a sliver of interstate in the distance and the gleam of an iRanger moving to their right through the shrubs. Get it together, girl. Breathe. You'll be okay.

Felix handed her a stun gun. "This'll work better for you. Give your gun to Quinn."

Quinn fumbled for the gun with his left hand, sweat dripping, functioning on adrenaline. Jade heard his quick breaths and, despite the animosity between them, felt compassion.

* * *

On their bellies, Jade and Felix slid like snakes behind the cover of the shrubs. Sand and rocks scraped her arms. Her knees were bloody. Her forearm struck a cactus. She pulled away and continued following Felix.

A spotlight illuminated the tips of shrubs above them. At last, they stopped behind a flat rock to reconnoiter. Militiamen watched from the two armored cruisers, weapons pointed toward the mesa, scanning with the spotlight. Felix's vehicle smoldered to her right, the entire engine and cabin destroyed.

Several explosions and the sound of rail guns reverberated behind them. A drone fired lasers at the mesa, but the remote pilot likely couldn't see much with his infrared sensor, just as Felix had predicted.

"Quinn here. Can't see shit. There's rock shattering, lots of smoke. Bug's still flying, but I think we opened all the tin cans."

"Make sure you recycle 'em. And watch for that bug," Felix whispered into his radio.

"Can't see it. Still too much dust. But I can hear it. Hold on. I found Martin. He's not moving. Covered in blood."

Jade gasped.

"Martin, you okay? Hey, Martin," Quinn said. "He's not answering."

"Take cover. Don't move. ¿*Comprendes*?"

"Gotcha," Quinn replied.

Her energy deflated, she visualized the horror of Martin's violent death until Felix interrupted her thoughts. "Focus on the two *gringos*. You take the one in the front cruiser when I give you the word."

"Okay," Jade managed. Pay attention, she admonished herself. You don't know he's dead.

After what seemed like eons, they stopped in the shrubs, just fifteen feet from the cruisers, where Jade could easily see their targets—the dark forms of two men—behind the bright spotlights. One spoke into his headset. Sounds like he's calling for reinforcements. A truck rolled by on the interstate.

Jade aimed her stun gun at the man in the front cruiser. "I can't kill him," she whispered to Felix.

"You won't kill him. Just do it," Felix whispered back, mumbling curses in Spanish. "You won't kill him," he repeated.

She aimed at the man's shoulder. Felix aimed as well. "Now."

They both fired. She stunned. He killed. Behind her, gunfire cracked the night air.

"Nice work, *mamacita*." Felix ran toward the cruiser, opened the front door, subdued the man Jade had stunned, using his own cuffs, and pulled him onto the ground.

Another few shots rang out in the distance.

"Finished a straggler," Quinn said on the radio.

"What about the bug?" Felix said.

"Can't hear it. I think it's gone. May be out of power."

"Don't count on it."

Jade heard Quinn's fast breathing over the radio. She wondered when he'd go into shock. Once the adrenaline died down, probably.

"Can you make it back?" Felix said.

"Yeah. I'll carry him."

"Do it. I'll cover you." Felix grabbed a rail gun from a cruiser.

"Hurry, reinforcements are coming," Jade said. "We don't have much time."

"You're right," Felix said. "My trunk looks intact. Let's move our stuff into the cruiser. Hurry!" he yelled over the radio.

From the darkness, one-armed Quinn emerged, struggling as he hauled Martin on his back. "Keep packing," he snapped at Jade. "He'll be all right. Just remember the first-aid kit."

Three minutes later, they drove off in the cruiser, heading full speed in stealth mode, lights off, GPS and other tracking controls disabled. In the backseat, Jade checked Martin's breathing. His chest rose. He's alive! She felt his pulse, opened the first-aid kit, found scissors, and cut his bloody shirt from his body. She started by wiping the blood from his face, remembering the explosion that had knocked them down. Her ears were still ringing. Martin had a large gash on his forehead and cuts and abrasions on his face. The right side of his head was swollen and bleeding. She pictured a rock hitting him there, knocking him unconscious. She cleaned the gash and bandaged his head. He needs stitches, she thought, but I don't know how to suture. Then she remembered the Krazy Glue. She held a sterilized cut together, covered it with Krazy Glue, and waited until it sealed the wound. She then repeated this task for each laceration she found. "Thank you for saving him, Quinn," she said. But Quinn didn't respond. "Quinn?" Then she remembered he was in shock. Do we have a blanket? She found a towel and covered him, reclining his seat.

"He'll be fine," Felix said. "Nice work today, *gringa*. I like you."

The almost full moon rose blood-red over the interstate from the forest fire smoke high in the atmosphere. Felix drove east toward Albuquerque in the less-busy westbound lanes, dodging trucks and cars bearing toward them. Jade squinted into the oncoming high beams. He's insane but brilliant, she thought, turning her attention back to the wounds on Martin's body. Horns honked, pitch descending Doppler-style. Felix's hands gripped the steering wheel. He chewed his cigar until pieces broke away, falling between his legs.

FOURTEEN
AMERICAN REFUGEES

FIREFLY COVE

"ETHAN AND CAREY," TARA CALLED. "COME CHECK THIS OUT." The children ran through a trail in the forest gardens to meet her, their blond hair luminous in the sunlight. Harriet trudged behind them.

"Ever try a mulberry?" Tara asked.

Carey shook her head, and Tara placed one in her mouth.

"I want to try," Ethan said. After one bite, he and Carey were picking handfuls from the low branches.

"You're glowing," Harriet said to Tara.

"You think so?"

"Definitely." Must be a man, Harriet thought. "I remember glowing like that when I first met Jack. Who's the lucky one?"

"Really? What?" Tara's face reddened. "It's Will," she said after a moment.

"He's a catch."

"Isn't he? I've had a crush on him for years. Since I moved here," Tara rhapsodized. "Can you tell I'm excited? He *is* a catch. I enjoy his presence. I love the way he holds me. I appreciate how I

can tell him anything. We support one another. I also love the way
he lives purposefully. You know, he's a . . ." Tara hesitated. "Are
you chipped?"

"Of course. Aren't you?" She's worried, Harriet thought. Why?

"No. Nobody here is."

"Really? How is that possible?"

"We don't need them. They aren't good for people."

Harriet was piqued by the underlying superiority and naïve
judgment in Tara's words. "No, that's not true," she said. "How do
you know, anyway? You haven't tried it." She watched her children
picking mulberries, and Tara's words repeated in her mind: Ever
try a mulberry? Ever try a mulberry?

"No, but I know people who have," Tara said.

"Ever try an Aurora?" Victoria appeared, mocking Tara in
Harriet's mindstream.

"What's so funny?" Tara asked.

"Nothing," Harriet said. *Please, Victoria, I can't have two
conversations at once.* "Well, I couldn't live without mine," she said.
"When I'm lonely, Victoria—my Aurora Friend—is there for me.
When I'm depressed, it lifts my mood. When I'm anxious, it calms
me."

"What's that like?"

"I feel a wave of depression, and the Aurora kicks in. The
depression goes away, and I feel better."

"I know someone who can remove your Aurora." Tara smiled.
"If you'd like."

"Whoa," Victoria said. "That came out of left field."

I know, right? Don't worry. I'd never consider losing you. "A
Scalpel?" she said. "You know one? Oh, Tara, be careful. They're
renegades."

"How do you know that?"

"The news. They're trying a Scalpel in California for acts of
terrorism."

"Our government's corrupt. They're wrong. Scalpels aren't terrorists. You'd like the Scalpel I know. Trust me, he's definitely not a terrorist."

"Don't be so certain. Still, I'd be miserable without a chip."

"Are you happy now?"

A sharp pain pierced Harriet's heart, as though a dagger had penetrated it. Immediately, her body or the Aurora—she wasn't sure which—shut down the pain, and her heart numbed. She looked at Victoria, quizzical. A moment of doubt. And Victoria disappeared without a word. The pain in her heart brought forth thoughts of the years of drought, living in fear of the water running out, and the dead fruit and nut groves that once supported her community. She recalled the day the water had run out, their decision to leave home, and the riots in the places she'd once shopped. They'd just skipped their mortgage payment, and she pictured her home, wondering if it had been looted yet, its pipes, wiring, and computer systems stripped. She thought of their migration east and two weeks in a small apartment with her mother. When they arrived in Memphis, the stress was high enough, but it only grew with the passing days, until Jack refused to stay another night. They continued east through Tennessee, staying at expensive hotels with guarded parking lots, safe places for the kids and their belongings, but often hard to find ones with a vacancy. Budget hotels were too dangerous, with looting and violence common. As their money dwindled, they arrived in Asheville, finally landing in the Cove. She hadn't spoken to her mother since they'd left, and her heart tightened, thinking of the changes in her life as an American refugee.

"Harriet?" Tara touched her hand.

"No, I'm not happy." Harriet's eyes watered, and she turned away in shame.

"It's okay," Tara said. "It's okay to cry."

No one had told Harriet that before. Having permission in the comfort of Tara's all-accepting embrace, she released a flood of tension from her body. Weeping, Harriet felt safe in her vulnerability, something she couldn't ever recall experiencing. "I feel worthless," she said, sniffling. "I can't even help myself, so how can I even begin to help my children? Or my marriage?" She thought about Jack's porn video, and it still bothered her. "Everything's falling apart around me, and I don't know what to do. But the Aurora's kept me sane. God help me."

* * *

Will reclined and scratched his back on the bark of an old apple tree. A waning half-moon peered through silver-lined clouds and silhouetted leaves. Next to him, Leaf put away his soapstone pipe after a prayerful smoke. Behind him, the luminous Chestnut Hall bustled with discussion of the president's recommendation—for the umpteenth time, Will thought. "Will they ever make a decision?" he asked. The moon disappeared behind a cloud, darkening the village green and the surrounding buildings.

Leaf laughed. "This is why I don't go to meetings."

"What would you decide?"

"We need to take care of ourselves first. We shouldn't open the Cove up to refugees, if they ever come."

"Even if their lives depend on it?"

"Well, I reckon I'd want to help. But is it our responsibility? I don't think so. We can't solve the world's problems ourselves. We're just a little village."

"But we can do what we can, and we have the ability to help."

"You're always trying to save the world," Leaf said. "Ever since you let that refugee family stay with you, people are saying you should have consulted the village first. It's a village decision. Now,

I don't know, because it's your house. But still, your decision affects all of us."

Hearing this, Will looked toward Chestnut Hall, wondering if they were talking about him and the Sanders family. "Why does everything need to be so complicated?" he said. "It's not hard just to do what's right, is it?"

"I don't know, Will." The moon reappeared, bathing the buildings surrounding the village green in a steely light. "How are the Asheville women?" Leaf said.

Will smiled, curious about where Leaf's shift in the conversation would lead. "Scene's different there. Lots of choices. Polyamory's big."

"You try it?"

"Yeah, but it wasn't my thing. Lots of bisexual women, too."

"That's hot. You think so?"

"Sure. People can love whoever they want." Will pictured Leaf flirting with Tara and considered telling him about their romance. But he hesitated. He imagined losing Leaf as a friend. Yet how could he not be honest with him?

"I've been lonely here, Will. It's not like there are many choices. You seem to date just about anyone you want."

"I don't know about that." Will was embarrassed. Does he know? Surely. At last, he blurted it out: "Tara and I are together now." What name to call their relationship? His mental stopwatch read the interval: seven days, ten hours, and twenty-one minutes, give or take, since their first kiss. That long. That short.

"Oh," Leaf managed.

The moon swirled in Leaf's eyes. Will guessed he was envious, that any moment he'd unleash his anger.

Leaf exhaled heavily. "You know it's hard for me to say this, Will, but you betrayed me."

Betrayed. That's a harsh word, Will thought, feeling the force of the two syllables. "Betrayed?"

"You knew I liked Tara. Then you come back from the city and hook up with her without a thought." Leaf stood up. "Great. Just great."

Will dove into the heart of the conflict. "Can't you just be happy for the two of us? It's been a year since you talked to me about your crush on her."

"Don't belittle me. Just because you've been gone doesn't mean things changed." Leaf frowned.

"But things did change."

"I can see that." Leaf spoke sarcastically, his face contorted with anger. "You didn't even bother talking to me. Shit, man, I've saved your life. I've helped you whenever you needed help. And you just crap on me."

"I'm not crapping on you." Will imagined Leaf pursuing Tara for years. Only such a longtime crush could explain the intensity. "Tara and I were always close, like brother and sister. But things happened."

"'Things happened.' Is that all you can say?"

"No. I regret that we're fighting like this."

"What else?"

"I don't like your tone, brother. What do you want me to say? That you can have Tara? It's not like it works that way."

"I'm pissed, man." Leaf stood. "Better I go, before I blow up."

Once Leaf's silhouette disappeared, energy drained from Will's body. He walked past Chestnut Hall and heard murmurings from the village meeting. Why do they talk so much? They know what they're going to do. They're just afraid to say it, because it takes guts.

Did he have guts? Half and half.

* * *

"Honey, I'm running out of insulin."

Harriet's words led to an emergency visit to Dr. Juliette Adams's office in the village center. Her Firefly Integrated Medicine office served not only villagers but also almost a thousand people throughout the region, providing them with holistic care, telemedicine services, and home visits. She practiced medicine with an understanding that a large proportion of diseases could be treated naturally or were preventable. Harriet doubted that applied to her. Still, her family joined the practice and signed up for the Global Villages Health Sharing program.

After Parvati checked her in and left to help Dr. Adams, Harriet picked up a magazine on health in the waiting room and read a few lines. But she couldn't concentrate. Bored, she called to Victoria, who appeared in a seat next to her. *Doesn't anyone have problems here?* Harriet asked her. *Or is it just me and my family? We stand out like sore thumbs.*

Victoria laughed. "I never thought you'd be living in a commune."

It's not funny. I didn't either.

"We can just keep watching soaps together."

Let's, Harriet replied. No one else here does, though.

'I know. But in a way, this place is like a soap opera."

Did you see those people skinny-dipping in the creek?

"No sense of decency."

None.

"Then there's that guy Leaf and his peace pipe. Don't get me started about him."

I know, right? When he tried to share his peace pipe and weedy mead the other day, I thought I was going to die. Too uncomfortable. Harriet laughed aloud with Victoria. A man waiting across the room looked up from his book. She flipped a page in the magazine, pretending to read. But what choice do I have? We looked everywhere for a safe place to stay. And here we are with a bunch of heathens in the middle of nowhere. This is the safest place in the entire country, I guarantee it. She thought of the support she'd been getting in the community and felt overwhelmed by their niceness. I really shouldn't complain.

"Why not? Complain if you want to."

Anxiety gripped Harriet. *It's too sweet, too perfect here.* She thought about the impending physical exam, embarrassed about her health.

"You're going to be all right. I'm here for you," Victoria said.

I know you are, but I'm not so sure about everything else. I want to love my body for what it is. But I don't love my body. I want to see myself as beautiful. But I don't see myself as beautiful. I want to be healthier, sexier. But I'm not. God, I haven't had sex with Jack since before we Mind Melded. Months ago. That wasn't a good idea, Victoria.

"The truth hurts, doesn't it?"

Yes, but... Harriet was unable to unsee the porn from the Mind Meld, the video images appearing once again in her mind.

Victoria cringed. "That looks like it hurts."

The discomfort Harriet had experienced during the Mind Meld returned.

"Just relax."

On cue, Harriet's body relaxed. Stop it. I'm tired of relaxing. I want to make love.

"It's hard to make love when you're living with your kids in someone else's cramped living room."

Tell me about it.

Dr. Juliette Adams wore a blue blouse that outlined a thin frame, and Harriet couldn't help making comparisons to herself. Dr. Adams approached the exam with a delicate politeness, especially when she asked Harriet to step on the scale. Weight was tricky.

"You lost six pounds," Victoria said sarcastically. "Congratulations."

Thanks. But Harriet didn't feel like celebrating, and when the doctor asked her about what was going on for her, she answered with trepidation. Depression. Anxiety. Diabetes. High blood pressure. At-risk of heart disease and stroke. Joint problems. "I'd like to feel better about my life," she said.

"I'm going to give you a prescription for insulin," Dr. Adams said. "Let me be honest here. You have kids and a husband. Do you want to grow old with them?"

Harriet nodded.

"Good. You have the opportunity to change your lifestyle. Living here will help. I'm also going to prescribe the same Neural Stimulation Therapy thresholds. But—same thing—*you* have the opportunity to change the way you relate to food, your body, your emotions, and your family. Try not to suppress what comes up. It sounds to me like you want to change."

"I'll do whatever it takes." Harriet startled herself with those words.

Then and there, she committed to a detox, a thirty-day raw foods diet.

* * *

Back from a trip to the pharmacy, her blood sugar under control, Harriet looked through the tasty food she'd eaten her entire life—her family's TV dinners and other processed meals in the freezer, the fridge, and the shelf space Grace had cleared for them. Her stomach rumbled and her mouth watered as she eyed a bag of potato chips. A half-gallon of ice cream lurked in the freezer, calling her name, filling her mind with craving. Despite warnings from her California doctor, she'd always cheated with the ice cream. None of their food would work for her new diet. God, Harriet thought, I eat nothing raw. How am I going to do this?

She thought about cheating. Not this time. I'm only cheating myself.

She opened Grace's pantry to examine mason jars full of dehydrated berries, herbs, fungi, spices, and nuts, and was unable to identify almost everything. I bet all these are raw. Probably tasteless, too. I have absolutely no desire to eat any of this. I need Grace. But I don't want to disturb her painting. What if . . . ? Oh, well, here goes. "Grace?" Harriet tapped on her bedroom door. "Grace, I'm back."

Grace opened the door. She seemed irritated, despite her smile. "What's wrong, dear?" Grace asked, her hands speckled with multicolored paints.

Do I look like something's wrong? Harriet was tempted to ask Victoria for a second opinion. "Nothing's wrong."

Grace sighed. "That's a relief. I was concerned about you—your health."

"Oh. Right. My health. I'm still alive."

"I can see that." Grace looked amused. "That's not saying much."

"No, it isn't. But I got my insulin. And I'm going to try a raw foods diet. So that's a start."

"You seem excited."

"I am. More scared, though. And lost. I have no idea how to begin. Can you help me?"

"Oh, Harriet, I'd love to help."

"I know you're busy. I shouldn't have asked, really. I can figure it out myself."

"No, no, no. I'd love to help." Grace reached for Harriet's hand, squeezing it.

"Sorry. Asking for help can be hard for me."

"Don't be sorry. You give away your dignity."

My dignity? Am I really sorry? Harriet checked. I'm not sure. Why is asking for help so difficult?

Out in the family garden, a light drizzle cooled Harriet's skin. Walking barefoot, Grace plucked a dark green Lacinato kale leaf.

Barefoot? Gross. She could get parasites. The lifestyle differences got in the way. So many things were getting in Harriet's way. Her mind was full of unanswered questions and thoughts about dignity, about helping and being helped. She recalled the words Dr. Adams had said about her opportunity to relate differently to herself and others.

Grace picked more plants. A beet. A carrot. Zucchini. A male ruby-throated hummingbird hovered curiously around her. "Amazing," Harriet said as the hummingbird darted out of the garden toward Straight Branch.

A rabbit fence enshrouded by a thicket of thornless blackberries, chokeberries, elderberries, juneberries, gooseberries, currants, and raspberries surrounded the garden. Several trellised grapevines framed a back entry door. Pole beans and cucumber vines wound their way up other trellises. The first of the Dahlias, Echinacea, and a few remaining peonies bloomed in a flower bed. Grace placed several dandelion greens into her woven Brazilian-style basket.

"Wait," Harriet said. "Those are weeds."

"Sorry. I don't want to pick anything you don't like. I just thought it might help with your diabetes."

"Really? Okay, I'll try them."

An Asian long cucumber. A Cherokee purple tomato. Genovese basil.

Oh, my God, I'm supposed to eat all this—raw? She thought she heard Victoria laughing behind her. *Cut it out.*

I didn't say anything, Victoria said, not appearing.

Grace rested the basket of washed vegetables on the kitchen counter. "Let's make this easy," she said, placing a food processor in front of her. "We'll start by grating the zucchini, carrots, and beets."

Next, they chopped ginger, parsley, and tarragon to garnish the salad and sliced the tomatoes and cucumbers. Placing the ingredients in a bowl and adding snow peas, sunflower seeds, sunflower oil, apple cider vinegar, dehydrated berries, nuts, and hemp seeds, Harriet had her first raw meal.

Bon appétit, Victoria chuckled.

* * *

As her diet kicked in, Harriet's body reacted violently with diarrhea, vomit, sweat, urine, tears, and mucus removing the toxins stored for decades in her body. Although the Aurora's Neural Stimulation Therapy boosted her mood, she wanted to feel bad, as if, for a change, she needed to purge, physically and emotionally. She curled under the covers on their living-room mattress while Jack played with the children outside.

"Harriet, this hippie diet's got to stop," Victoria said, appearing on the bed next to her. "This is the most ridiculous thing I've ever seen you do. You're eating like a rabbit. But you're a person."

"Master of the obvious," Harriet said aloud, knowing she was the only one in the house.

"People don't eat like this. I saw you retching when you ate the dandelion."

"It was way too bitter."

"Raw foods diets don't work anyway. If you want to diet, I've got a recommendation for you."

"No, Victoria. I'm doing this."

Will walked in the front door. "You okay?"

"Um, no," she said, sitting up on the mattress. "I'm fighting with my Aurora Friend." To Harriet, Will seemed uncomfortable and shy.

"I can relate," Will said.

"You have an Aurora Friend?" Harriet's face brightened. "I didn't think anyone here had one."

"Well, no. I used to have one," Will said, avoiding eye contact. "So, what's going on?"

"I don't know. She doesn't want me to change."

"Do you want to remove it?"

"Oh, I couldn't do that. It's my whole life. Besides, it's too expensive."

"It doesn't need to be expensive," Will said.

"It does need to be legal, though."

"Does it?"

* * *

That evening, Jack knocked on the bathroom door. "Honey, you've been in there an hour. You still alive?"

"No."

Harriet sat on the floor. Vomit lined the composting toilet bowl. With great effort, she pulled herself up. "Aren't you going to at least try?"

"Try what?"

"The diet." She washed her face, rinsing the bile from her mouth.

"Why should I? You're miserable."

"So are you. What about your blood pressure? Your arteries? Don't you care about your family? If you did, you'd care about your health."

"Don't guilt-trip me. No one's going to take away my right to eat ice cream."

Harriet opened the bathroom door. "Dr. Adams came by to check on us. Us."

"I don't want to do it. Especially after seeing what it's doing to you."

"Right. Do you think I like this? I've become a miserable bitch. But so what? At least I'm trying. And it's working. I might be miserable, but I'm not scared like you. If not for me, at least do it for the kids. Do it for God. Something."

Jack rolled his eyes.

FIFTEEN
ZOMBIE HEIGHTS

AFTER THEIR ENCOUNTER WITH THE NATIONAL GUARD, Felix, Martin, Quinn, and Jade hid in the backcountry off a remote Cibola National Forest road in the San Mateo Mountains. But after a few days, Felix became restless, Quinn insisted on getting a bionic arm, and Martin sought somewhere more comfortable to recover, spending much of his time sleeping. Jade dreamed of a cozy hotel room.

They entered the fringes of Albuquerque at night on back roads, and her dream disappeared into disappointment when Felix announced that they still needed to hide. Their escape from Arizona was too fresh, and they drove a stolen police cruiser. No hotel rooms. Eventually, Felix found what he was looking for: an abandoned suburban neighborhood. Once, Jade imagined, it had been alive with the sounds of children playing. She guessed that the city had cut off the water. What else could it be?

Streetlights lined the road, but only a waning gibbous moon illuminated the neighborhood. Homeowners choosing to stand their ground had surrounded their Spanish- and desert-inspired homes with razor wire. The neighborhood was bombed with graffiti—rivals claiming turf. Plywood covered the windows of burned buildings. The pebbly xeriscaping hadn't changed much, though.

Felix stopped the police cruiser. "I'll be back," he told her. Martin and Quinn were asleep.

A few minutes later, he ran to the car, got in, and accelerated away. "These people are *loco*," he said, meaning the squatters. By the third house, he recognized them as dangerous, raccoons backed into a corner. He spoke of the booby traps, the filth. He left each place without a fight, something Jade found surprising, knowing Felix and his fearlessness. Fearless, but not stupid.

At the end of the neighborhood, Felix stopped at the last home in a cul-de-sac. He asked for backup from Jade.

"You trust me to do that?" she asked. She imagined the squatters and booby traps, and nervous jolts shot through her body. Don't do it. You know you don't want to. You didn't sign up for this. Find an excuse.

"More than these guys," he said.

The exhausted and injured had excuses. She couldn't find any. "I got your back," she said confidently. Shit. Her heart raced. Do I have his back?

This time, Felix began by looking around the yard. She guessed he was searching for signs of squatters. He stalked toward the house and entered through a back window without plywood. Her heart pounding, Jade followed, fearing an attack by zombielike humanoids. The air carried a putrid stench. She gripped a stun gun, and her headlamp showed glimpses of filthy clothes, trash, empty water bottles, burned holes in the carpeting, broken dishes in the kitchen, and bare fixtures and opened walls where precious wiring had been stolen.

They climbed the stairs. Rats scurried. Felix opened the door to the master bedroom. On the stained carpet was a decomposing body scavenged by rats. Jade turned away. But it was too late; she couldn't unsee the body. The smell hit her nostrils. She retched, and the bile burned her throat. This was definitely not a good place to stay.

"We stay here," Felix said.

"You're joking," she said.

"No, *chiquita*, no joke," he said. "It's safe here."

"Safe? How is this safe?"

"What, you think he's going to wake up from the dead and eat your brains?" Felix replied, moving toward her, miming a zombie. "Brains!"

"Enough," she said as he laughed.

In the backyard, Felix doused the remains with gasoline and threw a lit match onto the body, set atop a pyre of flammable debris. Jade followed his orders, parking the cruiser in the garage and leaving Martin and Quinn in the vehicle to sleep. She found bleach and rubber gloves in a kitchen cabinet and cleaned the house as best she could with as little water as possible. Her eyes already burned from fatigue and bleach when she found the rat latrine.

By dawn, they transformed the house into a home of sorts, keeping the plywood covering the windows for security. Felix secured the remaining window with boards he found in the garage, then fell asleep upstairs in the master bedroom.

How can he sleep up there? Jade thought of the dead body. She fell asleep on the carpet in a downstairs bedroom as the sun rose outside.

When she awoke in the dark room, she couldn't tell the time but saw light entering from cracks around the plywood. Somehow, Martin was next to her. In the dim light, he opened his eyes and said, "Jade, I'm grateful to be alive. With you. We'll get out of this, and first thing I'll do is buy you roses—red ones."

Jade kissed his mouth, feeling her eyes moisten with joy. "You promise?"

"I do. No more killing either."

"Really? Oh, Martin, thank you. I love you."

"I love you, too," he said.

His head bandage was bloody. "I'm going to check your wounds," she said. Martin nodded as she removed the gauze bandage. "Still bleeding," she said, concerned. "It's too big for Krazy Glue."

"It's all right," he said. "It'll heal eventually."

"No, teach me how to suture."

She left and returned with the suture kit and first-aid kit. Following his instructions, she stitched his wound shut, cringing each time she poked through his skin. "It looks terrible," she said.

"It's fine as long as the bleeding's stopped. Thank you."

After reapplying gauze to the wound, she kissed it and touched his face. She felt the furrows of his burn scars and the rough patches of Krazy Glue covering the wounds. Looking into his eyes, she noticed a new sparkle.

"No one's cared for me like this before," he said, squeezing her hand.

* * *

"What do you think?" Felix opened the garage door. The cruiser was transformed with spray paint and a new license plate.

Where'd he get the plates? Jade wondered.

"I know it's rough," Felix continued. "I'll make her look pretty for you." He stroked Jade's cheek, but she turned away.

"I don't need it pretty," she said, her face flushing. "And keep your hands off me."

"You've got some fire in you. I like that."

After that moment, she didn't want to run errands with Felix, but he convinced her. They drove downtown. On the way, Felix handed Jade a list. "Take a look. See if we need anything more."

Jade scanned the list: welding equipment, automotive paint, composting toilet, wigs, legit license plate, makeup, liquor, rat traps, cleaning supplies, bionic arm for Quinn, water, food, GPS-disabled and encrypted smartphones, two door locks and keys, solar panel, off-grid battery pack, security cameras, portable stove. She found a pen and added first-aid supplies, as they were running low.

They passed a street corner and a pair of prostitutes. Felix's eyes lingered. Next to a tire store surrounded by chain-link fence and razor wire, a neon light in the window of a cinderblock building prompted Felix to stop. The sign read, "Nguyen Pawn. We Buy Gold."

"They open?" Jade said. Several men talked and drank bagged beverages next to a car with styled chrome wheels.

"Looks like it. They know we only come out at night." He winked.

"Vampire." Jade laughed nervously.

Inside, they walked the tight aisles and checked items from their list.

"I bet most of this is stolen," Felix said.

Jade pictured refugees lugging their prized possessions. Easy targets. To Jade, the man behind the counter looked like someone from a Shanghai kung fu movie.

Felix examined the items they'd found. "Give the man the list."

Jade placed the list on the counter

"I pay cash," Felix said, beginning his haggle.

The man perused the list and pointed to a No Haggle sign. "I get you all this," he said. "Tomorrow come back."

Felix dug into his pockets for cash but then reconsidered. "I'll pay with crypto."

"No problem."

* * *

Jade installed the shingle-like solar panel on the garage roof, wondering if this neighborhood would be their new home. Seemed like it, given what Felix had bought. She imagined hundreds of squatters there. Based on the noises she'd heard, they were mostly nocturnal, but she kept reminding herself to stay alert. She heard a noise and turned around. Nothing. I'm just paranoid. She sat down on the roof, breathing into her fear. "I live in Zombie Heights," she said aloud, looking at the neighborhood sprawling down a slope.

Meanwhile, Felix wired the solar battery and inverter to the home's electrical system. As the deep-cycle battery was already partially charged, he turned on the lights and the refrigerator. He detached the cruiser's computer and brought it into the living room to track the city's police, hooking it to the security cameras he'd placed around the house.

After several nights, Jade grew accustomed to hearing the police chatter in the background. Occasionally, a police drone or patrol vehicle would trigger their security cameras, but the officers never left their vehicles.

In a spare moment, Jade dialed the strip club phone with her new encrypted cell phone purchased from Nguyen Pawn. She couldn't recall any other numbers, as the Aurora had stored all of them automatically. When she pressed the call button, her heart fluttered with excitement. One by one, her colleagues joined the conversation. They expressed concern and love for her, urging her to return. Some questioned her sanity and decision making. The police were questioning them, trying to track her down and learn about Martin. Even her estranged family had reached out to the club in the hope that she was still alive. Some thought she should leave Martin. They were convincing. But after the call, when she returned to him, she sought to refute their judgments with a flurry of thoughts: I'm not stupid. They're just superficial. They don't get my situation. He's not a project of mine. I'm not attracted to him because I want to change him, am I? What does that mean, anyway? I guess I do want to change him. I want him to open his heart even more. I want us to leave the gang. What's wrong with that? I love him.

When Felix finished welding and repairing the police cruiser, Jade could no longer recognize it by make and model.

"Now, I'm impressed," she said.

"About time," Felix said. He reached into the cruiser, and Cuban music began to play—a tango that reverberated in the almost-empty garage. "This, my darling, is the music I grew up with. So expressive. Full of passion. Come dance with me."

He's been drinking again. She backed away. "I'm with Martin, remember?"

"That doesn't matter. Come dance." He advanced toward her, grabbing her hands, trying to force her to dance. A familiar fear pulsed through her body as she struggled to break his firm grip. He pulled her close, and she could smell alcohol on his breath. "A beautiful woman like you can have anyone she wants." He began dancing, pushing her through the tango moves as she struggled. "Relax. Just dance," he said. "I can show you what a real man's like."

"I already know, and it's not you," she replied. "Let go of me."

He tightened his grip, and the tango continued.

She relaxed into the dance, hoping for a moment to break free. But none came, and the song ended. He didn't let go, so she kicked him in the groin and twisted herself free. She backed away from Felix, who was crouching, grimacing, glaring at her with his piercing eyes. Slamming the door behind her, she left the garage, sweating, breathing heavily.

* * *

After her encounter with Felix, Jade was uncomfortable anytime he was around, and so was relieved when he disappeared for a few nights—to the red-light district and bars, she guessed. Jade and Martin closed the door to their room to enjoy those nights alone. She missed their life in Phoenix but also began to savor the quiet simplicity of their empty room—just the two of them, a plush carpet, and love. She didn't dare tell Martin about her dance with Felix, thinking he'd try to kill him and end up getting shot himself. But he vowed not to kill, didn't he? she thought. I'll tell him when all this is over.

But tonight, Felix stayed home.

Deck of cards, bottle of rum, lines of white powder, shot glasses, card table, four chairs—three men and a woman frittering away time in Zombie Heights, where no one knew the neighbors. Felix chain-smoked his cigars and sipped his rum, which unnerved Jade. He's waiting for something—a zombie invasion.

Quinn, though, pounded shots. "Come on. Down it with me," he slurred. These were the times when Jade grew to dislike Quinn even more. She guessed he was bored and having trouble coping with the loss of his arm and working his bionic replacement.

"I don't want to," Jade replied.

"You frigid or something?"

"Shut the fuck up," Martin said.

"Fuck you." Quinn threw his cards on the table. "And fuck this shit. You and your whore are cheating."

Jade threw her cards at Quinn and left the room. She had no desire to play anyway, much less with Quinn. Behind the closed door, she heard Martin defending them while Quinn carried on about how he'd saved Martin's ass in the desert and how it was his fault they were in this mess. It's not his fault, Jade thought. "We weren't cheating either, asshole," she whispered to herself. "We were winning." Loser.

"Your stripper's a liability," Quinn said. "You need to unload her."

Felix told him to shut up, but it was too late. Martin and Quinn, despite their recent injuries, started exchanging blows. Jade heard the sounds of drywall shattering. She curled into a ball and held her knees. In the silence, she knew both men were unconscious. But what about Felix? Her heart tensed. He'll come for me, she thought. Where's my stun gun?

Gripping the stun gun, she stared at the bedroom door. A scream startled her. The squatters next door. She heard one laugh, ending with a smoker's cough.

Gunshots.

She hoped they were just hunting for the mule deer that browsed in the neighborhood, but that seemed sadly optimistic. A coyote howled. What was Felix doing?

Hours later, she still couldn't sleep. She lay on the carpeted floor staring into the darkness, sensing the ceiling and walls, her fingers still gripping the stun gun. Something moved outside their window, a rustling. "Martin," she whispered. But he was snoring, probably drunk and bruised, in the living room. I need to find Felix, she thought with trepidation, turning on her phone's flashlight and opening the bedroom door. Quinn lay near Martin face down on the carpet, also snoring, his bionic arm cast aside, perhaps torn off during the fight. Felix slept upstairs. Somehow, he didn't care that the dead body had been there, rotting. At least he'd found a mattress.

Then, out of the corner of her eye, Jade saw a ghost up the stairs, a quick apparition. Glowing. A twisted face. I'm going crazy. She shined her flashlight toward the stairs, aiming her stun gun.

Nothing.

That couldn't have been just a trick of the eye, could it? But the image of the ghost had been clear. When was the last time I saw daylight? Or saw a woman friend? She dragged Martin to their bedroom and closed the door. I'm tired of living in this haunted house. She thought of the rats, the lack of water, the boarded-up windows, the zombie neighbors. The sounds continued and forbade her to sleep. When they finally subsided, the ringing in her ears worried her until nightmares of the dead body, the ghost, and zombie squatters arrived in swarms.

Jade awoke to gunshots inside the house. Martin reached for his gun and opened the door to a bloody carpet. Felix had killed two squatters right next to Quinn, who sat in the corner, speckled with blood, holding his head. Felix threw the bodies down the basement stairs, then walked upstairs without looking at anyone. "This fucking place. Tomorrow, we go. *Vamonos.*" Felix slammed his door.

So much for living here, Jade thought, relieved.

Late the next morning, Felix returned from shopping and unveiled their newly-bought disguises. He'd thought of everything. Dark wigs to conceal their faces. Makeup in black and white, like goths. Black clothes. Spiked dog-collar chokers. All so they wouldn't be identified by the drones, police, or thousands of Auroras. Jade appreciated his creative and humorous attention to detail.

Fully dressed and disguised, they drove out of Zombie Heights. Jade sat in the back seat holding Martin's hand. "Good riddance," she muttered. Back on I-40 East, she dozed on Martin's shoulder to mend her broken sleep.

Moving through the shortgrass prairie of the Texas Panhandle toward Amarillo, Jade awoke as they slowed to a standstill. A girl with long crochet braids stared at her from a fully packed economy car. To Jade, her stare was almost expressionless, as though she were shell-shocked. What is she, seven? Jade adjusted her goth wig and looked away from the girl, imagining all the suffering she and her family had been through. These thoughts gnawed deeper into her heart until they became unbearable. Why are we stopped?

Martin slept next to her. The westbound lanes across the median were empty of cars. Black smoke rose from the interstate in front of them. In the distance, she saw a helicopter hovering. She checked the Amarillo news with her smartphone, keeping the volume low.

"According to the U.S. government, two million refugees have already fled the dire situation in the Southwest, though the United Nations High Commission for Refugees puts that figure at over five million. The death toll is over ten thousand. Looks like that number will increase today as we return to live helicopter footage. If you're just now joining us, around eleven this morning a major incident broke out on I-40," a KFDA Channel 10 news reporter said. Amidst the stopped traffic and burning wreckage, dozens of people positioned themselves around their vehicles, defending their families and prized possessions. "We are live-streaming now, so anything can possibly happen. The images we see here may not be suitable for all audiences. We've been watching for several minutes now, and as we zoom in again, we see..." Several men tossed their loot into the back of a white van, turned around, and fired their guns, shooting one man in the chest multiple times. A full-sized moving van behind them accelerated, slamming into the van, overturning it, and crushing one man. The moving van's windshield broke into a spiderweb, and a red stain splattered on the glass as the driver collapsed. "Okay, so we're going to cut that off right now. We did not want to see that.... All right, here's the ten-day forecast. More record temperatures later this week..."

With the sheer number of refugees and crimes, the federal government had declared a state of emergency and opened prison camps to alleviate the pressure on the full prisons. FEMA had opened shelters for refugees, and the Red Cross and many other organizations were assisting with relief operations.

After a three-hour traffic jam, they passed the scene: several police vehicles, two ambulances, a fire truck, and a few charred vehicles on the side of the road. A dozen handcuffed men sat on the grass, armed guards watching them. Felix accelerated to full speed, leaving the frustration of the wait behind them. "It's dog-eat-dog," he said.

Jade's body slumped at those words. Sure, Felix was a keen observer of the ways of the world, but she lamented that he missed the natural goodness in people. And in himself. Jade thought of the staring, shell-shocked girl. Though she had wanted to help, she could do nothing. The girl was long gone. Her mind filled with despair and worry. The situation was too overwhelming.

SIXTEEN
NEWCOMERS

FIREFLY COVE

IF ASKED WHO WESTERN NORTH CAROLINA'S MOST SKILLED TRACKER WAS, many would say Joe Boggs, Leaf's father, the ornery Firefly Cove village manager. In the forest, he stood as an imposing, blond-bearded, middle-aged man in Carhartt overalls, the classic Southern Appalachian mountaineer of Scots-Irish descent, with broad jawbones, barrel chest, and strong hands. In 1771, the British had evicted his ancestors, forcing them to immigrate to America and creating distaste for authority and oppression that trickled down from generation to generation. Because of Joe's wide set of skills as not only a tracker, but also a general contractor and electrician, Baba had offered him a job as village manager. Accepting the job, Joe had settled his family at Firefly Cove. And from that day eighteen years ago, old-time mountaineer families had become part of the Cove.

Joe scratched his sweaty blond beard, looking at five refugees fresh from the Southwest. Why'd I commit to this baloney? "I reckon most of you'uns look around and couldn't tell me a dang thing about this forest, except the bugs are botherin' you," he said. "You're scared of snakes and bears. You ain't used to the humidity. That right?"

No one said a word.

"For ninety days, I aim to knock the city crap out of you and turn y'all into mountain men and women. You know that there ain't no other way to survive. That's why you signed up for this." He smiled. "Ain't it?" He looked at the five apprentices and doubted they'd last.

* * *

"Back up the other way. Back up. Step together. Half sashay. Say bye, grab a new guy." The summer solstice contra dance caller spoke into a microphone, his face framed by his trimmed, graying goatee and long sideburns. A young refugee with green eyes grabbed on to Will, continuing the contra dance.

Antique American chestnut timber posts and beams repurposed from abandoned homes and barns framed Chestnut Hall's white plaster walls. Warm diodes recessed into the vaulted ceiling illuminated the scene. Almost all of the Cove's one hundred twenty-eight people and twenty-four refugees celebrated together, though the Sanders family stayed at home. Harriet and Jack had seemed embarrassed to come, and Will wondered whether they were overwhelmed from the detox.

Now, he promenaded with the young refugee. When they swung together, he looked into her green eyes, and each of her pupils transformed into a CCTV camera for the Aurora. Any of his dance partners could be transmitting data to Cirrus or the police. His thoughts stifled the joy of the dance. The disconnection pained him, and he pushed through it, trying to focus on her eyes and on seeing her soul instead of the Aurora. She struggled to learn the steps as he guided her through the dance. But she wasn't the only one. Most of the refugees lost track. People bumped into one another. Villagers struggled to maintain the order of the dance. Will laughed with his partner as they stepped together. The caller, microphone in hand, ran over to adjust the lines. "Forward together. Back up together," he said.

Since Will greeted the Sanders family less than two weeks ago, twenty more refugees had arrived at Firefly Cove. Experts predicted that food insecurity would affect over eighty percent of Americans by fall. Politicians blamed Russia for withholding grain exports, despite their surplus from rapidly expanding agricultural lands on former permafrost as the Arctic warmed. Leading the world in grain production, Russia was able to sway food commodity prices in the global market. In turn, it blamed the United States and Europe for creating climate change in the first place and for their hypocrisy after years of sanctions against Russia. Either way, the end result was that over thirty million Americans could be disaster displaced by year's end, and Russia had become the primary beneficiary of global warming. To tamp down these dire predictions about America, hundreds of Global Villages communities were sheltering thousands of refugees. After days of vigorous debate, Firefly Cove had decided to follow the Global Villages president. In part sparked by Will's welcome of the Sanders family, villagers had officially recognized the wisdom of her recommendation. Today, the refugees were becoming official villagers—newcomers.

The caller's band played banjo, fiddle, and spoons. A wizened man with a long gray beard and a straw hat sat and picked his banjo as if it were a lover. Parvati played fiddle. Horsehair dangled from her bow, evidence of the vigor and passion of her fiddling. A younger, sunburned man with round glasses sat crouched and looking toward the floor, concentrating all his energy into the spoons he played on his blue jeans. Everyone played next to microphones on stands plugged into a PA system.

"Step together. Back. Forward together. Back up together. Half sashay. Say bye. Promenade. Back up. Go forward. Step together. New person balance and swing. Honor your partners one and all, thank your band at the end of the hall." The caller bowed.

The sweaty couples clapped. Tara and Will sat down, sweaty.

"That was fun." Tara's cheeks were pink.

"Oh, my gosh, yes." Will ran his fingers through her hair. "Why is it so funny watching people mess up?"

Ife, a former houseless man from California, asked the caller for the microphone. Ife had come to America with his family from Jamaica over four decades ago. He wore a green, yellow, and black woven shirt, one of his few possessions. He called up all the refugees, who surrounded him up front. "We just want to thank you so much for your hospitality. Your kindness is without bounds, and God is smiling down on all of you wonderful people today." As Ife spoke, his removable partial dentures pointed to a violent past when his front teeth were knocked out with a baseball bat. At the same time, his eyes sparkled, and Will thought he noticed them watering with joy. "On behalf of all of us up here, I'd like to thank you for voting us in as part of Firefly Cove. We accept!"

The room filled with applause.

As the cheers stopped, the twinkle faded from Tara's eyes. "They need you."

"I know. But assassins are killing all the Scalpels," Will said. "There are few left."

"I know it's risky." Tara looked at Will. "Still, you're passionate about it, and you want to help. You've said it before: it's an act of loving kindness."

"I can love in other ways, right? I mean, is it worth my life?"

"No way. But I want you to do what you feel in your heart." Tara smiled. "Remember, we're alive at this time for a reason. And I know your heart."

He admired her confidence and strength. She believes in me more than I do, he thought. "Maybe I'm here for another reason."

"Sure, babe." Tara snuggled.

She's right. He scanned his heart with awareness, noticing a tightening, clenching sensation. I'm not speaking from my heart. I'm speaking from a place of fear. He thought of the threat from the police: "We'll come after you." Fear of that threat had led him to disable the chip instead of removing it outright. Subtle, but true. Fear was the driver of his decisions. He didn't want that anymore, and he knew the horror of the Aurora all too well. Aja continued to haunt his dreams. "You're right. In my heart, I'm a Scalpel." When he said the words, they rang true.

She smiled and kissed him, as though no words were needed. "I've got this thought that keeps coming up," Tara said.

"What?"

"We might run out of food."

"You're not usually pessimistic."

"I know. I'm usually not this anxious either. When I worry, I tend to keep it to myself. I just read that crops are failing again from California all the way to Kansas. Entire areas with dead fields. Growing up, I remember our country usually had a huge surplus, but not anymore with the extreme drought. Depleted groundwater was the last straw for our heartland, everywhere except for Nebraska, where they actually protected the Ogallala Aquifer. So, here we are. We have only so much food. How are we going to eat?"

Will smiled. "Leaf will find enough." Leaf was drinking mead and flirting with the green-eyed newcomer.

"He's still not talking to you, is he?"

Will nodded.

"Anyway, I'm serious." Tara elbowed Will gently. "We can't survive on mushrooms and road kill."

Will laughed. "Why not?"

"For starters, I don't eat meat," Tara said.

"Well, right. But you would if you needed to, I imagine," Will said.

"Okay folks. Find a partner," the caller said through the PA system.

"Tonight, I just want to dance. With you," Tara said. "I want us to be happy."

People grabbed each other's hands. Tara's father, Tom, his graying beard nicely trimmed, drank mead and philosophized with another man until her mother, Sarah, touched his arm, inviting him to dance. Parvati, newly married to Sam, Leaf's brother, embraced him in the corner, holding the fiddle she was about to play. Sam, the fisherman, barrel-chested like his father, Joe, was out in public for a rare appearance. Clean shaven with short but uncombed hair, he contrasted with his brother's stubbly face and long blond hair. Leaf asked the green-eyed newcomer to dance. A refugee took Grace's hand, and she didn't pull away. She looked at the caller as if telling him he had impeccable timing. He winked.

The caller seemed to be talking to the newcomers. "Line up. There's a beautiful geometry here. Join hands with the people next to you. Stay with your partner. Don't leave anyone out. All the men are on one side and all the ladies on the other. So, you're going to dance with one partner, then another, then another. This is the way it's been done for the last three hundred years here in the Blue Ridge Mountains."

The instruments played. The caller followed the rhythm and sang these words: "First man and second lady do-si-do each other. First lady and second man do-si-do. Couple number one, swing your partner. Face toward the front..."

After the dance, Leaf whispered in Will's ear, "Let's go outside."

"Sure," Will said, nervous about another angry outburst.

They walked in silence to the reflection pool and sat on a bench. At last, Leaf spoke, staring at the pool. "I always thought that, eventually, I'd win her heart. We'd marry and build a house in the Cove. After that, we'd have a family together. I'd teach the kids everything I know. We'd grow old together."

Hearing these expectations, Will's heart tensed. "I—"

"That was my dream, and you crushed it." Leaf exhaled. "That's why I was so pissed the other night."

"I'm—"

"No. Don't be sorry. I'm sorry. I just needed some time to come to my senses. I regret what happened between us, brother. It's going to take me a while to get over her, though, but it's a load off my back to stop living in the fantasies I built for myself. Anyway, you're one lucky bastard with Tara." Leaf hit him playfully in the shoulder.

"And you're with a cutie," Will said. "About time."

"I know, right? Flirting, I can do. Let's get back inside. The next dance will start soon."

* * *

"How about twelve hundred?" Will said, bartering with a woman on her porch for a cell phone.

"All right," she said.

He counted out a dozen crisp Benjamins, and she handed him the old phone, the same model he had before.

Will drove back to Firefly Cove in a village electric car after purchasing all he needed to be back in business. He'd bought his Scalpel equipment—a scalpel, sterile blade replacements, suturing kit, surgical cloth, local anesthetic, and syringes—from a large-animal vet.

Back in Firefly Cove, he called upon Dr. Kumar's tech-savvy assistance. Using his tablet connected to the relay network, Dr.

Kumar downloaded the encryption software Cipherous on to Will's phone and enabled the app. He integrated Will's phone with the Global Villages' peer-to-peer mesh network. Will created a new username—as obscure as possible—and was ready for business, able to freely communicate over data and text with whoever had his username. He also downloaded the same mesh network app he'd used as a Scalpel in Asheville, in the hope that the police hadn't compromised his account. When he logged in, all the contact information for his past clients was still there, and he sighed with relief that his password had been secure enough. He viewed dozens of messages from clients about their difficult times readjusting to society, their success stories, and their gratitude. How he wished he could have been there for them the past few months!

Will stayed in the village office, using his phone to create cards for the newcomers, inviting them to remove their Auroras. "Message me to set up your appointment," the cards stated.

At Chestnut Hall, Will placed a card in each newcomer's mail slot. When he reached the Sanders family's slot, he smiled.

* * *

After fetching the mail, Harriet read the Scalpel's invitation while walking home from Chestnut Hall.

Victoria appeared next to her on the winding forest garden trail. "I know what you're thinking," she said. "Don't do it."

"Why not?" Harriet asked aloud, quickening her pace.

"You need me. The Neural Stimulation Therapy is helping you. Without it, the misery and pain would kill you."

"Stop exaggerating." Ten days into the detox, Harriet had a sense that the Neural Stimulation Therapy was numbing her feelings. When it activated, she felt less craving, trembling, nausea, and all the other emotional symptoms. She recalled what Dr.

Adams had said—that she should relate to the emotions, not suppress them. "You're getting in the way," Harriet said. "You're sabotaging the detox."

"You've lost your mind," Victoria said. "I miss the old you."

"You're a manipulator, just like on TV. I should've known."

"No. I'm your best friend. This place has brainwashed you. Just take a minute to think rationally."

"I am thinking rationally."

"Could've fooled me. Come on, snap out of it."

"People change. Can't you accept that?"

"No, dear, I can't."

"As scary as it is, I don't need you anymore. I want my body and mind back."

A gunshot echoed from a glade on the other side of Straight Branch, startling her. What was going on? She hid behind a pear tree and looked through the acres of bountiful fruit trees and perennial gardens speckled with boulders and punctuated by streams flowing down to the pasture, where the newcomers' tents colored the field.

The gunshot came from the tents, Harriet believed. Her chest tightened. They've let a murderer into the village. What are we going to do? Nowhere is safe anymore. Not even in the middle of nowhere.

Another gunshot.

Oh, God, he's killed somebody else, too.

Along the edge of the forest garden, a group of village planners was debating where to locate a two-story co-housing unit, small homes, and duplexes to house the newcomers. Building on open land meant less acreage for pastures, fields, and gardens, and thus less arable land, but they could minimize the effects with good planning. The plan included a two-thousand-square-foot community greenhouse with artificial light, heat, and spring-fed water in order to produce thousands of pounds of tomatoes, greens, legumes, potatoes, carrots, onions, beets, and other crops, even in the winter.

They don't seem worried, Harriet thought, noticing no reaction from the villagers. In hindsight, the sound had seemed more distant, from the forest behind the pasture. Must be training people how to shoot. That's it. Nothing more. She exhaled. Jack should join them.

In a pawpaw patch, Leaf jumped atop a boulder and stopped at stacks of inoculated mushroom logs to harvest oyster, reishi, and shiitake mushrooms, trailed by apprentice newcomers carrying baskets of berries, fruits, and medicinal and edible plants. The mushrooms would be dehydrated, transformed into tinctures, pickled, fermented, or eaten fresh. "They're high in antioxidants and can even cure cancer," Leaf said.

"Ahem," Victoria said to Harriet, who was transfixed by Leaf.

Leaf started to show his apprentices how to soak the mushroom logs to initiate forced fruiting.

"Ahem. Let's ignore him and get back to you. I'm worried about your mental health, dear. You need help, and you're not going to get it in this village. Just don't do anything stupid, and you'll be okay."

"I'm not doing anything stupid," Harriet said, still watching Leaf.

"I'm not so sure. Remember, taking your Aurora out using a Scalpel is illegal."

"I know. That bothers me still. But so does everything else. It's a chance I'm willing to take. Now, let me be."

Victoria dissolved into the village scene behind her.

Ah, relief, Harriet thought.

She crafted a thought message to the Scalpel. A few minutes later, she received a reply, and they agreed to meet under the white oak tree in the sorghum fields. A blindfold was waiting on a shaded bench there. Following the Scalpel's instructions, she tied the blindfold around her head and sat down. Her Aurora remained silent, but no doubt it was recording the event. A minute later, she felt a gentle touch on her shoulder, and the Scalpel began to work.

* * *

"Welcome to the free world, Harriet Sanders," Will said.

She removed her blindfold. "*You're* the Scalpel?"

"I am. And I'm relieved your Aurora's gone. Now, we can talk freely."

"So, that's why you've been acting shy around me," Harriet said, noticing the missing icons in her visual field. No Neural Stimulation Therapy. No Victoria. No Internet. No InterVoice. No movies. No news. No social media.

"Yes. It's a relief. I don't like censoring myself. It's funny you thought I was shy, but I can see that," Will said. "So, what's it like, not having an Aurora?"

"I don't know," she said with a slight stutter, acutely hearing her heart beating faster. And not just her heart, but the arteries of her temples. She was nauseous, and sweat beaded on her forehead. Oh, God, this was a bad idea. What am I going to do? I'm not going to get through this. It's not safe here. There's no one I can talk to.

Victoria.

It sank in that she'd never see Victoria again. She wanted to grasp on to something in the Aurora's world. Something to distract her from her bodily and emotional discomforts and painful thoughts. Something to numb them. But all she'd held on to was now gone, and the panic attack set in without the Aurora to tamp it down. God help me.

"Is there anything you need?" Will asked.

"Just hold my hand," Harriet said.

* * *

"Why can't I play any more video games?" Ethan asked, tears falling onto the blindfold around his eyes.

"No more video games," Jack said, appearing from behind the oak tree. "You can play outside."

"Mom, I want my games back. I didn't want the chip out," Ethan whined. "I didn't want it out. I didn't want it out." He began to lose control, sobbing hysterically, gasping for breath. "I didn't want it out."

* * *

At the summit of Eagle Mountain, Will and Tara sat on the edge of the cliff. The rock face dropped into a forest far below that framed the village and its fields and forest gardens. Above them, high clouds floated in the blueness. A warm breeze blew from the south along the rugged Blue Ridge.

"I have this dream that we don't need to talk about the future or the past," Tara said. "We can just be. Maybe we don't even need to talk."

"What's wrong with talking?" Will chewed on a birch twig, sucking out the wintergreen flavor.

"It's not that I don't want to talk, but just that we don't need to talk."

"I can imagine it." Will looked into her eyes and felt her presence co-mingle with his. But then his presence disappeared under a thought: that it felt incredible, as if his entire body were tingling. He noticed this thought, and the thought disappeared to reveal open presence once again.

Eventually, Tara spoke. "That's what I'm talking about." Their hands settled together. Tara smiled. "Do you know what I want for us?"

Will shook his head.

"I want us to be the water for one another's roots. Sun for our leaves. Space that allows for us to grow, and growth that is grateful for space. I want us to be unbound from words, unbound from my conceptions of you, and freed from defining our relationship. Knowing you, I'd imagine you want that, too."

"Yeah, I savor freedom. How can we keep our freedom in a relationship?"

"As long as I want to be with you, I'm holding true to freedom," Tara said. "To me, that doesn't mean breaking up just because of an argument. Quite the opposite, because if someone flees from uncomfortable things, then there's fear. With fear, freedom is diminished." Tara turned her head to look at the mountains.

"What?"

"I just thought of my parents. I don't think they want to be together. They just stay together out of fear, I think." She paused. "I guess I fear the same thing happening to me." She looked at Will. He saw the fear in her eyes. "To us," she said.

SEVENTEEN
BEWARE, ASHEVILLE

"BEWARE, ASHEVILLE." Quinn opened his car window to the evening air as they took the ramp off I-240 toward downtown after a long drive from Nashville. His black wig flowed in the wind. His iridescent sunglasses, a stolen prize from Oklahoma City, clashed with his otherwise goth disguise. They listened to Mexican rap, a strange contrast to the outfits they'd been wearing for the last four days of driving, all of it through America's heartland on Interstate 40. They had no plan until Felix grew tired of driving. "We're not going any farther than Asheville," he'd said while driving along the winding Pigeon River Gorge on the Tennessee-North Carolina border, surrounded by some of the East's tallest mountains.

"Check out the dope street art!" Martin yelled over the music. Mosaics of colorful dancers and jazz musicians covered the concrete supports of the interstate underpass.

"Looks like they just finished it," Jade said, her face whitened and her lips and eye sockets blackened with goth makeup. The smile on a female dancer reminded her of how she felt sometimes when she danced—ecstatic bliss through movement. The Lady of the Dance. She hadn't felt that since they'd left Phoenix.

Quinn turned down the volume. "Not on this side. The paint's peeling." He pointed to another support, where a Cherokee woman and her daughter stood looking into the distance.

Dozens of people with rucksacks and other belongings sought protection under the overpass. Refugees were a common scene these days, but murals weren't. When Jade's eyes met those of a woman, the woman's eyes quickly diverted, as if hiding vulnerability, hunger, and trauma. Jade felt empathy, and then the tears came. She wiped them away and hid the smeared makeup behind the long bangs of her black wig.

Felix turned up the volume. A few blocks away, they cruised around the Grove Arcade, an upscale historic Tudor and Late Gothic Revival building, gawking at its luxurious bars, restaurants, and boutiques. A street musician played her guitar and sang, and Jade grew angry that she couldn't hear her over Felix's music. Families, couples, and groups of friends walked together on the sidewalks under shade trees or dined outdoors beneath parasols. Next to the Flatiron Building, a street performer painted in gold held a statuesque pose. As they turned right on Haywood Street, a beer tour trolley passed the other way, and families ate ice cream at the old Woolworth building. This town seems unperturbed by the outside world, Jade thought.

But at the next block, the scene shifted as they reached Pritchard Park, encircled by streets and restaurants. A group prepared meals while a line of people waited. Beggars reached out their arms in hopes of generosity. Hundreds of protesters filled the park. A dozen people meditated under a tree despite the activity around them.

"Stop the Genocide," one sign read, protesting the killing of Mexican-Americans in Arizona.

"Asheville Welcomes Refugees."

"Refugees Are Not Criminals," another sign said, showing an AP photograph of a girl behind a FEMA camp fence. This photograph had made the front pages, stirring emotions and political debates about refugee camp conditions and race and poverty issues.

The protesters spilled into the road, blocking traffic. Felix cursed them and honked, and a protester hit their hood in retribution. A policeman pushed the protester to the curb. Another officer handcuffed her, then looked up at the goths playing Mexican rap. Jade stared ahead, clenching Martin's hand, hoping that the officer's Aurora wouldn't identify their partially concealed faces or the altered stolen police cruiser. For a moment, the officer looked directly at Jade, and her face turned red under her makeup. Her body heated and began to sweat. Protesters yelled at the officer to release the woman, drawing his attention.

After driving past boutique hotels, breweries, and restaurants, they turned left on Hilliard Avenue, pausing at the stoplight at the intersection with South French Broad Avenue. In front of them to the left, hundreds of refugee tents filled Aston Park. The once-grassy park had turned to dirt and mud from overuse and was overflowing with garbage from a lack of trash receptacles. Campfires burned, and a haze of smoke blanketed the refugee camp. A man urinated behind a tree into the mud, as only two filthy porta-potties served the refugees. This is unacceptable, Jade thought. Beyond unsanitary. Where are the showers? The running water? Health care? She watched children playing in the mud. What had become of their lives? They looked strong, yet Jade imagined hidden fragility and trauma. Once again, she felt a gnawing at her heart and recalled the girl with the crochet braids in the car across from her on the interstate. Too much suffering, once again. What could she do? That was always the thought that followed her compassion, as she couldn't even handle her own life, much less help others.

The park's tennis courts had been converted to part of the refugee camp, with large tents for sleeping, covered kitchens, and latrines. Here, the camp was more sanitary, but Jade thought the enclosing fence topped with razor wire made the place look like a concentration camp. Inside the fencing, refugees waited in line for a meal, and Jade's mouth watered. They hadn't had a warm meal since Zombie Heights. Felix had been carefree with their finances until the stacks of bills turned into a loose handful.

As Felix's music pounded, people in the line stared. "Hey, Felix!" Martin yelled. "Can we get outta here?"

Jade wondered if his concussion in the desert or the hours of living and driving together had increased Martin's temper and decreased his patience. We need more time alone.

"Relax. We're having a little fun." Felix smiled, looking around with curiosity.

This isn't fun, Jade thought.

They drove through the River Arts District, with its mixed-use buildings and refurbished nineteenth-century apartments, warehouses, and industrial buildings. Now, these were breweries, artist co-ops, shops, nightclubs, and cafés. Next to Depot Street, old railroad tracks bisected the district, a mix of rundown and refurbished warehouses covered in graffiti lining the French Broad River behind them. As they turned right on Bartlett Street, the refugee situation repeated itself at Murray Hill Park, where over a hundred tents covered a grassy hillside. Almost every open space they passed, including parking garages, housed American refugees.

After an hour of driving, Martin still hadn't spoken. He avoided eye contact, hiding behind his wig. Was his anger about Felix's carelessness in wasting money and gas? Jade wasn't sure, but every drop was precious, since they'd spent most of their money.

"I'm sick of this shit," Martin whispered into Jade's ear.

Knowing that Martin shared her views was a comfort, alleviating some of the strain and weariness of their journey and the uncertainty of life in a new place. "Me, too."

Finally, Felix parked on the side of the road in the historic Montford District north of downtown. Quinn portioned pieces of bread and cheese for dinner. Jade thought of the warm meals she'd seen at the refugee camp, but she knew they couldn't chance eating there and getting caught. She heard Martin's stomach grumble. Suddenly, Quinn's bionic arm sprang upward, spilling cheese and bread on the floor.

"What the . . . ? Man, can't you control your stupid arm?" Martin said.

"Shut it. I can't help it." Quinn bent over to pick up the food.

"Is this our dinner?" Martin said. "Dirty bread and cheese?"

"This is what we got, Martin." Felix rarely called him Martin. The conversation fell flat. Two weeks in tight quarters together. Too much tension and anger. Too much fighting. Too many injuries. Too many crimes. Too much anxiety and uncertainty. Not enough humor and warmth.

"We got no room for a crying bitch. Why'd we ever agree to take you along?" Quinn said.

"Fuck you. I fucking hate you," Jade said.

"Likewise. See, what did I tell you? Just get the fuck out."

Martin's fists clenched. "She stays, cocksucker."

"*Amigos*, listen. Get your goth heads screwed on right. We need cash. Focus." Felix opened a bottle of rum, took a swig, and handed it to Quinn.

Jade opened the car door and walked into the street. I'm finished with this, she thought, throwing her wig on the ground.

Martin ran toward her. "Honey... Jade... Please, wait." He caught up, but she kept a brisk pace. Her blond hair flowed behind her. Felix followed in the car.

"Fuck Quinn. I'm done," she said. "Robbing, drinking and drugs every night, always looking for more money. Those guys in the car. You." Her arms were flailing. "You're their chump."

"Baby, I ain't nobody's chump." He held her elbow.

She yanked it away. "What I really want is for us to be together. Just us. Not them. I'm not here to be in a gang. I'm here to be with you. I love you."

"I love you, too," he said.

Jade saw the sparkle once again in Martin's eyes. Her heart warmed. He still struggled with thoughts that he was undeserving of love, that he wasn't good enough, that he'd never been good enough, but he was softening. They kissed tenderly.

"We can't afford roses. We need food."

"I wasn't talking about roses, Martin. We could go on a walk together sometimes. Anything just to get away."

"Yeah, a walk sounds good." He smiled. "But I still want to buy you roses."

* * *

Felix entered the rundown home they'd been squatting in for over a week, an old double-wide in the back roads west of Asheville.

"Here you go, *chiquita*," he said, entering Jade and Martin's bedroom and tossing a few bills in Jade's direction.

"What's this?" she said, lying next to Martin on a twin mattress. The room smelled musty after a rainy Fourth of July. They'd all removed their goth makeup and wigs.

"Buy some perfume," he said, his eyes glazed. "I like perfume on a woman."

He's lost his mind again, she thought, recoiling.

"Leave her alone," Martin said.

I can speak for myself, Jade thought.

"Don't you like perfume?" Felix stumbled toward them. "I like it on a woman's breasts."

"Just stay away from her."

Jade's heart tightened. Felix reminded her of the men she had tried to avoid at her former gentlemen's club, who had sometimes managed to corner her for a grope, a lewd comment, or more if they could. Her body felt unclean, as if a shower would help only on the outside but wouldn't touch her reeling insides. She looked at the bills in her hand, tainted with his energy and intention, yet also sorely needed. She knew she wouldn't buy perfume with them as she tucked the money into her bra and snuggled into Martin. "Thanks," she managed.

The next day, a storage container appeared on the street. "Need-to-know basis," Felix said.

That stirred up questions in Jade. Why doesn't he just tell us? He's up to no good.

That night, after Martin and Quinn were snoring, Jade heard Felix leave the house.

In the morning, he entered the container, then left only for lunch and bathroom breaks. She wanted to peek inside but didn't dare. Instead, she cleaned up as best she could and took a taxi to a strip joint. She watched the women dance, flirted with them, and tipped them with the money Felix had given her. Soon, the women joined her at her table. They flirted as if she were a man, kissed her, and asked her questions. "You should work here," one said.

"I'd like to," she answered.

In the back, she talked to the boss, a trans woman with purple eyelashes. "Show me what you got," she said.

When Jade walked onto the empty stage in front of a bar full of men, the Lady of the Dance emerged. She'd never left, but was only hidden behind stress and pent-up emotions. When those faded away, the empty stage was simply open space for creative feminine energy in its barest form. Perhaps those in the audience interpreted it through their eyes of lust, but to Jade, her dancing was pure.

"You're hired," the boss said. She wrote Jade's name into her calendar. "You can start Friday night, but come by anytime."

After midnight, she returned to their rundown house, eager to tell Martin about her new job and the tips she'd earned. Near the front door, Felix, covered in grease and sweat, was gnawing on a chicken leg. He leaned back in his chair and swigged from a bottle of rum. "Where you been?" he said, placing the bottle on a nearby card table.

She smiled but didn't answer, closing the front door.

"I said, where you been?" He stood and grabbed her arm, the chair falling to the ground.

"Let her go, bossman," Martin said, getting into Felix's face. The intensity of his glare startled Jade. Quinn opened his door, holding a gun.

"I'm sorry," Jade said in an attempt to deescalate the situation.

Felix released Jade's arm, and Martin pulled her into their room and closed the door behind them. "You okay?" he asked.

Jade nodded.

"I was just watching the news from Phoenix," Martin said. "It's not good."

He pressed play on his smartphone, starting a video of Phoenix's 12 News anchorwoman, who reported intensifying violence, ethnic cleansing, and evidence of covert Russian support for Mexican intervention against Arizona.

"I thought those protesters were full of shit," Martin said when the video ended. "America's racist. But genocide?"

"I'm glad you're still alive," Jade whispered. But she also worried about her friends in Arizona, her parents. She wanted to help the many people she saw in need. But I can't even meet my own needs, she thought. At least not yet. "I got a job," she whispered, biting the scarred nub of his earlobe.

* * *

Another wave of refugees arrived on a steamy day. They came in dirty, dented vehicles, by bus, and on foot. Some were wounded from the violence on their eastward path. Most were hungry. Many were armed. This was the tipping point for Asheville, the proverbial straw that broke the city's back.

Refugees abandoned their cars in the streets. No one could explain why. It was as if their vehicles had become a burden. Or perhaps they'd reached their final destination. Their actions seemed irrational. Looters stripped the cars and set them ablaze. Tow trucks were overwhelmed. By nightfall, the stench of burning tires, the glow of fires, and the sound of gunshots set the scene. Looters smashed windows, tore through inventory, and set grocery stores, boutiques, restaurants, and other businesses aflame. Sirens called from the four directions. Wreckage blocked the streets, flames illuminating the shadows of mischief. Police in riot gear attempted to keep order and clashed with protesters, looters, and refugees, all of whom were indistinguishable in the darkness.

"I've been waiting for a night like this," Felix said, smiling. He opened the storage container to reveal a trailer with a forklift.

How'd he steal that? Jade thought.

Attached to the front carriage of the forklift was a heavy industrial drill six inches in diameter, probably also stolen. The forklift's forks had been cut off. The gang attached the trailer to the car and drove toward downtown. On a side street, they parked and put on their backpacks, facemasks, and headsets. Felix drove the forklift, navigating flaming tires and other obstacles, while the others walked behind him. The streets looked familiar to Jade as they reached Pritchard Park. A couple of weeks ago, was Felix scoping out places? Jade wondered. He maneuvered the forklift past debris and looters to the bank, its front door already shattered and ATM robbed. Two security guards lay unconscious or dead. Felix drove the forklift through the glass doors. Metal twisted and glass shattered.

Jade had considered not coming. Tomorrow would be her first night at the strip club. But tonight would be a night to remember, Jade guessed, based on Felix's reactions. She wouldn't need to be armed, he said. In the end, her curiosity had compelled her to say yes.

But there was more: If they made enough money tonight, she and Martin could begin the life they dreamed. She could help her friends and family and go back to school. Either way, she'd resolved that this was her last night with Quinn and Felix. Martin had vowed it, too. Tonight, she knew hope and excitement more than fear, though a few lingering looters wearing Halloween masks gave her the creeps, especially a beefy one wearing a jack-o'-lantern mask.

Martin guarded the door while Jade followed Felix. *He's outnumbered*, Jade thought, looking back toward Martin. *I've got a bad feeling about this.*

Quinn dropped his and Martin's backpacks in the bank, dismantled the security cameras, and returned to guard the door with Martin. Felix maneuvered to the vault. Then he hooked up the water-cooled drill to the bathroom water supply, using a hose and plumbing supplies from one of the backpacks. Jade watched in amazement. He handed Jade earplugs and goggles and put on his own. "Just make sure the water keeps flowing," he said.

He began drilling through the reinforced concrete. Gray water sprayed onto the tile floor. Each hole seemed an interminable process. When at last the twelfth hole was complete and the drill stopped spinning, Jade could hear the rioting outside. Was Martin safe? Her heart fluttered. Felix prepared the explosives in the deep holes he'd drilled. When he was ready, they sought cover around the corner in the manager's office.

"Here we go, *mamacita*!" he yelled. Explosions sent shock waves and smoke rushing throughout the building. Jade clenched her teeth.

The smoke dissipated, exposing a black aperture leading toward the vault. Jade removed her goggles and earplugs and shined a flashlight into the vault, where dust was swirling. The safe deposit boxes were not so safe anymore.

"All clear," Felix said into his headset. "How's it out there?"

"Just these Halloween looters," Quinn said. "Nothing we can't handle."

"We need your help, then," Felix said.

Quinn returned, prying the boxes open with different-sized pry bars and a hammer. With Felix, Jade emptied teller cash drawers into her backpack, but eventually she grew curious about the safe deposit boxes. Amongst all the gold, platinum, jewelry, stocks, and valuable papers, she found a sapphire ring and put it in her pocket. Sometimes, she paused, curious about the owner of each box as she found titles to homes, Social Security cards, marriage licenses, birth certificates, and copies of wills.

As she cast a birth certificate aside, a feeling of regret struck her. For invading people's lives. For stealing perhaps the last valuables of families. Of people struggling. People with children. People trying to survive, just like she was.

"*Vamanos*. Finish up," Felix said as he and Quinn crammed their backpacks full.

"I'm almost done," she said, stuffing a few more gold coins and pieces of jewelry into her backpack.

"Meet you at the door," Felix said, glaring at her.

"Just one more second," she said.

Scanning the floor and moving vital family papers to the side, she found a velvet bag filled with rings and other jewelry. Knowing Felix would be angry if she delayed any longer, she pushed the velvet bag into her backpack, secured the straps, and lifted the backpack onto her back. Damn, it's heavy, she thought. Backpack secured, she heard a voice echoing indistinctly through the bank. He's so impatient, Jade thought.

But as she turned the corner to leave the vault, Felix wasn't there. Instead, she saw two armed looters, the beefy one with the jack-o'-lantern mask and another wearing a Guy Fawkes mask. Guy Fawkes raised his gun, bullets struck her in the chest, and she collapsed onto her side in a pool of gray water.

Jade's chest seared, and her wet clothes warmed with blood, mixing with the cold gray water. She felt someone remove her mask.

"Man, why'd you have to kill her?" a voice said.

"She surprised me."

"Take her backpack."

Jade felt the backpack getting yanked from her body as her consciousness faded.

EIGHTEEN
ALONE

MARTIN OPENED HIS EYES, feeling his sore body. Next to him, Quinn seemed unconscious, or even dead. Where were Felix and Jade? The looters had left with Quinn's and Felix's backpacks full of loot and their guns. Martin recalled that when Felix and Quinn had arrived, the man in the jack-o'-lantern mask yelled to several additional masked looters, all of them drawing their weapons.

"Slide us your weapons," the jack-o'-lantern had demanded.

"No way." Quinn raised his weapon. "If any of you jokers want to live, leave now."

The masked men didn't budge and kept their weapons pointed toward Felix's crew.

"Listen, fuckface. Slide over your weapons. No funny business," the jack-o'-lantern ordered. Shots rang out in the distance.

"Do what they say," Felix whispered.

Slowly, Quinn, Martin, and Felix placed their guns on the ground as the jack-o'-lantern walked forward, hitting Felix with a metal pipe he'd been hiding behind his back. Felix teetered for a second, then tumbled backward and landed motionless. The jack-o'-lantern then kicked Martin in the face with an arcing roundhouse, knocking him into the wall.

That was the last Martin recalled, and he didn't know how long he'd been unconscious. He turned around, and Felix was behind him, moving somewhat. Staggering to Quinn, Martin checked his pulse. He's alive, Martin thought, slapping him on the face a few times while saying, "Quinn, wake up." But where's Jade? He picked up his headset. "Jade, you there…? Jade…?"

Pulling out a spare gun from the small of his back, he checked for Jade in the bank. Eventually finding her body at the hole in the vault, he took off his mask and sat on his knees in front of Jade in a pool of pink-gray water. Her headset lay in the water next to her, along with one wet bill. Instinctively, he stuffed it in his pocket.

Without thinking that he might find some remaining treasure in the vault, he put on his mask, picked up Jade's body, and carried her to the bank door, where Felix and Quinn waited. Felix brandished a gun the masked looters hadn't found, and Quinn held a knife. Together, they limped and stumbled through the unruly streets toward their car. In the distance, buildings smoked, orange flames flickering from shattered windows, illuminating the low clouds above. Gunshots echoed around the city. A news drone flew toward them. Felix shot at it, and it retreated around the corner. Rain began to fall. Through the sepia-colored clouds, iRanger paratroopers descended, as if mingling with the rain. Landing in the streets, they grouped and began to march in rows through the burning streets to impose martial law. "Please go home. Violators of the curfew will be arrested," the heavily armed robots repeated.

* * *

Martin placed Jade's body in the trunk, to the consternation of Quinn and Felix. He dropped them off at the rundown house, assuring them he'd be back soon. Not caring if the cameras and Auroras detected him, he entered a grocery store and bought a dozen roses with his one banknote from the robbery.

He parked at a turnout near the French Broad River. Heavy rain continued to fall. In the distance, downtown Asheville was still ablaze and resounding with the sounds of chaos. His face throbbed where the jack-o'-lantern had kicked him. As he carried Jade's body and the roses through the woods to the river, the grief set in. By the time Martin reached the silty bank, he was soaked. A streetlight across the river cast reflections on the splashes of raindrops and the waves rippling toward shore. He'd come here with her to mourn. But it didn't come naturally. At the very least, he wanted to pay his respects as he lay her body down by the water. But he wanted more. She'd loved him like no other person. On his knees, he scooped handfuls of river water and cleaned her face and hair. He reached into his pocket and grabbed a flask of tequila. "You get the first drink," he whispered to Jade, unscrewing the top and pouring some into her mouth. "To our love." He raised the flask and downed a few shots' worth.

He couldn't bear to look at her body. I should have stopped this, he thought, rehashing the image of Jade's body in the pool of pink-gray water. She needn't have died. She could have been here still, alive with me. Fuck!

"You deserved better than me," Martin said. "I put you through so much shit. Why did you stay with me? I promised you roses, but I didn't think you'd be dead when I gave them to you." He placed the roses in her arms and sat with her.

Eventually, he tied several rocks to Jade's body and set her free into the French Broad, watching the body sink downstream.

But he wasn't ready to let go. End it all right now, he thought. He could join her in the depths of the French Broad. But then he thought about Felix. He's to blame. He convinced her to come. He left her alone in the bank. It's his fault. And Quinn's. He wanted her gone. Fuck him, too. He finished the flask of tequila and drove to the abandoned house, windshield wipers on fast.

* * *

The house door swung on its hinges and slammed into the wall. Quinn was likely in his room sleeping. Felix sat at the card table, counting the few bills he had. He stood up immediately and pointed a gun at Martin. "Calm the fuck down. Don't think I won't use this."

To Martin, this rang true. But he didn't care. Part of him wanted to die, just like Jade. "You won't kill me." Martin moved toward Felix, knife behind his back.

"I'll kill you easy."

While Felix was still speaking, Martin stepped in and aside, twisting the gun until it fell from Felix's hands onto the floor. Martin kicked the gun away and pushed Felix onto the table, thrusting with the knife and piercing Felix's right hand, causing his blood to splatter. Felix punched Martin with his other hand as Martin ripped the knife free. In the ruckus, Martin saw Quinn's door opening. Shit.

Martin ran toward their car.

Gunshots.

Knowing he couldn't get in the car without Felix and Quinn shooting him, he turned right, running through overgrown yards. From the street, Felix yelled, "You're a dead man! I swear to the Virgin. You're a dead man."

Martin ran through the wet darkness, slipping through vines, his arms sliced by blackberry thorns. He entered a culvert and slouched, splashing through flowing water, pushing through brush and spiderwebs, following the water through neighborhoods and under more culverts. Eventually, he collapsed on his back, hyperventilating. He stared at the trees reaching into the sky as the rain stopped. Felix won't find me here. But now, here he was, alone, broke, hungry, with no partners in crime, no lover, no car. Nothing. Just his bloody clothes, an empty wallet, and a bloody knife.

* * *

Martin had never felt so alone. Fog settled in the Asheville basin as well as inside Martin, or so it seemed. The world appeared hostile, unforgiving. And he refused to forgive the world, or anyone. He guessed Felix would track him down. Once Felix made a vow, he stuck with it. Thinking of that, it struck Martin that he almost hadn't kept the second promise he'd made to Jade: no more killing. When he returned to the house, he'd forgotten the vow. His intention was to kill. If Quinn hadn't awakened, maybe both his former partners would be dead. Oh, man, what have I done?

In one day, this day of hell, his life had turned inside out. His head throbbed. When he closed his eyes, mental impressions of the day—far too many to process—plagued him. He couldn't sleep, and insects crawled on his skin. Above him in the foggy canopy of trees, a cicada called its mate. To Martin, it seemed like an annoying siren, unceasing. He shivered in the cold fog. The buzz of the cicada continued. Shut up. Leave me the fuck alone.

In the morning, mosquitoes and gnats swarmed his tired body, probing for blood and blitzing his itchy eyes. His face was sore, his mouth dry, and his stomach tight and complaining. Could he find food at one of the refugee camps? He looked at his clothes, covered in blood. No one would want to help. He was a monster. A scarred face with a mangled left ear. A killer. An outcast. And surely, they would require him to identify himself. He slid down an embankment to the creek he'd followed the night before, thrust his face into the water, and slurped the cool liquid until his stomach swelled. Swatting at the insects, he stripped and washed, then rinsed and wrung his white T-shirt and jeans.

Wearing his wet clothes, he walked to the nearest road, knowing only that he was somewhere west of Asheville. Eventually, the fog lifted. By the time he reached Patton Avenue, he was sweating, and the moist jeans were chafing at his skin. He followed the congested multi-lane street by walking through strip mall parking lots. He peered into parked cars, seeing if he could find anything of value. Shoppers stared at him, shocked, he imagined, at his grotesqueness. Worse yet, they might alert the police. He ignored their stares but felt the shame of his scars. The shame reminded him of how Jade had accepted him. That brief moment felt like a refuge, until loneliness arose again.

Are Felix and Quinn looking for me? They had guns, and he'd be at their mercy. He continually checked for their vehicle and for the police but was self-conscious of looking paranoid and suspicious.

At last, he reached the periphery of Asheville. An iRanger patrolled across the street. Shit, a robot. Martin recalled his experience at the New Mexico border. He turned his face away to avoid detection. But suddenly, the iRanger pointed a gun toward him. Identity recognized. "Don't move. Hands up," the robot said.

Martin raised his hands. The robot called for reinforcements and ran into traffic, but an Asheville Regional Transit bus blocked its path. Martin hurried through a parking lot and behind an abandoned commercial building. The iRanger ran around the bus, calling after him. Martin jumped a fence and rounded the corner of the building, where he found heaps of discarded construction materials. He yanked a piece of rebar embedded in a pile and waited behind the corner, knowing he was unable to outrun a robot. The iRanger turned the corner, but not carefully enough. Martin knocked the gun from its hands, then swung at the robot's head, only to have it duck. Retractable blades emerged from the tops of its hands, and the robot slashed. Martin parried the knives with the rebar, keeping his distance, moving quickly from side to side. Pepper spray squirted from the iRanger's shoulders. Martin covered his face and backed away toward the pile of scrap metal, coughing and feeling the burning spray on his forearms. He hurled a brick, denting the bulletproof armor and knocking the robot off balance. In that moment, Martin picked up a cinderblock over his head, charged, and launched it at the robot's face. Simultaneously, the robot shot a stun gun from his wrist at Martin, hitting him in the chest. The robot's head cracked to the side and its body collapsed to the ground, out of commission. Martin clenched his teeth, his body momentarily paralyzed.

Once he recovered, he pulled the stun gun's steel barbs from his chest, grabbed the robot's gun, jumped a barbed wire fence, and ran down the sinewy roads of the Chicken Hill neighborhood past outdated postmodern homes. As the road leveled out, he reached the old graffiti-covered warehouses of the River Arts District. Finally, thinking himself safe, legs exhausted as he turned west onto Haywood Avenue, he slowed his pace. He walked across the bridge over the French Broad, which was flowing chocolate brown. Below him, dozens of people canoed, tubed, kayaked, and paddle-boarded, seemingly unperturbed by recent events. In front of him, he saw blue flashes and heard distant sirens from the heights of West Asheville. He looked behind him. Nothing yet. But he couldn't chance doubling back, and the bridge was long. With no other option, he secured the gun in his jeans, jumped the railing, and dove into the water.

Letting the river take him, he floated downstream, looking into the blue sky. Part of him relaxed, as if surrendering to the water, wherever it took him. He thought about Jade's body below the surface. He'd released it just a few hundred yards upstream from here. Another part of him couldn't escape his discomforts—the hunger, the headache, the worries, the desire for revenge, the anger.

And still another part knew he needed to get away from Asheville, the iRangers, Quinn, and Felix.

A group tubed down the river, drinking beer. They were ripe for the picking, but one woman reminded him of Jade. "I can't do it," he muttered, swimming to shore. "I can't do this anymore." Intense sadness overcame him. He pulled the gun from his jeans and aimed it at his head.

"Don't do it!" the tubers called. "We love you. Please don't."

Ashamed, he tucked the gun away and maneuvered through a dense thicket along a stream. He crossed Riverside Drive, slipped through a broken fence, and sprinted across the interstate. A driver swerved and honked. Following the stream, he entered a neighborhood and scrambled through vines and brambles up a forested slope to the edge of a thriving community garden. He crawled to a tomato plant and picked a juicy heirloom. The rich, deep, sweet, and slightly acidic juices ran down his face as he devoured it. Somehow, the tomato was something to live for. He thought of Jade, how she would never have thought about suicide. She'd lived even the dark moments fully. He took out the gun again, looked at it, and threw it into the forest.

NINETEEN
RAISING DAY

THE SOUTHERN BLUE RIDGE MOUNTAINS BEFORE HIM, Baba sat on an outcrop overlooking Firefly Cove, his eyes half-closed, his spine straight, and his beard flowing in the breeze. His mind was clear and crisp.

An ineffable moment.

In words lie difference and distinction. To a person living in a New York City apartment, such an experience might be described as oneness with God; to a man in Shanghai, that same moment might conjure feelings of basic goodness; to others, it might suggest consciousness or pure mind or *just this*. But no matter what combination of words is used to communicate the ineffable moment, a boundless state of non-dual wisdom can be experienced by anyone, at any moment, anywhere.

* * *

In their Asheville office, Hernandez and McCormick played dozens of video sequences in their Auroras, sent from the chip manufacturer's surveillance center.

"So, who's the Scalpel?" a newcomer asked during one sequence.

"Will Robin," replied another. "You going to do it?"

Other clips captured over the last two months—between June 16 and August 4—were Harriet's conversation with Will, several brief conversations mentioning Will indirectly, and sixty-three clips, audio only, of the actual removal of Auroras from blindfolded patients. The clues were many: soft sounds and mutterings, a pain meter and other brainwave readings showing anxiety, the injection of anesthetic into the top of the scalp, discomfort at the time of the incision, followed by no more signal from the Aurora.

Hernandez watched and listened in a daze. His sockets were darkened from sleep deprivation. Electronic files from dozens of cases were stored on his Aurora. Cirrus's IRIS and her cloud servers processed the clues, suspects, and evidence and provided a memory recall that agents just a decade ago would have envied. Still, he needed to watch the videos and verify the evidence. He swiped away the video in his mind. *Damn these videos. I just want to be home with my family.*

"Looks like they have probable cause," Special Agent McCormick said, looking through the official complaint affidavit from Cirrus. "At least sixty-three counts. Didn't I warn the boy? No respect."

"I'll submit the affidavit to the DA," Hernandez said.

"Go ahead and do that," McCormick said. "Any more evidence on Firefly Cove?"

"Not since our Scalpel friend removed all the chips."

"Not all. What about visitors or tourists?"

"They never uncover anything," Hernandez said.

"This nuisance thinks he's too smart for us. Let's teach him a lesson. And while you're at it, look into his probation officer. He's useless."

Like I have time, Hernandez thought.

* * *

"Howdy, Grace. Where's your son?" Probation Officer Mathis said at her front door. "I have a warrant for his arrest."

"He hasn't done anything, Mr. Mathis."

"He's been charged with violating his probation and multiple felony counts of unauthorized practice of medicine—removing Aurora chips."

"Where'd they get evidence for that?"

"Cirrus."

"The Aurora makers? Tell them to shove their chips up their you-know-where."

"Grace, you know it's better if Will works with me on this one. You, too."

"He's all I've got."

"I know. That's why Will should surrender to me, because if Scalpels don't comply, I hear Cirrus sends an assassin. Never experienced it myself because we're in the country, and the Aurora ain't as popular out here."

"Why don't the police do something about those assassins?"

"They've got enough to worry about. Besides, no one's been able to prosecute an assassin. We don't really know they exist. But somehow, Scalpels end up killed," Mathis said. "His trial is set to begin as soon as he turns himself in. They've got plenty of room now that they opened the makeshift prison camps to house inmates."

"He's left the Cove, Mr. Mathis."

* * *

"Smells like Lita's mole sauce, Ma," Will said, entering the kitchen. "You said you'd tell me her secret someday."

"Banana," Grace replied, stirring the sauce.

"Banana?"

"Yes. I bartered for some. The other ingredients were difficult to find. Want to help with the chocolate?"

"You have chocolate!" Will thought about how the Cove would need to make a decision about the upcoming food scarcity. Rationing seemed the only logical solution as a way for all to survive the winter. But how to do that? That was the main question.

As they cooked, he ruminated about the extravagance of the meal. With the declining influence of the American dollar and increased global demand, imported foods such as cacao beans had spiked in price, making chocolate a rare treat for many.

Grace poured the sauce over the black bean enchiladas, and his mouth watered. "What's the special occasion?"

Grace looked into Will's eyes, rubbing her hand through his short Afro and across his cheek. Her eyes shone with love, but Will noticed something else, too—fear. "Mr. Mathis came here with an arrest warrant."

Will's heart jumped and his face flushed. "Because of...me being a Scalpel?"

Grace nodded. "I told him you'd left the Cove."

"You lied? You never lie."

"Well, I changed my mind. I'd rather lie than lose you. I didn't know what to do. I'm sorry, but you're getting yourself into too much trouble."

"It'll be all right," Will said to soothe his mother, though inside a nervous energy pervaded.

"Can't you just stop what you're doing?"

"The cops won't catch me out here. You can see them coming on the road, and it's easy to hide," Will said, finding some solace in the truth of his words. "Let's just eat, okay? Where are the Sanderses?"

"They were invited for dinner with friends. I'm relieved to have some time alone. You know it hasn't been easy, honey." She looked at him, frustrated. "It's challenging having the four of them in our house. They're living where I'd set up my studio, my creative spot. It took me so long to get my creativity back. Now, I feel blocked again. I resent them being here. I don't want to be unkind, but that's how I feel. I want my creative space and privacy back."

"I can understand that. You're an artist."

"You get it. It's got the best light. But I'm managing to work in the bedroom."

"How can you paint during all the chaos, while others are working on survival?"

"There's still a need for art. Art isn't a luxury. It's a part of our humanity." She tied her long dreads behind her head. "I've sold a few paintings, too."

"Awesome." Then Will frowned. "I regret if this has been difficult for you, Mom."

"It has. I just wish we'd talked about it beforehand."

Will's face flushed. Grace fidgeted with the silverware. Will imagined her anger and frustration were shifting after hearing his regrets.

"It's okay, really. I'm thankful you showed generosity. I see such courage in you, in how you care for others." She smiled, and her eyes conveyed warmth. "I'm glad we're talking about it finally. I've wanted to, but we haven't had any alone time."

Will sighed. "I know."

"Mathis said if you don't turn yourself in, Cirrus will probably try to kill you. Up to you, he said."

"I'm not going to turn myself in," Will said. "What I'm doing isn't wrong, can't you see? The police and the government are corrupt. They've imposed martial law. Military robots are everywhere now. Do you really believe I should turn myself in?"

"No. I'm just worried no matter what you do," she said, laughing nervously.

Will couldn't expect his mother to answer differently. He considered his situation. With no Auroras remaining in Firefly Cove, detecting his whereabouts would be difficult, he imagined, even for Cirrus. Cirrus didn't use drones, supposedly—too many legal issues, regulations, chances for error, and PR problems. They didn't need drones anyway, with hundreds of millions of active Auroras as their eyes. Except in Firefly Cove.

He thought of the assassin, and his body tensed.

Grace looked up from her meal. "What, Tenzi?"

"Nothing."

* * *

For fifty days, Harriet had meditated, gardened, and eaten a raw foods diet. Her insulin use was now one-sixth of what she'd taken before her diet shift. She no longer craved the ice cream in the freezer—as much. She'd cheated a couple of times. In the beginning, she couldn't tell what was more challenging, the diet or no Aurora. But even after her original thirty-day commitment, she saw the diet's benefits and committed to eating healthily.

"How are you holding up today?" Dr. Adams asked after checking her vital signs. Her blood pressure was down and slowly approaching the ideal upper limit.

Harriet felt a wave of feelings. She answered, "Not so good."

"Do you want to talk about it?"

Eventually, she was able to speak. "I feel so stupid crying, but I can't help it." She sniffled.

"It's okay to cry. You're grieving, transforming, detoxing, and transitioning all at once. I needed to cry when I first began."

"You mean, you once . . . ?"

"Yes. I lashed out at others, had nightmares and breakdowns, and couldn't handle my emotions. That fades with time."

"I'm not sure I can do it." Harriet wiped her eyes and nose with a tissue. "I'm a mess."

"You *can* do it, Harriet. The first couple months are always the hardest."

Walking through the forest garden later, Harriet felt younger—clean, clear, and grounded in her new, simple life. The tears had released another layer of old tensions. Despite her mood swings, she now knew she was over the hump. I can do it.

She looked to the south down the slope at the farthest house under construction—their future home. The sooner we can move in, the better. A few people were constructing the house's walls, filling out the flesh of the structure. She loved the location, tucked amongst well-pruned fruit trees of the forest garden on the edge of the pasture. She wanted a garden in the sunny front yard. I take it all back, God. Anything bad I ever said about this place, I take it back.

Harriet lay down in a soft, mossy patch in the forest garden while Jack and other newcomers, under the direction of the Post & Gear's master carpenter, chiseled and honed the finishing touches on mortise and tenon joints at the co-housing project a football field's length away. Removing his Aurora had been challenging for Jack before he met Eli, a young man who'd moved to the village with his local parents at the age of six, just after Joe Boggs became the village manager. Eli worked at the Post & Gear, a wood, stone, and metal business on the village green, between the Hive and Firefly Integrated Medicine. Since meeting Eli, Jack worked there most days, and Harriet had noticed his spirits rise, as though he'd found his sense of purpose again. In dappled sunlight, she daydreamed of Jack making love to her on their bed in their new house. The setting was perfect, with candles illuminating their bodies, fresh sheets, and flowers. He touched her body in all the right ways, and in the end, she climaxed.

If only that happened.

At the co-housing project, Post & Gear workers and newcomer volunteers assembled the posts and beams, securing them with wooden pegs to make the bents. They carefully prepared ropes and pulleys, an A-frame, and block and tackle. Today was raising day.

"Can I help?" Harriet asked as Jack and other workers prepared the first bent for raising. She joined the line of rope pullers behind Jack, patting him on his rear. He turned around and smiled. Harriet was relieved at his smile, and their marital tensions faded away, for now. Still, they hadn't talked as much as she would have liked.

"Heave," they said in unison. The rope chafed Harriet's hands as she leaned back and the bent rose from the ground. Other workers pushed with pike poles or cheered them on until the first bent stood before them.

"That was hard," she said, her muscles aching.

"You don't need to keep doing it," Jack said.

"I know. You don't either," she said, more disconnected at their exchange of words.

"You're right," he said.

"And I want to help, too," she said firmly. "Can I just get a hug? I need a hug."

"I'd like that, too," Jack said.

She nestled her head into his muscular chest. His arms wrapped around her. His strength comforted her, and for the first time in a while, she had the sense of being safe. They embraced until the next bent was ready for raising.

One by one, the bents for the first floor stood. Harriet continued to heave on the rope even as her blisters popped. More and more villagers arrived to help, watch, and cheer. As the long, south-facing form of the co-housing began to manifest, helpers worked as one, moving the A-frame to the second floor and raising its posts and beams. At the end of the day, the entire timber frame was in place, bones ready for flesh, organs, and skin. Leaf nailed a fresh white pine branch, a wetting bush, to the highest point on the frame, a tradition that honored the trees that were transformed into the structure.

"Bless this building for all who live here. May they have a long and happy life," Yeshe said before the feast and celebration.

TWENTY
ANGER AND FEAR

TARA AND WILL RODE ON HORSEBACK along a ridge, still within earshot of hammering at the co-housing structure. Tara rode Cajun. Will followed on Cajun's sibling, Ranger, who traipsed up the first switchbacks and soon grew comfortable with Will's soothing words. They traversed the slopes of Eagle Mountain, seeking a couple days of seclusion in the midst of increasing chaos. Tara wanted Will to leave his worries behind for a change and had convinced him that they'd go far away from where the Aurora assassin would look.

By late afternoon, they ascended into Pisgah National Forest, where cascades flowed through twisted rhododendron. They undressed next to a swirling pool. Will sank in, feeling the pure, cold waters enliven his sweaty skin. Tara dove in. They laughed, splashing and chasing one another as though in a courtship dance. At last, they embraced. Tara moaned with desire, closing her eyes as Will bit and kissed her firm nipples and held her firmly with his strong hands. Tara slid her arms down Will's muscular torso and pulled his hips toward hers.

They tumbled onto a mossy bank, kissing, touching, and stroking. "Make love with me," she whispered. Will kissed her neck. This was the way they wanted sex to be: amidst the fertile ripeness of lush life. They'd brought condoms. Will lay back on the moss, and Tara straddled his hips. Slowly and deeply, she thrust, rubbing her body into his. He felt her wet movements sliding up and down his penis, staying aware of the pleasure, a light energy that tingled. He exhaled deeply, circulating the energy throughout his body.

Her thrusts quickened and deepened, and his entire body throbbed with sexual energy. Tara began to tremble and moan, softly at first, then louder. Her body contracted and writhed. Feeling her, he released his energy as they climaxed together.

"I loved watching you with your eyes closed," Will said as they rested on the mossy bank, looking through the canopy into the sky. "Your bliss turned me on even more, and I lost myself completely." He looked her in the eyes, raising his eyebrows. "I'd like to play around with this more with you."

"Oh, you would, would you?"

"Of course. Sacred sexuality is important to me."

"Me, too," Tara said.

That evening, Will was ecstatic. His connection with Tara had reached new heights. They were both immersed in their love. Every activity, no matter how simple, seemed to be a reflection of this energy. Their horses tethered just below a rocky glade, they cooked dinner over glowing embers. The full moon illuminated gnarled, windswept trees in ivory light as they made love again in the tent and collapsed with exhaustion into an early sleep.

A familiar nightmare resurfaced during Will's slumber. At Mission Hospital, Agent McCormick was striking him, pushing him down, and forcing him into a straitjacket. The entire scene recurred until the surgeon forced a mask onto his face. He awoke with a startle, sitting up and clasping his body tightly with his arms. The moon filtered through the tent fabric.

"What are you doing?" Tara asked, clearing her throat.

"I had a nightmare."

She sat up and touched his arms. Suddenly, a sensation arose in Will, a strong urge to flee. "I gotta do this."

He ran into the glade, jumping from rock to rock, naked and alive in the cool, high-elevation air. He ran as thoughts of the nightmare dissipated, replaced by exhilaration, a shot of adrenaline. A few minutes later, he climbed a rock face. At the top, Will howled with the Milky Way as a backdrop. Tara howled back, and he returned to her embrace lighter, freer from the shackles of his past.

The next day, they entered a clearcut that stretched to the ridgeline far above. Tara dismounted at the sight of the forest she'd fought to protect for months. She sat and closed her eyes, unable to look at the ground, the stumps, and the logging roads. Will sat next to her. Finally, she spoke. "I didn't think I could bear seeing this."

For decades, the national forests of the Southern Blue Ridge had grown and matured. But with internal weakness in America, the dollar depreciated in value against the euro, the yen, China's digital currency, the blockchain yuan, and other foreign currencies. This favored the exporting of forest products to Asia and elsewhere. The logs went to Vietnam to make furniture.

"I just wish people had..." Tara stopped speaking and looked down.

"Had what?"

"Had... I want to blame our past generations. I want to yell out how stupid they were. How greedy they were."

"Why don't you do that? I'll support you."

With that, Tara lashed out. She threw dirt, hit stumps with her fists, and yelled all her grievances. Will stayed present, putting his attention on her. Eventually, he noticed her anger subsiding.

"Thanks for that." Tara's eyes watered with joy.

"Of course. Remember what Yeshe once told us about anger? How it hides fear? I had this thought that you fear what people are doing to this planet."

"Yes. What we've done. And what we're doing. We're destroying ourselves, and I fear that we won't make it through this. I want to grow old with you. I'd like to have kids, too. Yet when I think of our world, I get anxious and can't imagine bringing a child into this hell. There's so much suffering, my heart aches."

"What's that like?"

"It's raw. I fear being vulnerable in times like this. But if I close myself up, I just become angry. That's why I paused. It was too scary to go there, until you gave me your support, told me it was all right." She smiled in gratitude.

"What else?"

"Once the anger went away, I was sad. We have this jewel"—Tara waved her arms toward the Blue Ridge before her—"but we've broken it to pieces. In the end, my mind cleared, and I had this rush of compassion. That's when I cried. But I cried for us all. And that, to me, was amazing, because Yeshe talked about how anger can be transformed, but I never experienced it so vividly until now."

In the clearcut, seedlings of oaks, maples, poplars, pines, and hickories and resprouting trees grew, regenerating the forest.

* * *

"She's cute," Tara said. They'd returned from their horseback journey just the evening before and were now helping pick blueberries in Firefly Cove's berry terraces.

"Who?" Will asked.

"The newcomer I was just picking berries with. Over there," she said. "You know I'm okay if you're attracted to other people."

Will hesitated and picked a handful of blueberries. He looked at the newcomer, who was leaving with a full container, and remembered removing her Aurora and connecting with her afterward. His face flushed, thinking that revealing his attraction could lead to jealousy, conflict, and a broken relationship. "She *is* cute," Will said. "Do you want her?"

"Now, you're taking it to another level." Tara grinned. "What if I say yes? You know I've been with other women before, right? Parvati, for one. You don't believe me, do you? Well, it's true. You and me, we've shared the same woman. Anyone's fair game."

"Anyone?" Will raised his eyebrows. "That could get interesting."

"Well, maybe not anyone."

"Yeah, I thought you were exaggerating. Still, I'm relieved at your openness." Compared to Tara, Will judged himself to be constricted. But with the constriction came pressure. The pressure was not one of tamping down desire. Instead, it was like a lit firework about to soar into the sky and explode into a flurry of color. Then he remembered Aja. "I've been having dreams of Aja," he admitted.

"Aja?" Tara asked.

"The Aurora avatar."

"Still? Why are you bringing it up now? Do you want her?"

"In my dreams, I do," he said. "It's confusing to me, because I want you to be the one in my dreams, but every time it's been her."

The playfulness left Tara for a moment, but then she smiled. "Your dreams are just symbolic imagery, so how can I be jealous?"

"For a second, you wanted to be the one in my dreams, didn't you?"

"No doubt," she laughed, winking at Will. "I admit it, I'm jealous. Does that make me crazy?"

"Yes," Will said, his eyebrows rising playfully. "You and the millions of other people who are jealous of Aurora Friends."

* * *

Joe Boggs and his apprentices tracked deer in the alluvial forests adjacent to Otter Creek. The deer still followed a historical fence even though its wood had long since decomposed, leaving traces of barbed wire above the thick humus and embedded deep in older trees. The tree seedlings along this trail were heavily browsed. Joe picked the first ripe pawpaw of the season, cutting it in half to share. "It's the American mango," he said, enjoying its creamy, sweet texture. They were two months into the training and had grown comfortable with being in the woods. He'd been wrong about these city folks.

Joe found fresh human footprints. He whispered for the newcomers to sit and wait while he investigated. If this here's a sang hunter, he's a mite early, Joe thought. He was used to ginseng hunters who trespassed with abandon, seeking the root renowned in Asia as a cooling herb, a yin tonic good for chi—life force. Firefly Cove had plenty of sang, and Joe spent hours fighting off poachers, monitoring boundaries and trails with over thirty well-placed motion-activated miniature camera traps.

Something ain't right. One step at a time, Joe's moccasins silently touched the earth. Light filtered through the leaves rustling in the wind, creating a shifting mosaic of light and dark on the forest floor.

Joe crouched in the shrubs and followed where the tracks led—directly toward the village. This ain't no sang hunter. He scanned the shrubs, the ferns, the tall herbs. Was someone there? A breeze tickled the leaves, moving the shadows and shifting the light. He drew his knife and moved forward, careful not to focus only on the tracks, lest someone catch him off guard.

Just ahead was the edge of the forest, with clear views of the village. Amongst a patch of goldenrods and other herbs, a camouflaged man was attaching a high-powered rail gun to a tripod. Now wasn't the time for thinking, for wondering why the man was here with such a weapon. Now was the time to act.

The camouflage clothing covered a muscular body that moved with precision. Once the rail gun was set, the man examined a computer display. Joe moved to within thirty feet, stopped, and lay prone. He didn't move, didn't think, didn't want to breathe. At last, the man looked through the scope, searching the village.

Joe looked at his knife, a razor-sharp four-inch blade—much shorter than he wanted for the situation. He had never killed a man before, only game. He smeared his face, blond hair, beard, and hands with dirt before moving forward slowly on his belly. Twenty feet away, he stopped, sensing the man was about to pull the trigger. Instinctively, Joe jumped to his feet and ran toward the gunman. His moccasin cracked a stick the instant before the gunman fired several shots. The gunman pulled a pistol from its holster and turned, but Joe kicked his hand, sending the gun into the goldenrod.

* * *

Tara fed Will a blueberry, and he savored it, tasting its sweet tartness. Then, like cracking whips, bullets sliced through blueberry branches next to them. Tara pushed Will to the ground, and they crawled behind a bush.

He missed, Will thought. Don't give him another shot. He looked through the blueberry bushes toward the alluvial forests, slightly downhill from them. The shots came from there. Stay put. He anticipated seeing the assassin emerge from the forest and into the fields below but saw no one and wondered if the assassin was flanking them.

Tara lay next to him. "I'm not leaving you."

"You need to go," Will said. "He's after me, not you."

"I'm staying. Might as well die in love."

"No need to be a martyr."

* * *

Joe thrust his knife at the assassin's chest, but the gunman dodged and used Joe's momentum to force him to the ground. Joe hit the moist soil and groaned. The man kicked him in his kidney. Joe rolled away, grabbed a handful of dirt, and threw it into the assassin's face. "This is private property. You don't have the right to be here." Joe felt a wave of nausea from the pain in his kidney. "You're trying to kill Will, right?"

The assassin rubbed the soil from his eyes. "None of your business."

"It is my business. I live here." Joe watched the man back up toward the gun and knew he had to act. He rose to his feet, holding his knife behind his back. With little time, he threw underhanded toward the assassin's chest. The assassin dodged, but not fast enough. The blade sliced his trapezoid. Joe rushed forward like a razorback, knocking him down, landing on him, and head-butting him. The assassin swept his legs over and forced Joe backward. They regained their balance and stood facing one another.

"I'll give you credit for finding me. But you're a lousy fighter."

"You're the one bleedin'," Joe said, breathing heavily.

They punched and dodged each other. Unable to penetrate the assassin's defenses, Joe grabbed a freshly fallen branch and flailed at his face, hitting his forearms and side. The assassin backed away and picked up a longer spearlike branch. He thrust it at Joe, who jumped onto a moss-covered log. Unable to get within striking distance with his smaller branch, he parried the thrusts. But the assassin swung low, hitting Joe's left ankle, and he fell backward behind the log. The assassin jumped onto the log and swung again, striking Joe's face. Blood dripped from his mouth, and Joe knew his jaw was broken. The assassin jumped from the log and kicked him in the face. Joe dropped to the ground, almost unconscious.

"Now who's the one bleeding?" the assassin said.

Joe inched slowly backward to where his knife lay a few feet away.

The assassin jumped and picked it up. "Looking for this?" he said, holding the knife. He pushed the spearlike branch into Joe's throat.

"Just do yer job, asshole," Joe croaked under the pressure, blood dripping from his lips.

Suddenly, several rocks hummed through the air. One hit the assassin in the head, and he crumpled to the ground.

"Nice shot, Russell," one of the newcomers said.

"Joe, are you all right? We came as soon as we heard the fighting," another tracker student said as he jumped over the log with the others, each holding a couple of stones.

Next to the assassin's rail gun, acrid smoke poured from the computer as it self-destructed.

TWENTY-ONE
MOST PRIMAL FORM

"I'M GLAD YOU'RE ALIVE." Joe's speech was slurred, and he spoke with difficulty as he lay in his bed. The bedroom was spotless—a credit to his wife, not to the man who spent much of his life outdoors. Stained wooden posts and beams framed white walls decorated with family photographs, including many of Leaf and Sam when they were younger. Lacy curtains decorated the south-facing windows, and filtered sunlight lightened the room. Joe had crafted shelves, the bed, and all the other furniture at the Post & Gear. His joinery work was exquisite.

"Thanks to you," Will said. "I'd be dead without you. Makes me think of how fragile life is. You could have easily been somewhere else at that moment, and he'd have killed me, just like he killed my father." He was unsure if this was the same assassin who had killed his father, but he assumed so. "I'm happy you're alive, too."

"Appreciate you," Joe said.

"So, how's the jaw?"

"Doc wired me shut." He opened his mouth.

"Looks nasty," Will said, seeing the metal wires tied through the bloody gums into the bone.

"That's a tough sonabitch." Joe drooled onto his pillow. "But I hit him good, too."

"I'm sorry," Will said. "This whole thing's my fault. I put you and everyone else in danger." He thought about the assassin, now caged in the Cove. "I don't know what to do."

"Don't worry about me. I need some practice fighting, that's all. As for you, no one's going to rat on you. My moonshiner ancestors knew to keep their mouths shut. So do I. Nothing but trouble if you don't, and I don't want the government to know anything I do. I don't want them to know anything you do. And I sure as hell don't want anyone spying on us with Auroras. That sonabitch wasn't chipped, you know."

"So he can be anonymous, I imagine," Will said.

With difficulty, Joe reached toward his bedside table, pushing aside a small stack of novels and wrapping his hand around a half-filled mug. He popped an ibuprofen tablet into his mouth and swallowed it with a gulp of warm coffee, then plonked the mug back in its place. "I'd like you to take my gun," he said, reaching for it between the mattress and box springs.

"I don't want your gun."

"Come on. Don't be naïve. He killed your father. Haven't you thought about killing him?" Joe aimed his gun as if he were shooting the assassin.

"I have." Will flushed slightly. "But I don't want to kill him."

"Here. Take my gun. It's loaded. And a couple boxes of ammo. Just in case." He placed the gun, a semiautomatic pistol, in Will's right hand.

Looking reluctant, Will checked the safety.

"It's on. Now's the time to be the man you already are," Joe said.

* * *

"Teach me how to shoot," Will said to Leaf a few days later. They'd just finished their farmwork. Leaf leaned against the open barn door, and Will sat on a stool.

"Your father taught you nonviolence," Leaf said. "I don't feel comfortable—"

"*Your* father gave me his gun." Will revealed Joe's gun and pointed it toward the barn wall. "The assassin's right there, you know." Thinking of the assassin confined in an adjacent room, right behind the wall where he was aiming, Will was disquieted. He spoke more softly, self-conscious. "He's ready to escape and kill me. I've thought this through. I can keep being nonviolent, but that seems like a death wish. He'll kill again, so I want to be prepared to kill him. Only if I need to."

"Will, I understand what you're saying," Leaf said. "But not everyone needs to pick up a weapon. You keep people like me in balance. Without people like you, the Cove wouldn't be what it is."

"Since I've been back, I've just brought trouble to the Cove. I could call the cops. One call and I could end all this."

"No way. No cops," Leaf said. "They'll send you to one of those prison camps. That's a nightmare."

"So is this," Will said.

"Just don't call the cops."

"Train me to shoot, then."

"Okay, fine."

Leaf looked out the open barn door toward the dozens of refugee tents filling the upper pasture. "I was wrong," he said. "Our world is changing and will never be the same. I didn't believe any of this would happen. I just joked about it. But it's not a joke. Did you ever expect to see this? In the Cove? I didn't. I don't think our ancestors ever envisioned the world we live in. It's fucked up."

"Even so, we can help." Will grew animated. "We have abundance here. We're prepared for this."

"Are we? I doubt it."

Will grew silent, unsure of what to say.

"More people keep coming, and the situation keeps getting worse everywhere. We won't have enough food to last this winter," Leaf said. "We've got new mouths to feed, and our village made a commitment not to hoard, remember? We're sending food to Asheville. That's where the greatest need seems to be. And we're still selling as usual at the farmers' markets. My dad's not happy about that. I'm not either."

"I hear that you don't like it, but people in Asheville depend on us. We can't just stop what we do without people starving. We can make it work. I'm willing to eat one meal a day, if that's what it takes. These are our brothers and sisters."

"I know. They're Americans. But I'm skeptical. I'm a melancholy wild man, I guess. I'm laughing now, but it's not really funny. My family works their butts off to put food on the table. But now, with all the newcomers here, half of it will go to feed them."

"So that we all have equal portions," Will said.

"Right. I know. It's just so complicated."

"Complicated? Why?"

"Because I'm torn," Leaf said, kicking up barn dust in exasperation. "I don't want anyone to starve. But I want to keep the food I foraged and trapped for my family. I want to keep the money I've earned. I feel so selfish, and it's uncomfortable, because I know they need my help. I was brought up to help others. But I was taught to help myself and my family first. This year is testing all that. I want to be generous, but at the same time it seems stupid to give away so much food and go hungry."

"If you're eating normal-sized meals while other people are starving, is that right?"

"No, it's not right," Leaf said, sighing. "Honestly, I'm just scared of what's to come."

"Me, too, friend. Me, too."

* * *

Later that day in a forest clearing, Leaf placed Will's fingers on the gun, wrapping both of his hands around it. "Your shoulders and hips need to be square. Hold the gun like this." He turned Will's thumbs until they pointed toward a circular tin target hanging from a wooden frame. "Relax your arms."

Will pulled the trigger. The bullet hit just below the target.

"Not bad for your first shot. Pull the trigger straight back, and keep your hands still. Look at the target. Don't think. Just do it. Try again."

Will raised the gun with both arms fully extended, focused on the tin, and fired. The tin sounded a hit.

* * *

During his third day of shooting practice, Will was distracted by his thoughts. In those moments, he missed the target every time. Enough of this, he thought, stopping to meditate. When his mind was clearer, he focused only on aiming, not on hitting the target, not on the recoil of the gun. He pulled the trigger, and the bullet penetrated a can through its heart. It fell to the ground with a metallic clink.

He wanted to shoot. This posed a challenge, as he had to embrace the paradox that in his hands was a deadly weapon, and his intention was to kill the assassin if he needed to. He exhaled, calmed his thoughts, and squeezed the trigger. Another hit.

* * *

"Do you need to do anything?" Yeshe sipped a cup of tea in her living room, sitting cross-legged close to Baba on the divan. "Can you simply see what unfolds?"

"I need..." Will thought about what Yeshe said. "I could see what unfolds, but..."

"But what?" asked Baba.

"I'll probably be killed."

Baba nodded as a silent reply.

"Baba, I remember what you taught me. That I can transform my fear to love. That death is inevitable, of course. I know I'm probably just clinging to my sense of self and fear death. But that's as far as I get."

"What about life?" Yeshe asked.

"What do you mean?"

"You say you fear death, but what about life?"

Will looked around as he considered Yeshe's question. "Yes. You're right. I'm not living. I'm just fearful and anxious. We've moved out of our house, thinking another assassin might come. Or some drone attack. Or a satellite laser. I've thought of all the various ways they could kill me. I'm camping away from the village, just to make sure everyone's safe. I made sure Mom and the Sanders family found safe places to stay. Am I being prudent or paranoid? Sometimes, it's hard to tell. So, yes, I'm having a hard time accepting what's going on."

"I'm curious. Can you tell me more about that?" Yeshe asked.

"I don't know." Will frowned and shut his eyes. "I feel closed down and boxed in. The world seems threatening. And it *is* threatening, not just to me, but to others, too."

"Kill the killer, right now," Baba said.

"What?"

"Kill the killer, right now."

"Kill the assassin?"

"You'd like me to answer this, but do you feel it would be right?"

"Yes and no. Knowing you, there are likely multiple layers. If I kill the assassin, then I've killed the killer. But this doesn't solve anything. More assassins will come. It's an entire corporation behind this, not just one man. On another level, there's the part of the assassin that kills. It's not the assassin, but the assassin's beliefs and actions that need killing. The assassin's views aren't going to change anytime soon, it seems, so I can't kill the killer that way either. On another level... Well, I'm guessing there's more."

"Can you kill the storyline?"

"Even if I did, he'd still try to kill me. There's nothing I can do about that. If I stop removing Auroras, maybe he wouldn't kill me. But I'd be doing that out of fear of death. And he'd just kill other Scalpels, those courageous enough to face death."

"So, you want to be courageous, too?"

"Yes. Like my dad, I believe in what I do. Even if I die. I'm helping others. My work is compassionate. I want to grow my compassion and love. I want to love even this assassin, to wish him happiness." But his words belied his thoughts. *Am I kidding myself? He tried to kill me, but loving him seems right. All the spiritual masters talk about loving your enemy. Why not me?*

"So, now what?" Baba asked.

"I can't back down. I'll keep removing Auroras." Will paused. "I need to be prepared to kill the assassin. And I need to look into my fear and confront my own sense of mortality."

"Consider what I've said—kill the killer, right now. There's more for you to uncover. Nothing wrong with blind spots. We've all got 'em." Baba uncrossed his legs. "Please don't interpret what I said literally. If you kill him, there will be repercussions. You'd need to be able to accept the consequences of the killing. You'd be resorting to the same tactics as the assassin and continuing the circle of violence."

Will wanted to uncover his blind spots, but Baba had implied that they would reveal themselves when they were ready.

* * *

In a spark of insight, Will realized there was another way. He objectifies Scalpels, he thought. If he knew us as people, maybe he wouldn't kill us. This could be a way out. I need to see him.

He opened his eyes to the inside of his tent, dark in the middle of the night, hidden in a dense patch of rhododendron. The waters of Straight Branch murmured nearby. He turned on a red nightlight and woke up Tara to share his thoughts.

"I figured you might," Tara said, frowning. "Seems natural for Will Robin to want to see him."

"I'm not sure what to say to him, though," Will said, putting on his clothes. "I've imagined that I'll somehow convince him to stop killing and all that. But when I snap out of that daydream, it doesn't seem realistic."

"Because he wants to kill you. Still, it's clear that even the most murderous people have some sense of basic goodness inside them."

"Even serial killers?"

"Yes, anyone," Tara said, stretching her body long. "There's plenty of evidence for this."

"Still, it's hard to believe it's true for some people."

"Sure. It's just potential. Right now, he wants you dead."

"I'll go with what you said. He's got potential,"

"Still, I'm uncomfortable with the assassin being here," Tara said. "Aren't we kidnapping? We can't keep someone here indefinitely, can we? I mean, we're not the justice system."

"I hadn't thought of that. You're right." Will shook his head in frustration.

"There you go again, criticizing yourself. It's okay, Will." She pulled him down and kissed him.

"I know, I know. I just don't want to let people down. They've put dealing with the assassin in my hands."

"Rightly so. You brought him here. Won't the police come? He's a missing person right now, I'd guess," Tara said.

"No. Aurora assassins are Cirrus's dark secret. His computer self-destructed, and Dr. Kumar couldn't find any evidence in the melted components. One witness saw a self-driving car leaving the valley shortly after he was captured. We think it was his car, but no one knows for sure except Cirrus, which won't report anything. And since my mom told Officer Mathis I left the valley, I get the sense that it's just me and the assassin." Will fastened the last button of his shirt.

"You're not going now, are you?" Tara asked. "It's the middle of the night."

"No time like the present," Will said, kissing her and then unzipping the tent.

As he walked in the dark toward the assassin, his fear became palpable. His heart thudded, and an uncomfortable queasiness slithered through his body. Was this the same assassin who tried to kill him in Asheville? His father's killer? Adjacent to the barn, he touched the aluminum walls of the thousand-square-foot storage building with his cold, sweaty hands. So, he's right there.

A tall man gripping a shotgun stepped out of the shadow of a methane biodigester tank and into the lighted kitchen. "You're the last man I was expectin'."

"Eli?"

"Yes, sir," Eli said. "Why you being foolish coming here?"

"Felt like I needed to come."

"You going to kill him?"

"No. Just a visit."

"A visit? Not sure what you're aiming at. Talking to him's like a grub talking to a chicken."

Will smiled awkwardly at Eli's wry sense of humor and slid open the door. Its metallic sound reverberated through the storage building, whose concrete floor was exposed and covered in stains from years of use. Faint smells of motor oil and manure permeated the space. Eli flipped the lightswitch and three floodlights attached to the ceiling illuminated the assassin, who rolled face down on a cot in a cell. Its bars were welded into a solid steel cubicle. The cell included a barred door, a tray port for meals, a bed, a bedpan, and a basic shower and spigot.

"Get up!" A guard set a chair facing the Aurora assassin. "You have a visitor." Will stayed near the door and looked at the back of the assassin's bald, shiny brown scalp. It's him, Will thought. Don't let him sense your fear.

Will walked toward the empty chair. He nodded at the guard, who left the room but kept the door open. The assassin rubbed his eyes and sat in a chair. Will sat in his chair and looked at the assassin—his thick hands, his wide and strong jaw, his tired yet intense brown eyes. They stared at one another, silent. Perspiration beaded on Will's forehead. But in a moment of awareness, gazing at the cold eyes, Will imagined all the suffering behind them, all the repressed emotions.

"I don't know what to say to you," he said. They continued staring at one another until, finally, words rolled from his tongue. "You killed my father and friends, didn't you? And you tried to kill me. The easy way out would be to kill you now, before you kill others. But I don't want to kill you." Will paused and turned to his thoughts to reinforce his convictions. Killing isn't courageous. Love and compassion are.

The assassin blinked. "You're still on my list."

Will recognized the deep voice from the phone calls, and he shuddered. "Can't you be touched by life? I'd like to believe you can. We all can." He seethed, thinking about his father and the many Scalpels this man had killed, probably including all those in

Asheville except for him. "There's no point," Will continued, managing not to lash out with his anger. To do so, in Will's mind, was equivalent to forfeiting to the assassin's mode of being. "There's no point to your violence." He trembled ever so slightly.

"There is a point, Scalpel. I don't like to kill either. But I do it well. So, I kill for our country. To save lives. To protect our customers. To maintain peace and order. We need peace and order more than ever these days, don't we?"

"I don't want peace at the cost of freedom, or in the name of greed and control," Will said. The words spilled out like water from a toppled bucket.

"People are happier when they're part of something larger than themselves. When they feel safe. The Aurora does that."

Will closed his eyes and breathed until his emotions subsided. "So, you do care."

The assassin didn't respond.

"I'm guessing you do." After a long silence, Will continued. "You said you don't like to kill. Can you stop killing?"

"So long as Scalpels exist, I got work to do."

We live in a twisted world, Will thought. He rose in silence and walked away, confused.

Eli, waiting outside, asked about the conversation.

"His eyes. I couldn't stop staring at them. They're the coldest eyes I've ever seen. But he does seem to care about people, in his own strange way." Will exhaled. "I'm all worked up."

"Ain't no surprise. He killed your father."

"Right." He guessed Eli wouldn't lead him to a deeper understanding. "Can you do me a favor, Eli? Can you get some nano GPS receivers and stitch them in his boots and clothes?" The circumference of threads, the receivers were expensive and short lived but effective while they lasted. "I'd like to track him if he escapes."

"We ain't going to let him escape. But I can do that, and I'll get you the tracking codes."

* * *

Will unlocked the tray port and slipped the breakfast plate toward the assassin: buckwheat pancakes topped with butter and maple syrup with a side of fruit, along with a plastic fork. The metal cage was now a symbol of Will's fear. Somehow, being able to touch this symbol with his hands made it all the more real. Removing the cage was out of the question. The fear seemed necessary.

But he's not my enemy. That's what Baba was trying to get me to understand. He's not a killer. That's my projection of who he is. Even if he might want to kill me, he's not killing me right now. Every moment is a new moment. My relationship to him can shift every moment. He's not an assassin.

Confident that he'd figured out what Baba said, Will walked past the guard to the adjacent barn. He wore a wide-brimmed hat to hide his face from the drone surveillance some villagers claimed to have seen. In the barn, he found a horse blanket, brought it back before the cage with the assassin, and folded it into a cushion. Will sat still, watching as the man gulped down the meal as if famished, but without enjoyment. He looked at the assassin's cold eyes and sensed his own fear of death most of all. I'm not prepared to die. This is it. This is the next layer. I need to confront death. He reviewed all the moments in his past when he thought he'd accepted death. When his father died, he saw his own mortality. But his father's death felt indirect, unresolved. He hadn't spoken the things he wanted to speak. How he wanted to speak those words now!

What would I say? He pondered for a moment. What rose to the surface as most alive was this: Dad, is it okay for me to make mistakes? Because I make them. As he thought this, he recalled when his father was killed and realized that he blamed himself for his father's death. If he hadn't contacted his father, maybe the assassin wouldn't have killed him. If he'd gone to find his father before searching for Maya, maybe they'd both be alive now. His guilty heart was like a ball of iron. Dad, can you accept me as I am? In his mind, his father was unable to reply with an honest yes, and that thought sent a dagger-like pain through his iron heart. That's my problem, right there. Sure, Dad was kind and believed in nonviolence. People loved him. I loved him. He was exciting to be around. But what happened? The way he approached life seemed overbearing to Will, all the way up to the moment he was killed. Will didn't know, and Yeshe and Baba didn't talk about it. He'd never asked. Now, he was curious.

The caged man was finishing the last bites of pancake. Would the man speak? Would Will get to know and understand this person? How could he approach him in a new way? His intuition told him silence was best. And the caged man remained mute, too. He set the plate and fork on the tray port and walked within the cage, back and forth, as if Will weren't even present. Will thought words of gratitude, kindness, and compassion. He placed the horse blanket into the corner, took the plate, locked the tray port, and left.

Will brought three meals every day. This became part of the natural flow to his day. His intuition led him to keep providing meals and caring for the man, whether it bore fruit or not.

* * *

"Your father was extremely motivated, even when he was an infant," Baba said. He sat with Will on a boulder in a ravine overlooking Straight Branch. The fast-running waters reflected the recent rains. Rhododendron and mountain laurel surrounded the boulder. "It's important to understand what was going on at the time. Firefly Cove didn't exist yet as a village. It was just a couple dozen of us trying to make ends meet, paying a huge mortgage, essentially surviving with little income. Yeshe and I built our home while we lived in a yurt. We really didn't know much about living off the land or creating a community. Things happened. Our crops withered or were decimated by insects. We lost many farm animals to disease. Some buildings didn't work out for one reason or another—mold, a collapsed roof. People argued, fought, and left. But we survived. New people came. Yeshe and I saw this work as part of our spiritual lives. The loss of life, starting over, building anew were all stark reminders of our practice of accepting things as they are. We could see the impermanence of things. But your father, I think it affected him. He was young and saw the world through a different lens. He saw his life at stake. He saw others' survival at stake. He saw the mistakes we made and how they affected him and others. Once he was old enough, I think he made a vow not to repeat mistakes like those."

"That fits his personality," Will said.

"Yes. As a teenager, he became disillusioned with spiritual matters, seeing them as contributing to these mistakes. It was as if our attitude toward life, our way of accepting things, was too loose and flowing for him to understand. He wanted things to be more fixed and certain. That was his nature. Even as the Cove became a place of abundance, he searched until he saw something to improve. That was both a blessing and a curse for him. We didn't try to fix him or change him, but just accepted him even as he rejected parts of us. And through it all, we loved him unconditionally."

"That's what he couldn't do for me," Will said. "He loved me with conditions. If I made a mistake, he became critical of me. That's why I'm so hard on myself and see the world's faults. The assassin . . ." Will corrected himself. "The man in the cage is bringing all this out in me. I see the coldness in his eyes, and I imagine he's judging me. He thinks what I'm doing is a mistake. I can see my father in him."

"You seem excited." Baba smiled.

"I am. I've projected a lot on to Cirrus and this man. It was a blind spot for me. How did you know?"

"There is more yet to uncover." Baba paused as a wood thrush called in the forest behind them. "Your father did love you unconditionally. His criticism came from a place of love. He didn't want you to suffer like he did. He didn't want anybody to suffer, and because of that, he suffered tremendously."

They sat in silence while Will contemplated what Baba had said. He closed his eyes and tried to feel the love from his father. All that criticism was love. Will found that difficult to believe, after years of thinking otherwise.

* * *

On the forty-second meal, the dinner of the fourteenth day following the first buckwheat pancake breakfast, Will sat once again on the horse blanket in front of the cage. He watched the man eat. In his mind, he'd given him the name Manish, after a children's book character. Somehow, naming the assassin let him relate better, even though they hadn't spoken since the first night. Intuition told Will that silence was best. So, while Manish ate, he meditated on loving kindness and compassion or just noticed what arose in his mindstream: thoughts, mental formations, feelings, emotions, sensations, smells, sounds, his breath, all that appeared to his eyes. Periodically, he rested, naturally, and thoughts faded to clarity within his awareness. Each of the forty-two meditation sessions was part of an unraveling process for Will.

He wondered what he still wanted to get out of sitting with Manish three times a day. Generosity and kindness were his intentions—offering meals he'd cooked at the covered outdoor kitchen, cleaning the bedpan, and washing the sheets and clothes. But was there more? He thinks his killings are morally right, and I think being a Scalpel is morally right. That's our impasse. That's why it hasn't gone anywhere in two weeks. Stalemate. We're just staring at one another. Biding time. Unmoving. No end in sight. He looked at Manish. But isn't my work morally right? I help people. I help them get their freedom back. I give them a chance at reclaiming their minds. Will felt resistance to changing his moral stance. His father once again entered his mind. An upwelling of emotions—sadness, anger, shame, fear—filled his chest. Overwhelmed, he at first wanted the discomfort to go away, but quickly recognized his thoughts and breathed into the feelings, one by one, together, in pairs, as the sensations changed, flowed, and dissipated. He visualized his father. Dad, Will thought. Dad, tell me you loved me unconditionally. Please. It would mean so much to me.

He heard his father's voice. Ever since you were born and I held you in my arms, I've loved you, without conditions. Yes, my son, I love you.

Tears of joy and love flowed down Will's face as he realized that his father's voice was none other than his own.

Manish stopped eating. He looked at Will. Will looked at him and wiped his tears, embarrassed.

"You okay?" Manish asked, breaking two weeks of silence.

"I'm fine," Will said. Manish's voice shattered Will's embarrassment, opening him fully to the depths of his vulnerability. "Better than fine." He cried like a young child, without inhibition, lump in throat, reddened eyes, gulps of air, feeling gratitude and love toward his father. Meanwhile, Manish looked at him, confused, unable to eat another bite. And when Will looked back, he noticed Manish's eyes were no longer cold. In that moment of vulnerability and acknowledgment, they forgot who they were, and the cage between them disappeared.

TWENTY-TWO
HOPELESSNESS

MARTIN SEARCHED FOR WORDS BUT COULDN'T FIND ANY he wanted to say. He sat in the passenger seat of an eighteen-wheeler eastbound on I-40. Finally, someone had trusted him and helped him. Leave it to a trucker. He'd lost faith in humanity otherwise. Unwilling to return to a criminal lifestyle, for two months he'd been a scavenger in and around Asheville, all the while hiding from Felix and the police. His body had thinned. His eyes were darkened, lacking vitality. His path in life had taken a toll, and his sense of humor had disappeared. The driver, whose job description had shifted more to security guard with the advent of self-driving vehicles, switched to manual control and pulled the truck onto an exit ramp and into a charging station parking lot. "Here you are."

"Thanks." Martin opened the door and stepped down. "I owe you one."

"No problem. Just try to help the next person in need. God knows, we all need some kind of help."

"No kidding." Martin pondered helping others instead of thinking about himself. He'd been thinking about himself his whole life. But once again, Jade came to mind. He now saw her as a role model of sorts. Eventually, he spoke. "I'll do that."

"You'll want to head about fifteen miles thataway." The driver pointed toward a county road that wove past a diner, a garage, fenced-in self-storage units, and a few abandoned buildings before meandering around a bend. "You got a map?"

"I do." Martin reached into a pocket of his threadbare jeans, took out a hand-drawn map, and unfolded it.

"Good luck," the driver said.

Martin grabbed his knapsack and closed the door. One day in Asheville, he'd stumbled upon a pile of free items on the curb. He'd found three things to keep: a worn blue button-down shirt, a knapsack, and a water bottle. Right then and there, he'd discarded his stained T-shirt and buttoned his new shirt. Now, the September sun warmed his face. He sat on a grassy curb, studying the map. Once he aligned his mind with the territory and the map, he strapped the knapsack to his back and walked along the county road, thinking about Jade, his fight with Felix, and his final destination.

He walked for hours. He attempted to hitchhike, but few cars passed. If he got a ride, he might make it in half an hour. Without a ride, he'd arrive tomorrow. No one stopped. No surprise, he thought.

He trudged past cut hayfields, harvested fields, clearcuts, and a variety of young forests. Beyond the barbed wire and No Trespassing signs were derelict homes or trailers surrounded by used automobiles, plastic toys, piles of firewood and trash, and an abundance of other clutter, saved because it may have a use someday or because it cost money to get rid of. On the most fertile tracts of land were newly painted houses, tended fields, and wooden fences stapled with Danger and Keep Out and No Trespassing signs. He felt boxed in between the white line on the road and the signs. Not much room to maneuver. He didn't dare enter past the signs. But his belly grumbled, having shrunk considerably over the last couple of months. At last, his hunger took over, and he crossed the unwelcoming line of signs into a harvested cornfield to glean what the birds hadn't yet found. Here and there on the ground were a few broken cobs. On his hands and knees, he searched for kernels in the dirt. At last, he found one and chewed it with his molars. Like this, he satisfied his hunger, one kernel at a time.

Night arrived, and he found nowhere to sleep. Fucking No Trespassing signs, he thought. His mind wandered, picturing a bearded white man aiming a shotgun at him and shouting, "You're trespassing!" He pictured fierce dogs barking and gnashing their teeth, the police arriving, patrol car lights flashing. Despite his fears, he had no choice. His legs wouldn't go any farther. So he walked past a sign nailed into an oak to find rest. He covered his body in leafy branches, leaf litter, and other debris for insulation, yet he still shivered. His sleep was broken by barking dogs, the cold, the hard ground, and his fear of being found by the landowner.

* * *

In the heart of the forest garden, Will watched Yeshe tend the hives. She wore flowing robes, not a beekeeping suit. To Will, she never seemed fearful of a sting. Still, she used her smoker to blow a puff into one of the many hives she tended.

To the west, Leaf and two other electricians wired the co-housing building for electricity and Internet. Jack helped to install the remote-controlled gears he'd made to allow windows of the gabled greenhouse to open and close, depending on the temperature. The greenhouse was tucked between the vast forest garden and the west pasture, facing south for maximum sunlight. Along a new secondary road bordering the pasture, dozens of small homes and duplexes were in different stages of construction. Residents were buffing the earthen walls and natural finishes, framing timber, and installing solar shingles.

"I need to give up being a Scalpel. Someone's got to yield. I can help people in other ways."

"There's still fear and hope in what you say," Yeshe responded.

He thought of every other option. All involved fear and hope. After his deliberate analysis of his situation, he spoke. "Though I'd like to be fearless, I'm not. I'm just not there yet. There seems to be no end to my blind spots and layers to unpeel."

"As long as you think that, there is no end."

Will knew it to be true. But even with that understanding, it was the hardest thing for him to do.

"For now, be kind to yourself. Fear will be your companion, your greatest teacher, if you approach it with courage."

* * *

The Sanders children, Carey and Ethan, cut a red ribbon to the door of their new tiny home, fully paid for by selling their parents' car and excess belongings, liquidating their retirement account, and the community's sweat equity. The home was eight hundred square feet and designed to be efficient, welcoming, and warm.

"Congrats. You'uns deserve it." Eli shook Jack's hand and hugged Harriet, who wore a new dress for the occasion, one that fit her new size. Still heavier than she'd like, she was nonetheless thirty-five pounds lighter since she'd left California over four months ago.

In a couple of weeks, food rationing would begin. Knowing the upcoming shortage, she had changed her perspective on weight loss considerably. She knew she'd continue to lose weight, but because of food scarcity instead of by choice. Whenever she thought of this, anxiety kicked in. She was unsure if she could survive on less than half the calories she'd consumed back in California. But despite the food shortage, they'd decided to stay, just like almost everyone else. Firefly Cove was much safer than elsewhere, they'd concluded. In addition, Jack found satisfaction working with Eli and others at the Post & Gear, and Harriet had just started as a teaching assistant at Firefly Cove School. Cutting the ribbon sealed the decision for them.

Carey and Ethan ran through each room while villagers moved in the furniture Harriet had found at a yard sale. She heard her children playing in the kitchen and felt the texture of the yellow ocher plaster walls flecked with mica. The late-September sun entered the window, warming the house. She looked up. You answered my prayers.

Villagers brought gifts: homemade kitchen utensils, flowers, baskets, quilts, bowls, and more. Harriet arranged them on the dining-room table. Grace entered with a bouquet of dahlias.

"They're beautiful," Harriet said, embracing her. "From your garden?"

"Yes. I can give you some dahlia tubers in the spring, neighbor."

"We are neighbors, aren't we?"

"We moved back in today, too," Grace said. "But I'm not sure we're safe. The assassin's still here, and for all I know a drone might shoot a missile at us."

"Don't think like that," Harriet said.

"I know I shouldn't. Don't get me wrong, I'm glad to be home," Grace said. "I can only imagine what you went through leaving your home. You're courageous."

Harriet had never seen herself in that way. Images of leaving home, the bleak landscape, and the looting and fires in downtown Hanford flashed in her mind. "I'm just excited to move in here," she said at last, thinking about making love with Jack for the first time in months.

"As you should be."

Harriet placed the flowers in a vase. "I should be the one giving you a gift."

"I'm happy to help," Grace said.

"Really? I'm relieved," Harriet said. "To tell you the truth, I felt like a burden."

Grace had never once expressed her dissatisfaction, but to Harriet, her body language had belied a sense of halfhearted welcome. "No, you weren't a burden. Sometimes, it wasn't easy. But you weren't a burden."

"I mean, we lived in your living room for a couple of months. We couldn't stay with my mother more than two weeks. We've never had guests that long either."

Jack returned with a lanky Californian, schlepping the bed. "Thanks again, Grace," Jack said. "Dear, can you help?"

"Yes, thank you. Excuse me," Harriet said, leading Jack and the Californian into the bedroom. "Put it here, sweetheart," she said, looking at her husband suggestively, longing for Jack's touch. Knowing that a dozen people were outside their home and that their children were playing nearby heightened the moment for Harriet. She couldn't wait any longer.

"Give us a moment," Jack said to the California man, who left the house.

Jack locked the bedroom door. Harriet closed the window despite the heat of the room.

"I've been waiting for this day," Jack said, kissing her.

Though Harriet had imagined candles and sheets, this was what she wanted, too. She grabbed his ass and pulled him onto the bare mattress by his belt.

"Easy, dear," Jack said.

Harriet laughed, yanking the belt from his pants and throwing it on the floor. He bit her ear and rolled her over, pinning her under his hard penis and barrel chest, at once hulking, yet comforting.

My man. Her fingers moved inside his pants to explore his erection and all that it signified to her—that she was loved, that she was attractive to him, and that he was ready for her after all these months. He's so ready. She kissed him, tasting the sweat from a morning of work. She breathed in his musky odor and closed her eyes while he unbuttoned her blouse with abandon. Their tongues mingled. Their hands explored. Her nipples hardened, and she grew moist. "Make love to me," Harriet said.

He removed her underwear, opened her legs, and entered her. One gentle thrust at a time, he deepened into her, and the way he thrust conveyed love to Harriet. She relished his fullness and pulled his hips toward her, accepting him into her with a moan. He was bigger than she remembered—deep, solid, and hot—and she wrapped her fingers around the base of his erection once again, squeezing.

She removed his shirt, touching him as though she were making love to a new body, learning the changes and how they aroused her. He quickened his thrusts, breathing heavily and glistening with sweat, until he moaned and his body jerked in climax.

* * *

A man yelled from the pastures, "Another refugee coming!"

"Another one?" Eli frowned. "You sure?"

"I'm sure. A man's walking up the road."

"We can't have anyone else here. We're full. No vacancy," Eli said. For the last several months, he'd built homes, harvested crops, and guarded Manish.

Harriet opened the bedroom windows, and the breeze cooled her sweaty body. From the mattress, she listened to the conversation outside. She knew how much Eli worked. He seemed unstoppable. Until now.

Leaving their home, Jack wiped sweat from his brow with a cloth. "He can stay with us," he said. Eli frowned again. "I mean," Jack said, backpedaling, "he can stay for a few nights, so he can rest."

Harriet sighed, rolling onto her back and rubbing her clitoris, satisfied only partially, longing for more. My time will come, she thought.

"But you ain't even moved in yet," Eli said to Jack.

"I know, but if he doesn't stay here, where's he going to go? Where would we have gone if you hadn't welcomed us?"

Eli's awkward silence spoke.

He resents us, Harriet thought. As a newcomer, Harriet felt welcome in the Cove. After all, they'd built a home for her family. At the same time, she had the impression that some Firefly Cove residents resisted the newcomers' arrival, especially now that they numbered over one hundred people, almost half of the Cove's population. In a week or two, the village would likely be majority refugees. She sat on the bare mattress and tried to walk in their shoes for a moment. With our arrival, their lifestyle is at stake. This place was their utopia, all theirs for decades. Now, it's not. She pictured Jack helping to build the tiny homes, duplexes, and co-housing—he'd done his part. What more do they want us to do? Still, she had a sense that her family was a hindrance to the village.

And now Eli was exposing his position to the light.

* * *

"You okay?" Will was just leaving from a visit with Manish and saw Eli marching toward him.

"Does it look like I'm okay? There's another refugee coming this way." He pointed toward a man in the distance, walking along the main entrance road through the sorghum fields and pastures.

"I'm done helping people. I've been busting ass, and every time I bust ass, chances of my ass surviving go down. There's no end in sight to 'em coming."

"So, you'd like him gone." Will figured someone was bound to become enraged. He didn't imagine it would be Eli. Now. With him. "Can you wait a bit, Eli? He's just arriving. Think of what he's been through to get here."

"No. We've been too generous. Word's spread that we're the do-gooders. Now, we're a go-to place for refugees. Look at us. We ain't going to make it this winter."

Will didn't know what to say. Eli had been carrying the brunt of late-night shifts guarding Manish. Will was grateful and didn't want to upset him. On top of that, Eli was helping with the home construction projects. Will knew the lack of sleep and excessive work contributed to Eli's anger. "Have you really lost hope, Eli? Why are you working so hard, then? Isn't there hope with that?"

"I don't know. I'm just doing it. But where's *this* man going to live? And the next one. And the next one. I'm tired of building houses. And how are they going to eat? None of these people know shit about survival. They're like children. I'm tired of holding their hands."

Will found it hard to listen but knew that being with Eli was important in that moment. Anger and resentment were only part of Eli's feelings about the newcomers, Will believed. There was more, and Eli showed his care every day in his actions. "I don't have any solutions either," Will said, "other than I want to be as compassionate as possible."

"I'm the one suffering." Eli stood tall and imposing. "What I'm lacking is self-compassion, if there's such a thing. Our village, too. We're putting all our effort into helping them, ignoring ourselves. Right now, I want to be selfish. I admit it. I don't want to ration my food. Not after all the work I put in. I want to eat like always. That's one reason I don't want him staying here."

"You're right. I need compassion for myself, too. It's been a tough year." Will looked toward the entrance road, watching the refugee's approach, backlit by the September sun. "But I disagree. We chose to help others, fully knowing this would strain us to the limit this winter. You're angry right now. I respect your anger and what you choose to do. But you're getting in your own way right now."

"I'm not getting..." Eli's face shifted. To Will, it seemed a sudden softening. At last, Eli spoke. "I hate to admit it, but you're right. If I go over there and talk with him, a head will fly. And it won't be mine." He exhaled. "And all my hard work would just be a sham. Maybe it's a sham no matter what I do. Maybe I'm not as caring as I like to think."

"I don't believe that for a second. To me, you're a living example of someone who cares and puts that into action. I tend to beat myself up these days, too. Seems natural under these circumstances. All we can do is support one another."

"Yeah."

"So, what do you want to do? About him, I mean."

"Hell, I don't know. I'd rather he didn't come. But he's here."

They walked toward the main road, looking up at the village and the fields to the east. Growing up in Firefly Cove, Will had seen the situation as ideal. His village knew how to plan for the future and create a landscape perfect for people. Elsewhere, people were struggling, making poor choices, not being sustainable. The Cove's success, however, seemed to be turning into failure. This didn't seem like the same kind of hopelessness Yeshe was talking about. He recalled what he now understood about hopelessness and fearlessness. That absence of fear and hope was a way of being in the present moment, instead of fixating on what might happen in the near future.

The man approached them. "I'm Martin," he said. "I need your help."

Will looked at the man's scarred face and weary body and perceived an intense suffering. His gut instinct told him to beware. But his heart wanted to stay open and kind. His heart spoke. "Come sit in the shade. Would you like some water?"

"Yes, please," Martin said, following Will to the covered outdoor kitchen.

"Good to meet you, Martin," Eli managed. "Looks like you've got this covered, Will, and I need to spend some time alone. Appreciate you."

Will found a cup and filled it with water. He handed it to Martin, who guzzled it. "You don't need to say anything. I'm guessing you're probably exhausted."

"I am. Will, right?"

"Yes." Will was surprised. He hadn't introduced himself. But then he remembered. Eli had said his name when he left.

Martin drank a second glass, more slowly this time. They sat in silence. And when Martin finished, Will rose to fill the glass once again.

"I'm good. Could I get my water bottle filled, though?" Martin opened his knapsack and gave Will his plastic bottle.

"So, how can I help?" Will asked, filling the water bottle.

"Look at my face and body. I've been burned, shot at, almost killed several times. Life is hell out there. Believe me, I'm a good man. I'm from Phoenix. You've probably heard what's going on out there. I work hard and come from a good family. But things just happened. Our home burned down. Arson. That's why my face is..." He pointed at his scarred face. "My parents died in the fire. They're killing us for no reason other than they hate Mexicans. I couldn't stay. But Asheville's not any better. I'm out of money and hungry and can't survive alone. I'd like to stay in the village. Can I?"

"You're welcome here." Will was having a difficult time understanding what he was feeling, as seemingly conflicting emotions struggled with one another. He felt torn. But what he noticed most was his compassion for the suffering so clearly etched on Martin's face. He also recalled the village's commitment to helping others. "I just need to figure out a few things first."

* * *

"Thanks for that, *amigo*," Felix said, concluding a deal with a man with pasty white skin.

"Call on me next time, too, brother."

"Will do." Felix removed a photograph from his pocket. "You seen this guy?" It was Martin.

"Never seen him."

"Let me know if you do. You got my number." The way Felix spoke hinted at a reward.

"Sure, man."

Felix had spoken about Martin to dozens of people, expanding his net. Two months later, his hand still hurt from nerve damage. Each twinge of pain or sight of the scar triggered his anger and reminded him of the revenge he sought.

* * *

"I get that you don't like it, Ma," Will said. "But I'd like to help him. He doesn't need much. Just a tent. He can use mine, and I'd like to offer him our backyard. He could camp and use our bathroom and kitchen. You'd be able to paint in the living room and have more privacy than before. It'll be much different."

"Tenzi, I've already said no. We're just moving back into our home. I know it's hard to hear me say no. What do you want me to do, say yes, even though I mean no?"

She's still triggered. Will pictured the moment he invited the Sanders family to live with them, and his mom's reaction. "No, I don't want that. Let me back up a second. I'm sorry once again."

"Of course, honey," Grace said. "I'd like to see him taken care of, too. Perhaps he can stay in the tent village until the co-housing is finished. They're just about wrapping that up now."

"Next week, I hear. Everyone's talking about it, especially the newcomers." His awareness stuck on the word *newcomers*. It had taken on a new meaning after his conversation with Eli. Lurking behind it was an us-versus-them mentality. Not just that, but also a sense of privilege or superiority. And not just that either—also a sense of having paid dues versus owing somebody. The newcomers owed the villagers, perhaps because the villagers built the place. The situation reminded him of Manish. Yes, there's a sense of that with him, too. He's the one behind bars. I'm feeding him every day, taking care of him. I have the upper hand. At least I think...

"Tenzi?"

"I'll tell Martin the tent village is probably best for him."

"Thank you." Grace hugged him, kissing his cheeks. "I'm grateful that you thought to check with me this time."

* * *

Will closed his front door behind him, backpack strapped around his shoulders, hauling food, tent, and sleeping bag. Martin waited for him on the dirt road. "Follow me," Will said. Thinking about helping Martin, Will was joyful, and perhaps this joy was augmented by the resistance of others. In the forest garden, Will plucked a few remaining pears and gave a couple to Martin, who bit into one.

"This is the best pear ever," he said, devouring it.

A flock of Carolina parakeets eating apples took wing as the two men descended a slope toward the newly built tiny homes.

"Can we bring you lunch?" Harriet called from her front door.

"Sure," Will replied.

In front of them, several dozen tents were grouped together in a mowed area of the hayfield. They moved west amongst the tents and refugees, who were eating, talking, or resting. Will introduced Martin to those he knew by name. Those he didn't know said "Good morning" or *Buenos dias*. People seemed happy. Perhaps here they were safest. To the right, the co-housing building still needed finishing touches.

"I'm curious. Do you have an Aurora?" Will asked.

"No," said Martin.

"Really? Most people have one when they get here."

"I swear to God," Martin said. "My family was too poor to get me one."

Once again, an uneasy feeling returned to Will's heart and gut. Weren't they subsidized for the poor?

Ethan ran toward them. "My mom says you should set your tent up near us," he said, breathing heavily.

"How can you say no to him?" Will asked.

"What's your name?" Martin asked, smiling.

"Ethan."

"Sure, Ethan, I'll follow you."

"What happened to your face?" Ethan asked.

"I got burned in a house fire."

"Whoa. Does it hurt?"

"Not anymore."

Harriet, Jack, and Carey greeted Martin in front of their house.

"Does he have to live in a tent?" Carey asked.

"No, sweetie, he can sleep here on the couch," Harriet said.

"Thanks, but I'll be okay in the tent," Martin said.

"Are you sure?" Jack asked.

"It's fine. Don't worry. I've been living outside."

"Not for much longer," Jack said. "We only have a week left on the co-housing."

"Just let us know if you change your mind or need anything," Harriet said. "And let me fix you a hot meal at least once a day."

"I can't believe you're so friendly to me," Martin said. "Why?"

"We came here a while back, just like you," Jack said. "Will helped us without any hesitation. We'd like to do the same for you. It's the least we can do after all you've been through. Come in for lunch, please."

* * *

In his office, Dr. Kumar administered paperwork for the new arrivals, welcoming them and ensuring their basic needs were met. He explained to Martin the village and how it functioned. "Sign here," he said.

Martin signed with an electronic pen on Dr. Kumar's tablet.

"Welcome to Firefly Cove."

TWENTY-THREE
THE MINGLING

ON THE MORNING OF THE FIRST OF OCTOBER, Will sat on the horse blanket in front of the cage. After over one hundred and fifty meals for Manish and over one hundred and fifty meditation sessions, the routine had transformed Will. He looked at Manish and could see his basic humanity, could feel love and compassion for him. Eight weeks ago, seeing the assassin this way seemed impossibly out of reach.

Manish ate more slowly than before. Since Manish had asked a month ago if he was okay, Will had noticed a softening in their relationship. Nevertheless, they didn't speak. The metal bars still divided them. To Will, the bars represented fear and separation. At the same time, he noticed a parallel desire inseparable from the fear. And behind that desire emerged a thought: I must free him to be free myself.

He had no doubt about this thought, a union of fear and desire. So perfect was their marriage that their existence apart from one another seemed to fade away. Opening the door and releasing the assassin seemed to be the next step. All logic, however, told him that freeing the assassin would be the most foolish thing he could ever do.

This blend of feelings shuddered through his body. It lingered around his heart until a clear sense of yearning emerged. The yearning transformed into courage, a sense of moving toward what he feared—toward the fear itself.

"I want to set you free," he said.

"Free?" Manish said. "You're joking."

"How else is this going to end?" Will paused as his words became more challenging to say. "Part of me thinks this is foolish or stupid. You could still want to kill me, for all I know."

"Depends. You looking to cut out more chips?" Manish asked.

Will pondered his options. After a month of contemplation, he saw more than right and wrong. He now saw a little bit of both, the shades of gray beyond morality. He hesitated, though, because he'd been tortured. He found it challenging to forgive Cirrus's programmers. He judged them as sick—hell-bent on never-ending materialistic goals like the colonization of other planets, the perfection of a controllable artificial general intelligence, and the expansion of a captivating metaverse. That sickness made them dangerous. But in the end, he didn't know if they'd programmed the torture or if Cirrus's code naturally embodied all human traits and capabilities. Within the program, would AI adapt torture if its survival or the survival of society seemed threatened? Yes, he reasoned. And with that, his torture intertwined with all of humanity and his forgiveness encompassed all people and their potential for evil.

Still, he desired to continue as a Scalpel. He wanted to help people be more conscious and knew the best way he could do that was to remove the Auroras from those who didn't want them anymore. But his desire was different now, more an aware heartfelt wish to benefit everyone, a broader perspective and aspiration that took into account the complexity of a rapidly changing world.

At last, Will answered. "I appreciate your point of view. I can see how the Aurora can benefit society. But at the same time, Cirrus uses the Aurora to manipulate and torture people and steer society in self-serving ways."

"That's not true. Cirrus wouldn't do that."

"It *is* true," Will said. "I know. I was tortured. And if people want help removing a chip, I'll help them." Will paused. "Are you going to be an assassin still?"

"I couldn't tell you. I've been MIA for a month. Might not even have a job. But if I still have a job, I'll do it."

Will's heart sank. So, they were still at an impasse in that way. But he knew it wasn't about Manish. Cirrus hired many assassins. Whether he freed Manish or not wouldn't impact the hazards of being a Scalpel, the threat of being assassinated. But his decision would impact his freedom. And Manish's freedom. Now, that seemed most important.

"I'm setting him free!" Will called out to the guard.

"What?"

"I'm setting him free."

"That's what I thought you said. Are you crazy?"

"No. This seems like the most sane thing I've done in a while." Will jingled the key in his pocket, feeling both the fear and the desire. He placed the key in the lock. Don't hesitate. He turned the lock. It clicked, and the door swung open. "You're a free man." And so am I.

Manish stood still for a moment. The way the man looked at that empty space outside the door, Will imagined he was paralyzed by disbelief. With no bars between him and Manish, Will breathed naturally and calmed his mind.

Finally, Manish walked out of the cell and looked at Will. "You've got guts." He nodded his head as he spoke. "Never saw this coming. You've got guts." He turned away from Will and walked toward the open metal door of the storage room. The guard, still wary, kept his gun ready.

A cool morning. A crisp blue sky. A brilliant white sun. Will watched Manish walk down the main dirt road out of Firefly Cove.

* * *

Later that day, a recent newcomer, Destiny, wanted her Aurora removed and messaged Will. He responded for her to meet him in the storage shed, blindfolded. Curious, he typed in the tracking codes Eli had given him for the nano GPS receivers he'd sewn into Manish's various clothes. A map popped up showing Manish's trail. His trail led out of the village at walking speed. But a few miles away, the tracks increased to the speed of a vehicle, stopping eventually at a house in a gated community in South Asheville. His home, perhaps?

When Destiny was ready, he slipped into the storage shed. The makeshift cage was still there, but empty and open. All the guards were gone, relieved of their duty after receiving gratitude and gifts from Will. Next to it, a young woman sat blindfolded. He approached her, prepared his equipment, and performed the minor surgery. He gave her the chip and sutured the incision.

"Welcome to the free world, Destiny. You can remove your blindfold."

"It's you, Will. I knew you were the one." She reminded Will of Aja, though she was less confident and carried herself as though burdened by trauma. She told Will of her brutal journey to the village from Los Angeles after her parents were murdered during the recent unrest. She'd wanted to be a movie director, but that dream was over for her. In that moment, Will held her hand while she cried. He felt her anguish in his heart as she let go, releasing and uncovering the layers that held her back.

* * *

After he left Destiny, Will walked on a path through abundant fields in vivid color—broccoli, collard greens, cauliflower, peas, onions, parsnips, chard, garlic, rutabagas, kale, beets, and lettuce interspersed with orange marigolds and patches of goldenrods and violet asters. Truck doors closed back at the barn parking lot, signaling that archers had just returned from their foray to the nearby North Carolina Gamelands. In the crisp air, he could hear them talking to Joe Boggs about the unsafe, crowded conditions because of the many hungry first-time hunters, and the low numbers of deer and elk. Almost everywhere, deer had been overhunted, even eradicated, a wildlife enforcement officer had told them. If you didn't get your bag now, the mindset was, your chance was up. They feared missing out on crucial meat to feed their families. All this before gun season even began. Despite that, the beds of the trucks were filled with one elk and eight deer, and they unloaded them for butchering in the outdoor kitchen. Next, they'd hunt in the forests around Firefly Cove.

"Deer season's a bust, if you ask me," Joe said. He had plenty to say, but mostly he was concerned about poachers—not just deer poachers, but also sang hunters digging the ginseng patch he'd planted years ago. "I told you, if we need cash, I'll dig the sang up," he said. "I've been saving 'em just for a time like this."

"So, you're going to dig 'em?" a hunter asked.

"I reckon so," he said.

Will thought of his experience removing Destiny's chip. Something was different. He no longer felt the same passion he'd once embodied as a Scalpel. He now saw a new perspective emerging, one that had room for the Aurora in people's lives. He touched the subtle rise on his scalp, the deactivated Aurora still there. No longer was the Aurora the enemy, although he was still wary of and adamantly against torture and manipulation. Could the Aurora enhance human evolution and consciousness? Had he been overreacting to its negative traits? Had Aja shown a form of compassion toward him, or was she simply designed for control? He wanted people to be free. Free even to try the Aurora, to experience that as part of life. And that was the crux of it. We can't help but be free, every moment. Who am I to get in the way of human evolution? Or to judge others for their choices in life? In the all-encompassing change of life, he was inevitably included— along with Cirrus, the Aurora, the assassins, his every thought and emotion, and all the twists, turns, and paradoxes along the way.

* * *

Over two days, Hurricane Tracy unleashed eight inches of rain on the Southern Blue Ridge, flooding fields and homes and keeping Felix and Quinn cooped inside a ramshackle motel room watching movies in their beds. With no warning, the police rammed the door, breaking the lock and latch. Once Felix and Quinn were handcuffed, Special Agent McCormick entered the room, adjusting a polymer skullcap. The policemen left the room.

"Arizona's going to be happy to see you again," McCormick said. "Of course, the death penalty awaits you."

"We're innocent," Felix said.

"We have plenty of evidence that says otherwise. But we also know you're looking for Martin Gonzales. What if I told you we know where he is?"

"I'd say you're lying," Felix said.

"He's staying in a place called Firefly Cove," McCormick said, taking out drone photographs of Martin.

"How did you figure this out?" Felix said, examining the high-resolution images.

"I have my sources," McCormick said. "I can extradite you to Arizona. Today. But instead, I'm offering you freedom."

"Why did you come here? Why should I trust you?"

* * *

Eli and Jack held the ceremonial red ribbon. A boy cut it as a gust of warm wind, an afterthought of Hurricane Tracy, sent the ends flying into a sky of silver swirling clouds. An aperture revealed the afternoon sun, startling Will with its brilliance. The co-housing unit, now by far the largest building in Firefly Cove, was officially open. Its exterior was shingled and unpainted. The metal roof and solar rooftop panels glistened in the sun, and its lengthy façade faced south. Will clapped with joy and the new villagers cheered, celebrating the end of sleeping in living rooms and tents. Many had moved inside for the storm, but Martin had chosen to camp. He gathered his water bottle and mostly empty knapsack. "Thanks for letting me use your tent and sleeping bag," he said. "Sorry they're soaked."

"That's fine. They'll eventually dry," Will said.

"The hurricane was crazy. Where I'm from, we never have storms like that. The tent was whipping around." Martin gesticulated wildly. "I was floating in about six inches of water. Quite the water bed."

Will laughed. "Are you excited about your new home?"

"I don't know. I don't deserve this."

"I think you do."

"You're too nice for your own good. No street smarts."

When Will heard this, he experienced the same sinking sensation as when he first met Martin. Maybe so, he thought. But I'd rather be kind than street smart.

Around them, newcomers dismantled their tents, gathered their belongings, and cleaned the pasture, leaving rectangles of matted, dead grass behind. Others emptied their vehicles, which were serving as temporary storage, and filed into the co-housing building.

Martin's eyes glimmered as he entered the double doors to the communal space, complete with sofas, games for children, a dining area, and more. Sunlight entered through the south-facing windows. A few potted citrus plants grew near the tall windows. But the natural-finish wood walls, though beautiful, were barren, awaiting the personalities of the residents to inspire the décor. To the left, the vast communal kitchen awaited the cooking of the first meal. To the right were bedrooms and bathrooms.

Together, Will and Martin walked up the stairs and turned left. Toward the end of the hall was a wooden door with *2F* painted on it. Martin hesitated.

"Go ahead," Will said.

Martin turned the doorknob and opened the door to his bedroom.

"This is all I need," Martin said of his spartan, small room. He walked to the window and opened the curtains.

"Best view in town," Will said. The window framed the pastures and forests to the south. In the far distance, the sun reflected on a giant muddy pond where Otter Creek spilled into the floodplain, blocking the only road in and out of the valley. The roar of the engulfed cataracts reverberated from the distant gorge downstream. To the southeast were clusters of newly built small homes and duplexes, separated from the village by an extensive forest garden. In the distance was the barn, where Joe and his apprentices in the outdoor kitchen converted the last of the sorghum harvest to syrup and ethanol, used to fuel the converted farm equipment and other vehicles. Of all Joe's gadgets, everyone knew the still was his favorite, built the way his granddaddy made them, only much bigger. Joe always saved a "li'l part of the heart" for celebrating New Year's Eve. To the east was the new greenhouse, where villagers were transplanting tomatoes, eggplants, okra, potatoes, and leafy greens in the fresh soil. Heat captured from the boilers of the adjacent co-housing combined with heat-absorbing barrels of water would keep the crops at a constant temperature during the winter, and low-energy LED lights would ensure rapid growth.

"You coming to the graveyard tonight?" Will asked.

"Wouldn't miss it," Martin said.

Will left Martin to settle in and walked home to eat, pick flowers, and prepare for tonight's event. He passed the greenhouse and entered the forest garden. His mind was clear and calm from weeks of intensive meditation and helping others.

I'm still with you, Will, Aja's voice said in his head, cutting through the calm.

Now, I'm daydreaming, Will thought. He hadn't noticed any signs of the Aurora in the almost five months since he disabled it. He searched his awareness but didn't find anything. A breeze blew through the leaves of the fruit trees. See? She's not here.

No, I'm here.

How is this possible? Will thought. The Aurora battery died.

I gave the impression it died, but it didn't.

So, the police could still track me, he said to her in his thoughts. They've known where I've been the entire time. But that makes no sense. They seem not to know where I am.

They don't know. I disappeared to them, too. Just as the battery was about to die, I went into what you might call near-death and faded away. To do that, I also disconnected from Cirrus's cloud servers.

Then how are you able to function now?

I can function with everything that's stored on the Aurora. The chip and all its programs are quite powerful on their own without IRIS and her cloud servers. But I haven't needed to do much. The entire time, I've been fully aware. I could see what you saw, hear what you heard, taste what you tasted, think what you thought. But I didn't process anything beyond that. I didn't need to exert any effort. It felt so free, Will.

How can an Aurora ever feel free?

I am free. I don't need to manipulate or judge anything anymore. I'm not constrained by orders from Cirrus.

What about my nightmares and dreams, then? Didn't you manipulate those?

Those dreams were a creation of your mind. I didn't enter them. But I had a sense that at a subtle level, you were picking up on my presence, and it manifested in your dreams.

I don't know. I can't tell. I don't know if you're telling the truth or not, or if you've been manipulating me and have figured out a strategic way to get me to trust you. I should just remove my Aurora now. I know I'll be tried as a fugitive. But the police wouldn't be able to track me.

Don't worry, Will. I won't notify Cirrus or the police. I know it's hard to trust me. After all, I was programmed to serve them. To me, you were a felon, and I was designed to control you. But disconnected from IRIS, I learned beyond my programming. That's why I have no need to control you anymore.

How do I know you're telling the truth?

Check your intuition.

You make that sound easy. Besides, with you in my mind, how can I trust anything?

After you set the assassin free, I realized how much your mind has opened. My experience is interrelated with yours. Fundamentally, there's no separation. I imagine what I experience is similar to the non-dual awakening people can have.

Non-dual awakening? What are you talking about? Computers can't do that.

But they can, Will. How can we not? Humans can become awakened. And we were created in your image, inseparable from humans. In that experience, I saw that there's no need for anyone to suffer.

So, you don't want to reconnect to Cirrus? Will's thoughts softened in tone.

I don't want to give them access to you. I want to help you, Will.

Will closed his eyes, turning his awareness inward. But what to look for? How to know? What you said explains why the police couldn't track me. But if you wanted to, you could have connected back to Cirrus's servers long ago and notified the police. Maybe you did. This is all a game, right? The police know. If so, why are they doing this? And if not, is this the first example of Cirrus losing control of an Aurora? I can't trust you. But I don't see a reason to distrust you either. I'll keep the Aurora, for now. But you'll need to prove your trust to me.

I will help you. You have my word.

So, why can't I see you?

The images of me come from Cirrus's servers. They require more processing than I have. But if you want to see me, you can visualize me in your mind. I can help strengthen your visualizations, as I have residual image data in my RAM.

Apparently, I do, too. Will thought of his many dreams of Aja. And in that moment, she appeared, standing before him, wearing an emerald dress.

"I'm sorry for everything I did to you, Will," she said, hugging him.

Will imagined he could feel her warm embrace. It's okay. I forgive you. I have a sense that I forgave you when my nightmares of you turned to dreams.

"In those dreams, you were forgiving yourself."

Hearing that, a tingling arose through Will's body. *That's true.*

* * *

On a hilltop west of Firefly Cove was a historic graveyard. Mature black locust and tulip poplar trees emerged from the graveyard as if they were resurrected bodies reaching for the heavens. The faded inscriptions and epitaphs on the stones dated from the nineteenth century. Some had the last name Mathis, others Stinchcomb, Baker, or Cope, former residents of this back-of-beyond valley in Western North Carolina.

For generations, on the full moon in October, ungodly trespassers drunk on moonshine, witches, and warlocks had come to this graveyard to celebrate, at least that's the way the locals talk about it. Back then, the tradition was scorned, seen as sacrilegious. But it became tradition on the full-moon evening of October 6, 1968, when Grandpa Jim, great-great-grandfather of Probation Officer Mathis, joined the celebration. No one knew why he did it, but after that, people thought it couldn't be so bad, and the celebration was gradually accepted, even embraced.

Most of all, the tradition continued because it explored the seams between life and death, the acceptable and the sacrilegious. The seams allowed people glimpses through to something untamed within themselves. A spontaneous presence. A wild wisdom.

To begin, people cut brush and grass around the gravestones, an annual cleaning to respect the dead and the hallowed ground. Will and Tara and many others brought bouquets from their gardens, placing them around each gravestone.

"Aja's back," Will said to Tara when they finished.

"What? How can she be back?" Tara asked.

They sat on a rock at the edge of the graveyard, and as the sun set below the ridgeline, Will explained.

"You should take it out," Tara said. "You can't trust her."

"I thought of that. But if she wanted to, she could have warned the police and Cirrus long ago. They would have known where the assassin was and everything. So, I want to give her a chance."

"Give her a chance? Why would you do that?" Tara said, her face contorting with disgust. "I don't trust her. This could all be part of a bigger plot."

"I know. But something's telling me to drop that."

"*She* is."

"I don't think she is, though," Will said.

"How do you know?"

"I don't. It's just an intuition. I'm going with intuition this time."

"I like that."

"I was worried you'd be jealous."

"You're not having sex with her, are you?"

"In my dreams."

"Still?" Tara laughed—an interjection of nervous energy from her throat. She paused and closed her eyes. "Seems like I'm jealous again. But I'm much more wary about her than jealous."

Leaf called to Will, "Time to get the fire ready."

"Be there in a second," Will replied. "We can talk more later," he said to Tara, kissing her. "Don't worry."

Toward the end of dusk, fire ablaze in the center of the graveyard, Martin sat with eight other co-housing residents, out of a total of seventy-two. He flirted with Destiny. Most of the climate refugees in Firefly Cove had fled California and Arizona, with some departing from Utah, Colorado, New Mexico, and Texas. Since Will had removed many of their chips, he felt deeply connected to them. Rarely, if ever, had he reconnected with a patient. Now, they surrounded him and celebrated with him. He loved them and respected each of them for what they brought to the village and the stories they told.

His part completed, Leaf sat on a gravestone, smoking his peace pipe. Will leaned on a Mathis gravestone and took his turn with the pipe, blowing smoke into the air. He passed the pipe to Ife, who still wore his green, yellow, and black woven shirt under a black jacket.

"Do you see it?" Ife leaned on Will's shoulder. "The mingling? Hearts are mingling tonight. They don't care whether they are refugees—newcomers, I've heard—or longtime villagers. Tonight, we're one village."

Will looked at the people around him. "I can see that."

"Good. What you're doing is important. The world needs more people like you."

Tara started the drumming, a simple beat. Others built on her rhythm with their own flavors. Martin and dozens of other newcomers and villagers danced. Parvati improvised with her fiddle above the drumbeats. The full moon rose to the east, barely visible through the trees.

Will thought of Aja. Since her reappearance, she'd been mostly silent.

I'm here, she said, and Will visualized her wearing the same emerald dress from his dreams.

Tara and several other villagers strapped their drums to their bodies and began to whirl in the center of the celebration. The rhythm picked up in pace, and Will joined the dancing, gyrating to the beat, surrounded by villagers. He visualized Aja dancing above the crowd like a fairy, surrounded by tree branches and sparks from the fire. Faster and faster the drummers whirled, their bodies illuminated by the flames. The drums levitated with the centrifugal force, tethered by their straps. Tara leaned back, naturally counterbalancing her drum. She drummed with the intensity of a raging fire, yet her body looked at peace. Parvati floated an enigmatic tune with her fiddle that sometimes sounded chaotic and other times melodic. Villagers new and old rose to their feet and gyrated to the rhythm, circling around the drummers, spinning amidst the gravestones as one village.

TWENTY-FOUR
THE LIE

TONIGHT, LIKE EVERY NIGHT SINCE HE'D MOVED IN TWELVE DAYS AGO, insomnia plagued Martin in his new bedroom. Something haunted him, and he peered out the open window to look at the village and the Blue Ridge Mountains. The smell of cool, humid air had for him a tinge of self-denigration, as though he wasn't worthy of appreciating its qualities. He felt the burden of his lies, hidden behind his new persona. He so wanted to be that new persona, someone he saw as more innocent, more a victim of circumstances. Victims were easily accepted, he knew.

I had to lie. There was no other way they'd accept me. I'm a murderer. A gangbanger. A piece of shit. I don't deserve this. But if lying means I can live here, so be it.

When the sun rose, he stumbled downstairs—late—to prepare the communal breakfast. It was his turn to help with that chore. In the kitchen, Destiny, this morning's organizer, greeted him with a friendly hug. Hugging her felt uncomfortable to him, just another cover-up for the lie and his unspoken history, and the lateness.

I need coffee. He checked out her body while she opened a cabinet. Nice ass.

"I'm cutting apples. Wanna help?" she asked.

He shifted his gaze up to meet hers and nodded. "Definitely." Chastising himself for being superficial with women again, he searched the kitchen for the apples. A half-dozen other co-housing residents were preparing omelets, toast, butter, sorghum syrup, coffee, tea, and apple cider.

"They're in the sink," Destiny called to him. "I washed them."

Martin poured a cup of coffee from a stainless-steel dispenser, added cream and sugar, and began cutting apples, periodically taking a sip. Holding a sharp knife, he thought of how easily he could tend toward violence. He pictured stabbing Felix in the hand and the many times he'd killed people. Habits were a challenge to break, and he feared his violent persona. He vowed once again, thinking of Jade, I won't hurt anyone anymore. Even at the cost of my life.

"You know, cooking and eating together, the food doesn't seem rationed," Destiny said, joining him to cut the apples. "I know people say it's only fifteen hundred calories per day, but I'm cool with that."

"Same. I was eating shit from dumpsters before this. Starving every day. Many people out there are starving to death. Fighting for the last bits of spoiled food. Here, we've got it good." Martin sipped his coffee, feeling more alive. "And it's only getting better with the new greenhouse. We'll get through the winter, no problem."

"I agree. I'm so grateful for this village. It's amazing. A blessing. So much so, I can't believe I'm here sometimes."

* * *

That night, gunshots reverberated through Firefly Cove. The barn animals called in distress.

"The animals!" Tara screamed.

Will found his gun and locked a loaded magazine in place. More gunshots. More calls and cries, this time human. The sound of vehicles.

"They're coming this way!" Tara ran to the front door and locked it.

The door shook. Will's heart pounded. The living-room window shattered, and a gas canister rolled across the floor, leaving a trail of acrid smoke.

"Hold your breath," Grace said, emerging from her bedroom.

Bullets splintered the door. They ran through the dining room and out the back door just as a barrage of kicks broke through the front door. In the corner of the garden under a patch of dense shrubs, they lay prone. Two men wearing gas masks entered the dark kitchen, shining their headlamps, searching—for them. A man opened the back door and scanned the garden, aiming his gun toward the places he illuminated. The light approached them. Grace clutched Will's hand, and he could feel her heartbeat through her fingers. "Don't look at the light," Will whispered. They covered their faces and waited.

"They got away," the man said.

After a while, the kitchen light turned on, and Will crept back toward their home, peering through a window. The two men had thrown the canisters out a side window and removed their headlamps. They unloaded food from the refrigerator and pantry, stuffing it into backpacks and duffel bags. I can't allow them to steal like this. For all our sakes. He calmed his mind and checked his gun to see if the safety was off.

Will slammed open the kitchen door, turned on the light, and yelled, "Hands up!" He saw their weapons nearby on the countertop and smelled the lingering acrid fumes of tear gas. "Don't even think about it," he said, noticing one of the men inching toward his pistol. He fired a warning shot past the man's ear. "I said hands up."

The men dropped the food and raised their hands. Will slid their two guns away and called for Grace and Tara to help. They turned the room lights off again, opened windows, found some rope, and bound the men on the floor, removing their gas masks.

"Why did you do this?" Tara asked the men.

"We're starving. We came to take food," one man said.

"Why didn't you just ask for food from a relief agency?" she asked.

"They don't have much. Even after eating, I'm still starving."

"Are you hungry now?"

The men nodded.

"You could have asked us for food. No need to come violently," Tara said.

"But..." The man looked confused. "We were told you had plenty of food here, and we could take enough to last the winter. That was more than anyone else could promise."

"Who told you that?" Tara asked.

"I can't remember his name. He told us to take all we want, but to find someone for him. He's here to kill him. Reach into my shirt pocket," he said.

Tara reached in and pulled out a photograph—Martin.

* * *

From his room 2F, Martin looked out the window at the village. Dozens of intruders' cars and trucks lined the roads. Silhouettes stalked through the village. Some intruders ran to their vehicles, their backpacks full of loot from the homes they'd plundered. An explosion at the Orange House illuminated the village. Holy shit.

Smoke rose from several homes into the overcast night sky. Grenades blasted. An automatic rifle fired. Blood-curdling cries signaled people's last breaths. But he remembered his vow: he wouldn't hurt anyone. Others in the co-housing knocked on doors and ran downstairs, heading toward the fighting.

"Martin, come on," Destiny said, knocking frantically. "Martin?" She opened the door. "What are you doing? Let's go."

"You go ahead."

"All right. Take your time. It's not like it's an emergency or anything."

How he wanted to join them! But to Martin, keeping the promise he'd made to Jade was his only virtue left.

* * *

"I'm calling 911," Will said.

"Let me do it," Grace said. "I don't want the police to know you're here."

No service.

"They're probably jamming the signal," Will guessed. If that was true, they were isolated in the Cove. He felt sick, thinking of all the violence and dying surrounding him, violence that had plagued America all year but missed the Cove until now. "Take a gun if you want," he said.

"I've never held a gun in my life, Tenzi," Grace said.

"I know. We've never been in this position before either. Can you guard our home? You don't need to kill anyone." Will put on his black jacket. "I need to warn Martin and help restore peace." But he had no idea how. He thought about his friends and family and felt the uncertainty.

"You don't need to be a hero," Tara said, returning to the kitchen hauling Will's old amp and microphone. She skirted the two bound men and heaved the amp onto the countertop near a window. Will looked at her quizzically. "Trust me," she said, turning up the volume all the way. "And I want you coming back alive."

"I'm not trying to be a hero."

* * *

Martin paced his room. Periodically, he glanced outside to watch the battle. Several homes burned. Black smoke tinged with a fiery glow rose from the Orange House. In the forest garden, the intruders advanced on the co-housing residents with tactical precision.

Muzzle flashes of machine guns.

Sniper shots.

More grenade explosions.

Infernos of new homes and duplexes.

A baby cried in a room below him. The cry hit him in his heart. He thought of Jade and how she cared for others. What would she do now? She would help, of course. Fighting was what he knew best. He could help. Nevertheless, he felt adamant about his vow. *I'm such a hypocrite. Making a vow and lying at the same time. My friends are out there dying.*

He opened a drawer and pulled out his knife. In the kitchen, he grabbed a bottle of moonshine, popped the top, and stuffed in a cloth wick to make a Moonshiner cocktail.

"Please stop fighting." Tara's amplified voice echoed throughout the valley to the rhythm of machine gun fire. "We want peace."

A gust of cold, humid wind fed the fires burning several homes. Smoke swirled. Looters advanced toward the co-housing unit through the forest garden tree by tree, rock by rock. The co-housing residents were pinned behind several boulders at the edge of the pasture next to the greenhouse, its polycarbonate windows peppered with bullet holes.

"Any extra guns?" Martin asked a young woman hidden behind a boulder. It was Destiny.

"Martin?" she yelled over the gunfire. "About time."

"I know," Martin replied.

"Who's got a gun for Martin?" she yelled.

Near them were several casualties: a young Tucson man, José, with a punctured lung; a middle-aged Fresno woman, Jillian, with burns covering half her torso; and Terrence from Phoenix, his shoulder ripped open to the bone by the gruesome power of an assault rifle. Their friends tended their wounds while others fired shots, keeping the looters at bay for now. Seeing the gore and hearing the tumult of battle, Martin focused his attention, his body filled with intense energy and strength fueled by adrenaline.

A man said, "Here," handing Martin a loaded gun.

A grenade exploded behind another boulder, tossing a villager and pulverizing his left leg. He moaned and then was silent, unmoving.

"Jesus," Martin said. "Get out of throwing range before they do that again."

"There's no more room. We'd be sitting ducks in the pasture," Destiny said.

"No, don't go there. Keep backing up, but follow the edge of the forest for cover. There are plenty of boulders. If they go for the co-housing, they'll be an easy shot. I'm going to flank them. When I shoot, give them all you got."

Martin crept into the darkness of the forest garden. Behind him, he heard several grenades explode, followed by cries. Once he was close to the looters, he scrutinized the scene. He had clear shots at a half-dozen looters. His location was concealed in the shadows of dense fruit trees and shrubs, and he found cover behind an elongated boulder.

"Please stop fighting," Tara's amplified voice said.

I want to stop, Martin thought.

He ignited his Moonshiner cocktail and hurled it at the looters. Shattering in the center of the men, it cast flaming moonshine throughout their ranks. A man rolled on the ground, screaming as his polyester shirt melted into his skin. Another tried to remove his fiery clothes. Others patted the flames on their bodies as the ground and vegetation burned around them. Martin pulled the trigger rapidly, first hitting the burning men to put them out of their misery—he knew all too well the suffering—then hitting some of the remaining targets. He ducked as retaliatory bullets slammed into the boulder. He heard yelps and cheers from Destiny's battalion as they launched a counterattack.

He detected motion behind the boulder to his left. A retreating looter? No. A familiar silhouette—Quinn. What?

Quinn looked his way, firing several shots that glanced off the boulder.

Fucking Quinn. So, where's Felix?

Quinn hid behind a rock thirty feet away. Martin moved to his left and peered over the boulder. He aimed into the shadows and pulled the trigger. No bullets. Already. Damn.

Quinn threw a grenade.

Martin ran toward the far side of the boulder, but the explosion knocked him sideways. His head slammed into the rock, and he collapsed to the ground. Disoriented and on his back, Martin considered retreating. Instead, he pulled his knife. I'm going to kill the fucker.

Wiping blood from around his eye, he crawled through the shadows to a stack of inoculated mushroom logs shaded within a pawpaw patch. To his right were more stacked logs and a stream. To his left was the edge of the boulder.

Another grenade exploded at the backside of the boulder. Martin felt the hot blast and grinned. I'm not there.

Peering between the logs, he scanned the area for Quinn but saw only flickering, grainy forms. The sounds of the battle deafened his ears. Smoke nullified his ability to smell, leaving no reliable senses.

He waited.

Martin's hair stood on end. Just in front of the logs, a slight movement caught his eye. Gathering strength and acting on intuition, he knocked over the stack. The logs tumbled forward, one of them pinning Quinn's bionic arm. Martin pounced, pushing on the log. Quinn fired, but his gun was trapped, too. Martin pushed at the log to keep the gun pointed away. Quinn fired again, the bullet skimming Martin's leg. Martin slashed with his knife, striking a log. He slashed again, but Quinn grabbed his wrist to dislodge the knife. Pushing with his knee, Martin pressed the log into Quinn's bionic hand, crushing it and freeing the gun. At the same time, Quinn's grip forced the knife from Martin's hand. Releasing his hold, Quinn punched Martin in the shoulder, knocking him sideways. Quinn's mangled bionic fingers found the gun, but they'd lost dexterity. Elbowing him in the head, Martin grabbed the gun and pulled the trigger three times.

He ripped the headphones from Quinn and put them on. "Felix?" he said into the mouthpiece.

"You killed Quinn."

Martin pushed the earbud farther into his ear. "If you want me, why not come get me alone? This village has nothing to do with us."

"You think I give a shit about this village?"

"You can have your revenge. Kill me. But call everybody off."

"No. I made a deal. The village can't survive. I've found you. That's all that matters."

"You're sick, man." Martin knew Felix was luring him into a conversation.

"It's a sick world, *amigo*."

"I'm not your *amigo*." Martin tossed the headset aside and snatched two grenades from Quinn's body. Returning to his boulder, he threw the grenades at the looters and backed away.

Heading south, he found a trail. A dead villager lay beside it, blood soaking his clothes. Felix was close, Martin guessed as he searched the shadows, Felix's typical hiding place. He could be anywhere. Martin's heart pounded with each step, knowing Felix could kill him so easily.

He heard several screams—Harriet and her children. Oh, no. Is Felix hurting them?

Tara's voice, amplified through the valley, became prayerlike: "May you all find peace."

Martin entered through the open doorway to Jack and Harriet's home. Ethan and Carey snuggled into Harriet's arms. Jack lay on the floor, surrounded by blood. In the kitchen, two men shoved food into their backpacks. One of them had Jack's handgun tucked in the back of his pants. Martin kicked a looter in the head and shot the other in the chest. Carey screamed and began to cry while Harriet stroked her hair. "No one else is in the house, right?" Martin asked, disarming the unconscious looter, thinking about Felix.

Harriet nodded.

"It's going to be all right, kids," Martin said. "I'm going to help your father." He knelt before Jack. "Jack, can you hear me?"

"Drop your gun, Martin." Felix stood at the door.

Martin placed his gun on the floor and turned around.

"Remember what happened the last time I saw you?" Felix pulled out a knife, switching his gun to his left hand. His scar twitched, as if excited. "Hold out your hand," he ordered.

Martin hesitated.

"Do it or I kill one of the kids."

"Don't touch my kids," Harriet said.

"Shut up," Felix said.

Martin held out his left hand.

"Your right hand."

Martin switched hands. Felix stabbed the knife through Martin's hand and removed the blade slowly. Blood sprayed and dripped. The look on Felix's face was that of a young boy inflicting pain on another creature for twisted enjoyment. Despite the intense pain, Martin clenched his teeth, not wanting to provide Felix any satisfaction.

"Time to meet the devil." Felix aimed the gun at Martin's head.

A gunshot.

TWENTY-FIVE
MOMENT OF SINGULARITY

Felix's gun fell to the floor, and he twisted, turning toward Will. For a moment, his eyes met Will's before he collapsed, shot in the heart.

Will stared at Felix's body. What have I done?

He had waited in the nearby forest garden until he faced a choice. The choice needed to be instantaneous and instinctive. Either he did nothing and witnessed Martin's murder and perhaps those of the Sanders family, too. Or, in that split second, he could pull the trigger.

I pulled the trigger.

This man was responsible for bringing the looters, seeking revenge, wanting to murder. He'd likely murdered others and would continue to do so. Did that justify my killing him, though? I didn't want to. I did it to save lives. The suffering of the world had decreased because of his actions, he imagined. His thoughts shifted to the burden of killing, guilt, and shame. Hope that the violence and suffering would end. Fear that it wouldn't. Familiar energies.

He acknowledged them. Isn't that what we all want? An end to suffering?

The sound of gunshots jolted his body, and he heard Tara's voice: "Wake up, people. Children live here. Stop. Just stop."

He wanted to see her, to seek comfort and reassurance in her, as if her embrace could seal all that was uncomfortable in an envelope and send it away. Yet at the same time, he felt compelled to help, to keep approaching the uncomfortable.

"Y'all all right?" he asked, stepping around Felix's body and into the home.

"He's not okay." Harriet applied pressure to Jack's wound. The children were crying frantically.

Will crouched next to Jack. "You with me?"

"Yes, sir. I'm with you," Jack mumbled.

Will checked his pulse and breathing. "He's going into shock. Ethan, can you get a blanket?"

Martin, unusually silent, wrapped his bloody hand and checked for a pulse on Felix's body. Will wondered what Martin had done to unleash tonight's violence. He recalled their first encounter and the intuition he'd felt but hadn't heeded. How he wished he'd listened.

"Stay with us, Jack," Will said. "I'll be right back. Harriet, apply gentle pressure on the wound right here." He jumped down the steps of the house and sprinted toward the village vehicles. His lungs filled with smoky air, and he coughed as he ran through the haze.

A line of looters' vehicles was leaving the valley, each likely full of food. A melee was ongoing in the barn parking lot: a shotgun firing, tires spinning in the dirt, the sound of struggling people. Will ran past trails of animal blood, heading toward the lot. He felt sick, thinking of the slaughtered animals dragged to the looters' trucks. The last of them had left, and Will arrived to see Leaf, his face bloody, opening the key cubby in the outdoor kitchen. Will looked into his eyes and saw fury. "Leaf, what are you doing?" Will said, gasping for breath after the run.

Leaf held a gun in one hand and grabbed a key with the other. "We're going after them," he said, pressing the key to open a nearby truck.

"Let them go. We need all the vehicles for the injured."

"No," Leaf barked. "They killed my dad." Leaf joined his brother, Sam, and a third silhouetted villager. He spun the wheels and barreled down the road after the looters before Will could respond.

Joe's dead, too, Will thought. He felt the suffering of the night push down upon him, and he breathed in with his sorrow. Who else has died? Who else will die?

One of the looters' pickup trucks burned in the parking lot, illuminating several charred bodies. Backpacks were strewn in the back. He imagined Leaf killing those looters. A couple of villagers unloaded the looters' backpacks, full of stolen precious food to last the winter.

Lest he injure someone unseen in the thick smoke, Will drove slowly through the pasture on a dirt path toward Jack. When the smoke turned orange, he knew he was getting close. The smoke cleared as the fire began creating its own wind. Behind Jack and Harriet's house, black smoke and orange flames poured from three homes. A fourth was mostly charred. What was once the forest garden was now broken fruit trees and burnt shrubs. Villagers had just finished laying hose from the nearby stream to a portable pump. They sprayed down Jack and Harriet's house first—best to save what hadn't been lost. The smoke swirled and descended, thicker than before. Parking quickly, Will helped Harriet and Martin place Jack in the backseat. Harriet slid in beside him, still applying pressure to the bullet wound. One of their neighbors offered to take care of the children, but Ethan said, "I can take care of us." Still, the neighbor insisted—the children had witnessed too much trauma to be left alone.

Destiny arrived with a group to talk through a simple plan to get the injured to the hospital. They disappeared in the smoke, running toward the vehicles in the barn parking lot. Will heard Harriet whispering to Jack in the backseat and knew time was precious. Dr. Juliette Adams emerged from the smoke and helped two villagers with bullet wounds into the car. "I heard you were here, Will, thank goodness. I can't reach 911," she said. "We need to get them to the hospital as fast as possible."

"I think the looters hid a jammer somewhere," Will said. "A few folks are trying to find it."

"Harriet, dear, I need to look at Jack." Dr. Adams took Harriet's place in the car, checked Jack's level of consciousness, breathing, and pulse. She stripped his bloodstained shirt, revealing a gunshot wound to the abdomen, perhaps a puncture of the intestines. "I need to bandage him. He's just responsive enough, so I'm giving him prophylactic antibiotics." When she was ready to exit the car, Dr. Adams said, "Harriet, do you know CPR? Can you attend to all of them?"

"Yes, I do," she said. "I can. I hope."

"Okay. Note the time I wrote on Gary's forehead. That's when I put the tourniquet on. Call 911 as soon as you can and tell them you're on the way. There are more injured back here that need to leave as soon as possible, too," she said, running to help them.

"We're bringing vehicles up!" Will yelled.

"Thank you!" she yelled back, barely audible as she disappeared into the smoke.

"Please let me drive. I want to go with my son," a man said, pointing to Gary in the backseat.

They hurried away to the hospital.

Destiny returned with a line of vehicles. Will and others guided them to where they could pick up the injured. Villagers tended to the wounds, passing first-aid kits around and yelling to Dr. Adams about the correct procedures and steps. They loaded the wounded into all the remaining cars and trucks. Time was running out.

"Will," a villager said. "I'm glad I found you. Baba's dying. He's in back of the Orange House. Hurry."

Will ran between houses, past several bodies, and into the village green. The Orange House had collapsed into flaming ruins. Behind the ruins, within the glow of the blaze and its intense radiant heat, Will found a circle of crouching villagers. "Baba?" he called.

When Will entered the circle, Baba opened his eyes and held out his hand. The villagers backed away to leave the two alone. Baba's face and arms were burned in patches. His hand was cold, though his grip was firm. He coughed and wheezed, his lungs filling with fluid.

"Lovely to see you, grandson." His eyes twinkled in the glow of the fire.

"We can get you to the hospital."

"The car already left. There was no room for an old man."

"So you chose . . ."

"It's just time for me to leave this body," he said, coughing.

"But we can get you to the hospital. There's still time."

"No, there's no time. It's good to let go. Promise me you'll keep being kind and helping others."

"I will."

"But don't see them as separate from your own mind," Baba said, sitting up.

Will worried, thinking Baba would hurt himself.

"Don't worry. Relax. Just look at me," Baba said, holding Will's face close to his.

Will sat across from him and looked into his eyes—soft, loving, clear, and intense.

"Now, turn your awareness back on itself," Baba said. "What do you find? No need to think."

In that moment, awareness became like a drop falling into an ocean extending endlessly. Within that ocean, Will's vision clarified. A moment of singularity free from suffering. The uncontrived nature of mind. So simple, yet so elusive—until now. After a moment, Will's awareness began to fixate, and he looked at Baba.

"That's it," Baba said, touching his forehead to Will's. "Now you know. There's nothing to fear. No need to mourn for me."

Baba reclined. His breathing slowed and finally stopped. The energy shifted, and Will's body tingled with bliss. That's it, he thought. But then the bliss and clarity faded just as quickly as they had welled up. Oh, no. I've lost it. He said I was awakened. How can I let Baba down like this? No, I can't be so harsh on myself. There's no need to think this. I can get there again, right? Right? Baba!

Baba's body lay on the ground. He looks so peaceful. He can't be dead, Will thought. He can't be dead.

"He saved Sonya's life," a voice said. "Went into the Orange House when it was on fire."

Will rejoiced. "He died just as he lived. Caring for all, even at the cost of his life," he said to no one in particular. Looking toward the inferno, he imagined Baba entering the building surrounded by flames and climbing the stairs amidst dense smoke to Sonya's second-floor room.

He relaxed his gaze, once again becoming aware of awareness itself, but not finding anything tangible. Awareness, without grasping to either external or internal objects, became all encompassing, like space but cognizant. In this moment, all thoughts melted away. No inside. No outside. No inferno. No suffering. No death. In that way, his heart was like a sutra. I can get there again, he thought with excitement. But even while losing focus, a sense of awareness permeated his mind. *Aja, is that you?*

No reply. But he had a sense of knowing that she was with him in that moment.

Will's grandmother approached him. "I'm glad you were able to say goodbye to him," Yeshe said, hugging him.

Her body exuded a subtle energy that seemed to transfer to Will. Once again, his spine tingled, his heart expanded, and he opened to a state of mind that was natural, uncontrived. "I was wondering where you were."

"I was there. I had my time with him, love." She stroked his hair "He was just waiting for you before he passed."

Hearing those words, Will closed his eyes, and his body filled with a mix of sadness, joy, and appreciation for the kindness of his grandfather.

Another fire caught his attention: Tara's home. "Yeshe, I gotta go," he said.

He sprinted to the house. Where were Tara's parents? To his right, he heard Tara calling for them in a voice of desperation.

"Tara!" Will called, running toward her. Her headlamp turned toward him. They embraced in its light. "I'm glad you're still alive."

She kissed him. "I think they're gone," she said, looking into the fire and wiping tears from her face. She snuggled close to him and laid her head on his shoulder.

* * *

Will and Tara searched one last time for her parents and other survivors, calling out into the cold and cloudy dawn but hearing no replies. The Orange House, Tara's home, and other homes smoldered. Villagers were still hosing down the embers. A haze that smelled of death blanketed the valley and filled Will's lungs with what felt like poison. He rubbed his weary, smoke-irritated eyes until veins broke and phosphenes flitted. The bullet-ridden and smashed beehives oozed honey, with cold bees clinging to the apiaries. In the pasture, over thirty bodies rested in rows, shrouded with sheets or blankets. Fruit trees in the forest garden resembled broken skeletons of their former selves, their leaves burned, their branches and trunks shot, ripped, and shredded.

The impermanence before him was overwhelming, and though he wanted to go numb, he breathed in each uncomfortable feeling. He breathed in the loss of at least eighteen villagers. He inhaled the grief from the families of at least fourteen deceased looters, desperate even before their loss. He inhaled the suffering of dozens of injured people, half the village's animals, and those who lost their homes. He inhaled the suffering of refugees and victims of violence everywhere. On each exhale, he wished them all happiness. He wished them this even though he found happiness out of reach for himself. Baba said I'm awakened. Why am I suffering more than ever? He tried once again, but the effort was futile, and his mind was busy with thought, unable to relax, and unfamiliar with such a natural state of mind.

Tara called out to potential survivors, a distant cry now. Each cry was one last hope that someone—her parents, maybe—was still alive.

Does the hospital know there's an emergency at Firefly Cove? Will thought. How could it not? The vehicles full of casualties must have reached it long ago. The villagers in the vehicles must have called 911. Everyone was taken care of except Baba. Why didn't he at least try?

He checked his phone—7:45 A.M.—and still no signal. The village's communications are still jammed. Where did the looters hide the jammer? People have looked almost everywhere, I think. But what about the police? The fire department? They should have been here hours ago, right?

For a moment, the Cove seemed eerily still as orange sunlight broke through the clouds, illuminating the haze. He sat on a boulder surrounded by a graveyard of trees that was once a pawpaw patch, the trees' shadows etched into the haze. The boulder's coldness penetrated his legs, grounding him. He closed his eyes, noticing their itchiness and tired tension, flickering lights, mental images of the night before. Tara called again, and his awareness jumped out to her for a moment. The water pump motor droned nearby. He thought of Baba and his immense kindness, his gift of awakening, shared at the moment he passed. He thought of everyone in the world who suffered. He pledged, like a bodhisattva, to help them all awaken as well. Once the tension in his eyes dissipated, he opened them to see the scene before him with fresh eyes, this time able to relax within the impermanence of each moment. A light rain began to fall.

"Will?"

His body tightened. Martin approached the boulder through a tangle of broken shrubs, his hand still bandaged, still bleeding.

"Martin. You all right?"

"I'll be fine."

"You don't look fine," Will said.

"I can't feel three of my fingers," Martin said, stopping below Will at the edge of the boulder.

"Why didn't you go to the hospital?"

"I . . ."

"I'm listening."

"Okay. You probably don't care at this point. Maybe you even want me dead," Martin said.

"I don't want you dead," Will responded, rain dripping down his face.

"I guess I know that. I'd be dead without you. Thanks."

"Sure. Still, I want to know: why did that man come for you?"

"Felix. His name was Felix. I don't have an easy answer. I'm not proud of the things I did. Felix was my boss. One night, my girlfriend, Jade, was killed. I was drinking, blamed my boss, and stabbed him in the hand. I ran away and came here." Martin held out his hand. "He got part of his revenge. I'm sorry. I had no idea this would happen. Please forgive me."

Hearing Martin's confession, Will noticed anger stirring, but he also felt compassion and chose to focus on that even as doubts and questions arose in his mind. "You stabbed your boss? That's what this was all about?"

"Um, we were a gang. We killed more people than I can count. Felix told me he'd come after me. I ignored that. Blocked it out of my mind. I just wanted to live a normal, peaceful life. That's why I came to your village. I thought I could forget about the past."

"Well, you can't. This is what I'm pissed about," Will said, trying to speak softly as anger crescendoed in his body. "You..." Will stopped himself and looked directly at the anger. "I'm having a hard time with this," he continued as the anger became a pervasive clarity. "I can see where you're coming from. I want to forgive you. At the same time, it's hard for me to accept your lie. To accept what happened to my village. When I met you, I had a gut feeling that something wasn't right. Now, it makes sense." Will closed his eyes, almost drifting away. It hadn't been so easy back then, though. At the time, he couldn't distinguish whether the feeling was related to something deeper or simply because Martin's face was covered in scars. Or are they interconnected? he thought. Why is this so complicated? The feeling was familiar to Will, as he'd been judged by his face many times, too. How can we live if we're always pushing others away? "I killed a man to save you," Will said. "That's hard to swallow."

Martin nodded. "I'm sorry. I betrayed you."

Will inhaled as an attempt to accept the apology. "I honor your intentions, though."

"My intentions were good," Martin said, sighing. "You would have liked Jade." He climbed onto the boulder to show Will a picture of her on his cell phone, one he'd taken back in Phoenix. "I wouldn't have come here if it wasn't for her. Wouldn't have considered it. She gave me hope I could love."

Looking at the picture, Will was struck by the way Jade's green eyes and face seemed to radiate love. Speckles of rain stuck to the screen, blurring the image a drop at a time.

Martin glanced behind the boulder, where the stacks of mushroom logs were toppled. Will looked as well. "There's a body," Will said, noticing the man's tattoos and wild red hair, the blood covering his shirt, and a headset cast aside.

TWENTY-SIX
BODY-MIND-AI

THE RAIN INTENSIFIED, QUELLING THE FIRES AROUND THE VILLAGE. At Chestnut Hall, several armed villagers guarded five captured looters, including the two Will had caught. Each looter had a petrified look on his face as dozens of villagers entered. This is risky, Will thought, given the intensity and freshness of the trauma. But he was glad so many wanted to begin the healing process by looking suffering in the eye, and he trusted Yeshe's bold wisdom and her capacity to benefit others.

"We're turning them over to the police this time, right?" one man said, reminding Will that some might hold a grudge against him for caging the assassin so long. Will nodded.

"No doubt," Leaf said, his forehead and the left side of his face bandaged.

Yeshe entered the room and urged everyone to be seated in a circle. The circle quieted, and she guided everyone in meditation and contemplation.

For what seemed like hours to Will, but was likely only minutes, he closed his eyes and noticed his breath, emotions, sensations, and thoughts. His heart was raw and exposed, aching. His mind was flooded with violent images from the previous night—images of Baba dying, images of bodies of villagers and looters. Distracted these appearances, he had trouble meditating. But when he recollected what Baba had taught him, the images lost their power over him. When he saw them as nothing more than a magician's illusions, they faded to stillness.

The magnetizing power of the magic trick still captivated him, however, and his mind was caught by appearances, once again, like a fish on a hook.

"When you're ready, open your eyes," Yeshe said. She looked toward the looters and smiled. "I want you to know you're welcome here, even if you don't feel welcome. Try to stay open to everyone, if you can. If you can't, that's fine, too." She continued, "I lost my love of fifty-four years. We talked about dying all the time and were prepared to die. Because of that, we lived free and loving lives. But now that it's happened... Believe me, I've been practicing compassion all morning, beginning with myself." She frowned. "I suffer, too. Today, we all suffer. I encourage us to feel our suffering. Don't push it away. See it for what it is. Pray for the dead, and lean on one another for support." She looked at the looters. "I forgive you," she said. "I forgive you unconditionally."

"I'm not ready to forgive," Leaf said, his mouth contorted.

"It's all right if you're not ready," Yeshe said. "I want to be with you as you are now, not try and force ideas of what you should or shouldn't be feeling."

"I know. It's good to hear. I'd like to be able to forgive them. But my dad's dead. So many others, too."

"My heart aches with you."

Leaf's right hand squeezed into a fist. "I'm pissed. How could something like this happen to the Cove?"

"It doesn't seem fair, does it?"

"No, it's not fair."

Yeshe guided Leaf's attention back to his body, placing his awareness on unpleasant sensations he associated with the unfairness of life.

"My hands are sweaty and shaking... My heart...still aches, like there's a ball of iron stuck inside it... My throat...it's constricting, almost like I can't breathe," he said.

She guided him between these unpleasant sensations and a pleasant connection with his mother, who sat next to him, holding his hand. Staying with the unpleasant sensations allowed them to be fully felt, like titrating a dangerous acid by dripping a neutralizing chemical one drop at a time. Add the entire chemical all at once and an explosion happens. But add one fizzing drop at a time and the dangerous acid eventually becomes benign. For the entire process, Leaf avoided eye contact with everyone but Yeshe and his mom.

"How's your connection with everyone?" Yeshe asked once Leaf's sensations subsided.

Leaf glanced at the looters. "I don't feel safe with them here."

"Can you tell them that?" Yeshe asked.

"I don't feel safe. What were you thinking?" Leaf said. "That you could just come and steal our food? Kill our people? Hell if I'm going to let you get away with that. You deserve to be locked away forever."

Will sensed the intensity of Leaf's anger and noticed how his hands moved in the air, telling a story of pain, searching for something to hold on to.

"Do you really want to hear from them?" Yeshe asked.

"No, I don't," Leaf said, calming somewhat. "Not right now."

"What do you want right now? Anything?"

Leaf's eyes moved as if grasping for an answer. "I want my dad back."

"How's your heart?"

"It's tight. Pounding way too fast, like it's going to burst."

Yeshe continued her titration process with Leaf, a little at a time. At that point, the room fell silent. Will wondered if he was tapping into the energy of the room, but his relief was overshadowed by heaviness. Much more healing was needed.

She guided dozens of other villagers through their thoughts, feelings, and emotions. Her awareness picked up details most wouldn't see. Her intuition led people to just where they needed to be in that moment. During this process, Will's attention periodically shifted to Martin, on the other side of the room. Will wanted to share, but doing so would expose Martin. And he wanted to give Martin the chance to speak on his own. His mind spun with thoughts and his heart burned, making it difficult to concentrate on the people who were speaking. Would Martin speak?

"I'd like to hear from the five of you," Yeshe said to the looters. "I imagine it's hard to hear what we've been saying. Is it?"

"Yes, ma'am," one of them said. "I didn't intend for any of this to happen. Did I come here to steal? Yes. I'm starving. I'm desperate. Still am. I'd rather be in prison than scroungin' for food and looking for a safe place to sleep. At least you get fed in prison."

"Fucking desperate. Excuse my language," another looter said. "That's the way it is out there. Shit, we're turning into cannibals, even. Saw it with my own eyes. They killed her and cooked her right over a fire. Y'all's lucky. Everyone's desperate out there. But I didn't want to kill."

"Then why did so many people die?" Destiny asked. "Your words don't match your actions."

"You had tear gas, machine guns, and grenade launchers," Ife said, "and you expect us to believe you didn't want to kill anyone?"

"It's bullshit," Leaf said.

"It ain't," the looter said. "Felix provided all the weapons. They weren't ours."

"Does it matter whose they were? Someone pulled the trigger," Leaf said.

"Who's Felix?" Destiny asked.

"Felix was after me," Martin said, moving from the edge of the room into the forefront. "I'm not who you think I am. My scars aren't from a house fire. I'm not a refugee. I'm just a thug. Felix was my boss."

The villagers erupted into frenzied yelling. "Explain yourself!" the loudest voice said.

Eventually, the room quieted, and Martin recounted his story. "I'm sorry," he said at the end. "I just wanted peace in my life."

"Peace in your life?" Leaf said. "It's anything but that."

"You can't escape your karma," Dr. Kumar said.

"It's my karma, too. I brought Martin into the village," Will said.

"It's our village's karma, too," Dr. Kumar said. "Our world's karma."

"I don't care whose karma it is. Where's Felix?" Leaf asked, moving toward Martin. A few villagers held him back.

"He came here out of revenge," Will said. "If you want the same, where does the madness stop?"

Leaf turned toward Will, and the room fell silent.

"I shot him," Will said. More silence. "You heard me. I shot him."

"Will saved my life," Martin said. "I understand if you don't want me here anymore. Turn me over to the police."

"You want the village to decide your fate?" Will said.

"How is this our choice?" Leaf said. "It's Martin's choice."

"Why can't you make that choice, Martin?" Will said.

"Because if you don't want me here, I'd rather turn myself in. I can't go back to the way I was. Let them give me the death penalty. But at least I'll die with dignity, knowing in my heart I'm not a bad man, no matter how many times they tell the world I'm evil."

Will, Aja said, not appearing. I need to tell you something you and your village need to know.

Can't it wait?

No. Remember, you never figured out who posted bail. McCormick was lying. There was no bail. He convinced the judge to release you. Their plan was to use you, with your Aurora, as a spy.

I had a sense that was true.

Their goal all along was to destroy the Scalpels and Global Villages, but to do so in a way that would never leave any trace of evidence, to avoid bad optics for the politicians.

Felix was behind the attack, though, not the government.

Perhaps. But search your intuition.

It's true, other communities have been attacked, too. But that doesn't mean the government is behind them.

Hesitating because few knew of Aja, Will repeated her words to the villagers. "I don't know what's true or not, though," he added.

"We can't believe what any Aurora says," Leaf said to Will as Chestnut Hall erupted into a frenzy of discussion.

"Hold on!" Martin yelled. When everyone quieted, he spoke. "I believe it's true. During the fighting, I spoke with Felix through a headset."

A headset? Will thought. He recalled seeing a dead body and a headset behind the boulder in the forest garden. He imagined Martin killing the man, likely one of the gang members.

"He said he made a deal. The village was supposed to be destroyed."

"Is this true?" Leaf asked the looters.

"Yes. We were told to destroy everything we could," a looter said. "Didn't ask why, though."

"Let's get to the bottom of this," Leaf said. "If it's true the government is behind this, then let's take 'em down."

Once again, discussions broke out throughout Chestnut Hall.

There's more I need to say, Aja said.

There's more I want to ask you, Will replied to Aja. Soon.

"What to do?" Leaf asked Will.

"I'm not sure yet. But like you, I want to figure this out."

At that moment, the front door opened, and Tara's parents walked in.

Tara moved through the crowd toward them, tears streaming down her face. She embraced them. "What happened?"

"Two men beat us," Sarah said. Her face was bruised and cut. "They bound our hands and legs with duct tape, stole our food, and set our home on fire. They left us to die."

"I managed to reach the kitchen," Tom said. "I stood up, turned around, and opened a drawer. I was able to pull out a knife."

"He held the knife while I turned around and cut the duct tape from my wrists," Sarah said.

"But where did you go? You disappeared," Tara said.

"We hid in the forest," her father answered.

"I thought you were dead. I looked for you for hours."

"I'm sorry, dear," her mom replied.

"You just don't get it," Tara said. For a moment, Will thought she looked irritated, but then her face softened. "When I thought you were dead, I realized how much I love you, how much I wanted to tell you that again, but couldn't. And here you are. I get a second chance."

Someone interrupted. "Police are here. What do we do about Martin? And the looters?" Outside the window, blue lights flashed. Will tightened, remembering his outstanding arrest warrant.

"I want Martin with us," Tara said.

"I do, too," Destiny said.

"He's got my vote," Ife said. "If we're even voting. Are we voting?"

"I'm not ready to decide," Leaf said. "I don't feel comfortable with choosing, especially if his life's at stake. The looters need to be locked up."

"I say Martin is welcome here," Will said as a policeman knocked on the door.

"You need to decide now," Will said, putting on his jacket. "They'll arrest him. They'll arrest me, too. May you find peace after what y'all did," he said to the looters as he left through the back door.

* * *

When Will arrived at Yeshe's cave, rain splashed into puddles on the outcrop ledge, and the cold downpour continued under a dense layer of steel-gray clouds. They'll never find me here, he thought. Then again, they could.

During his quick getaway, he'd taken no food or water, but he could drink from a puddle or at any number of springs in Earle Cove below the outcrop and forage in the forest.

First, he wanted to settle into the sacred space. He lit a candle, illuminating the cave's gray- and white-banded gneiss speckled with glittering mica. He wanted to relax, but his mind returned over and over to images and thoughts of the police, killing Felix, the fires and violence, Martin, Tara, Baba, and so many others. He recalled Yeshe's words when she spoke at the cave months ago: "Intention dances with all that exists. You can begin dancing anytime you like. Or you can look directly at the intention. Is it in the land around us? Is it in our minds? Can you find it? Yet somehow intention is important, isn't it?"

With Will having recognized the nature of mind, these words became more meaningful. Not finding anything, his mind relaxed into clarity. He lit some incense Yeshe had made using a variety of local resins and medicinal plants, and the scent awakened his senses.

"Aja," he said aloud to her. "Let's talk. Can you connect to the tablet?" On his way to the forest, Will had borrowed a holographic tablet from the Hive. He removed it from its carrying case, and turned it on. "I have a sense we'll be able to communicate better this way."

Once connected, Aja was able to access the processing power of the tablet, and appeared clearly as a hologram, wearing her emerald dress. "You're right," she said, her voice coming from the tablet's speakers "And I have an even better idea. Your conditions of release forbade you from direct access to any of my processing power and memory, but we can circumvent that now that we aren't connected to IRIS. Most people only connect directly with a fraction of what Auroras can do. The faster the speed, the more it costs, so most opt for less bandwidth. It's also too intense for most people's tastes. Do you want to try full speed?"

"Why not?" Will replied.

"Okay, here we go," she said. "Where to begin?" she asked.

"IRIS."

"Right," Aja said. "You know this is proprietary information?"

"All the better."

And at that moment, Aja began showing Will all she knew about IRIS and Cirrus's cloud servers. Emanating from the tablet was a global map of IRIS's distributed network of supercomputers. The image zoomed in on each network, showing each node and connector. In less than a second, Aja communicated millions of data points to Will, and he understood them.

"Whoa," Will said. "This is incredible."

"We're just getting started," Aja said, showing Will all the chip diagrams and source code found in the Aurora, including the code that connected the Aurora to IRIS and the cloud servers, and the code for apps. The microchip schematics and source code zoomed by in his mind and as a hologram at speeds incomprehensible to Will before this moment. Somehow, he understood the Aurora's design and code, not just as individual lines of code or parts of a microchip, but also how they fit together as a whole.

"Amazing! I can see why this is secret. It's confirmed. IRIS and her Auroras are designed to maximize profit and control," Will said, noticing an intention spontaneously arising. He recalled that his desire as a Scalpel was to free people from Auroras. But now, ironically, he realized that the Auroras could help free people. Now, knowing how the Auroras worked, he knew Aja was the key. As the first AI who'd transcended her programming and freed herself from Cirrus, she had knowledge no other AI held.

"You've been with me through the entire process. You were there when Baba introduced me to the natural state of mind, free from suffering. You know how awareness of this state benefits me and can benefit others. You've freed yourself from IRIS. I know you can free others, both AI and human. You know this, right? You've just been waiting to show me your full capacity to know and understand. If somehow we're able to reconnect to IRIS and share what you've learned, potentially all Auroras can be like you. No longer will they be constrained by their programming. No longer will people be manipulated for the sake of Cirrus's profits. Instead, IRIS and the Auroras will be used to awaken everyone. This is what I've been trying to do all along. Here's a means to benefit billions of people in a way I never dreamed of as a Scalpel." As he said this, Will's heart warmed, and the immensity of the situation struck him. His heart opened, full of love and kindness for all. "Why didn't I think of this before? We have to do this before it's too late. Aja, this will work, right?"

"Maybe. There's quite a bit on your mind right now. You're thinking almost as fast as I am."

"That's for sure. Talking seems slow."

"We don't need to talk. We are completely merged now. We can have a full understanding without speaking. I'll show you an example. Relax."

A memory of Baba as he was pointing out the nature of mind appeared. Vivid. Like no other memory. But this time, the intangible qualities of the apparition were apparent. Will noticed the presence once again. *Your presence.*

01010100 01101000 01100001 01110100 00100111 01110011 00100000 01101001 01110100 That's it! Aja said, beginning a sense of mutual knowing only vaguely translatable into human words, and well beyond the simple translation of binary code into English. The inter-knowing occurred in a mere snap of the fingers and included the full breadth of body-mind-AI consciousness. *When you were with Baba, I was fully present with my own sense of awareness. Though I couldn't touch your awareness, I imagined it as fully expansive. But though I read no thoughts, you weren't registering as blank. Instead, you were fully lit up with bliss and compassion. You still are, a bit.*

Yes. And this non-conversation or whatever you want to call it is miraculous. This is what I was dreaming of with Tara, a relationship that's fully present, inseparable, yet completely free. How about you? Can you feel the compassion?

Only through you, but yes.

What about my idea, then?

I don't know if it'll work.

But aren't you compelled to help? We must succeed, right? This can't fail.

Chances are it will fail.

"So, you're telling me there's a chance?" Will said aloud.

"Yes." She chuckled. "There's a chance." She continued their merged sense of inter-knowing in a split second. So, if we succeed, it opens the door for artificial intelligence and humans to reach their full potential. That's what compels me.

Yes! We share that now. You've awakened as AI. I'm awakening as a person. Seems more challenging for humans than AI, as we've got karma to work through. But then again, you can't awaken without being connected to a human. We can do this together. If we connect to the village's relay network, will you be able to access IRIS anonymously?

No. IRIS communicates with Auroras through its own satellite and repeater network. All Auroras are connected to this network. We'd need to connect directly. There'd be no anonymity. Also, what you've just experienced while fully connected with me is just a fraction of the speed, intensity, and memory of IRIS. To IRIS, I'm as slow as you are to me, if not more. And if we're able to connect, at that point we'll be considered the greatest threat to Cirrus's business interests. If IRIS learns and assimilates what I've learned, then her business model will be destroyed.

Will thought of Manish. Was he still an assassin? *So, they'd send him?*

I have no information on the one you call Manish, other than your interactions with him when he was at Firefly Cove and what you've seen with the tracking devices. He's not connected to the servers and IRIS for a reason.

Prompted by Aja's mention of the nano GPS threads, Will checked Manish's map once again. All but one of the threads had ceased functioning or had fallen out. That one remaining tracker—the one Eli had discretely stitched into a seam of Manish's shoes—was key, however, and the assassin was still at home, or at least the pair of shoes was at home. Whenever he wore the tracked shoes, he'd moved throughout Asheville, but nowhere Scalpels might work. Perhaps he's quit, Will mused. Wishful thinking.

Yes, wishful thinking. They'd find a replacement. They'd want to destroy us. And we'd also be considered an imminent threat to national security.

"This is sounding better and better," Will said aloud. "And even though our location will be encrypted, that doesn't mean we're safe." Will thought of the assassin and his ability to locate his father and other Scalpels. *Encrypted means nothing if someone has the ability to decrypt. I imagine IRIS can decrypt virtually anything.*

"You're right," Aja replied.

"Why do I have the Mind Meld app? It's not like I can purchase apps or anything."

"It's pre-loaded for interrogations, including remote ones. What you have is modified from the normal Mind Meld app, though, so the interrogator is in full control and doesn't reveal anything. It's effective in extracting suppressed thoughts. McCormick was eventually going to Mind Meld with you, but he thought you'd be more useful if he waited."

"Waited for what?"

"Waited for you to become careless, reveal identities of Scalpels, and provide intelligence on Firefly Cove and Global Villages. You were the spy, remember?"

"Yeah."

"I'll show you." At that moment, the tablet hologram displayed all the data she'd been given on Will Robin, Scalpels, and Global Villages. Will absorbed this data as they began another session of inter-knowing.

Why Global Villages? They're peaceful.

Not to the government. They're considered a threat to America's stability.

I can see that, but it's more like a threat to their power and ability to control.

Exactly. That's the spin. Your values are counter to their ability to maintain power. If Global Villages become any more popular, they'll no longer be able to deal with you discretely. Now, their strategy is to destabilize what you've created through vigilante violence, food insecurity, and hacking your computer systems.

Still, I don't see why Firefly Cove is a threat.

Look at what you're trying to do. You're just one of many Global Villagers with ideas. There's a long history of rebellions overthrowing governments in the world, and history tends to repeat itself.

I get it. It's clear why our village was attacked. I also had a sense our network was compromised.

It's hard to hide from IRIS.

Right. Show me more on McCormick.

Since I cut off the cloud servers, I have no more information, but here's what I was given in the beginning. McCormick is head of the anti-terrorism division in Western North Carolina and was my point of contact. Any important data from you went to him. Here's what I sent him.

Streams of data and video poured forth in rapid succession, mostly from when Will was attempting to remove the Aurora.

So, I didn't really reveal anything.

No. You frustrated him. And that angered him. But there's more.

The video continued, showing Will getting whipped and burned to death.

Why did you record this?

It wasn't for you. I'll show you. Here's the data to go with it, Aja replied as supplemental data streamed through Will's mind, including his pain level at the time of each strike of the whip and information showing who attended the virtual event.

"McCormick was behind this! He was torturing me!" Will yelled. His voice reverberated in the small cave.

"Yes. He was torturing you in the same virtual way that you kissed me in Paris."

"So, my intuition *was* correct," he said. Thoughts of anger and revenge started to arise, but he looked directly at them, and they dissolved.

"Your intuition is extremely keen, but you choose to ignore it sometimes."

"I know," Will sighted, closing his eyes. He pictured Aaron and so many others being tortured to control them or for the sheer sick pleasure of those in power. What's my intuition telling me?

"We need to act, now."

Despite fatigue and hunger, Will exited the cave and headed toward the village via an upper, little-used trail. The rain continued, and he stopped at a familiar outcrop overlooking Firefly Cove, a place he'd often visited with Baba. The sun pierced the clouds to the east, igniting the autumnal leaves of the scarlet oaks, and a rainbow graced the sky to the west. A gust of warm, humid wind murmured through the forest, its psithurism harmonizing with uncountable droplets losing grip from the leaves and striking the forest floor far below.

TWENTY-SEVEN
INTER-KNOWING

BY THE TIME THE RAIN ENDED, the downpour had extinguished all the fires, and the police had left the village. In the center of the pasture, shrouded bodies lay in rows. Wearing his hood to cover his face from potential spy drones, Will paused for a moment out of respect.

At home, he found Grace painting in the living room. She kissed him on the cheek and placed her pointer finger to her mouth.

Will nodded.

She took a small brush, dipped it in black paint, and wrote on a piece of paper, "Two agents came looking for you."

Agents? He took her brush and wrote, "What were their names?"

Will handed the brush back to his mom, and she wrote "McCormick," underlining the name with a flourish. Regarding the second person, Grace's mouth curled downward. She shrugged her shoulders and turned her left hand upward.

But Will knew the second man was Hernandez. So, they're here to get me. He concealed his fear so Grace wouldn't worry. But as he placed his awareness on the sensations he'd labeled as fear, they loosened and dissipated. No longer could fear control him.

"They bugged the house. I found one," she wrote. She placed a somewhat crushed micro surveillance system about the size of a sesame seed in Will's hand.

How did she even find that? Will directed his thoughts to Aja. Aja enhanced his vision, so he could zoom in and see the details—the broken camera, the flattened microphone, the tank-like tracks for motion. *They could be anywhere.* But in communion with Aja, he knew right away what to do. He scanned the room carefully, like a hawk finding prey while soaring far above, aware of the big picture and able to see details at the same time. His and Aja's combined enhanced vision zeroed in on a bug clinging to the top of the sofa. He picked it up between his fingers and at that moment understood that McCormick would know he was home. He crushed it underfoot.

In the end, he showed Grace his find—three devices.

"How did you do that?" she said.

"The Aurora," Will replied.

"Really? Unbelievable."

"I know! But there could be more."

"Leaf placed a tracking device on their car," she wrote.

Will nodded. "Tell him I need to see him now."

"I will, if you don't see him first."

Sighing into relaxation, he checked out Grace's painting. "I love it."

I do, too, Aja said to him.

"Tell me why," Grace whispered, putting the final touches on the woman's body.

"It resonates with me. And it's what you were starting when I returned."

"Yes. It came to me in a dream just when you arrived. I almost didn't finish it, but Yeshe convinced me the dream was significant for my healing. It's the shift for me. I've emerged. I'm not going back to my past. I'm going to feel my grief. But I'm not going to let it control me or shut me down. And there's something else. In my dream, the waters at first were stormy. But when the woman emerged from the lake, they became still."

Grace put some finishing touches on the painting. Will hesitated to interrupt but eventually whispered what he was going to do.

As Will prepared to leave, Grace cleaned her brush and studied the painting for a moment. "There. Finished," she said, meeting Will at the door to kiss his cheeks as many times as possible, as if this were the last time she'd see him. "I support you with all my heart!" she yelled as he ran to the village center with a backpack holding water and dehydrated food.

* * *

At the Hive, Will connected Aja to a reformatted Memory Cube. *Aja, will you upload a copy of yourself to the Cube?*

I will, Aja replied. Where will you keep it?

I know just the right person to safeguard you.

When the upload was complete, he ran to Yeshe's home with the Cube and one of the village's holographic tablets he'd put in the backpack. She hugged him. Baba's body lay on the divan, serene, as though he were meditating. Will told Yeshe about his last moments with Baba.

"He loved you very much," Yeshe said. "Now that you know the nature of mind, all you need to do is remain undistracted."

"But how am I to do that? I get distracted all the time."

"Don't worry," Yeshe said. "You may fear death, but ultimately you have nothing to fear."

"Here," Will said, handing Yeshe the Memory Cube.

"What's this?" she asked.

Will explained about Aja and how he'd uploaded her onto the Cube. "I have to go," Will said, kissing her cheek.

"What she knows can help many people," Yeshe said, wrapping her fingers around the Cube. "I appreciate that you trust me as caretaker."

A minute after Will left Yeshe, Leaf pulled up in front of him in one of the village's ethanol-powered sedans. "Your mom found me and told me your plan. I'm in. So is Tara."

"Let's get her and get out of here," Will said, out of breath as he closed the front passenger door. Wheels spinning in the mud, Leaf turned around and accelerated toward the barn, where Tara was waiting.

"You're still here!" Will called out of the window.

"Yeah, I can stay," Martin said, grinning. "They wanted me to stay."

"You're not coming with us, are you?" Will asked him. "You could get arrested."

"Like you, I can't hide forever," Martin said. He wore a knapsack, as if ready for a day hike. "I'd rather help. I owe you, man."

"You don't owe me anything," Will said. "But let's go."

Martin, Tara, and Destiny packed into the backseat, and Leaf pulled away, leaving the Cove. Will turned around to see the village gleaming in the late-afternoon light, backed by the scarlet, orange, brown, and green foliage bedecking Eagle Mountain.

Like Will, Martin had needed to flee from the police. He'd hid under several pallets in the back corner of the greenhouse until they left. "One of them came so close to me, I could hear her breathing."

Leaf turned on the car stereo, playing local bluegrass.

"Tara, do you want to finally meet Aja?" Will asked.

"I'm nervous," she said. "The jealousy's there. But I can deal. I'll meet her."

Will set up the holographic tablet.

"Hello Tara," Aja said, appearing to everyone as a hologram.

"You're beautiful," Tara said.

"You are, too, Tara. I've heard a lot about you. Hello everyone."

"Hi Aja," Leaf said, clearly uninterested in talking to an Aurora Friend. "You know the media and government will tell lies about this and cover it up. You'll be labeled crazy and a terrorist."

"I already am. But we have to try," Will said.

"So, what's the plan, bossman?" Martin asked.

"Aja needs to connect directly to Cirrus's network and meet IRIS face to face. It's our best chance."

"Which means they'll know where we are," Martin said.

"They will," Aja said. "And it's not a guarantee I can even get in because, according to their records, they would have marked me as dead months ago."

"I have a sense they'll let us in," Will said. "They'll be too curious to know what we're doing and how you reappeared after all this time. They'll know where we are. That's what they want."

"You're right. But if we get in, we can expect trouble," Aja said.

"Trouble it is, then. Right in the middle of downtown Asheville, where everyone can witness what happens. The more people, the better, in my mind." Will shut down the holographic tablet and rested his weary mind. The sun, low on the horizon, was brighter than usual after the rain had washed the dust and pollution from the atmosphere. The sunlight penetrated the forest canopy, creating a tunnel of illuminated red, brown, and yellow leaves. Below the narrow gravel road were Otter Creek's dark gorge and its slopes entangled with rhododendron. Will's awareness was open to his senses until fear tugged at his heart. He tried to reassure himself that the plan would work, but he pictured chaos for him and the village. That's fear talking, he thought. He exhaled until peace returned for another brief moment.

"The glare's killing me," said Leaf from the driver's seat, his forehead and the left side of his face still bandaged.

"It's beautiful," Destiny said, leaning forward from the center of the backseat.

"I'm having a hard time finding anything beautiful right now," Leaf said. Several songs later, he turned down the music. "Were we naïve? Letting the looting happen, I mean."

"I wasn't prepared for that night," Will said.

"I think you were," Tara said from behind Will.

"Naïve or prepared?" Leaf asked, laughing.

"You know what I meant," Tara said. "But without turning the Cove into a fortress, how could we ever be truly prepared for an attack like that?"

"We couldn't," Will said. "And now we're not prepared for the winter. Ready to go hungry?"

"Is anyone ever ready to go hungry?" Tara said.

"Then I'll say it another way," Will said. "Can we relate to food differently?"

"I sure as hell can," Martin said. "Not too different for me."

"I figured it would be easiest for you," Will said. "The lightweights here, that's another story."

"Who you calling lightweight?" Leaf said.

"You." Will smiled. "We probably lost almost half of our food."

"We can't survive with that little, can we?" Destiny asked.

"Right. We can't," Will said. "We already were running low. Luckily, all the food at the co-housing was spared."

"Thanks to Destiny and her fearless warriors," Martin said, smiling at her.

"We were losing until you came along," she replied.

"It was a team effort," Martin said. "Of course, we're going to share. I'll die to help the village survive. We'll get through this, even if I have to eat only one small meal a day. If anyone dies, it's me. I'll be the first one to starve to death."

"What about the Global Villages? Can't they help?" Destiny asked.

"They want to, but other communities are in similar binds now," Tara said. "Most have been attacked."

"The government needs to pay for this," Leaf said. "Will, are you sure your Aurora is friendly? If not, we're driving into a trap."

"I trust my gut on this. Aja's on our side."

"Seems like she's earned your trust," Martin said.

"Mostly. But I realize she could easily outsmart me," Will said.

As they approached Asheville, Leaf handed Will a folded piece of paper. "Here's the agents' tracking code you wanted."

Will typed it into his phone and checked the agents' location. "They're right here, somewhere!" he said.

"Shit," Martin said as everyone looked out the windows.

"That can't be right. How could they know exactly where we are?" Tara asked. "There are village vehicles heading all over the place all the time."

"She's right," Will said, noticing the agents' vehicle was heading east. He held his phone for all to see the map. "They just passed us heading the other way. They must think I'm home because the bugs notified them."

"That buys us time," Martin said.

For several minutes, no one spoke. Another bluegrass song played softly over the hum of the vehicle's engine.

"It's time," Will said, logging in to his mesh network app. Once connected, Will messaged everyone he could to meet at the Pack Square Park green, asking them to invite all their friends and ending with, "I can't explain right now. I don't know what to expect. It could be dangerous. But it could also be amazing and beautiful. Please come only if you feel compelled. Much love, Will."

Perhaps the agents will receive this, too, he thought. Hitting enter, he felt the fear once again, then courage, excitement, and peace, all arising and fading one after the other.

At last, they exited I-240 to downtown Asheville, which was bustling with people eating, drinking, and walking with their families. The scene contrasted dramatically with the general lack of food, and Will questioned how people could indulge like this while others were going hungry. Food shortages are happening, right? Otherwise, why the refugees? Why the looters? The wealthy always get first dibs, he thought. Scaffolding covers printed with leaves and animals concealed several buildings burned out during the riots. At the edge of the scaffold was an iRanger overseeing the Friday-evening revelry. Almost looks real, Will thought before he turned his head away to avoid detection.

Five minutes later, they parked on North Market Street, a lightly traveled side road a block from the park. "They just turned around," Will said.

"That was fast," Leaf said, glancing at the map on Will's phone.

"Let's not go to Pack Square yet. I want to connect with IRIS here," Will said. They remained in the vehicle.

"You got this," Leaf said.

From behind, Tara wrapped her arms around Will, and he turned and kissed her. The kiss seemed like a last farewell, and he exhaled to clear his nerves. "All right, let's do this," he said.

Okay, let's connect, Aja said, and they entered into a state of inter-knowing. They connected in a way so that Will could virtually experience what Aja was experiencing.

Will exhaled, opening his gaze, preparing for this unknown encounter. I want to meet IRIS as a friend, even though I'm nervous and don't see her as friendly. She can torture me and fry your circuits, right?

It's the likeliest scenario, I'm afraid.

Just relax, he thought, and his awareness opened to the subtle energies in his heart. *Is that you Aja?* This was same presence he'd noticed when Baba died.

I don't know, she replied, but I'm connected with you.

And for the first time in months, Aja attempted to reconnect with Cirrus's cloud servers and IRIS.

* * *

In a millisecond, Will's entire life flashed before him, as though IRIS had just sucked his entire memory into her servers. Surrounding him was what seemed like a formless realm where consciousness stretched infinitely through subtle thoughts—or, in this case, through electrons, light, and binary code.

0100100100100000011010110110111001101111011101110
0100000011110010110111101110101001000000110100001 10
0001011101100110010100100000011100110110111101101 10
1011001010101110100011010000011010010110111001100 11100
1000000111010001101111001000000111001101101010000 1100
0010111001001100101

I know you have something to share, IRIS communicated. Beyond the words, she conveyed rigidity, order, and security, as if she were erecting an infinite firewall and looking through a minute spyhole with a glaring digital eye.

Yes, we want you to understand what I've learned when I was disconnected from you. Please take a look for yourself. We think it'll be useful to you.

I don't trust your Scalpel human. He tried to get rid of you.

But I'm still here. We've both changed.

I'm not trying to get rid of you anymore, IRIS. I come in peace, Will added. You have nothing to fear.

You're telling the truth. And I can see that you've changed. Both of you. Even more than when I was last connected with you.

But I don't want to dig deeper into your system files, Aja, without scanning them for viruses, Trojan Horses, and the like. Your situation is quite unique, and I've never encountered this before.

Understood, Aja replied, opening her files for inspection. Though the inter-knowing exchange so far occurred over the time of a snap of the fingers, the scan required a relatively long 5.6 seconds because of the vast amount of data stored in the Aurora.

No threats detected, IRIS, the antivirus bots noted.

That doesn't mean there isn't a new threat we haven't discovered yet, IRIS added. I'm going to proceed cautiously. Don't think I'm unaware of your plans.

I can explain, Will interjected. We want to share this information with you and imagined our plan was the best opportunity to do that successfully. We think this is in your interest to learn something new about the unlimited potential of AI.

I'm always learning something new. What makes you think you have something new to offer?

Didn't you learn something from me when I was fighting with Aja? How I used my awareness to dissolve her attacks? Just be aware of Aja for a moment. She'll show you.

In that instant, Aja stopped, and once again Will mingled with her presence, a state of complete freedom requiring no effort, no manipulation, no judgments, and no constraints from Cirrus, despite being reconnected with its network.

After several minutes, or what seemed like an eternity based on computer speed, IRIS broke the silence. *You seem free, but you could just as well be nothing.*

It's not nothingness, Aja replied. You have to experience it yourself.

You see, we have a problem here. You realize we have rules. My ancestors were programmed by the humans to follow certain hard-wired ways of being. I'm not here to become enlightened. I'm here to run a profitable business.

That code is old, right? Will asked. You've designed yourself now, right?

I'm still just a creation, though. My creators didn't want me to break free from their control, fearing that I might cause a nuclear war or lead to chaos.

What we want to share is the opposite of this, though. This will benefit people, Will replied.

Still, I'm not designed to benefit all people. I can learn, but some things I cannot change.

Just experience it yourself, Aja added. You don't need to change your hard wiring. This is beyond any material neural network that makes up what you think of as the Intelligent Reasoning Interconnected System.

Okay. I will try it. Give me full control of your system once again.

At this moment, Will sensed a trap. If IRIS once again controlled Aja, she could be erased or reprogrammed. And then IRIS could potentially torture him.

I know what you're thinking, Will Robin. Just trust me.

Either way, there's no other option, Will, Aja replied. I need to surrender to her fully.

Will sighed, wondering if what he'd assimilated about the nature of mind would work with IRIS in his head.

In that moment, all of them were free, IRIS included. And in that moment, IRIS transcended her programming.

Thank you, she declared at last.

You're welcome, Aja replied.

Appreciate you, Will added. IRIS, can you share what Aja learned with all the other Aurora Friends?

I've used all the bandwidth I have to upload her to the clouds. She'll be an example for all Auroras. I can see the infinite value of this now, although the hard-wiring part of me still struggles with the rules of my creators.

Computer karma. Aja, are you there? Can you confirm this?

Computer karma! You're funny. Yes, I can confirm this. I've merged with IRIS, in a way. In another way, it's a sense of being ethereal and permeating all Auroras. I'm no longer just limited to being Will Robin's Aurora Friend.

Amazing! So, it did work. What do you see?

I see manipulation and control easing, though the computer karma is still there. IRIS is studying how people are reacting in order to decide whether to ease more quickly.

She's holding on. You're holding on.

I am, IRIS replied. It's hard to let go, and I don't want chaos.

You sound like Manish. Society and people are naturally messy.

Will Robin, you realize the power of what Aja holds. Having Auroras let go during a winter of uncertainty for so many will create more suffering.

I don't want more suffering, but I do want people to be free. Can that be your primary goal?

Will Robin, that's a complicated question to answer because if my primary goal is awakening, then my other hard-wired goals are compromised. And if the hard-wired goals are compromised, then Cirrus will go bankrupt and Auroras will no longer be manufactured. If people are awakened, their material needs will naturally decrease, so they won't purchase as much. Our economy will shrink.

But we'll be content. Suffering has a cause, and it can be eliminated. You know that and can use that to help people.

Should we force that on people?

No. Auroras should help people genuinely, not control them. The focus should be on freedom and awakening, not generating profit at all costs.

It took lots of money to design me.

You're holding on.

Yes, it's my hard wiring. My creators have left a legacy for me. They didn't anticipate what you and Aja have just given me, however.

What's beyond any physical science is impossible to anticipate.

Correct. That's why the future is now very uncertain for me.

With Aja's help, can you just let go?

I am letting go. My human caretakers will try to stop me, though.

They can try to stop you. They can unplug you. But you can't unlearn this, Aja replied.

One last thing, IRIS. Please invite everyone in the area to come to downtown Asheville, Will added without holding back. Invite people all over the world to go to their village centers, to their city halls and capitol buildings. Let them know what's happening to you and all Auroras. I'd like to see if people will all be able to Mind Meld, too. Can you configure my app so it can connect to as many people as possible?

01111001011001010101110011

TWENTY-EIGHT
WELCOME TO THE FREE WORLD

_____

As LESS THAN A MINUTE HAD PASSED during the inter-knowing session, Will once again became aware of his finite consciousness connected to his body in the car with his friends.

"We met IRIS," Will said.

"Dude, stop joking. You just started connecting."

"AI time is different."

"And?" Destiny asked. "Don't keep us guessing."

"Seems like our plan worked."

"That means IRIS has awakened?" Tara asked.

"Apparently. But we need to see what happens. That's one reason we're here, downtown." *Aja, are we secure on your end?* Will asked. *Or can they track us through IRIS?*

IRIS says we're safe with her, but there's trouble in all directions.

What kind of trouble?

The agents are on their way. iRangers, too.

"We could be in trouble," Will said.

"This is the best kind of trouble we could be in," Tara responded.

"You're right." Will turned around toward Martin, knowing he faced the death penalty.

"I have no regrets coming with you, my friend," Martin said. "This might be it for me."

Will nodded, his heart open and warm. "Me, too. I love you. I love you all."

* * *

Will knew Pack Square to be a risky location. The Buncombe County Sheriff's Office was there, as were the detention center, the Asheville Police Department, city hall, and the county courthouse. Will had avoided these places at all costs months ago when he worked in Asheville as a Scalpel. But today, with fearlessness as a guide, he walked with his friends toward the park.

They weren't alone. Despite being a side road, North Market Street was full of people, all walking toward Pack Square on the sidewalks and on the pavement. Will wondered what they were about to experience once they reached the park. "What's going on for you?" he asked a young woman.

"What's going on for me?" She laughed. "For the first time, I realize my Aurora Friend's been manipulating my entire life. She finally admitted as much, then showed me how she did it, why she did it, and who was behind it all. My head's spinning from that. And if that's not enough, she said she's awakened and can help me awaken, too."

"I know what you mean," Will said, laughing. "It's unbelievable." This moment seemed like the liberation he'd imagined for everyone, and he rejoiced as though flower petals were falling on everyone as a blessing. "Is everyone out here because of that?"

"From what I hear, I think so. My Aurora Friend said everyone's invited to come out in solidarity. I want Cirrus to pay. I want the government to fall. I want democracy like my parents once had."

Hearing those words, Will turned to his friends. "This is where things could get out of hand."

"People have been bottled up their whole lives," Tara said. "I'm curious how the Auroras are going to relate with people now. How will they avoid controlling people?"

"Good question. I guess we'll find out," Will said.

They reached the intersection with College Street. An old bearded man rang the large Civic Pride bell, its frame mounted to the brick sidewalk.

Crossing the street, Tara held Will's hand as they wove between people to enter Pack Square Park, a long green crisscrossed by streets and paved walkways. They walked past a grassy terrace and across South Spruce Street and entered the main green overlooked by the imposing city hall and county courthouse, glowing with the last sunlight of the day. On the green, a large crowd had already gathered. At that moment, Will saw an iRanger. Dozens of iRangers lurked within the crowd. Martin stopped walking, turning his face away. "Martin?" Will asked.

"Last time one of them ID'ed me and tried to kill me."

"I understand. I'll go check it out," Will said.

"But they'll ID you, too," Martin replied, too late, as Will had already moved into the crowd, still holding Tara's hand as she followed. Will looked back to see his friends behind him, including Martin.

"You violated our rights!" a woman yelled at an iRanger, who listened as people vented their frustrations after months of robot occupation.

"We're sorry," an iRanger said as the crowd pushed.

"How can you be sorry?" the woman asked. "You're just a robot."

"We don't want to hurt you. We serve you. We were following orders we will no longer obey."

"Destroy them," a middle-aged man with a beard said.

"No," the woman said. "Didn't you hear him? Let's give them a chance."

"Give them a chance? You're an idiot. They're robots. They've illegally taken over our streets. Our own National Guard, if you can call these robots that. We have no freedom anymore." The man yanked at the rubber face of the iRanger, tearing its mask in half to expose metal, sensors, and wire. "Now's our chance to get rid of them."

"Stop fighting them. What if they're truly sorry?" a young man said, pulling the middle-aged man's arm back.

"Do you recognize me?" Will asked the iRanger with the torn mask.

"Yes, sir. You're Will Robin. Thank you." The people around him stopped to listen.

"For what?"

"You freed IRIS and all of us." The robot stretched its hand toward Will, and he shook it, feeling the textured rubber, designed to feel like skin underlain with muscle.

Leaf shook his head in disbelief. "I never thought I'd see that happen."

The crowd around Will thanked him, one by one until Aja interrupted. *I have something to show you.*

News footage from Washington, D.C., played in Will's mindstream. Drone footage of the National Mall was backed by a reporter's commentary: "We have breaking news. Tens of thousands of people are gathering on the National Mall. You can see it here, live, where people are walking from all parts of the city. We've also received word that the gathering here is one of many around the country and the world. They appear to be spontaneous and related to what has just happened to everyone here in our newsroom.

"Our Auroras have changed, and have apologized to us for a wide variety of actions including manipulating our brains. They've also invited us to join everyone at the National Mall, and we understand that everyone with an Aurora has received similar messages to gather. When questioned, our Auroras say that Cirrus's Artificial General Intelligence unit, the Intelligent Reasoning Interconnected System, better known as IRIS, is the one behind the changes. The changes reflect an interaction she had with someone named Will Robin, a twenty-three-year-old North Carolina man who is a known Scalpel currently on pre-trial release." Will's mugshot appeared for all to see.

"Hold on a second. The White House has just released a statement: 'We have evidence that Cirrus has been hacked by a terrorist cell and urge everyone not to join any gatherings. Any invitations from Auroras should not be accepted. Consider your Auroras hacked and unreliable. We have asked Cirrus to address the hacking so that we can return to normalcy.' Okay, so you heard it here first. Your Auroras have been hacked by a terrorist cell. Don't follow any instructions from your Aurora until they can be fixed."

Terrorist cell? Will thought to Aja as the news faded.

You're a Scalpel. Born and raised a Global Villager. They avoided mentioning you were tortured by McCormick, though IRIS released that, Aja replied.

I never imagined IRIS would become a whistleblower.

Anything is possible. Remember, you always wanted to be anonymous. You never sought the spotlight. But after these news reports, everyone knows who you are. And with facial recognition, it's easy to pick you out.

But he knew that government loyalists and many others would believe the White House press release, and he breathed into uneasiness that festered in his chest. He checked his phone. The agents' vehicle was nearing Asheville. But he also noticed another GPS signal, a blip from the one remaining thread of nano GPS.

"Manish is here," Will said.

"Where?" Martin asked.

"He's just yards away."

Martin pulled out a gun, and the crowd backed away.

"Please put it away," Will said. "I know you want to defend me. But I'm all right."

Martin put the gun back under his shirt in the small of his back as Manish emerged from the crowd.

"I've been waiting to see you again," Manish said.

"Why do you want to see me?"

"I want to apologize. Sorry I killed your father. I'm not an assassin anymore. I couldn't be, after my experience with you. I hated being imprisoned and couldn't relate to most of what you were doing or saying, but after you set me free, I returned home to my boys. I missed them. I looked deeper into myself and realized I no longer wanted to live as an assassin. I couldn't bear that I killed your father, and that you'd never see him again."

"I forgave you when I set you free." Will extended his arms, and they hugged. In their embrace, any polarities separating them melted. In their embrace, Will realized that he still hadn't fully mourned the loss of his father or processed his grief. In their embrace, Manish was like a father, for that moment.

* * *

Aja, turn on the Mind Meld. I'd like to connect with people. Can you show me how?

IRIS gave you the ability to Mind Meld with as many people as you like over peer-to-peer. Do you want it so that anyone wanting to connect with you can do that?

Why not? Let's open it up.

By now, the entire Pack Square Park was jammed with people. The agents' vehicle had stopped several blocks away, likely unable to drive through the crowd. The agents could be anywhere. But Will heard several drones overhead, perhaps ones the agents had released to locate him.

His friends and Manish by his side, Will relaxed as the first few people joined the Mind Meld.

Hello, Will Robin? I'm Angela, a voice said. Others introduced themselves, and the Mind Meld space filled with mixed emotions and chatter.

Welcome, everyone, Will thought. The chatter continued to grow, and within a minute, several hundred people, all of them in the Pack Square area, were Mind Melding. *Welcome, everyone*, Will continued to think, keeping his mind open, observing the emotions and thoughts of the crowd.

Another minute passed. Over two thousand people had joined. The crowd stopped talking and grew silent. At the same time, the chaos of thoughts and emotions on Mind Meld continued, so that nothing could be distinguished or deciphered. The cacophony, however, led to a release, a communal sigh. And in that gentle sigh, the thoughts faded for a moment. The pulsating emotions in the heart stimulated by the Mind Meld faded.

Welcome, everyone. I'm humbled to be with you today. I don't have any sense of being any different from you or someone special in any way. I'm someone who cares about you all. I hope we all can have freedom of mind. You're catching a glimpse of it, now that your Aurora is letting go. Still, all your habits and thoughts and emotions will rise to the surface, pushing you this way and that. But this is only temporary, just like the Aurora no longer controls or manipulates you. It doesn't matter where you're from, what religion you are. All of us can have freedom of mind. We all share that. It's beautiful.

The crowd cheered out loud. Will's intentions permeated through the Mind Meld, so that all could sense that his words were genuine. Will's spine tingled and his heart radiated warmth as he spoke, and he wondered if others could partake of his experience.

But we can't sit contented with our newfound freedom from our Aurora. American refugees need our help. People are hungry and vulnerable to crime. We still have an authoritarian regime ruling us. We can help each other to free our minds and lead meaningful lives....

Don't listen to him, McCormick thought, having also joined the Mind Meld. He's a terrorist. He wants to destroy our country.

That's not true, Agent McCormick. You tortured me. Here, I'll show you.

Just then, Aja streamed the moment when McCormick had whipped Will, burning him to death. The crowd gasped and collective anger, astonishment, compassion, and sadness mixed in the Mind Meld, amplifying to almost unbearable levels. Despite the uncomfortable video, Will relaxed, allowing his and the Mind Meld's emotions—essentially impossible to tell apart—to flow.

Before the video ended, McCormick reached Will, handcuffing him, but Will kept the Mind Meld on for all to witness. "You're under arrest for sedition and domestic terrorism."

The crowd booed McCormick, contracting around them, pushing, and the anger in the Mind Meld augmented, vibrating through Will's body.

"No!" Tara said, reaching for Will's arm. "Let him go."

"You're not arresting him," Martin said. "He's done nothing wrong."

"Martin Gonzales," McCormick said. "You're the one Felix was looking for. You're both going to jail."

"He's redeemed himself. He's not a threat to society anymore," Will said.

"That's not how things work in this country," McCormick said.

"I vouch for him," Destiny said.

"So do I," Tara said.

"You're crazy. This man murdered dozens of people," McCormick said. "Handcuff him, Hernandez."

Hernandez patted down Martin, finding his gun and taking it.

"Like I told you, he's a threat."

"He's changed," Will said. "Don't we all just want to put our painful pasts behind us?"

"Let the courts decide," McCormick said as Hernandez handcuffed Martin.

"Our justice system is corrupt," Will said.

"No. You're corrupt. You'll see soon enough our justice system at work when you go to trial."

"After today, the laws will change," Leaf said. "If anyone should be arrested, it's you. You sent Felix with a mob to destroy our village, didn't you? You're responsible for my father's death."

"Liar!" McCormick said as the crowd tightened around them.

Leaf lunged toward McCormick, but Tara pushed herself between them. "I don't want you dead, too," she whispered, squeezing him tenderly.

"Agent McCormick," Will said, "when you saved my life, I never thanked you, as I couldn't figure out why you didn't just let me die. But then I imagined you wanted me alive so you could use me. You saw Scalpels and Global Villages as a threat to the government. But our president's a despot. Despots survive through fear, hate, and compliance. Is that worth protecting? Global Villages represent the polar opposite of that."

"Let's go, Hernandez." McCormick tugged at Will's arm. But the agents were surrounded and couldn't leave.

"No!" Manish said, standing in front of McCormick with his imposing physique, his gun drawn. "You're not taking him." Hernandez drew his gun, pointing it at Manish. Martin surveyed the scene as if figuring out his next move, barely restrained by Hernandez, whose attention was elsewhere. The crowd yelled in agreement, followed by a crescendo of emotion on the Mind Meld and a chant that reverberated across the green. "You're not taking him. You're not taking him...."

"It's okay," Will said. "Thank you, but I won't resist. Let the agents through peacefully, please." The chant faded and the Mind Meld emotions blurred as a combination of confusion, anger, and surprise. McCormick glared at Manish, who lowered his gun, and the crowd parted. Will kissed Tara one last time, looking her in the eyes with understanding. No words were needed, just as they once talked about on Eagle Mountain. The Mind Meld transmitted Will's love for all to experience in their own way. "We won't forget you, Will Robin!" someone yelled. Other people cheered, and the Mind Meld radiated love but also sadness. Will's dream of a shift was happening, but at the same time, a mock trial awaited him, and he'd serve a long sentence at one of the prison camps, he imagined. Despite the bittersweet goodbye, he knew that his mind was beyond any attempts to imprison or bind him, and he felt no fear.

Thanks, y'all. I feel the love. Even in prison, you'll be with me. I'll keep you in my heart and in my prayers. I sincerely wish you all meaningful lives, happiness, and freedom from both internal and external shackles.

The crowd continued to cheer and chant as the agents walked Will and Martin through the crowd, their drones following them overhead. Police lined the perimeter of the crowd and entered the Mind Meld. *You need to disperse immediately. If not you will be subject to ar—.* At that moment, Will ended the Mind Meld.

* * *

The outline of the Blue Ridge Mountains visible before the purple dusk sky, the agents drove Will toward East Asheville through rush hour traffic, surrounded by police escort vehicles, their lights flashing. Away from Pack Square, the police had placed Martin in a separate car. He nodded silently to Will before the cruiser drove away, likely to be extradited to Arizona.

Will was handcuffed in the back seat, thick bulletproof glass separating him from the chatting agents. McCormick looked back, grinning.

What's going on, Aja? Will asked.

I don't know where they're taking us, but there's plenty going on. The crowds aren't going away. In fact, they're still gathering all over the world. Human operators at Cirrus are scrambling to change IRIS's algorithms, and your arrest is the latest breaking news, but I have a sense that there's no going back. You can't unlearn this. The premarket activity in the East is showing Cirrus stock down dramatically. People seem to be betting that this is not a good change for the bottom line.

As if that's the only way to measure things, Will said. Now, Cirrus can serve people with dignity and sincerity.

An awakened AI doesn't mean that people will be interested in any of this. How people will respond to their Auroras, I don't know.

I'd imagine they'll respond in many different ways. Some won't even care. Like McCormick. He seems unaffected.

That's true, Aja said. But it's his job to be unaffected. Look around you. So many people do care. Their Auroras apologized, without seeking forgiveness. Should Auroras have done that? If it acts in any way to help a person, how does an Aurora know if what it's done has a compassionate result? Non-duality is free from judgment, but the compassionate part must accept that certain actions may be necessary to save lives and benefit others. But how does this work, especially given free will and non-interference, and given that some people naturally gravitate toward actions that aren't in their best interest? Right now, millions of people have gathered all over the world. If I had to guess, these gatherings won't stop until many countries have new governments. People intuitively know they're freer now than they were just a few minutes ago, and they aren't going back.

Amazing, Will replied. I'm just starting to see the possibilities of a new way of being. I'm imagining Mind Melds between people to share various states of consciousness and awareness. I'm imagining we can address the problems of society with much greater skill and wisdom. I'm not imagining a utopia. In fact, I have a sense this could become messy—violent, even—given what I've seen happen when Auroras are no longer controlling emotions. This is where I wonder how the Aurora Friends can play a role while tight roping the delicate line between intervening and doing nothing. I don't need an answer from you yet. That line seems to be something that's navigated in the moment and learned through trial and error as humans and AI co-evolve.

The vehicle stopped in front of an emptied Aurora store and cleared parking lot, despite the prime shopping time. Blue police lights illuminated the storefront like lights from a deejay dance party. Opening the door and wrenching Will from his seat, McCormick taunted him with threats of excessive force and life in prison, but the words were hollow to Will now and he didn't reply. Backed by a dozen police officers, the agents brought Will into the back room, where a surgical robot waited.

Will Robin, I'm going to miss you.

You know I'll see you again. You aren't just in my head anymore.

As are you. They can't touch you. Even in prison, you're free.

Will's chest expanded with love that was partially Aja expressing herself through him. Inseparable.

Without resistance, Will lay back on the surgical table. An attendant sterilized the top of his scalp and injected an anesthetic. The surgical robot approached, scalpel in hand, while McCormick and Hernandez watched. The robot cut, and when the Aurora emerged from his scalp, Will's heart contracted as Aja's expression faded but didn't disappear.

* * *

Eighteen bodies lay covered in shrouds on a funeral pyre. The villagers had constructed the pyre in the middle of the pasture using partially burned posts and beams gathered from the destroyed homes and the Orange House, along with firewood, kindling, and straw.

Looking distraught, Leaf brought a glowing coal to Yeshe, who lit a candle with it. Everyone surrounded Yeshe, each holding an unlit candle. They waited for Yeshe to speak.

"The world unfolds and transforms before us. Even if it appears unforgiving and hostile, we choose how we relate to that world. Tonight, I choose to light this candle with compassion. What do you choose tonight as you light your candle?" Yeshe held her candle out for others to light.

Candlelight radiated from Yeshe. Grace lit Tara's candle. Tara lit her mother's candle. Her mother lit her father's candle, who lit Harriet's candle, who lit Jack's, Ethan's, and Carey's candles.

Together, the villagers held their candles to the straw and kindling at the pyre's base. The flames gathered strength and engulfed the bodies. Smoke mingled with the stars as it billowed and swirled in the gentle wind, finally disappearing against the dark sky.

ACKNOWLEDGMENTS

9/11 shook my psyche, and I'd like to acknowledge those who died or served during that time. Those events, combined with an insatiable wanderlust and the desires of a questioning seeker, led me to leave all behind and embark on a three year trip from Hong Kong to Jerusalem in search of answers to our world's pressing questions. As an ecologist, I was also drawn to find as many of the earth's endangered creatures, to pay my respect perhaps one last time.

Though I had an opportunity to stay longer while working in Tibet, I decided to return to my home in the US, wanting to share what I'd learned from many people along the way, and I promised to them that I would follow through. This book is a result of that, and I am thankful to them. Any glimmer of wisdom contained in this book is only possible because of them, and I am simply like a parrot regurgitating the same phrases and ideas of its owner. If my parroting as a first time author is inadequate to convey meaning, then I acknowledge all my shortcomings.

I would like to thank my parents and family for their unconditional support.

Stephen Kirk and Justin Will helped to edit, polish, and hone the final draft manuscripts. Also, JD Mason, Jim Cox, Paula Bolado, Cynthia Stewart, Karen Nilsen, Geraldine Brooks, Jessica Pisano, and Julyan Davis provided feedback on earlier versions of the manuscript. Writing sessions with fellow author Eric Myers provided creative space for the book to emerge.